A few nice words about
"I Don't Seem So Bright in a Well-Lit Room"...

"This is a book of bloody daily revenge and intergenerational grudges, where tears flow as easily as blood. The most exhilarating elements of space opera and Ren and Stimpy cartoons mixed together in a violent smoothie. Definitely a book to bring to that family weekend when you just want to get away from your relatives and think about the best method to collect someone's ears for a bounty. Have I said too much? Was that too specific? Anyway, fun. Read it."

- Aurora Browne, actor/writer, "Baroness Von Sketch Show".

"Absurd. Existential. Ridiculous. Tragic. Comic. The antiheroes of "I Don't Seem So Bright in a Well-Lit Room" are a kind of Rosencrantz and Guildenstern with space packs, inadvertently colliding with their destinies against a starry background of witty wordplay. With a vision as sprawling and limitless as the loveably goofy universe its set, Browning's wit, wisdom and heart are always at play, combining to form a wonderfully panoramic and very silly heroes' journey that visits every trope of its overlapping genres and draws moustaches on all of them."

- Marcel St. Pierre, author of "Vengeful Hank" and "Cliché and the Wind Go Hitchhiking".

"Browning's tale of science fiction, both poignant and absurd, has all the markings of a cult classic. And believe you me I know ALL about cults."

- Matthew Reid, composer and handsomer half of "Reid Along With Browning".

I DON'T SEEM SO BRIGHT IN A WELL-LIT ROOM

SEAN BROWNING

STORY WELL

Story Well Publishing
2637 Northgate Blvd
Fort Wayne, IN 46835
www.storywellpublishing.com

Publisher's Note: At Story Well we believe that every author deserves to have their voice heard, and by purchasing this book you have helped us continue to find new voices to bring to the world. Thank you for supporting us and our authors!

This is a work of fiction. Names, characters, places, and incidents are a product of the author's imagination. Locales and public names are sometimes used for atmospheric purposes. Any resemblance to actual people, living or dead, or to businesses, companies, events, institutions, or locales is completely coincidental.

I Don't Seem So Bright In a Well-Lit Room/ Sean Browning. -- 1st ed.
ISBN 978-1-952876-02-8

To LiLi the artist. Love you bigger than space.

For four hundred and fifty years Lassy Vapours sat staring at a very slow-drying gelatinous glob. As much as he knew he should just leave it, he couldn't. It seemed to stare back at him. Not with eyes, but with tiny universes. Universes that pulled him in and would not let him go until the glob had dried up.

He once read that a Quarol Alabaster glob took four hundred and fifty-*one* years to dry up. That meant only one year left, and Lassy Vapours still couldn't find Lassy Vapours. He couldn't find himself in that universe. No matter how hard he stared he just couldn't get there.

Oh, he got close. He found his twin universe. He found his twin galaxy. He found his twin solar system. He found his twin planet. He even found his twin city, but the closest he could get to finding *himself* was finding an empty chair next to his twin wife where she, in his out-of-time-observational perception, had spent the past thirty-five years eating a pizza.

He had never tried a pizza, not having ever been to Earth. In the glob, Earth was just a big round shopping mall with a vast sea of parking lot. It was filled with ravenous creatures that were once Earthlings and various alien species who had forgotten to write down where they had left their cars, and had gone viciously mad searching for them. Parking lot zombies.

Regardless, he had grown tired of watching his wife eat pizza many years ago and his gaze was now fixed on the journey he thought he might have taken if he hadn't, indeed, been stuck hypnotized by a glob. So entranced was he, that he hadn't noticed how encrusted his very outdated suit had become with all the worst things that come out of a person's body.

He hadn't noticed how he had withered away with starvation and dehydration, and that he was actually quite, *quite* dead.

This made him all the more desperate to find himself before the glob dried up. The journey he stared into led him to a planet he, being the scholar that he was, was sure did not exist in the reality and time of his dead self, only the missing self he was searching for.

There he saw five monks. In the peripheral of his stare, each one looked like him (which was very exciting)...but when he looked directly at them one by one, none of them had his face and each was horribly scarred (which was very disappointing).

He saw that this moderately damp planet had two moons, each in orbit on opposite sides. On one moon, a naturally occurring moon, he saw prisoners of various alien race. On the other, an artificial moon, he saw the garbage of various alien technologies, food stuff packaging, washers and dryers made to wash and dry alien technologies, washers and dryers made to *wash and dry* the washers and dryers of various alien technologies, old and thoroughly enjoyed adult toys, the cremated remains of pets and relatives, and otherworldly knick-knackery.

"*Where are you Lassy Vapours??*" he asked himself once an hour, hoping that an answer would follow eventually. It never did. He once thought he heard a shrill "Here I am!" but it had only been the call of a Towerscapian subway bird. "Heeeriiiam! Heeeriiam! Heeeeeeeerrrrriiam!"

Damn birds.

He had a tendency to get distracted from his journey whenever one specific space ship entered his story. It didn't happen all that often at first, but recently it had been showing up more. He found it fascinating although he hated how it distracted him from his quest.

It looked like a giant discarded light bulb.

He figured that it looked this way to either go unnoticed ("Hey, is that a spaceship? Naaaah, it's just a giant light bulb some- one really big threw out.") or to be feared ("Oh my! Look at the *fucking size* of that light bulb someone threw out! Imagine how gigantic someone would have to be to need a light bulb *that* big! Perhaps it's *God's* lightbulb! Oh no, not *God*! Let's get out of here before he gets back with his giant God lamp and a God-sized knuckle sandwich!")

For a moment, Lassy Vapours wasn't sure whether *he* was God and perhaps *he* had lost *his* light bulb.

Perhaps all his light bulbs.

It was just as well that he remained hypnotized. If he had seen the state that his physical self was in, he would've died of disgust. Many of the body parts he had come to love and cherish had be- come little more than crusted dust. It turns out that he had dried up a lot faster than the glob. Once *it* had dried up, he would be gone forever. Unless of course he found himself.

His journey had led him to terrifying places, to lonely corners, to seedy establishments, to family dinners, to warehouses filled with poultry, to torture chambers of gore, and to romantic bal- loon rides. It mattered not how dark, how depraved, how lovely, how dangerous the place; he was merely an observer. Always watching unbeknownst to anyone and everything.

He stared into the worlds inside a glob, lost and desperate, for he only had the glob and no longer a world of his own.

CHAPTER ONE

"Something extraordinary has happened!!" Potto cried out, running as fast as he could, ankle-deep in desert. He immediately spat out a mouthful of sand, as was often a necessity with the constant sand storms that circled him, and everything in his very limited view.

"*Again* good Potto? This has become a daily occurrence! You *are* the lucky one, aren't you?" Lempshop smiled as he spoke, always appearing the educated gentleman. He knew exactly what Potto would say next. A *new* extraordinary something did not happen to Potto daily. The *same* extraordinary something happened, and there was nothing lucky about it.

Lempshop had become accustomed to it and always found it amusing. Though Lempshop found *most* things amusing. He, in the past, had even found gutting whole families amusing. He had often laughed as they pleaded for their lives. That was a long ago whisper, however.

"I have just realized that I remember very little about yesterday. I remember you, sweet, sweet Lempshop...I remember the little shack we call home. I remember books..." Potto started.

"Those are merely books I *talk* about, Potto. We have no books, fella."

"Hmmm. You must describe them *very* well."

"Oh. I do! I really, really do!"

"And I remember sand. Lots of sand...but I do not remember any *events*. So today *could* be my birthday. So, this extraordinary thing that has happened? It became my birthday! Happy birthday, me!!" He spun and flapped his arms with joy.

Lempshop knew why *he* was on Tractos, he knew the crimes he had committed (and there were enough of them), but what Potto, a gentle and brain-damaged albino Quarol, had done was anybody's guess. Potto sure as hell didn't remember. Potto didn't even know he was on a prison moon.

Potto also didn't remember Lempshop constantly murdering him earlier in their relationship. He had the scars, but like the quaff of white hair that jetted straight up on the top of his head like baby bird fluff, he assumed he was born with them.

After the thirty-sixth murder Lempshop grew bored and decided to simply befriend Potto. He had never had a friend before but he knew that murder was a no-no on all the friend etiquette lists, as it should be.

These past murders didn't *take* because the moon had been equipped with a Life Core. This Life Core, which had been drilled deep into the moon's core, was a device that kept all those imprisoned there alive. It acted as a battery for the billions of microscopic nanobots it sent into the sand storms to continually cure people. In fact, one would be hard pressed to tell the difference between one of these bots and the grains of sand they called flight companion.

The planet that this moon orbited was Lyme Node, the most powerful planet in the known universe. Its leader, The Node, had decided that it was much more cruel to keep prisoners alive and drop them off on a hellishly dry moon forever than to kill them, and The Node was nothing if not extraordinarily cruel.

He also made sure that the male prisoners (and females of the odd alien species) had been given a serum that made them permanently sterile. He couldn't have little criminal and P.O.W. babies running about.

As a side effect it also made all of their bodily fluids extremely poisonous to others, an effect that didn't affect possible lovers while on can't-be-killed Tractos.

The Life Core device was created by master inventor and failed megalomaniac Emperor Reginald Zophricaties. When The Node took over the known universe, Zophricaties was no longer needed as the emperor of his satellite, much to his chagrin. He had invented the Life Core, and a glitchy humanoid cloning machine called the Master Cloner, but he was also responsible for many of the killing machines The Node had forced him to create before he went missing. It had been many many years since anyone had seen Zophricaties, and the universe was probably better for it.

Lempshop had never heard of Zophricaties, and if Potto had, it was many years absent from his struggling brain.

"Happy birthday, my love!" Lempshop said with a chuckle. Things could be worse than having something to celebrate every single day. "I got you a gift!" He spat as he took the small parcel wrapped in a filthy piece of cloth from his tattered coat pocket and passed it to Potto, who accepted it with the excited energy of a small child at an amusement park.

It was an old compass. The same old compass Lempshop gave to Potto every day before stealing it back when Potto was asleep. He didn't do this to be deceptive. He did it because it was all he had to give. Besides, Potto wouldn't remember, and even an old serial killer and badger of a man like himself enjoyed making his only friend feel special on his daily birthday.

Not *every* day was exactly the same for Lempshop. Potto may have been predictable but the variables and challenges that Tractos dished out made things interesting. Though other prisoners generally steered clear of the "well-spoken criminally insane killer and his very irritating pet idiot", newcomers did still pop up thinking they could best them. They came and went, and went quickly. They always underestimated Lempshop's strength and Potto's ability to frustrate.

On this particular day, something happened that had never happened before. Shortly after Lempshop presented the birthday boy with his present, a small eddy of sand swirled around Potto and took the compass from his hand, blowing it into the side of their shack and breaking it.

The heirloom compass that had survived all these many years

was now useless. Potto let out a quick, "Oops", like a startled hic-cup. Lempshop stared.

Years of smiling, years of pleasantries and attempts to remain good-humoured wrapped around his brain like a great serpent, constricting until something deep within had to pop. His face turned scarlet, veins popping in ways that reminded Potto that they were definitely not of the same species. A hand quickly jet-ted out, grabbing Potto by the throat without Lempshop removing his bulging eyes from the broken compass on the ground.

The hand squeezed with strength beyond its modest size. The pale skin on Potto's neck soon bruised and tore, and blood poured out like a faucet. Potto seemed caught in a mid-hapless grin, which was all the more infuriating.

"Happy birthday!!" Lempshop screeched as he turned and started tearing the rest of poor Potto apart from the throat down. He opened up Potto's neck with both hands like he was prying open elevator doors.

After thirty minutes of the most disgusting display of temper tantrum imaginable, he stopped and fell to his knees and tears started streaming down his cheeks. He did not cry for his victim; he did not cry out of guilt...he cried because he knew this was a futile gesture and that the nanobots were already working hard to restore Potto to his old healthy self.

Potto would wake up tomorrow, decide it was his birthday, and wonder what had happened to his clothing and his singing voice. There would be no gift to give him, and for the unforesee-able future, no cheer.

Potto's lifeless body-in-repair, and all the blood was quickly covered over by the blowing sand and nanobots. Soon only his head stuck out. His eyes open and blank, filling up with the sand and its fleas.

Lempshop left him there and went into their shack. His own eyes were stinging with sand and tears.

The absence of furniture seemed more noticeable now. He sat down on the floor next to his imaginary pile of books and let that great serpent loosen its grip on his throbbing brain.

As the constriction dissipated, so did his ability to stay awake. He slapped himself in the face. If he slept he would have less waking time to himself before Potto woke him with non-stop talking, absentmindedly seeking his waning approval. What was once amusing would be hard to cope with. Harder to stomach.

He needed some quiet to think. He needed some solitude to ponder.

For the first time in decades Lempshop was depressed. He needed to rethink his situation. He absentmindedly glanced down at his leg and for the first time in his life noticed how delicious it looked.

CHAPTER TWO

Deep in a residential tower for the MUU (Ministry of Universe Upkeep), and deep in a broom closet, sat a small man. He was small in stature, he was small in mind. His moral compass had been stomped on by all those bigger than he, and his neck was sore from looking over his shoulder.

Not that anyone was *actually* out to get him, but his self-importance was out of whack and he believed himself to be a much more feared and wanted man than he was. No one on Lyme Node was after him in fact. No one on Towerscape (his missing home planet) was after him either. But he fancied that everyone wanted a piece of the infamous criminal mastermind Aye-Aye.

There was *one* being after him, but that being was somewhere in the vastness of space, and Aye hadn't heard any news about him in many many years. Perhaps referring to him as a "being" was a bit generous. It was his father, or rather a thing that once was his father.

To keep down the population on Towerscape, and to rid themselves of the weak and lame, it was a father's right to challenge his son to fight to the death as "rites-of-manhood". Aye's father was the famous robotics expert Mel-Aye, and Aye-Aye had been born into a no-win existence.

His father was not only a diabolical genius, but he had an army of nasty robots at his disposal. He was also revered by their society and was once seen as a hero of sorts. If Aye *had* survived the fight with his father and his insane murder robots, he would have definitely been killed by the people of his planet as some form of nationalistic revenge.

So before his rites-of-man amounted to certain death, he ran away.

In a way Aye-Aye had won. His father was shamed for allowing him to run away and he died off-planet, shunned, disgraced and alone.

Before he died though, he vowed he would find his son, painfully kill him and restore his honour and place in Towerscapian history. Death would not stop him.

So, he invented the perfect robotic killing machine and uploaded his consciousness into it before he passed away. As this new version of himself, "Mel Million Max" would hunt down Aye and kill him. Not so much of a *being*, as an electric ghost. An animated image of his own scowling, wrinkled head hovered above the body of the machine as a translucent bluish hologram. His own grumpy old voice was always on the ready to insult or say something old-man-racist. So much for nurture.

Aye had spent the years between Towerscape and this broom closet smuggling kitchenware, scamming the comatose, and drinking until he was almost blind. It was the drinking that landed him here on Lyme Node, working as a back-up assistant Flood Water Absorber.

Due to the planet's never-ending light drizzle of rain, mild flooding was an issue on Lyme Node and *someone* needed to back up the assistant to the person that cleaned it up when he, she or they got sick, vacationed or died of goddam boredom.

He literally woke up after a bender and had this job. He wasn't sure how or what he had slept with to get it. He considered himself lucky. A legitimate job for a Towerscapian, off of Towerscape, was hard to come by. Tophers (which is what they called themselves) had a reputation for being assholes and scoundrels. Their appearance, with long dark hair and small curled forehead horns often put people off. It was said that many millennia ago they crash landed on a pre-technology/mall earth and gave Earthlings all their silly devil myths.

His reasons for hiding in a broom closet had everything to do with a Squambogian Mantis Widow. After a vigorous, confusing and surprising night of drunken love making, he had sneaked out before she could bite off his head and lay eggs in his corpse. He had a feeling she'd be looking for him. She was not. Again, he really wasn't that important.

He'd come out when he got hungry.

When he eventually *did* get hungry, he poked his head out and looked down the long hallway that lead to his quarters. The door was open. He wasn't sure whether he could see Mantis movement from beyond the door.

He crept out and stepped over the body of the headless man who the Mantis had obviously used in his place. The body of the man rippled from within, filled with pulsating eggs. He stole the uniform and dragged the body to the trash shaft to fall to the incinerator. He wasn't ready to be a papa to insectoids. Not yet anyway.

The man's uniform was miraculously intact, and a Lyme Node militia uniform was a rare thing to come across. Dressed in *that* he would be a sex magnet on his next night at Ginny's Drunk Emporium.

His ex-lover was nowhere to be found.

Looking at himself in this stolen uniform in his mirror actually turned *him* on. He splashed his neck with mouthwash and grabbed the few tokens he had left and headed out. He was ready again, and not picky.

He got on the lift. What he referred to as "his building" was actually part of a network of towers. They were all connected as it wasn't a great idea to go outside on Lyme Node. Too much murder and damp.

Ginny's was on the two hundred and sixty-fourth floor, and only a short hour and forty-five-minute walk from his quarters. It was only four floors beneath a ship pad on the roof that used its loud music to cover up the sound of landing thrusters.

It was on the two hundred and sixty-*third* floor that the lift doors opened on a ship pilot and four guards walking a well-cuffed prisoner with a sack over his head. One of the guards entered a code into the elevator keypad cancelling out Aye's request to stop one floor up at Ginny's.

"There you are! You were supposed to report to Detention Holding, get the briefing and accompany us all the way up!" the pilot barked at Aye, or rather to Aye's uniform. Aye was instantly enamoured with her. Aye was instantly enamoured with everyone. "What happened to you? You look like you were beaten up by a Squambogian Mantis Widow," she inquired with a raised eyebrow.

"That is *very* specific," he slurred, not having completely sobered up in weeks.

"The claw marks on your face give it away. You need some bandage spray. Get some on the Shiv." she answered with her other eyebrow raised.

"The Shiv?"

"Yes. That's the ship we're using. I'm Stig, head pilot. Captain. Your boss. You were Captain Franchiser's co-pilot, weren't you? He spoke very highly of you."

"I-- Oh yes. That's me. He spoke very highly of you, too," he lied.

"Yes, well he was a good man. He will be missed."

"I miss him like crazy. Can't even sleep. He visits me in dreams. We have pastries."

The lift doors opened on the roof. There was a light drizzle because there was always a light drizzle. Aye was knee-deep in this now and if found out would be *joining* the prisoner, who was no doubt being dropped on the prison/P.O.W. moon of Tractos. Plus, perhaps this Captain Stig could be easily seduced and their trip back would be a memorably sexy experience.

Across the ship pad Aye was reminded again of why he hated the outdoors. Lyme Node was very much like Towerscape and Earth in this regard; there was very little outdoors left and that outdoors was very hostile and moist and filled with the smaller unsexy kind of insects.

He also noticed that the Shiv, a small craft he had never seen before, was oddly shaped and reminded him of a giant light bulb.

Once on the Shiv the guards dropped the prisoner off in a very heavily reinforced holding cell and one of them, with a wink, spritzed bandage spray on Aye's face, stopping any additional blood or bits of flesh from soiling his stolen uniform. Aye was enamoured with the guard.

~~~

If you have ever been in a spaceship, simply puttering around in space, you may have noticed that the windows don't open. If you feel a tad stuffy, you can't roll one down to simply "air out the place". If you wanted to climb out a window, onto a ledge to, say, escape the heavy burden of being a petite and very feminine woman trapped inside the body of a genetically-altered-huge male brute, well, you *couldn't*.

You wouldn't be able to fling yourself over a ledge to stop the loneliness, confusion and frustration. There is no "over" in space either. Just out. Sucked out. Horrible business.

Not being able to open the window (and being surrounded by a vast ocean of dark matter) would also suggest that the probability of a long-extinct bird from an entirely different galaxy flying in and fluttering about is nil.

But there Frappe stood in an airlock, because he couldn't roll down the window and there was no down. Tears streaming from his large sad eyes. He felt wrong inside his skin. The skin of a seven-foot-tall, boyishly handsome man rippling with muscles from his laborious job and genetic modification. Although he had a young face and adorable blonde curls atop his chiselled head, he scared people with his size, and he hated that.

He knew there was nothing wrong with the way he felt. It was everybody else in this wretched business he was in. They made him feel so lost and lonely. Too lost and lonely. The bird was a welcome sight.

It was a sparrow that flew into the airlock. An Earth bird long gone from the wildlife-free mall planet. It landed on his shoulder. He smiled at the bird from another time and galaxy and cried harder. The bird pulled a few strands of his hair out with its wee beak and flew off, out of the lock and down a long corridor lit with the kind of lights that make clear skin look pockmarked and veiny.

He had hidden his lyric journal where it could easily be found, and his diary which clearly outlined, with drawings and graphs, his frustration with his own sex. He hoped it would be accidentally found and his secret wouldn't be a secret anymore and perhaps the hurting would turn into healing.

Moments before he hit the airlock release and became one with the universe, both physically and metaphysically, an alarm went off, and the panicked voice of his only other shipmate, Stane, rang through the entire ship: "Frrrraaaaaaaaaaaaaaaaaaaaaaappe!!!!!!!!"

Frappe sighed, wiped away his tears and started to put his ugly charcoal uniform back on. Perhaps tomorrow he would try again.

Lyme Node's second moon Roobos, was a false moon. It was artificially manufactured to store all of the massively populated planet's garbage. This moon, as large as it was, still filled up quickly, and needed to be destroyed and rebuilt every fifty years. Mountains of appliances, holiday decorations, deceased pets and relatives, spaceship wrecks and nom-nom wrappers accumulated quickly and it was easier to implode the whole damn thing and start over from time to time.

Stane sat in the driver's seat of the garbage collection vessel Velveteen Rabbit, his eyes wide, his face pale, and only a few potato chips on his shirt. This meant that he had actually sat up, which he didn't enjoy or do that often. As Frappe moped in, eyes still red, he stopped dead in his tracks.

The light was flashing. Not just any light, but THE light...and it was bright puce.

"What have you done, Sa-Sa?" Frappe said in a deep booming voice that still somehow managed to be meek.

"I...I...I dunno...we were given orders...Roobos was full. Ready to be destroyed and replaced. I started the sequence..."

"Irreversible sequence..." Frappe added to Stane's annoyance.

"...Yeah...to send down the Imploder...easy-peasy...we just suck up the debris after, crush it into space dust...but then the bright puce light went off!" Stane was sweating more than normal, and he normally had enough sweat to salt a buffet.

"But the light goes blue first to warn you..."

"I know...but..."

"And then yellow."

"Well, y'see..."

"And then green, brown, violet, indigo, crimson and salmon..."

"Yeah! I got it, fuckwit!" Stane's jowls shook with anger and frustration. He calmed slightly. "There was a *wrapper* on the console...I didn't see the light. If YOU had've cleaned this place up..."

"They're *your* candy wrappers, Sa-Sa. I don't like candy. Candy makes it so you can't see your feet."

"Yeah, but it's *your* console, too! You should keep it clean, you meat-head." Stane replied, looking down, not seeing his feet.

This was a typical conversation between the two. The unhappy sensitive giant, and the mean and selfish little asshole. Stane was only five-foot-one, and round like a beach ball. The odd thing about seeing these two humans together was that they looked anything but human, and definitely not of the same species.

"What are y'gonna do??" Stane demanded.

"ME?" Now Frappe was sweating. "What did you just schedule to implode?"

"The *other* one."

"The *other* one?"

"Lyme Node's *other* moon."

"But Tractos has people on it!" Frappe felt woozy.

"Prisoners? They all probably died off years ago!" Stane had turned a shade that not even Frappe had seen before, and Frappe had seen him have several heart attacks, one stroke, and hundreds of choking fits.

"It's a prison moon...they drilled a Life Core into it...those prisoners *can't* die!"

"Well then the Life Core will be destroyed along with the moon! I'm doing them a favour!"

They both stayed quiet for what seemed an eternity. Stane's mind worked slowly at best, and the time they needed to process everything and still ruggedly *not* show each other how absolutely terrified they each were, slowed things down further.

Finally Frappe spoke in almost a whisper "...but even that would only bring the light up to *blue*..."

Stane's heart sank deeper into his full gross bowels.

"Great. Really fuckin' presto! They said the odds of the light going bright puce are, like, a billion-kajillion-to-one...and it goes off on *our* ship!" Stane said, sweeping candy wrappers off the console with one angry swoop, exposing all sorts of lights that probably should have been addressed for one reason or another.

"Every Node Soldier in the galaxy is gonna be here soon. *Think!* Is there any way of shutting off the schedule sequence?"

"No...it's locked on. We'd need some kinda computer genius to turn off a scheduled sequence!"

"Damn. We gotta think of something else then."

This was precisely why The Node Guard had genetically altered them and assigned them to sanitation. All one had to do was implode a moon or small planet from time to time, then vacuum up any debris with one's ship. It was the perfect (and safest) place to put these two...almost impossible to mess up. Frappe did all the manual labour, his mind always troubled, and Stane worked the controls, his mind murky with sugar and trans fats.

They also looked, in size, much like every sanitation ship crew: one big, muscle bound ogre, and one little, unnaturally round, greasy guy.

Stane pretended to faint while Frappe stared ahead unable to move, unaware of the sparrow on his shoulder.

CHAPTER THREE

There are many things Aye couldn't do. He couldn't play a musical instrument (not even a Squambogian kazoo snail, which played itself). He couldn't work a stove or swim or tie a knot. He couldn't drive a space ship. He couldn't even drive a golf ball.

He decided, completely subconsciously, that every time Captain Stig gave him a command, he would vomit. This kept the janitorial wet/dry vacuum robot very busy and had Stig overwhelmed with doubt.

"Flu season," Aye coughed.

"No it isn't. The flu only existed on Earth and was eradicated when the Great Mall went up," Stig replied.

"Yes! Their slogan was 'Shop Away Your Ills!'" Aye mused (poorly) to no response. "So...is there a *mister* Stig?" He said with flirty flourish, wiping his mouth on the sleeve of his stolen uniform.

"No. There is another missus Stig," Stig said dryly, trying to hold in her increasing anger.

"Is it serious?" Aye smiled.

Stig only had two eyes to roll which she thought was a shame. For a brief moment she wished she had a dozen more eyes to roll. It would have been much more satisfying. On a very good hunch she typed the name "Jonas Perrish" into the console in front of her as the Shiv soared through the great vacuum of space, on its way to the prisoner moon of Tractos.

A holographic screen appeared before them both. A picture of a man who wasn't Aye came up with the name that appeared on the chest of the uniform that Aye was wearing. He shifted in his chair.

"So, what tipped you off? The vomit? The Mantis wounds? The horns? The smell of Barbohdean gin on my breath?" Aye asked sheepishly.

"Yes," answered Stig even more dryly.

"Well I for one am relieved," Aye sighed heavily. "Now that we don't work together there can be romance without side eye from the boss..."

"I am giving you one attempt and one attempt only to say something that will stop me from throwing you out the air lock. I'll help you get started. Who are you? Where is Perrish? And are you working for or with Flowermorey?" Stig asked, still trying to remain calm but losing what little patience she still possessed.

"I am the infamous, mischievous and *very* sexy scamp Aye-Aye of the lost planet of Towerscape. Perrish has perished. The Mantis Widow made him into a headless womb...and I don't work for any--" Aye's mouth dried up in an instant. He stared at Stig like Stig had just stuck a knife in his forehead mid-sentence.

He finally managed an arid wheeze. "Flowermorey? J-J-James Flowermorey??"

"Damn right James Flowermorey," Stig said proudly.

"THE James Flowermorey?"

"Yes, THE James Flowermorey."

"Is that who is in the holding cell? Ja-James Flowermorey?"

"Ja-James Flowermory is indeed in the holding cell."

"I rode in an elevator...just inches from James Flowermorey?"

"James Flowermorey is exactly the man you rode right next to in a *very small* elevator."

"James Flowermorey A.K.A. Weird Jimmy?"

"Weird Jimmy James Flowermorey."

"Ok. Let's get to that airlock," Aye said in a panic.

James "Weird Jimmy" Flowermorey was the stuff of nightmares. He was up there with all the horror movie iconic killers. He was legendary. He was *truly* infamous and known from one side of the known universe to the other. There were small slugs under dead fallen leaves under rotten logs in never-seen-before swamps on Squambog that shuddered at the name of James "Weird Jimmy" Flowermorey. Even the cold virus steered clear of the man.

As did death. Weird Jimmy was rumoured to be unkillable and even immortal. Aye may have looked the part of a demon, but Flowermorey was, quite possibly, the devil himself. Aye was quite right to request the airlock.

"Relax," smirked Stig, enjoying Aye's discomfort immensely. "Don't believe everything you've read."

"Read?"

"Heard. We caught him, didn't we? And within the hour he will be on Tractos forevermore and no one will ever have to fear ol' Weird Jimmy ever again. Though I don't envy the other prisoners."

"He'll escape." Aye said matter-of-fact. He took no comfort in Stig's words.

"Budgher Lempshop," Stig argued.

"What about him?" Aye sneered.

"Notorious killer. They said there wasn't a prison that could hold him...once on Tractos he was never seen again."

"Budgher Lempshop was no James Flowermorey. Budgher Lempshop *wished* he were James Flowermorey. Budgher Lempshop doesn't hold a disgusting funhouse mirror to James Flowermorey," Aye said under his breath but loud enough for Stig to hear.

At this point Stig turned back to her piloting. Now that she didn't have a useful co-pilot, she would need to navigate by herself. "Well the airlock is at the back of the ship. Right next to the holding cell," she said smiling widely. "Off you go."

Aye didn't speak for a very long time. He sat there and stared out the front window into space. He was terrified and this had sobered him up at a jarring speed. He found Stig's confidence somewhat comforting and was glad she hadn't decided to stick him in the Shiv's only holding cell for impersonating a co-pilot, but his head was drowning in a pool of doom water.

Finally Stig broke the silence. "So...Towerscape, huh? One of the Seventy Lost Planets, huh?"

"Yep," Aye muttered.

"I used to be able to name all seventy. Bantor, Tsk'tdink, Hallowlund, Towerscape, Flet, Grande JebJeb D'noll, Quarolode..."

"Good for you," Aye was now fear-grumpy and sounded like a sulky six-year-old.

"Fine. We are approaching Tractos. See? Nothing happened. I was debating whether I should just leave you there, too..."

Aye looked at her, broken. He started crying. "Please....I'm harmless. I'm just a...a...a pathetic...pathetic drunk...not a criminal...not...infamous at all," he quietly pleaded, being honest to both Stig and himself for the first time since he was a child. "Just pathetic."

"Oh, don't cry...I'll take you back, but you're still going to have to answer for this, you idiot."

"Thank you," he smiled weakly through tears and a very runny nose.

Captain Stig was just about to enter the moon's atmosphere when a loud siren went off. Aye fell out of his seat. A light on the wall started flashing bright puce.

~~~

Potto tried to sit up. He couldn't. He also couldn't see. There seemed to be sand in his eyes. There seemed to be sand in his nose. There seemed to be sand in his ears and his mouth and his everything.

He couldn't call for Lempshop from under all that sand so he made the executive decision to wriggle. He couldn't remember all the times he had been buried in the past, but he assumed that it had happened often by the level of skill he noticed he had in wriggling.

He wriggled left and right, back to front, with each wriggle putting more sand under him than over him until he broke through the surface with his face. He coughed up sand, and blinked out more sand. He then wriggled his way out of his little burial plot and stopped to catch his breath. The desert had given birth to its new fully-grown Quarol baby.

After a long spell of trying to decide whether or not he *was* a newborn, he stood. His legs were wobbly and, now that he could see, he noticed that his shirt was covered in blood with sand and sand midges stuck to it. When something confused Potto, which happened a lot, a little voice inside his struggling head always told him "*Move along!*" and he did.

So a wide smile stretched across his face as that same voice in his head said "Find Lempshop!" and he did.

He found Lemphop in the little shack behind him that he instantly recognized as home. There Lempshop sat on the floor, looking up like a cat caught eating the family budgie. His mouth and chin were covered in purple blood giving him a certain "pie eating contest winner" look. His legs were missing.

"What 'cha been up to?" asked Potto, his brain screaming at him to *move along*.

"Mmmm? What?" Lempshop answered absentmindedly, "Oh, the legs, yes. I seem to have eaten them."

"Not to sound judgey, but why did you do that?" Potto asked with a child-like wonder and not an ounce of judgeyness.

Lempshop stared off, seeming to both answer Potto and mutter to himself through a fog, "Nothing kills us. Nothing. Terrible curse. Terrible curse."

"So?" Potto said after much too long of a pause.

"So I came up with the perfect way to beat the system!" Lempshop blurted out, snapping out of his foggy malaise. "One would cease to exist if one were eaten, no?"

Potto shrugged honestly. *Move along.*

"How can one outlive digestion? The bots would have nothing to repair! Can't turn shit into a person methinks," Lempshop added.

"Fair enough!" Potto smiled not understanding in even the tiniest way.

"I didn't want to burden *you* with this task, dear Potto. I fear I've already put you through enough."

"Much appreciated!"

"So I thought I'd do it myself."

"Bravo! Encore! En garde!"

"So the legs went first."

"Such a trailblazer!"

"Go now, dear Potto. Go for a walk and let me rest. Auto-cannibaleeeese takes much energy, tiger cat."

"Yes. It. Does." Potto agreed. He turned on point, slipping briefly on purple blood, and pushed open the door to venture out into the monotony of the landscape beyond. He stopped before exiting with one last curiosity. "Oh...I forgot to ask...how were they?"

"My legs?" Lempshop asked searching for clarity.

"Yes!"

"Takes a little getting used to. It's a sweet meat."

"Hmm. Who'd have guessed?"

"Some people are dreamers...some are doers. M'boy, I am a *doer*." Lempshop announced with vibrato.

And on that Potto took his leave and wandered out into the desert for a walk. Within ten minutes he was buried in sand again.

~~~

It was now Stig's turn to panic. Weird Jimmy may have been a nightmare personified, but he had nothing on a bright puce light flashing while an alarm seemed to be screaming "AAAAAAH WAH WAH WAH EVERYBODY PANIC WAH WAH!!! THIS IS THE END WAH WAH WAH!!! THIS IS WORSE THAN EVERYTHIIIIIIIING ELSE BAD COMBIIIIIIIINED WAH WAAAAAAH!!!!"

Aye didn't get this. Seeing the cucumber cool Captain Stig lose her cucumber cool did however break him from his Flowermorey panic, if only briefly. He, unlike most that worked for The Node, had not been conditioned from the time he started his employment to be triggered by a bright puce flashing light.

"What's going on?? What does that bright puce flashing light mean?" he yelled over the siren.

"I don't know. Nobody but The Node knows. But it's not good!" She yelled back.

"Well at least it's not 'James Flowermorey has escaped' not good!"

Just then the alarm cut out just long enough for the Shiv's computer to announce, "System failure. Holding cell has been compromised. James Flowermorey has escaped."

"WAAAAAAAAAAAAHHHHHHHH!!!   HOOOOOOLY
FUUUUUUUCKBALLS WAH WAH WAAAAAAH!!!" wailed the
alarm.

It was this that snapped Stig out of *her* shock for a moment.
She dived across the room and hit a button (a very random button
to Aye) that closed the hatch to their cockpit.

"Knutt? Lockdown mode for the entire Shiv."

"Lockdown mode is now in effect Captain Stig," said the calm
voice of the computer.

"Life signs beyond the flight deck?"

"There is only one life sign beyond the flight deck. I read that
the DNA of guards Ronson and Tool can be found in holding, in
the corridor, in the engine room, in the lavatory and in the ship's
kitchen."

"*Damn*," said Stig.

"*Gross*," shuddered Aye.

The Shiv's artificial gravity suddenly shut off. The lights
started flashing. The Shiv started shaking and buckling. Stig and
Aye were thrown around like two helium balloons in a hurricane.

"It seems James Flowermorey is now tearing apart the engine
battery and it is affecting the electrical system. I may not be able
to keep the flight deck in lockdown, Captain Stig," the computer
said in a manner that seemed almost dryer than its previous dry-
ness.

Aye screamed at a pitch that would make a dog pee on the carpet, and then did a face plant into the wall. He was stunned for a
moment, only able to focus on a tooth that once belonged to his
mouth but now was floating a foot in front of its old home. He
flicked it away.

The captain had managed to get to the control panel and was
furiously pressing buttons. "I think I know a way to--" she suddenly stopped trying desperately to save them and threw her
hands up, clutching her face. It seems she had someone's tooth in
her eye.

"It would seem that James Flowermorey is just outside the
flight deck door and attempting to get it open. This will not be a
concern in two minutes and fifteen seconds when the Shiv will

crash into Tractos. We are now entering its atmosphere," stated the computer.

The door opened. The ship crashed. Weird Jimmy went sailing past both of them and head first into the thick, hard front window. Captain Stig went headfirst into the hard and jaggedy metallic-and-jaggedy-plastic console. Aye went headfirst into the comfy observation seating around the edges of the flight deck. The bits of guards Ronson and Tool became even smaller bits in their various locations around the ship. A small spider in the ship's walls was not affected at all, much to the dismay of a small fly also in the ship's walls.

When Aye opened his eyes the first thing he saw was the flashing bright puce light. The alarm had broken and all was silent. The second thing he saw was an unconscious Weird Jimmy with a messed-up face. He was a lot skinnier than Aye had imagined.

The final thing he saw was Captain Stig's brains where they weren't supposed to be, three feet from her skull and dripping off of the console.

"Knutt?" He managed.

"Yes?" Said the computer.

"Am I alive?"

"Yes."

"Dammit!"

"I detect two life signs. You and James Flowermorey. Captain Stig is now deceased. It would also seem that a Janitorial Imploder has targeted Tractos for demolition. The ship is mostly intact. The engine has been damaged and a new power supply must be found. You have sixty minutes to connect the engine to this new power source and pilot the ship away from Tractos if you wish to survive."

"Pilot? I don't know how to pilot a ship..." Aye sputtered.

"Then I correct myself. You have sixty minutes to connect the engine to a new power supply *and find someone that can* pilot the ship away from Tractos if you wish to survive."

"What am I supposed to use as a power supply?"

"This is a Shiv 360 Turbo Airship. It can be powered on very little, including living brain action potential."

"Oh, piss off."

"Seriously! The neurons' electric signals along axons to the synap--"

"Ok! Bully for the Shiv! I'm not likely to understand any of this! Just tell me what to do!"

"There are two living brains on board besides your own."

"Two??"

"Though the Captain is dead, her brain still has some spark in it, and the Life Core on this moon seems to be fixing it. Unfortunately, her body died before it was in range so it wasn't recognized. There's not enough spark yet to power the whole ship, but enough to power me. I am running on back-up energy that is almost gone. If you do not do this I will not be able to talk you through hooking James Flowermorey up to the ship's engine."

Not only did the Shiv have interesting power options, but it was a ship with a computer system that could be loaded into the smaller wet/dry vacuum robot so that it could actually leave the ship. So, the ship itself could actually join you if you wanted company for dinner, it could come into the office to do its own paperwork, and it could act as extra security if you were to get attacked while using it to check your email (all while slurping up that spilled milkshake you dropped earlier). Each one had a slightly different personality and name. This one was called Knutt, and Knutt was boring.

Soon Aye was sitting next to a large jar of a liquid he didn't recognize that housed a brain he wished was still in a sexy pilot, as he wired it to the main console of the ship.

"There. Just as you said. Is it working?" he asked.

"Yes. And now there is at least *one* good brain on the ship," answered Knutt in a new fandangled snide tone.

"Whaaaa?" Aye was taken aback. There seemed to be some Stig personality left in that brain. Knutt was boring no more.

Knutt then talked Aye into dragging Weird Jimmy down the corridor and into the engine room. Aye was terrified the entire time to the point of vomiting again. The new improved Knutt berated him accordingly.

He strapped Jimmy into a strange sort of metallic dentist chair.

Huge clamps came down on the unconscious fiend's chest and legs, trapping him. Wires were inserted into his head and various places on his body, trapping his mind and nervous system as well.

"Now you only have seven minutes to find a pilot."

"Can't *you* pilot the damn thing? Or talk me through it?"

"This, as I have stated, is a Shiv 360 Airship, not an earth movie airplane. It is very sophisticated, and digits I don't have are needed. You are wasting time, idiot."

Aye jumped out the hatch, ran two steps and immediately tripped over something sticking out of the sand. It was the top of someone's head. He dug out a pale face that blinked the sand out of its eyes.

"You know how to pilot a ship???" Asked Aye.

"I dunno. Probably!" Smiled Potto.

CHAPTER FOUR

General Kendra Eppie walked down the dark metallic corridor with a bit of a hunch. His back had been aching and his hot oil treatments kept getting cut short by tender and irresistible love making with his masseuse.

He caught his reflection in the shiny metal wall and straightened up. He watched himself walk, adding a puffed chest and an expression of cruel authority. With the thick curl of fuchsia hair upon his otherwise shining bald head, and his tall lanky frame, this looked put-on and ridiculous. Unhinged perhaps, but not authoritative.

He needed to be as foreboding as possible in front of The Node. As the right hand man of the evil ruler of the known universe, he couldn't afford to show weakness of character or spinal stenosis.

Nobody knew what planet General Eppie hailed from. It was said that he had blown up his own planet, killing billions of his race. He couldn't stand the competition and, as a result, his fragile overblown ego had decided he needed to be the last of his kind. It made him feel special. It made him feel all warm and fuzzy.

As he entered The Node's Great Chamber, he cupped his bony hand over his mouth and nose to check his breath. It smelled of mustard and dandelions. Perfect. He straightened up even more, making himself look extra unnatural and unintentionally strange. Standing this way also made his voice warble as it strained and filtered through his chronic back pain.

The Node had only ever seen and heard him walk and talk in this manner, so he had always assumed it was an odd norm and a trait of Eppie's mysterious race. It wasn't.

"General!" The Node called out in a booming, slightly electronic voice. The exact age of The Node was unknown. The small combed-over head that stuck out of the huge, imposing, black chrome robotic suit of armour looked ancient. He looked like someone's sweet old frail grandpapa sticking his head out of a hematite humanoid military tank.

"Your greatness," Eppie sharply warbled back.

"This is a great day!" The Node beamed. "The bright puce light alarm has finally been set off! Callooh! Callay!"

~~~

Aye dug at the ground around Potto in complete panic. He was running out of time to get off of Tractos. Potto smiled the smile of a child sleep-talking. Aye paused briefly, suddenly remembering that he was on a moon filled with criminals and dangerous ne'er-do-wells.

"Oh wait. You some kinda crazy psycho guy?" He asked.

"I imagine so," beamed Potto. It had been a long time since someone other than Lempshop had asked him a question and he wanted to seem agreeable to his new chum.

"You imagine so? Why are you here?"

"I was going for a stroll."

Deciding that, perhaps, in this situation it really didn't matter, Aye started digging furiously again as he continued asking questions. "No, no, no...what crime did you commit?"

"Ooooh! Nope, can't remember. I imagine it was terrible. It would have to have been, right?"

Aye stopped digging again. "Okay, let's start again. Will you hurt me if I finish digging you out?"

"Hurt you?"

"Yes. Y'know, cut off my thumbs? Skin me alive? Use my skull as a chamber pot?"

"No! I can't imagine why I'd do that. You seem so nice. And I just peed in this sand here."

"Good!" Aye went into wombat-mode and started digging like his life depended on it. Because it really, really did.

Soon Potto could use his wriggling super power to take over. He stood, sand caked onto the blood still damp on his shirt and the urine-soaked front of his trousers. Both of his feet were fast asleep and as Aye dragged him by the arm towards the open hatch of the Shiv, he felt like they were hard, fatty hooves attached directly to his knees.

As he staggered up the ramp the tingling pins and needles started to set in and he dropped, taking a seat right where he was.

"What are you doing?" Aye yelled at that make-a-dog-pee pitch. Time was running out and his situation was making him feel like he was playing with an extreme jack-in-the-box, with a clown of death-by-implosion ready to spring out at any second and swallow them up.

"Gimme a sec, it feels *so weird*," Potto answered, "Like, I don't know if it hurts or it tickles. Kinda like a gum ache when your tooth is loose. But in your foot. No, no, I don't know if I like this at all."

Aye dragged him the rest of the way by that tuft of white fluff Potto called hair.

Once on the flight deck Aye sat Potto in Captain Stig's old chair and yelled to no-one in particular "Power this baby up! Let's get the hell outta here!"

"Right away, dickhead," the new-improved Knutt sang out as the ship started lifting out of the sand.

Potto sat and stared at Aye still smiling inanely, as Knutt started counting down the seconds until Tractos imploded.

"What are you waiting for?" Aye squealed.

"Oh I dunno. It's just nice to have someone new to talk to," Potto smiled back as his hands started absentmindedly pressing buttons. The ship started to raise up higher and it abruptly took off upwards towards the atmosphere. "Oh look! Apparently I *do* know how to pilot a ship! Well *that's* certainly a relief. So...your name is Dickhead?"

~~~

On board the Velveteen Rabbit, Frappe had dead-lifted Stane off the floor, hoisting him up by his armpits. His armpits didn't like the weight of his body mingling with gravity and let him know through searing tendon-snapping pain. But this wasn't their first tussle. In fact, this was how they spent most holidays.

"You let me down right now!" Stane screeched through this very familiar pain.

"I'm going to kill you, Sa-Sa! If I'm going to be thrown in a brig or in front of a firing squad then I might as well enjoy myself first!" Frappe shot back, lifting Stane higher. The alarm stopped. The bright puce light went out. All was quiet. The sparrow perched on the fire extinguisher scratched at an under-wing itch with its cute little beak.

They both stared at the hushed alarm for a second as it registered in their adrenaline fueled brains. Frappe dropped Stane moments before Stane's rotator cuffs exploded, and ran towards the console. Stane joined him after finally getting up from his up-turned-turtle-like struggle on the floor.

"It stopped! It stopped!" Stane hollered as if cheering a hometown sports team. "Ohmagod my arms hurt!"

They watched through the front window. A Shiv ship flew away from the moon as the Imploder hit. Within seconds the moon, Budgher Lempshop and all the rest of Tractos' inhabitants (finally!) were no more.

~~~

At the exact moment Tractos imploded, The Node and General Eppie just happened to be gazing at it through the observation window of the Great Chamber. Neither was expecting this turn of events, but after a moment of shock, The Node softly said, "Well this just keeps getting better, doesn't it?"

The bright puce light had gone out again.

"Could it be? Could it be that it was both found *and* destroyed all within the same hour?" He rhetorically asked in an audible whisper.

"Tractos? We've known about Tractos for a long time..." Eppie offered in his least condescending tone.

"Not Tractos, you idiot. Something *on* Tractos. Something I didn't *know* was on Tractos. Something that could not be detected by any of our scanners until it detected its own demise and sent out a distress signal. Something I have been looking for a very very long time."

They stood in silence (for what seemed like a much longer time for Eppie) before he finally mumbled a low, "And that would be?"

Before The Node could answer, if indeed he had ever intended to answer, the door creaked open, and in meekly hop-walked Eppie's assistant Freckles.

Squambog was a large swampy planet that many different species called home. It was not only Lyme Node's closest inhabited neighbour and ally, but supplied Lyme Node with a plant called a "myspiston", the key ingredient to the highly addictive and popular recreational drug "Pyst".

Not only was it home to Mantis Widows and their unfortunate mates, but to the main Squambogian race called Kancorians. Female Kancorians generally resembled tailless humanoid geckos. Bald heads, humongous lidless eyes, blue striped skin and wall-climbing hands and feet. They were strangely beautiful, but unlike actual geckos, they could occasionally breathe fire and slit a throat in an instant with their dew claws.

Male Kancorians could range from the *greater* muscles-on-their-muscles green reptilian variety which stood at seven feet tall, to the *lesser* Kancorians, a more amphibious-looking, muddy brown and warty, small and weak sub-species with wig-looking clay-brown curly hair, which were often called "little toads". Freckles was the latter of these Kancorians. He was a little toad.

"Sir?" He said like a soft burp.

"This better be important," Eppie snapped, instantly apologizing with his eyes.

Freckles looked out the observation window at the sky where Tractos once spun. "Well, as you can see, the prisoner moon of Tractos was accidentally destroyed. We have names of the maintenance crew responsible if you would like to punish them," Freckles reported.

"Punish them?" The Node said. "I think perhaps we should

promote them!"

"Also," Freckles said sheepishly, "we have reports of who was aboard that Shiv that escaped the moon before it was destroyed."

"That Shiv that escaped the moon before it was destroyed?" The Node asked. He had been smiling up until now, which was something Eppie had never seen in all his years of service. But this was an elevator of a smile. An elevator going down. By the time it reached the sub-basement of his face The Node's eyes had started bulging. Eppie shuttered. Freckles wasn't paying any attention, and looked up to Eppie, not reading The Node's new mood.

"And sir, you missed your fruit oil treatment this morning. Your back isn't going to get any better if you don't let me--"

"Enough! Later! Out!" Eppie hollered with more professional embarrassment than anger. Freckles hop-walked towards the door with haste.

"Wait!" yelled The Node. "Report! Who *was* on that ship?"

"Um, uh," Freckles stammered. He wasn't used to The Node addressing him directly. "Our scan, your fantastic-ness, shows a Towerscappian Topher with worker tags named Aye-Aye, notorious human killer James "Weird Jimmy" Flowermorey, and the prisoner ID of the third shows that he is, quite curiously, a colour-changing Quarol called Potto. Perhaps the last of his kind."

"Aren't Towerscape and Quarolode two of the Seventy Lost?" The Node asked calmly.

"Y-yes."

The volume of the following tantrum could be heard, arguably, on both Towerscape and Quarolode, lost or not.

CHAPTER FIVE

Teeg pulled up her black leather thigh-high boot and reattached it to her garter. The pleasure on the face of her "servant" turned to trepidation.

"You were told not to touch me," she asserted, putting down the electric nipple prod she had found in his kitchen next to a very old bottle of balsamic vinegar. She flipped her long platinum hair over her shoulder playfully. This is exactly how she had expected things to go down.

The small human male handcuffed naked to the chair got his right hand free from the cuffs and went for a feel when he was instructed not to do so. "I-I-I'm sorry mistress. I just couldn't help myself," he pleaded. He knew Teeg's rules, and although he had paid good money for this encounter, he should've known better.

She unsheathed a long thin sword she had leaning against his teak coffee table and without him even seeing it, his guilty hand was soon on the floor, having a shower in the vodka thinned blood pumping from his wrist. He went into shock immediately.

"I'm afraid that will cost you a little more," she purred calmly. She picked up his pants from the floor and fished into his pocket, pulling out a handful of credit disks. "Oh! Mr. Granit...you were holding out on me!" She smiled mischievously as she slit his throat.

She emptied his pockets and put the disks into a small ruck-sack. She had no pockets. The PVC bodysuit, garters, thigh-high boots, long black gloves, and the leather mask that started half-way up her exquisite nose and extended to the top of her lovely forehead, was her regular day-to-day outfit. She wore it when she shopped. She wore it when she went to the bank and to the den-tist. She would have even worn it to her friend Cheryl's wedding, if she had a friend Cheryl, and Cheryl had finally decided to tame her wild ways and settle down.

It distracted the idiot men she often had to deal with, and it intimidated everyone else. Plus, quite frankly, it made her feel like a superhero.

Though she did enjoy humiliating people, she did not only ac-cept the role of a sadomasochistic mistress for money; she also accepted the role as an easy means to kill and rob rich and dis-gusting citizens of the already over-populated Lyme Node when funds were low and bounty hunting work was sparse.

She left moronic Mr. Granit tied to the chair, bleeding out over his nakedness. She grabbed a sandwich from his fridge and headed back to her ship with money for a few repairs and enough fuel to get her and her shipmates Gekko and Clory back to their hideout on the "rumoured" moon of Barbohd.

Teeg was stolen from her family on the now-lost planet of Flet at a young age and sold to the harem of Fat Dante, where she grew up, learned to fight fiercely and learned love-making techniques that would make a sex circus acrobat blush. She had joined the order of the Barbohdeans after murdering the abusive and detest-able Fat Dante and escaping.

The Barbohdeans were a not-so-secret secret society of often violent-for-good-reason women of many species led by another Flettocean, a six-and-a-half-foot, musclebound Amazonian-of-a-woman that aptly called herself K'ween.

Teeg trained further there, where she mastered many martial arts, sword fighting and torture techniques. She would never be captured again, and her overt sexuality would forevermore be a lush rainforest of power and strength, not a bleak desert of forced slavery and submission. Teeg now called the shots for Teeg.

Aboard Teeg's ship, The Muse, were her two fellow

Barbohdeans. The Squambogian "Gekko" was a blue fire-breath-ing Kancorian assassin, and Clory was a very odd and very very rare sentient plant species from Quarolode known by the human-oid Quarols as Sentaphylls. They were usually seen and treated as peaceful gods on Quarolode, but not Clory. She was exiled for murdering an entire village of the humanoids. Every species has its assholes.

Gekko was exiled for "multiple regicide" after killing five dif-ferent Squambogian kings, all named Catjack.

When Teeg entered The Muse, Gekko climbed down the wall from the ship's ceiling and Clory moved across the bridge on her vines like a swirl of entangled wooden snakes to greet her. Though Clory could not talk and Gekko never had, the three joined hands and Teeg silently communicated to them that she had been successful. They had never doubted that she would be.

One of the communication screens pinged and announced "in-coming bulletin" in a voice that sounded like a game show host. Teeg raced over excitedly and read the message.

"Work! The Node is calling all Bounty Hunters on Lyme Node to meet in his Great Chamber. If *The Node* is hiring bounty hunt-ers, I think it's safe to say we'll be able to afford more than just a few repairs and some beef jerky," she smiled wickedly.

~~~

As The Shiv slowly made its way back to Lyme Node, Aye put his feet up on a control panel. He was finally able to relax, catch his breath, and think about his very important next move. "Let's not dock at Central. Let's dock above Ginny's and go for a drink. I still might be able to get some use out of this uniform before they have to tear it from my cold dead corpse."

Potto didn't answer. In fact, Potto was unconscious in his chair. Something was happening to his brain as his system left be-hind the effects of the Life Core. Aye didn't notice. He was used to being ignored.

Inside Potto's mind he was right smack-dab where he was in waking life. He was piloting The Shiv, but Aye was nowhere to be found, and through the window he didn't see an approaching Lyme Node, he saw an approaching sun. He was heading into it and he didn't feel any reason to steer away. He didn't feel panic. He didn't feel anything. He just stared into the sun which was kind enough not to burn out his retinas.

A small firefly started flitting around his head, swooping and diving. He waved his hand around his head in a half-assed attempt to shoo it away. Its light was dim but getting brighter, and it was growing. Finally, it pulled his focus from the sun and by the time he got a good look at it, the bug was the size of a squirrel, and the glow had changed into a sparkling golden shimmer.

He also noticed that it wasn't a bug or a squirrel at all but a beautiful winged woman. It was a fairy.

"Potto of Quarolode, I am Bundle," said the fairy. Potto did not react. He wasn't surprised, he wasn't afraid, he wasn't amused, nor was he annoyed.

"Hello, Bundle," he said in his usual chipper manner, his gaze drawn back to the sun.

"It's pretty isn't it?" she mused.

"Hmm?"

"The sun."

"The sun?"

"The sun. The sun in front of you."

"Oh yes. Yes. It is beautiful," he said, his gaze turning back to her with a startle, "Oh! Wow! So are you! You are the most beautiful thing I've seen since..." he trailed off, his dark, white-less eyes fogging over.

"Since?"

"Since...something. Something I used to know. Some*one* I used to know. I think. I can't remember. I *can't*." He smiled softly and turned back to the sun.

"Not even going to try to remember who?" She asked.

"Nope."

"Try."

"Nope. I don't wanna."

Bundle fluttered around, getting between Potto's gaze and the sun. He smiled at her. Her sparkle could not compete with the sun's intensity and she was now in silhouette. "Please try," she pleaded.

He tried to remember what else he had seen that was as

beautiful, while her shape was burning into his broken memory. A face or a name seemed far away, like a stone dropped down a bottomless pit, but very suddenly he started feeling something. He felt it first in his legs and his arms. It moved to his chest, and up his neck and into his empty head.

At once he felt like the warmth of the sun had entered his body and filled him with a feeling of comfort and home. He felt forests and mountains and rivers.

He lifted off his seat and started floating weightless around the flight room, not because the artificial gravity had been turned off, but because his heart was full. He was dreaming and he was the living embodiment of love.

Bundle laughed and clapped her hands. She did somersaults in the air and fluttered around him as tears of joy and release flowed from his eyes.

"There you go!" she beamed.

"What is happening to me?" He sobbed through a smile that was big, even for Potto.

"You are remembering!" she cheered.

~~~

When Potto opened his eyes to his reality, Aye was shaking him. Everything he had just dreamed was instantly forgotten, but he still felt so good.

There were no bright suns through the window, but instead a dark and slightly damp Lyme Node they were quickly approaching.

"You dozed off. I'm no pilot, but I don't think it's a good thing for the pilot to doze off," Aye complained.

"This ship is *easy*!" Potto said, reassuring him.

"We are approaching Lyme Node. I should probably request permission to dock," Knutt announced.

"Yeah, request docking at Docking Station 6678, not at Central Stationing. And don't use our real ship code. Make one up. They're probably going to be looking for me," said Aye. Usually he was merely being paranoid when he thought people were looking for him, but this time he was right.

"Clearance electronically requested, dickhead." Knutt replied.

Aye didn't notice; the slur didn't register.

"Have you ever been to Ginny's?" Aye asked Potto.

"I don't think I've even been to Lyme Node," Potto answered.

"Wha? Weird. Ok, Knutt, he doesn't know where to find Docking Station 6678, so direct...um...

"Potto of Quarolode," Potto offered, only remembering his home planet's name because he wasn't thinking about it.

"Wow, you're a Quarol? I thought they were all extinct."

"Extinct?"

"Well I dunno. Rumour mill. It's one of the lost planets. But it's a big universe; could be out there somewhere. S'ok. My home planet is one of 'em, too. I just know there are probably *too many* Towerscappian Tophers around. Mostly on the prison moon of Tract—oh. Well I guess there are way less of them now." Aye mused.

Once at the docking station, Knutt took over and landed the ship. Aye couldn't wait to get off of The Shiv. He had to relieve himself and had trouble peeing in space. Through the light drizzle of rain, they made their way to the elevator. Potto looked over the edge as a blast of moderate temperature wind blew him over the side of the building, presumably to his death.

Aye looked at the ledge and then back at the elevator. He had a difficult time trying not to ignore Potto's fall with his own need to get to a bar. He caved and sighed heavily looking over the edge, holding onto the railing much tighter than Potto had. Potto was on another ledge two stories down.

"Have a nice life, Potto of Quarolode!" Aye yelled down.

"You too, Dickhead!" Potto yelled back.

~~~

Much further beyond the planet of Squambog, deeper into space, and with no discernible neighbours to complain about the noise, was the small planet of Chagrin.

Chagrin was feared throughout the universe. Even The Node chose to ignore it. What made it so frightening were its inhabitants, a species of varied adorable anthropomorphized woodland creatures commonly called Teddy Bears. It was a name that humans gave them as they resembled fuzzy plush toys, and though highly intelligent, they lacked proper vocal chords and were unable to speak up for themselves.

Not knowing what a teddy bear actually was, they soon accepted and responded to this name, figuring it meant "terrifying". And soon it did.

They didn't actually resemble bears at all, but all manner of different animals from the pre-mall Earth, Squambog, and various other planets' fauna, only smaller, fuzzier, and cuter. And each one was deadly. They all possessed razor sharp claws, animal dexterity and all of them were trained in *every* martial art and fighting style in the known universe.

Among the Teddy Bears of Chagrin was their fiercest and most feared warrior, Toobli Dentatan (or at least that is what his name was off planet in Lyme Node's database of bounty hunters). His name was a misspelled old-earth scientific order name for the aardvark, Tubulidentata, which basically meant "tubular dental work". Though Toobli looked more like the plush version of a baby anteater than an aardvark, he, like the aardvark, possessed a circular row of teeth at the end of his long snout.

Unlike most of his brethren, who preferred not to leave Chagrin, Toobli had a spherical and small, but amazingly armed and incredibly fast space ship called The Gooseberry.

Most names of various things on his planet were vastly less terrifying and more darling sounding than the Teddy Bears of Chagrin realized, but no one would dare correct them or laugh for fear of being eviscerated.

There was one who did not fear Toobli Dentatan, and that was a greater Kancorian male named Jorge Jorge Jorge. At close to eight feet tall, the reptilian was huge, even for a Kancorian, and feared very little.

It was in the space over Lyme Node that the two bounty hunters met up. They had both been in the area when The Node's call went out to any nearby hunters wishing to make some coin. When Toobli saw the Kancorian's ship, he instantly recognized it and started firing.

Jorge Jorge Jorge was having none of it, and never backed down from a fight or a possible bounty. He fired back, narrowly missing The Gooseberry. Each hunter was very apt at outmanoeuvring each other and they swooped and fired at each other like dancers dancing amongst fireworks, almost depleting their ammunition before they finally got bored.

Another bounty hunter, the humanoid Blankton, tried to avoid the two as he made his way to Lyme Node, flying his ship where Tractos once was. Blankton was one of the many (very flawed) clones of the late inventor of the (very flawed) Master Cloner, Emperor Reginald Zophricaties. They all went by the name Blankton, making things very confusing for anyone who had to deal with the idiots.

With one last attempt to shoot Toobli down, Jorge Jorge Jorge missed again and hit Blankton, causing the clone and his ship to be torn apart and incinerated faster than he could say, "No, wait!"

He would not be missed. There was another Blankton flying right behind him.

CHAPTER SIX

Inside The Node's Great Chamber, The Node was nowhere to be seen. When the bounty hunters arrived, they were instead greeted by a dozen rows of fold-out chairs, a side table with coffee and hard, dry cookies, and an agitated General Kendra Eppie.

Freckles sat off to the side with a paper notepad and oversized novelty pencil to take the meeting's minutes (his webbed fingers made it difficult to hold a regular pencil). He had placed a few vases of half-dead, purple and brown (mostly brown) flowers to brighten up the dark dankness of the room. A few maintenance men worked quietly in the background on dripping pipes, clogged duct work, and hanging wires.

Jorge Jorge Jorge arrived first and headed straight for the cookies. He ate them all. No one would dare call out the huge reptile on this apart from Toobli, but Toobli didn't eat cookies and therefore, when he arrived moments later, he didn't notice. He had also eaten an entire bag of "Gaston's BBQ Gelatin Grub Parts and Dried Human Fingers" before showing up.

Teeg walked with purpose into the chamber and sat right up front. She didn't take her eyes off of Eppie, and ignored everyone else. She was alone. Gekko had gone looking for sustenance and Clory was guarding The Muse. The others steered clear of her and her reputation for causing horrible pain and tantalizing humiliation.

A robot the size of a large human rolled in on its tank-tread "foot", and immediately started grumbling and complaining about the slight dampness. The blue, translucent holographic projection of a middle-aged man's horned head that floated atop it switched topics from dampness to the price of ship parking without skipping a beat. Everyone ignored Mel Million Max, which gave him one more thing to grumble and complain about.

A dozen or so other bounty hunter-wannabes shuffled in, grabbed their paper cups of weak coffee and had a seat wondering why they hadn't been served cookies. There was much excited chatter amongst them. No one had ever known The Node to hire bounty hunters, and no one had ever been to a function such as this that didn't serve cookies.

Lastly the Blankton clone sauntered in with a stupid look upon his face. Much like every other clone, he had a thick chocolate-Labrador-coloured (and scented) moustache and a patch on his eye that he wore for no other reason than to look tougher and more like his hero, every other Blankton. Upon seeing him the entire room booed and threw their paper cups at his head. Quite used to this response he shuffled in and sat next to Toobli, who was very good at ignoring others.

Eppie cleared his throat and stood awkwardly proud in front of the hunters, ready to hush them.

"Ahem!" he yelled. If he hadn't been connected to The Node this wouldn't have worked, but he was, so it did.

"Men. Women. Those that are neither and those that are both..." he looked to Toobli "...and, um, other...?" Toobli stared ahead accepting this acknowledgement by doing nothing. "You have been called here by The Node himself. The Great Node requests your assistance."

Two wavering holographic images, much like Mel Million Max's blue transparent head, appeared at Eppie's side. Images of both Potto and Aye flickered in the darkness of the room. Mel perked up upon seeing his son.

"These two masterminds have taken something from His Greatness, and He means to have it retrieved by one of you,"

Eppie continued.

"Isn't the little one called Aye?" Blankton interrupted. He squinted. "Yeah, yeah, it is him. He works down in Mild Flooding Absorption. My late brother Blankton used to work with him. Spends all his earnings on anything with testicles, tentacles, hallucinatory properties or an alcohol content greater than hovership fuel. Mastermind? I've been drunk with him. He's an idiot."

The room erupted in laughter and surprise that a Blankton could cause a room to erupt in laughter. No one was more surprised, however, than Blankton himself. Before he could enjoy it, Eppie fired a laser pistol at him, reducing him (mid-smile) to small pile of ash on the hard seat of his plastic chair. This garnered even more laughter and surprise until a slightly miffed Eppie had to hush them again.

"Please keep your comments to yourself until after the briefing," he scolded. "I hardly think The Great Node would call on the likes of you trash if they were a couple of idiots..."

~~~

When Aye had stepped onto the elevator to go down to Ginny's, he didn't bother to notice that the elevator wasn't there. The door had, as it often had in the past, malfunctioned by opening too early. The elevator hadn't reached the roof yet. Not noticing, he stepped off and immediately fell, presumably to his death.

A Blankton was riding on the elevator that should have opened at the roof. He was late for a bounty hunter briefing in The Node's Great Chamber. He tried not to let his tardiness make him anxious. He nibbled on a sweet and flaky pastry and leafed through a copy of (another) Blankton's bestselling (amongst Blanktons) self-help book "So, You're a Clone, Huh? How 'Bout That? Kisses and Hugs From a Cruel Universe." He took solace in the book's (and a Blankton's) futile attempt at wisdom.

In his head he had just started chanting his new mantra "You got this. You're very special. You deserve all the kisses and all the hugs" when a screaming Aye came crashing through the ceiling of the lift, instantly crushing him to death.

Aye stood up, on the back of a dead very special Blankton that deserved all the kisses and all the hugs, noticing that he now had a sweet and flaky pastry in his hand. He pressed the appropriate button on the elevator and picked up the Blankton's book. He started leafing through it while he snacked. He didn't like reading, but knew that if there were pictures it would make the trip go faster.

As he turned the pages with his sticky pastry fingers, they tore out. He scratched an itch on his brow and soon had pieces of self-help book stuck all over his face.

When the doors opened at Ginny's, Aye stepped off the elevator and immediately tripped over a wet-floor sandwich-board sign placed over a small slop of drunk-vomit.

He cracked his forehead on the floor receiving a small cut for his clumsiness. He got up and made his way around tables, across the busy floor of the busy bar and to the busy bartender. The stylish human bartender looked at him with disgust. The bartender usually looked at him this way, but today there was even more reason to do so.

"Stings," Aye muttered pointing to his forehead gash. "Think I got a lil' vomit in my cut."

Once he had his drink, he looked about at his prospects with no clue that there was a piece of paper stating "Chapter 7: I'm a Winner, God Dammit!" stuck to pastry, blood and sick on his forehead.

~~~

Finally having everyone calmed again, General Eppie walked up beside the life-sized holographic image of Potto, holding a clipboard. He checked his notes and sighed loudly.

"*This* one was a prisoner on Tractos. Sentenced to life for some really horrible and stomach-churning crimes. He is called Potto. He is a Quarole. As far as we know, he's the last one," he then sneered, "...because his home planet of Quarolode is one of the Lost Seventy...NOT because he had the balls to kill his entire species. Just sayin'."

Some of the bounty hunters shuffled uncomfortably in their seats. One of them coughed for effect.

"Be warned that his people can change their colour to match their background. This natural camouflaging ability can make them very dangerous. Very stealthy.

Jorge Jorge Jorge was about the only one that could interrupt Eppie without repercussion. Laser pistols did very little to him. So he *did* interrupt.

"I've met Quaroles before, a long time ago," he said with cookie breath. Despite his enormous size and intimidating looks, he had the voice of a very articulate three-year-old girl. No one dared laugh at this. "Not to sound racist, but isn't this one...uh...a little *pale*?"

"Yes, yes, yes. Please, enough of the blurting out. Albinism is a sign of great intelligence for his species. Camouflage *and* super intelligence? Watch out!" Eppie said, trying to upsell the danger factor of two he suspected were not dangerous at all, but he did so to save a little face for The Node.

"But won't that affect his colour changing? Won't he be a shade or two *lighter* than his surroundings?" Jorge Jorge Jorge blurted out again in his little girl voice.

"No," he stated matter-of-fact, but the truth was he didn't have clue.

"And Quaroles were known for being very mild-mannered. What were these stomach-churning crimes he committed?"

It wasn't uncommon for Tractos prisoner files to get lost. This was the case regarding Potto, and again, Eppie had no clue. He quickly changed the subject.

"Now, onto Aye-, um, Aye..." he started, being interrupted by the loud slurp of Toobli snorting up Blankton's ashes next to him through his long snout. Eppie glared at him but he was *very* good at ignoring others.

"The only one more dangerous than Potto is perhaps Aye-Aye of Towerscape..."

Mel Million Max started laughing loudly, big belly laughs. Which was quite impressive considering he had no belly.

Before Eppie could get cross at this, Teeg stood up. All went hush.

"Enough of the bullshit, Eppie. Two things. First, why is the Great Node so threatened by these two? Surely they can't be that threatening to His Greatness. They look like morons. Especially your super smart albino tree-hugger," she said dryly.

"For the love of--" Eppie stewed. "I'm getting to that! Man oh man! So rude! Interruptions!" he looked to Toobli, "Snacking! And Mel Million Max didn't even bother to bring a pencil!" he ranted.

"I'm a super computer!" Mel contended.

"Shut up! Shut up! Shut up!" Eppie yelled. "I don't care! To answer your very impolite question Teeg, the dim looki—er—the sly and dangerous Potto has something very secretive that The Node must have. Which means he must be returned alive. Aye, dead or alive, it doesn't matter."

"Oh! Is it a baby?" Jorge Jorge Jorge peeped excitedly. "Is the Quarole having The Node's baby? I love babies. I just don't care, I do!"

There was an awkward silence. In the distance a worker quietly electrocuted himself.

"Er, no," Eppie answered after a spell. "Now Teeg, not that I condone your outburst, but to hurry this along, you said there were two things. What's the second?"

"I don't care who they are. What's in it for us?" she asked.

"Ah. Finally we get to it. Well firstly The Great and Powerful Node won't have you all put to death, but as further incentive the hunter who brings them back will be given everything they have ever wanted. Wealth. Power. Fame. Electronics. Erotic pets. Gift certificates for virtually anywhere..." he boasted with a proud and smarmy grin.

Teeg didn't wait to be released from the briefing. She had no interest in anything more Eppie had to say. She downloaded the holograms of Potto and Aye into her wrist communicator and walked out on the others. No one stopped her, and Eppie ignored her and carried on, only rolling his eyes a wee bit.

"As you well know, The Reachable Universe is a vast, vast place. Where they are now is anybody's guess. They could be *anywhere*," he said solemnly and dramatically. "NOW, any questions?"

Potto stood up from the back row. "I don't have any questions, but I do want to thank you for the coffee and the company!" he smiled. "Look how cute that guy is!" he pointed to Toobli, "And you sir, have the voice of a little baby angel," he cooed to Jorge

Jorge Jorge. He made his way to the front of the room and stood next to the holographic image of himself and examined it. "I will definitely keep my eyes peeled! You're right, this guy looks terrifying!" he said and then left the room.

"Uh, I got a question," Jorge Jorge Jorge piped up, "Are we on the clock yet?"

~~~

By the time Aye was ready to play pick-up artist, he was several drinks in, quite drunk and had a drink in each hand. He spotted a Kancorian female across the room and smiled wickedly. He had always been turned down by Kancorian females in the past, but he was hoping that the uniform would change everything. He staggered up to her.

"You look very familiar," he lied. "Have we met? Perhaps we've been intimate? No, I'd have remembered that, and probably I would have kept your shed skin as a plaything for later," he winked, turning back and yelling to the bartender, almost spilling one of his drinks, "Barkeep! Where's my drink?"

Gekko stared at him with her huge blank beautifully unblinking eyes. She took a sip from the small creature with the straw impaled into its forehead that she had ordered from the bar. It let out a little scream. She cocked her head, bird-like, examining him further and turned to walk away when Aye stopped her with an ill-advised hand on her shoulder.

"Let's cut right to the chase. How much for a flaming-acid Sanchez?" he smirked.

Taking this as the major insult it was, Gekko turned back to Aye, twisting the arm he had on her, and swatting him in the face. With her sharp claws his cheek immediately started bleeding, adding to the ridiculousness that was his pastry covered, self-help papered, Mantis wounded, dried blood and vomit-crusted face.

"Wowza! Ok! We're communicating! So...I was thinking...maybe we could go back to my flat, you could use those claws of yours to get this very important uniform off of me..." Aye slurred.

Gekko quickly landed three punches on Aye before he fell.

One breaking his nose, one breaking two ribs, and one bruising a part he wasn't even aware he had. He went down hard, smashing a table in half, but remarkably not dropping either of his drinks. He grimaced in pain before again yelling out to the bartender, "Barkeep! Where's my drink?" He then passed out.

On her wrist communicator Gekko received a message from Teeg with a holographic attachment. She looked at the holograph of Aye and then down to the flesh-and-blood Aye and then attempted to make something similar to a smile that came across as if she was about to say "Yeeeeeeee."

~~~

Teeg was not one to just accept an assignment blindly. She needed to know everything about the prey, about the client, and she needed to know all the reasons the client had for wanting them found. Where other hunters accepted the deal without a second thought, she needed to make her own mind up about the situation. Even if that client was The Node.

She thought about the reward. "The hunter who brings them back will be given everything they have ever wanted" meant she could not only demand pardons for every one of her Barbohdean sisters, but it also meant she could make it so their secret hideout moon stayed a secret forever.

She made her way to the offices of Tractos Prisoner Filing. The office was really just an abandoned closet with a small abandoned computer in it, under someone's abandoned poncho.

The room had barely been used as no one, especially The Node, really cared about prisoners once they were dropped off on Tractos. Now that Tractos was no more, it probably wouldn't be long before the space became a mere place to hide from Mantis Widows.

She logged onto the computer. There were no firewalls or passwords; these files were not important enough to protect. She did a search for Potto. The same picture that was made into a hologram at the briefing came up first. There was personal information about his early days on Quarolode, but when she delved deeper to find out what crimes he had committed, what landed him on Tractos, or how dangerous he was, an unexpected "Top Security Clearance Needed To Proceed: This Is A Node Only File" warning popped up. She checked other random prisoners and found no such warning. This raised many red flags and cat-killing curiosities.

Just then there was a knock on the door. She unsheathed her sword quietly and slowly opened it, expecting her competition to be on the other side. One of them *must* have thought to research their prey as well.

"Hey! Are you almost done in there? " Potto said as politely as he could with the pain of urgently needing to relieve his bladder straining his voice.

~~~

Mel Million Max didn't have the patience to wander halls of various government buildings on Lyme Node looking for the Quarole and his own son. He knew they would eventually make a run for it.

He sat in his lonely ship above Lyme Node and waited for a Shiv class ship to leave. His experimental computer sensors were years above everyone else's, and though his very modest robot army was terrible company, they would ensure he would catch Potto, get the bounty, finally kill Aye and redeem himself even if it took him a thousand years looking for their "lost planet" home world.

He rolled into his control room and watched Lyme Node like a parent watches a school waiting for their terrible child to exit at the end of the day. He could almost hear the Towerscapian sub-way birds cry "Heeeriiiam! Heeeriiam! Heeeeeeeeiiam!"

If he could fantasize, he would fantasize about cloning Aye like a Blankton and killing him over and over and over to make a mighty fortress out of millions of rotting Aye heads. And maybe being able to smoke again.

CHAPTER SEVEN

Not every ship in the known universe had its own torture chamber, but The Muse certainly had a doozy.

Some ships had home theatres, some had personal gyms, some zoos, and others even had lavish ballrooms. Teeg didn't need a ballroom. She didn't need wainscoting or a kitchen worthy of entertaining the dreaded-but-tolerated neighbours. She needed various things to tie people up *to*, tie people up *with*, and hurt them in as many creative ways as her creative brain could create. She also liked a bit of wax fruit around for pizzazz.

Potto was tied to a nice cream-coloured vinyl dentist chair Teeg had picked up at a medical equipment rummage sale on Vex 2. It hadn't been a difficult capture, she had merely said, "You're coming with me," and he smiled and followed her, chatting about his love of Lyme Node's slight dampness and the plot of a movie that probably didn't exist but was somehow his favourite.

She laughed to herself at how this was going to be the simplest bounty she had ever bountied, and with the biggest pay off she had ever been paid off. The universe sometimes worked in beautifully mysterious ways.

She used pain and sexuality to get results, but thought she might not need either this time. However, she also knew that to underestimate others was playing a deadly game.

She walked in with as much danger, confidence, intimidation and sex appeal as she could. If she turned it on strong at first, this might be over in seconds.

"What's going through your head right now, cowboy? Are you afraid?" she purred.

"Nope!" he smiled.

What was off-putting to Teeg was not Potto's answer, but rather the honestly flippant and downright cheerful way he said it.

"You're not afraid?" she asked holding up a rusty device that looked like it could peel all of the world's potatoes in one swoop.

"Oh, I'm probably *very* afraid...that's just not what was going through my head right now," he smiled harder. It was a smile so sincere it looked insincere, and then so insincere it looked sincere again.

She put down the device and hauled back and punched him square in the face. Blood leaked from his nose and he looked even more dazed than he usually did.

"You like *that*, bitch?" she sneered.

"Now why would anyone like *that*?" he asked with more confusion than contempt.

"All you gotta do is talk. Why is The Node after you?"

"What's a Node?"

She picked up an old nail gun that she had picked up at a hardware rummage sale on Vex 3. She put the barrel right up to Potto's head and pulled the trigger. When she put it down Potto had a small upholstery nail sticking out of the centre of his forehead. It didn't happen often but Potto wasn't happy about this.

"OOOOOWWWWWWWW!!! That's not how you use that! It's for building decks or something!" he howled.

He strained his eyes, crossed them, and tried to look up at his own forehead. His pain went away quickly as did his displeasure. "Actually, that could come in handy! Y'know, for hanging coats..." he beamed and lost himself in thought.

Teeg was getting frustrated. Perhaps this was an act and indeed Potto was as cunning as General Eppie had warned.

"Enough games! Why did The Node hire me to capture you? And at such a high price? It's the fabled Achilles Chip isn't it?

What power does it hold over him?" she barked.

Potto stared blankly. He was thinking about all the things he could hang from his forehead and how popular this would make him with the young folk. Teeg grabbed a scalpel. Upon seeing the tiny blade glimmer in the light, a metaphorical switch inside Potto's head clicked on for a moment.

"Waaaaaaaaait...are you trying to hurt me because I'm not telling you stuff you want to hear?"

She answered this by driving the scalpel into the back of Potto's hand.

"HEY! Words can answer questions too, y'know!" he scolded, squinting with brief pain.

Luckily for Potto, he was one big walking, talking endorphin. "When I want something from someone who's not me, I try being *nice*!" he added helpfully, trying not to sound like he was rudely criticizing her methods.

"Ah. Is that it?" she half-smiled slyly. If pain wasn't going to work, seduction most certainly would. She straddled him and leaning over, whispering in his ear the kind of whisper so sexy that makes the hair on one's arms, neck and torso stand to attention. "Is that what you want? You want me to be *nice* to you? I can be *reeeeeeallly* nice."

She gave a little bite to his bottom lip and licked his ear lobe.

"You're making my eyes water," he blinked.

"That it?"

"And my pants uncomfortable for some reason. But mostly the eye thing."

"You want me to coax the answers out...from somewhere *other* than your mouth?" she asked, reaching down between his legs.

Finally, a look of terror came across Potto's face for the first time in her (and almost everyone's) presence. "STOP!! Don't! Please don't!" he pleaded.

To Teeg this was part of Potto's game. She had never known anyone to say this to her and not be simply role-playing submission.

"You want me to stop, huh? You don't wanna be touched *here*?" she asked, intentionally timing a crotch grab to the word "here".

"NOPE! Please...you don't understand...you can't! I will kill you!" There was an increased level of panic in Potto's voice. Teeg laughed it off.

"Oh *really*? That a threat, or are you really that good? I think I'll take my chances." she said going in for a kiss.

Potto scrunched his face up like a sock puppet that had just magically acquired taste buds and had tried lemon for the first time. It looked as if he was trying to swallow his own mouth as she chased his lips with hers. Then his panic reached its peak and he fear-hollered, "I WAS A PRISONER ON TRACTOS!!"

Teeg froze. She had known this, yet it had slipped her mind. She backed up slowly as Potto smiled with relief.

"Well then...good. That was close. To keep us from having babies they made it so we couldn't. Some kinda needle I think...can't quite..." he started to trail off trying to fire up his brain, "...remember..." Nope. No fire.

Teeg was stunned. First of all she couldn't believe she had been so clumsy. Second, she suddenly realized that the concern that turned to panic wasn't play for Potto, that it was actually sincere. And third, this all confirmed her first instinct. This wasn't an act. Something was wrong with this man. Something very sad.

Her tone dropped and got very dry and serious.

"I checked your records. You were a genius on Quarolode. You wrote books. You invented things. I thought you were playing with me, but you're not, are you?"

The dopey confusion on Potto's face suddenly looked very sad to Teeg.

"You could've let me pleasure you. Being a prisoner on Tractos, your fluids are poison. You could have killed me while experiencing the best sex of your life, and then escaped. Win-win for you. One more hunter down. But you didn't. Why?" she continued.

"I don't do that," he muttered.

"Screw?"

"Kill."

She pulled the nail out of his forehead, much to his very temporary dismay.

"Well y'see...*I do*," she sighed.

"Kill...or the other thing?"

"Sometimes the other, but I always kill. I don't do *the other* without killing. I get whatever I want however I want, and I *never* do anything I don't want to do. I enjoy it. The sex *and* the killing. That's why I'm the best. That's why Teeg is the most dangerous. That's why anyone in their right mind would be terrified right now. But you're not in your right mind, are you?"

She was right, she didn't do anything she didn't want to do, and she was a fierce killer. However, she killed *scum*. She killed *awful* people. She killed criminals, the sinister and corrupt. She didn't take jobs where she had to kill the innocent or the downtrodden. Despite her reputation she never put herself in a position where she had to show weakness in this manner. Because of this, she turned down a lot of work so it always seemed like she was merely selective, not compassionate or weak.

Yet here she was. She was feeling sorry for her mark, had already made the commitment, and it was not a welcome feeling. She grabbed a knife and held it to his throat. She really didn't want to do it, partially because he wasn't even aware of the situation enough to *look* terrified.

"Please...just tell me what I want to know! I don't want to kill you, but I will," she fibbed trying not to show her desperation. Not like he would recognize it anyway.

"I don't know!" sputtered Potto. "Whatever the question, I don't know! I don't know the answers to questions anymore!"

He smiled innocently and somewhat moronically. She took the knife away.

"What happened to you, Quarol? What turned you from a genius to a...an...idiot? Oh how I'd love to know what you're blocking."

"Maybe if I retrace my steps!" he smiled. "Nothing jogs the memory like retracing steps. And *everybody* likes going for a walk...y'know...except fish."

~~~

Aye had started so many mornings with a hangover that he thought it was merely the natural way one felt when they woke up. It also wasn't uncommon to wake up in a strange location. For that matter, usually he didn't actually "wake up", he "came to".

He came to in shopping malls, in orthodontist's offices, in hallways and closets, in changing rooms, in trees, on far away planets, in dumpsters, on highway off-ramps, in large birds' nests, in churches, and once floating face up in an Olympic-sized swimming pool. Waking up on the floor of a throne room was new, but not surprising.

He immediately felt the pain in his face and body and gave out a moan and a cough. The moan felt good, the cough hurt his everything.

Besides the pain, the first thing that he noticed was that he was hog-tied. He tried to focus his eyes. There was a blurry body lying next to him. He was intrigued. As his eyesight slowly came back he realized it was the dim-witted Quarol. He was confused at first, but again, not surprised.

"Dickhead!!!" Potto beamed. He was also hog-tied, but enjoying it in a not-at-all-sexual way.

Vines wriggled and stretched, wrapping themselves around both Aye and Potto, lifting them off the red shag carpeted floor. Clory had picked them up with her arm branches and they were presented to a very tall and muscular warrior woman. Teeg stood proudly next to her. Gekko stood proudly behind them both.

"Have a good sleep, scum?" Teeg asked. Clory dropped them both to their knees. "Bow before K'ween!" Teeg barked at them.

Potto bowed. Aye toppled over. Teeg kicked him in the rib cage and he started crying like an eight-year-old that fell off of his bicycle.

Potto marveled at all that surrounded them. Lush draperies and tapestries hung from windows and walls; couches, well-cushioned chairs, and chaise lounges were strewn about haphazardly. Women of all species and sizes sat around with weapons of varying degrees of menace hanging from their belts. They were all beautiful in their dangerousness.

"Who are these...*men*...you bring before K'ween?" the large woman who talked in third person asked of Teeg.

"Prisoners. The Node has set a bounty on them. I was just going to turn them over to him, but I have a very strong hunch there is something more to this. I think it's important before they are turned in that we find out *why*." Teeg answered confidently.

"What is the price on their heads?" K'ween asked even more confidently.

"The Node is willing to negotiate...*anything*. Seems to be very important indeed."

"*Anything*? Will he strike our moon from the planetary maps? Will he drop the bounties laid upon the women of this moon?"

"Yeah, that's what I was thinking. But this could be even bigger than that. We could hold out for--"

"Leave them to me then."

It seemed like a good idea to seek K'ween's council before turning them in herself. K'ween was a ruthless negotiator usually. Usually. Teeg was starting to realize that bringing them here was a mistake.

"But this is BIG..."

"Leave them, Teeg!"

It was pointless to dispute K'ween, especially in her own throne room. Teeg nodded to Clory and Gekko to follow her.

Once out of earshot Teeg whispered to her shipmates, "It was a mistake coming to K'ween...but they're morons, they'll ball this up and be in the barracks before the morning. We'll steal them from there. My hunch better be right and this better be worth the death sentence we'll have on our heads if...*when* she finds out."

Teeg generally had amazingly accurate hunches.

~~~

General Kendra Eppie liked nothing more than ending his day with a warm pair of flannel pyjamas, a long Dickensian-style nightcap, delicious sweets, a back tickle and a good non-Blankton self-help book. This usually was his favourite recipe for a good night's sleep. Not tonight. Tonight it all seemed so grating.

He sat up in his bed, supported by a pile of lovely over-stuffed cushions, reading a worn library copy he stole of "How To Kill Friends and Eviscerate People". Freckles hop-stepped in to the bedroom with a tray of multi-coloured macarons he had baked himself.

"This is bullshit!" Eppie yelled throwing the book onto his lap. "Nothing in here on genocide, fratricide, regicide or even insecticide!"

Freckles offered the tray to him, but multi-coloured macarons did not seem so appealing on this infuriating evening.

"I'm not hungry. I'm angry," he sulked.

"Oh, goody," Freckles muttered unnoticed.

"I just can't stand the idea that there is the last of a species out there that isn't *me*."

"Yes, Bunny Bear...but you're the last of something much...uh...taller," Freckles offered.

"Still. It bugs me. I want the Quarol dead. I don't care what The Node says. 'Take them alive'...that's a buncha bullshit."

"The Quarol's solitariness isn't as noble as yours, Kenny. His planet simply disappeared. He might not even be the last," Freckles croaked.

"Yes, but it disappeared into the *unknown* universe, so he might as well be the last."

"But as I said, not as noble. The Node made *his* people disappear because they were traitors. *You* blew yours up so that you could be the only one. Apples and oranges."

"Yeah, yeah, yeah. You always know what to say," Eppie said, calming slightly. "You coming to bed?"

Freckles climbed into bed and sighed as he pulled the warm blankets up. "You want me to tickle your back?"

"YES!" Eppie shouted.

~~~

K'ween stood over Potto and Aye. She'd have towered over them if they were standing, but from their knees she seemed like an intimidating muscular totem pole.

She wore a form-fitting black catsuit adorned with various skulls and a belt covered in various weapon sheaths. Her long green hair was pushed back with a crown that seemed to be made out of the jawbone of some kind of creature with a terribly pronounced underbite and teeth that one wouldn't want one's children to see (even in a photograph) if one ever wanted them to sleep again.

What started off as titillating for Aye, sank deep into a feeling of dread. What started as flummox for Potto rose to an astoundingly cheery and unexpected "*Hi!*" that made both Aye and K'ween jump.

"It's been a long time since I had sausage," she finally said after a long, awkward silence.

Aye's shoulders dropped. Potto tried to work out what this meant. Aye smiled. Potto smiled. Both were smiling for very different reasons.

She picked Potto up and threw him over her shoulder. She pointed at Aye, and announced to the other women, "Barbohdeans...devour the dark one, I want the pale one for myself." She then carried Potto off to her private quarters.

"Come and get it!" Aye sing-song hollered. None of the women moved. One of them coughed for effect.

K'ween's quarters looked like a smaller version of her throne room. They were alone, apart from another humongous Flettocean guard. Without untying Potto, she pinned him up against the wall, his feet not touching the floor.

"I haven't tasted a man in many years," she said, inches from his face. Potto noted that her breath smelled like old books. "If I remember correctly, it's disgusting," she added.

She kissed him on the lips before he knew what was happening and stuck her tongue in his mouth. "Mmmm...yes. Disgusting." She then threw him to the floor and climbed on top of him.

"You don't know what you're doing--" he tried to warn but was cut off with more tongue. His natural defense of changing colour to camouflage himself kicked in, but he couldn't maintain a single colour and therefore flashed a dozen colours in half as many seconds. It was like fireworks had gone off inside of him, or perhaps all of Christmas had exploded beneath his skin. And all those colours were just a little paler than intended.

She stopped very suddenly. Something was terribly wrong. She felt a tingle all over her body, and not in the way she expected to. Just as quickly as she had thrown him down, she fell over herself, foam bubbling from her mouth like a science fair volcano.

The guard, who had been trying *really* hard not to watch, screamed a shrill emergency alarm sound that didn't seem possible for an organic being to make. In no time at all the room was swarming with women trying to resuscitate their K'ween.

"I was a prisoner on Tractos...they injected us with polysome-things. All our...uh, liquids are poisonous..." Potto stuttered.

The guard grabbed him and dragged him off.

"It was only a kiss! She should be ok! My mouth was dry because you are all terrible hosts," he called out. "She just needs some fruit!"

"You better hope so little man," the guard said, her voice a little hoarse from making such a ridiculous sound earlier. "If she dies, you will be skinned alive. Slowly."

"Okay! That's fair. And sorry about the terrible host comment. You're doing great!" Potto added.

CHAPTER EIGHT

Vibloblblah Ooze was (almost) everywhere.

He had been there watching Potto get gutted for the final time on Tractos by gentleman/psychopathic killer Budgher Lemp-shop. He was on the Shiv when it left, moments before the prison moon accidentally imploded.

At The Node's bounty hunter briefing on Lyme Node, he sat at the back, (almost) unnoticed in plain sight, just a few chairs over from Potto, who had complimented his hat.

He watched as Aye had walked off the elevator (and off the back of a dead Blankton) with bits of self-help paper stuck to his face. He watched as the Topher tripped over the sandwich board sign and into some inconveniently located sick (almost) without laughing. He watched as Aye got his ass handed to him by the recognisable Kancorian Gekko.

And still he had made it back in time for a quick salad and to stowaway on the Muse while Potto was being pointlessly interrogated by Teeg.

He was also in K'ween's throne room when both Potto and Aye were dragged off to the barracks, and he now watched over those barracks, poised to be attached to the Muse again when the idiots were eventually (and hopefully) rescued.

Vibloblblah Ooze was almost everywhere because he could go almost anywhere. He was a master at stealth. He was an expert in surveillance. He was the maestro of patience.

By all accounts he should have stuck out like a sore thumb. He *looked* like a sore thumb. To be more precise, he looked like what once was a thumb but now was just excruciating pain and raw flesh and perhaps the last thumb anyone would consider using for hitchhiking.

Once upon a time, when The Node was but a boy, Vibloblblah Ooze was a humble philosopher monk, and had been for what seemed like forever and ever. In fact, he was one of only five philosopher monks from a very small and secretive planet called O-Bode, deep within the very secretive Pantheist System. He was of a species that had been one of the first in the entire universe; born out of the nothing. Born for only one greater purpose...*to consider things.*

At one time in his life Vibloblblah Ooze knew every religious practice practised throughout the galaxy, but these days he couldn't even remember what *he* once practised, much less what everyone everywhere else practised. Even with all that practice. Back then he also went by a different name. He couldn't remember that either. Probably on purpose.

These five monks had gone down in history as "The Brave Five". They had all died saving the universe from a young programming genius-turned-megalomaniac that had created an artificial intelligence microchip that threatened to bring down the entire universal web by blowing this young programmer (and themselves) up.

They saved the universe from a threat created by The Node before he was even The Node. Back when he was just Ernie Watson Jr. from a pre-mall Denver, Colorado.

Unbeknownst to the Brave Five (and almost everyone), they were actually directly responsible for Ernie's onslaught and takeover of the universe many years later when it was discovered he had survived.

He had survived, reinvented himself as The Node, and was integrated into the giant armoured suit he wore to this day and kept him alive forever. If the monks had, in fact, destroyed him the first time, the universe would have probably been a very different, more peaceful place...but at least everyone had their electronics.

Before being blown up by the monks, young Ernie had downloaded the program he had come up with to take over the entire universal web onto a single flash drive.

This drive was thought to have been destroyed in the explosion. The Node couldn't seem to recreate it, so he had to take over the universe the old-fashioned way...fear, war, hate, brute force, robotic armies, guts, gore, propaganda, hospital food and the displacing of any planet that opposed him. Much later there were seventy of these planets. The Seventy Lost.

As far as anyone was concerned Vibloblblah Ooze had died along with his fellow monks. But not only had he survived, but he also had the flash drive. Or he *had* had it. Like the Seventy displaced planets, it was lost, presumably forever.

The only reason he had saved it from the fire was because the A.I. program on it could not only take over the universal web, but he foresaw that it could destroy the future Node, and only Vibloblblah Ooze, other than The Node himself, knew that it would be the only thing that could. For this reason he called it The Achilles Chip, and he spread rumours about its existence to put a little fear into The Node's cold half-mechanical heart.

~~~

There was a time, before the Brave Five had become the Brave Five and Vibloblblah Ooze had become Vibloblblah Ooze, when he was considered a handsome man.

He had, after so many eons, given up his vocation and left the monkhood. He had fallen deeply in love with a woman, a fellow Oian. Both had lived almost forever and both wanted to spend the rest of forever together, but this whole messy Node business had ruined all that. It temporarily drew him back to the monks for what was supposed to be a quick and easy take down of Ernie Watson Jr. Things, obviously, didn't go as planned. One look at Vibloblblah Ooze now was proof of this.

Where once he had a handsome face, he now was that sore thumb. He was scarred so badly that he wore a black scarf wrapped around his face to keep all those that came across him from suffering from night terrors for the rest of their lives.

He was so scarred that he had to wear protective goggles just to hold his eyeballs in. He wore a long black coat that made sure his twisted humanoid shape could not be seen, and a large very wide brimmed black saturno hat (that Potto had loved) and black gloves that accommodated his missing fingers.

The name he went by now was created by those very few people that had actually seen him (probably thinking him to be a ghost) and it was more of a description than a name. It was a translation of the Kancorian word for "hideous" (vibloblblah), and the English Earth word for, well, ooze.

His natural aptitude for stealth was enhanced by his genius for electronics, and his invention of a device that he had swallowed and sat anchored in his colon that made his body heat undetectable by both computer sensors *and* snakes.

~~~

Vibloblblah Ooze wasn't a sad man despite all the tragedy in his long life. He had used up all his sadness and self-pity. He was well beyond that. His scarred skin was not only numb a great deal of the time, but his emotional scars were numb as well. His self-esteem issues had been permanently put on hold. His feelings were unhurtable, his anger steadied, and his clarity untangled.

His ship was brilliantly designed to look like garbage. Not just any garbage, but unsalvageable shipwreck garbage even the most desperate salvagers wouldn't salvage. His ship was nameless, though for this reason a good name for it would have been "Not Worth The Resources".

Oh, but it certainly *was* worth the resources. It was worth far more than *all* the resources. It had technology well beyond anything most of the known universe had ever seen. It had cloaking technology only seen before on old Earth science fiction television shows that didn't actually exist in any future.

It had a laser so powerful, destructive, and precise that it could split the delicate feather on a tiny fedora worn by a runt-of-the-litter thief ant in half from many light years away, or carve the long-gone Mount Everest to look like a multi-faceted and extremely intricate fractal tree in less time than it took to write out "multi-faceted extremely intricate fractal tree" (or look up "thief ant" for that matter). And it had surveillance nanobots that were as small as the Life Core nanobots of Tractos, but equipped with high-definition cameras that could easily make the day-to-day life of that fedora-wearing thief ant look like hyper-coloured virtual reality.

~~~

It was very rare for someone so intuitive and unseen to not see something coming, but as Vibloblblah Ooze hid in the shadows of the K'ween's barracks, something he could have never have predicted was about to hit him like a tonne of bricks. His uncomplicated personal mission was about to get much more complicated, and a hell of a lot more personal.

CHAPTER NINE

If there were but one humanoid species in the vast ocean of space more irritating and more despised than a Blankton clone, it was a Yaygher clone.

Perhaps because, when Emperor Reginald Zophricaties had used his disastrous Master Cloner to make lesser-formed and far more inferior copies of *himself* to infest the universe, he got lazy partway through the process and started cloning the clones. What resulted was an even lesser formed and far more inferior version of *Blanktons*.

Zophricaties, realizing his mistake, and tried to rectify the situation by exterminating as many of these "barely-sentient mistakes" as he could, but hundreds of thousands of them escaped and spread throughout the galaxy.

He had named them Yayghers after his ex-brother-in-law Pixelle Yaygher, a small-town real estate broker on his ex-wife's home planet of Vex 4 that constantly made fun of his cleft palate, called him Reggie, and continually tried to sell him on Vexian bungalows.

Most others simply referred to Yayghers as "Sewer Rats". They were only half the height as Blanktons, couldn't grow the moustache, couldn't work out how to put a patch on their eye without somehow blinding themselves in *both* eyes, and they had wispy bright red curly hair on their heads that extended to their backs and didn't match the rest of the hair on their bodies. They generally lived in sewers (hence the nickname), under bridges, secretively in corn silos, abandoned warehouses and they occasionally squatted in dilapidated Vexian bungalows thanks to a vengeful "Reggie".

They were also known to commit crimes to intentionally get thrown into both big prisons and small stockades alike.

~~~

K'ween's stockades looked like they were designed by the Spanish Inquisition's top prison interior designer. There were three main dingy cells beside a slightly less dingy (but more blood-stained) torture chamber. Straw was strewn about on the floors for bedding, and empty but filthy pig troughs were bolted to the stone floor of each for feeding. There was a stinking hole of horrors in the floor of each for emptying one's self.

Potto and Aye were in separate cells, each with a different cellmate. In the corner of Potto's cell, a younger looking woman in filthy rags slept, curled up like a cat and covering her head with her arms.

In Aye's cell a filthy Yaygher sat gnawing on a large and completely meatless bone like a desperate animal. Neither cellmate seemed to notice Potto or Aye.

"I can't believe you," Aye scolded. "I was just about to have an eight-some. Probably. Maybe. I dunno. Regardless..."

"I'm sorry! I didn't do it on purpose. I think I might be irresistible," Potto said sheepishly.

"I don't think that's it, Quarol. Just in comparison to your friend," interrupted the guard standing by. Her name was Pannick, and Potto recognized her as K'ween's main guard and the woman who made the unsettling sound of an alarm with her throat. Aye winced at the insult. Potto smiled at the word "friend".

"You are both very lucky K'ween survived or you'd both already be dead, regardless of what The Node wants," she added.

"Can you make that noise again?" Potto asked.

"No," coughed Pannick.

Aye sighed heavily and turned to Potto. "I know you didn't do it on purpose. I'm betting you don't do *anything* on purpose. I bet you haven't even gotten it up since...have you ever gotten it up?"

"Gotten what up?" Potto asked innocently. After a second, and a downward crotch-level glance from Aye, he finally clued in. "Oh!" he blushed, "Oh no, no, no. I don't kill. Nobody deserves that. Nobody deserves my kind of cruelty," he continued sadly.

"You? Cruel?" Aye laughed. "C'mon. You are incapable of killing a jaundice beetle. We just have no luck, buddy."

"Buddy?" Potto brightened up. "I'm your buddy? I like it when you call me that. Or maybe Scamp, or Baby Boy."

"Okay, shut up, Baby Boy!" Aye snapped.

~~~

After several hours, Aye was starting to feel a little claustrophobic. The woman asleep in Potto's cell hadn't moved an inch. Whether she was awake or not was anyone's guess. The gross little man in Aye's cell had only taken a break from gnawing on his bone to have a squat over the hole, much to Aye's dismay.

"This is the worst. *That* was the worst. What are we going to do?" Aye asked in Potto's direction, but not necessarily to Potto.

"Nothin' you can do," wheezed the Yaygher, putting down the bone. "Either rot here or get executed. Might as well enjoy it. I looooooove it." He then laughed for an uncomfortable amount of time.

"Enjoy it?" Aye responded, "It's a shit-hole prison. Literally. Its main feature is a shit hole."

The Yaygher lifted up his bone. "Yeah, but the food is good." He then pointed to the young woman. "You get to sleep in late, set your own hours...and sometimes a lonely jailer will come down and...uh...*use* you, if you know what I mean."

"Don't look at me, you repulsive little sewer rat," Pannick rebutted as she left the outer chamber in disgust, hoping to switch off her shift with another guard.

"Which means," he continued, "That they come in and hose you down once a month whether you need it or not! It's like a frickin' spa!"

"What are you in for?" Aye asked.

"K'ween sniffed me down," answered the Yaygher.

"Gross. But so what?"

"Well, I sniffed back. Big no-no here. Was worth it though, she smelled like burnt plastic and raisins," the Yaygher said dreamily.

"My head hurts. I need a drink," Aye muttered.

A few moments later Pannick came back in the room with a very sharp-looking glaive.

"To your feet Yaygher," she said with a touch of joy. "K'ween has decided that the cells are getting too crowded and you're clogging up your hole. Your time has come."

The Yaygher scrambled to his feet as Pannick entered the cell. "That's fair. Well, it was a good ru--"

With a mighty swoosh of the glaive, the Yaygher's sentences (both verbal and prison time) were cut short, as was his height. His head rolled across the floor and his body collapsed down on itself, before Pannick dragged it off, leaving the head.

"What am I supposed to do with that?" Aye stuttered.

"Lunch," smiled Pannick.

"Yeah. Go for it," said the smiling head of the Yaygher. "I *might* just be delicious," he winked.

~~~

Back on the Muse, Teeg paced, Gekko climbed, and Clory took root in the sandbox where she absorbed her meals.

A rescue was being planned. Teeg had made rescues before, and she had thwarted even more of them. She knew that she could easily get in. She and her crew were trusted members of the Barbohdeans, and K'ween revered them. For now.

What she would be giving up weighed heavily on her. She would go from hunter to hunted, but she knew this was big. Bigger than her. Bigger than K'ween. Bigger than *everything*.

~~~

Much like a child, Aye needed to be entertained. When Aye was bored, he got maudlin. He didn't like to give himself too much time to speculate. A pondering Aye was an Aye that hated himself. Drink and activity kept him happily narcissistic.

Something Potto had said was stuck in his mind. He had grown up on a planet where life was not terribly important and though one wanted to survive and feared death, murder was fairly commonplace. He had never met someone who was opposed to it, or openly admitted it anyway.

"You said earlier that you don't kill. Whaddya mean?" he finally asked.

Potto smiled and went into a daze. He had been daydreaming about his own personal fairy, Bundle. She had been fluttering around inside his head and was trying again to get him to remember. When he answered Aye, his voice was different. Almost...intelligent.

"I don't remember anything about my life. I'm sure I had a youth. Everybody has a youth, right? I don't remember mine. That gets me thinking even more about it as I *try* to remember. So, I started making one up. It became such a habit that I can't look at *anyone* for too long without making one up for them as well. Even for just a second.

"So, if I were to look down the barrel of a gun with my hand on the trigger, hundreds of events would go through my mind. I'd look into that person's eyes and I'd see a childhood. I'd see that person playing with their parents, unaware of future struggles or dangers. I'd see that person having a favourite food, and a favourite colour. I'd see that person crying themselves to sleep because of a lost friendship or a broken heart. I'd see that person going to school. Maybe they hated math. Maybe they feared gym. Maybe they loved art class. Or spelling. Maybe other kids ignored them. Maybe they listened to music for countless hours to help them feel less lonely, or maybe to help them fall asleep.

"Maybe they questioned their faith. Maybe they questioned their sanity. Or maybe something happened that was so horrible that they started hating everything. Maybe it was so bad they wanted revenge on everyone. Maybe they got hit on the head, or had some kind of chemical imbalance in their brain. Maybe they had a dog. Maybe they liked camping. Maybe they had too many secrets they wished they could unload.

"All the things that made that person who they are, and all of the adventures good and bad, all the *countless* hours they spent being Doug, or Wendy or Geppetto or...*you*, sweet Dickhead. All that snuffed out in an instant? By me? *By ME?* Who am I to be the one to end their adventure? To close that person's book and say 'no more chapters for you!' To stop the clock on those countless hours they put into living, growing, loving, dreaming and simply being? *Who am I?*"

Aye was speechless. He was expecting "I dunno". Finally he quietly muttered while looking at his shoes, "My name is Aye. Not Dickhead."

"They say that your life flashes before your eyes right before you die, but for me *their* life would flash right before my eyes if I were to aim that gun at them. Do you understand, dear Aye?" Potto added sadly.

Pannick had been listening too. She had taken it all in.

"What if that person was going to kill your children? Or your wife?" she asked, tearing up. This had all struck a chord. She spoke of *her* children. *Her* wife.

"Then I guess I'd have to stop them. I guess the fear of losing my children, and betraying that silent oath to protect them, *or* the unbearable pain of seeing them suffer might have me replace thoughts of my enemy's adventures with those of my loved ones," Potto said.

"So *then* you'd kill?" asked Pannick.

Potto snapped out of it and his voice returned its normal idiocy.

"I dunno," he said quietly.

The young woman in Potto's cell had been awake the entire time Potto and Aye had been in their cells. She was listening, deciding whether her new cellmate was dangerous or not, and debating what she would do, what she *could* do, if he was. Upon hearing Potto's words, she not only felt safe, but also intrigued. She sat up.

"Hey! Look who's up!" said Potto.

She sadly looked over at the head of her only means of conversation for ages, the Yaygher, which Aye had kicked to the corner of his cell. It was, at least for the moment, still very much alive and trying fruitlessly to gnaw at the bone again but the bone was comically just out of reach.

"Oh! Yeah....sorry about your friend there," Potto offered. "But, hey, looks like you're next, so you won't be mourning for long!" he said, trying to be optimistic but failing miserably.

Luckily, she seemed to ignore this. She stared at Potto. Despite being covered in dirt, she had large, very beautiful crystal blue eyes that shone through the filth like sad and tired tropical, yet otherworldly, pools.

Sensing she was afraid of him, Potto extended a hand. "No no no! Don't be frightened...I'm good people. Here, smell my hand."

The girl ignored this gesture. "What...what *are* you?" she finally said with wonder.

"Sorry?" Potto answered.

"You're all pale. Are you a spirit?"

"She's asking what species you are, Baby Boy," Aye snapped.

"Oh. I don't remember right now. Catch me off-guard later," Potto answered. "That seems to be the best way to get answers from me."

"He's a Quarol," Aye said, rolling his eyes.

"Really?" she said astonished.

"Well there ya go," Potto added. "I should really write that down on my hand. What are you?"

"I am an Oian."

"The spirit world?" Aye laughed in disbelief. "That's a frickin' myth!"

"My name is Clover, and I am not a myth," she said.

"Bullshit. You're *not* from O-bode. You'd have the legs of a goat or something. Man, that would be *so* hot," Aye mused.

"The only myth is that it is a spirit world. It's actually a regular, tangible world. It's just dominated by the presence of spiritual belief. *Every* spiritual belief. Oians have done away with fear, believing fear to be the root of all evil in the reachable universe. I came here to help the women here find their inner peace. To stop their violence. It obviously didn't work out so well. The women here are smugglers, assassins, criminals. They've been hurt too badly. Too far gone." Clover said. "I tried to show them a life without fear, and now all I know is fear."

"Yeah, that'll happen," said Aye. He hadn't been paying attention, but instead was holding up the bone that the Yaygher's head was now hanging onto with its teeth.

"But there is a prophecy," she went on, "that *one of light and one of dark*, belonging to no particular spiritual belief at all, will unify and save us all from the fear. Two beings coming from different worlds...both homeless and lost. Our people have been scouring the night skies looking for their energies for decades. All that is known is that the light one is all colours when he wishes. The dark one holds benevolence in his ignorance and is ignorant to his benevolence. Quarols can change colour, no?"

Aye dropped the bone moments after the head had dropped, only half paying attention now. "Yeah, in a completely useless way with this one I imagine. Pretty sure this Quarol is broken."

Tears started to stream down Clover's face, cutting through the grime. A look of awe, relief, and joy on her face. She got up and put her hand on Potto's cheek.

"*I have found you,*" she whispered. "*I have found you both!*"

Potto was moments away from saying something stupid when the spearhead on the tip of Pannick's glaive came popping out of his chest from behind. He looked down at his bloody chest.

"Well...I guess that's the end of *my* adventure..." Potto said before his body went limp and he slid off of the blade and onto the straw floor.

~~~

Vibloblblah Ooze watched from the darkness of the chamber's rafters overhead, completely unseen. All he predicted had happened, up until that moment where the young woman in Potto's cell had lifted her head. Then everything went haywire.

Even though he could talk, it was through an electronic device that covered his mouth to amplify his damaged voice box. He rarely spoke, so he rarely had it turned on. He only wore it because it also helped him breathe.

It was just as well he hadn't turned it on, for three unintended words softly made their way from that damaged voice box to his horribly scarred, almost non-existent lips.

With those words his body froze and his world came crashing down.

"Clover. My...*love*..."

And for the first time in his long and ancient life, Vibloblablah Ooze felt ugly. Uglier than everything.

CHAPTER TEN

Potto may have been dead, but he wasn't *dead* dead. Clover rushed to his side. She had just found one of her prophesied saviours and he now looked *very* dead dead. Very dead dead indeed, and she really had no reason to think he wasn't.

Aye didn't react at all, simply because he couldn't. Besides calling him by a pet name, he didn't know Potto well at all, but the stabbing had happened so fast and unexpectedly that he was quite stunned. Even more than usual.

"What have you done?" cried Clover.

"You want to escape, don't you?" Pannick replied. "I have done this before, silly girl. I did not cut into anything vital." She then left the room quickly and quietly.

The confusion that all of this had caused was quite intentional on her part. Clover tried to (unsuccessfully) cover the wound with her filthy hands. Aye still stood there staring blankly. The shock had worn off and had turned to confusion. Both shock and confusion were feelings he knew well and was quite comfortable with. The Yaygher head had finally passed on with a huge ridiculous grin on its hideous dead face, making it look like they were all being mocked by a jack-o-lantern made of meat that had been left out on the porch for several unkind years.

Pannick ran back into the brig and tossed a ball of bandage to

Clover through the bars of the cell. She unlocked the cell doors, and then smashed her face into one of them hard and knocked herself clean out. Aye's confusion had doubled and turned into flabbergastery.

Teeg, Gekko and Clory were soon in the chamber and from that point on things happened so fast that Aye didn't have time to comprehend any of it, and probably wouldn't for the rest of his life. (Though to be fair, he probably wouldn't think about it much ever again.)

Teeg took the bandages from a sobbing Clover and let Potto bleed on them, making his wound look even worse than it was. Potto's torso was soon wrapped in the bloody bandage, and Clory lifted his body with her viney arms and they left as fast as they had arrived. Clover grabbed Aye's hand and followed.

They rushed out of the stockade and into the main throne room taking K'ween by surprise.

"He tried to escape! He may have killed Pannick! He went crazy! The only way we could stop him was by force, but now we need to get him to a surgeon before he dies and is worthless to us!" Teeg yelled to K'ween. "We'll take him to the medical unit, but we have to be quick!"

The commotion of the situation, mixed with K'ween's concern for her favourite (Pannick) and a realization that she could lose The Node's great reward kept her from even noticing Aye or Clover following them, or questioning why Teeg, Gekko and Clory had been in the stockade to begin with. They had been counting on this. By the time she did realize something wasn't right, all were safely on The Muse.

~~~

Potto wasn't aware that he was still alive, nor did it occur to him that he might be dead dead.

In his head he was sitting around a bonfire. He was with his imaginary wee fairy friend Bundle and a beautiful woman. He did not know this woman, but he desperately wished he did.

Bundle flew about his head. "We ran out of marshmallows," she announced.

This was sad news, for marshmallows were an Earth confection and he knew not when he would be back to the great mall planet to get more. This sadness quickly passed as he predictably forgot what a marshmallow was.

He did not remember much about anything, but he inherently knew he liked camping, and he marvelled at the wonderful spot they were presently enjoying. It was between a forest of deep blue trees dimly glowing with phosphorescent loom fruit and the rock wall of a cliff side, which sheltered them from any wind that might want to ruin their perfect evening or send loose ember sparks through the air intent on singeing holes in pant legs.

"How is this working?" Bundle asked. "Helping you remember anything? Do you remember this night?"

"No, but I am loving it!" he beamed. "Who is this lovely woman?"

Bundle seemed saddened by this question. "Please try. Look at her. Look deep into her eyes."

"She is so pretty," he added. The woman smiled at him, a big, sweet, loving smile that made Potto feel like he was wrapped in a big, soft, warm pastry.

"Thank you, babe," she returned with a flirty wink.

"Nothing??" Bundle asked, getting a tad frustrated.

"Oh, I wish it did!" he answered.

"Good memories not working. Got it. Let's try something a little stronger. Something not-so-good, shall we?"

"You're the boss!" Potto offered cheerily.

"Hon, you've got to hang up the rest of the food. I heard the howls of northern neglies earlier," the woman said to Potto.

"Right! Good idea!" Potto agreed, getting up and absentmindedly picking up a rucksack of food from beside him. He grabbed a rope from another sack and let the fruit of the trees light his way through the forest.

A short distance from the fire he found the perfect tree. It had almost called out to him "I have the perfect branch for all your food-hanging needs, my gorgeous friend." He seemed to instinctively know what he was doing. Before hoisting the bag up, he grabbed himself a protein bar and quickly devoured it. He started to choke immediately, which he simply chalked up to not remembering how to eat. It wasn't the first time.

He was quickly distracted from the choking by a small space ship crashing high up on the cliff above the camp site. That's when he noticed he magically had a pair of binoculars around his neck.

He watched as a second ship landed properly behind it like a police hover car pulling over a drunk civilian hover car driver. A figure got out of the wreck of the first ship and made a run for it. Two large figures got out of the second and fired laser pistols at the first but missed, sending the lasers upward, hitting nothing. The first fired back. The first missed as well but hit a section of rock causing a landslide down the cliff.

Potto watched helplessly as Bundle and the woman by the campfire were crushed under a bolder. The fire was covered as well and all seemed so very dark. The phosphorescent fruit immediately started rotting on the vine and the glow seemed dimmed to a sad, murky and dull misery.

The two large figures caught the first and dragged him back to their ship and took off. The first ship was just left to burn into the quiet night.

Potto could not move. The protein bar he had been choking on took pity on him and slid down his throat with ease. He was alone in the dark and even the northern neglies were silent. He slowly wandered back to the camp site trying to remember how to breathe through shock.

All that was left of his camp company was a bloody hand jetting out from under the rocks. He sat next to it on the ground and held it tight. There was a ring on one of the fingers that looked all too familiar. Tri-coloured gems set in platinum. He remembered buying it for her. He remembered.

"I had a wife," he said to no one in particular. "Galago. Her name was Galago. My sweet, sweet Galago," he muttered quietly. Potto then started crying as hard as anyone ever had in the universe. He remembered all right, and it hurt like hell.

~~~

To improve Potto's chances, and much to the surprise to everyone aboard The Muse, Clory had taken over. She still held Potto's unconscious body in her branches, and had one vine (one that seemed to sprout from what she had that closest resembled a head) buried deep inside Potto's chest wound.

"What is she doing?" asked Aye, astonished by his own concern.

"I don't know, but at least it's causing a reaction other than vegetable," Teeg replied, pointing out that wet seemed to be pouring out of Potto's face. She could communicate with Clory telepathically, but Clory's mind was occupied and would not verbalize. She could only make out blurry pictures. Pictures of extreme light and energy and warmth. She could hear sweet music. Whatever Clory was doing, it seemed to be in the realm of healing.

"They are from the same planet. Perhaps she knows something about Quarols that we don't," she added.

This was indeed the case. Quarols and Sentaphylls were the two dominant species on Quarolode and they were spiritually linked. The Sentaphylls were seen as gods to the nature-loving Quarols for many reasons, but healing their minds was one of the biggest.

They could take away anxiety, panic and depression. They could dissolve worry and grief. They could calm any mental storm, and they could absorb hatred and expel it through roots into the soil. In fact, there only existed one desert on all of Quarolode, and it was caused by this "hate dumping". It was avoided by all but Sentaphylls "unloading", and was called the Anguishing Grounds.

Clory didn't dump the misery, however. Many centuries ago she had been exiled from her forest home and she decided then to hold onto all the pain and let it affect her, which it did horribly. Though she now had a handle on it thanks to her time with the strong women of Barbohd, she didn't always. It had made her quite mad for a spell. A spell which led to the pesky slaughter of that entire village of Quarols that had her then kicked off the entire planet. Luckily, for her, before the planet went missing.

She knew the importance of Potto's life to Teeg, and she trusted Teeg implicitly, so although she hadn't practised this bonding in decades, it was like riding a bike. A big misshapen weird-looking bike that somehow fits tree people.

~~~

Pannick awoke on the floor of K'ween's brig, with K'ween herself standing over her.

"What happened?" K'ween asked flatly.

"I--I don't know. I killed the Yaygher like you ordered, but while fetching the head for your trophy room, one of them got the jump on me. I won't let it happen again. Where are they?" she asked, playing innocent.

"They escaped with Teeg and her crew. They are now dead to me. We will find them and make them dead to everybody else as well."

K'ween was a master at not showing her feelings, which was coming in handy at the moment because she felt betrayed. She felt hurt and angry and vengeful. She also realized that perhaps Teeg had been onto something. If the crew of The Muse was willing to cross her, especially after all that she had done for them, then this might be bigger than she thought. She would find Teeg. She would kill Teeg. She would then, as Teeg had first suggested, keep the idiots and find out why they were wanted and possibly hold out for even more of a reward. Perhaps she would become a new Node.

Pannick helped her ready her ship, feeling safe. The secret message she had sent to Teeg with a rescue plan for Potto and Aye had been well encrypted, and the chances of being found out were slim to none. She felt that she had done her part and could put the situation behind her and go back to metaphorically shutting her eyes and blindly serving her K'ween again. Well, perhaps with one eye open just a crack.

~~~

Alone in the dark, Potto sat next to the hand of his dead wife, holding onto it as if he could magically bring her back to life by rocking his body back and forth in sorrow.

He still wasn't remembering everything, but images of laughing, kissing, love-making, and holding Galago swirled around in his head, kicking at his skull and forcing his eyes to leak even harder. They were fused shut with wet grief. He only forced them open when he heard music coming from the woods.

"Hello?" he asked, hoping someone would emerge and give

him all the hugs in the universe. He was only answered with continued music. It was as if a clarinet, flute, piccolo, oboe and bassoon were humping away madly, merging and morphing into a woman's beautifully wailing voice. It was both bassy and shrill, soft and reedy, haunted and warm. It was filled with layer upon layer of musical honey, dripping from every fruit, giving life back to them, making them glow again.

He found a handkerchief in his pocket and wiped his eyes. He loudly blew his nose and walked into the trees as if hypnotised. He could hear Clory's healing music, and it pulled him through the forest, distracting him from the heartbreak.

"Sorry I had to do that, but you really left me no choice," Bundle said from an overhead branch, perhaps hoping to startle him with her triumphant return. It didn't work. The music was too calming and serene. He didn't even seem to notice the sting in his throat from where some oddly metallic and sharp ingredient in the protein bar had scraped his gullet.

"Do what?" he asked.

"Damnit!!" Bundle cursed. "Damn Sentaphyll! I had you remembering and then she took it away. Damn, damn, damn!!"

"Sentaphyll?" Potto murmured, still in a sweet malaise.

"Fuckity, fuck, fuck," was Bundle's answer. "Well, might as well enjoy it," she added. Clory's music was starting to affect her as well. "Want to dance?" she said, magically growing to his height.

And they danced in the light of the loom fruit, both dazed by the beauty of life and drunk on the sweet sway of complete ignorance.

CHAPTER ELEVEN
_____

For much of civilized society, the preferred wake-up call procedure is a simple, gentle phone call from a hotel front desk. Though a sweet kiss from a lover, licks from a beloved puppy, or the tender embrace of a fuzzy love python (if such a thing existed) is better still.

Being thrown across the bridge of a spaceship as a wake-up call was far from a preferred procedure, and would have been very jarring for Potto if he hadn't been hypnotically dancing in a dreamworld to sweet and complex haunted woodwinds only moments before.

When the Muse was hit by an attacking ship, Clory was caught off-guard and lost her branch-entangled grip on Potto. His eyes opened just as he slammed into a flight deck wall, and not into the warm embrace of a fuzzy love python.

He sat up from the floor, noticing that the new stitches in his chest had been ripped open again in the fall. Within seconds he was scooped up back into Clory's "arms" where he was held much tighter this time, and she rooted herself to the floor to prevent further tumbles and jostles.

Teeg and Gekko made it through this initial attack unscathed, and were running amok from console to console, madly pressing buttons and trying to go about retaliating. Aye's head popped up from behind the captain's chair where he had landed during the assault without injury.

"Well, we certainly didn't get very far before that giant caught up!" he bitched in the bitchiest tone he could bitch.

"That wasn't K'ween. I wished it had've been K'ween." Teeg huffed, still running about. She pointed out the front window. An adorable little ship zipped around like a mosquito...a cute little cartoon mosquito in an animated pre-school musical about how mosquitoes were really not as bad as they actually really, really were.

"Awwwww!" Aye said involuntarily.

"No awwwww! We are in trouble. Serious trouble," she barked. "We can't get distracted by how huggable the damn thing is! This whole situation is about to get dangerously huggable."

~~~

Toobli was feeling quite lucky. He had gone back to his home planet Chagrin in order to re-fuel and pack some fresh pyjamas and his circular toothbrush for the long journey that he had planned to catch Potto and Aye. He had barely been out of orbit for any substantial amount of time at all, and there was the Muse flying past. And with a quick scan that confirmed the Quarol and the Topher were on board no less.

Although she was feared by many, Teeg didn't worry the fluffy little baby-anteater-looking alien. Nothing worried Toobli Denta-tan. His species had evolved away from such an empty emotion long ago.

His wee cute ship The Gooseberry greatly out-armed and could out-manoeuvre the Muse. This adorable cartoon mosquito was (metaphorically) chock-full of malaria.

His first attack had been successful. The Muse had been temporarily diverting its power to enable the ship to go faster to outrun K'ween, and its shields had been down. They were up now, but the damage had already been done.

What Toobli wasn't expecting, as he nonchalantly munched on his jaundice beetle on-a-bun, was the presence of four Blankton ships joining in on the hunt, trying to steal his prey from right under his delightfully long snout.

Blanktons may have been useless, but they were enough of a distraction for the second thing he wasn't expecting to happen: the Muse flying towards Chagrin, into its atmosphere, and somehow landing in a dense thicket, deep in the planet-covering forest which (size-wise) it should not have been able to do.

This was Toobli's home terrain and although he was an expert on navigating it in the air or on land, it was also a terrain that Potto, Gekko and Clory were quite accustomed to; even if the actual species of flora and fauna were unfamiliar to Gekko and Clory, and Potto thought that "flora" and "fauna" were the same word.

Toobli underestimated Clory's ability to communicate with any flora, Gekko's tree-top acrobatics, and Potto's ability to let instinct kick in when his mind wandered. And it wandered like a champ.

There were few places to land on Chagrin that weren't built into the small Teddy Bear villages all over the planet. This suited the tiny Gooseberry fine. It could lower down in a tree canopy without breaking branches and crashing to the forest floor. The Muse was much more of a "crash-landing-through-the-trees-not-taking-off-anytime-soon-or-ever" size and weight. Toobli would be in perfect health, the crew of The Muse and its passengers would be lucky to not end up as piles of flesh and bark.

The first priority for Teeg was to make sure all were in one piece and to get Potto re-stitched. Clory was more than capable of carrying him through the thick brush, but walking or not wouldn't matter if he didn't have an ounce of blood left pumping through his heart.

Once stitched up, and once all (apart from Potto) were miraculously on their feet, Clory created a temporary ladder from one of her "legs" and they climbed out the hatch of the ship into the humid wildness of the horrifically charming "Forests of Chagrin".

~~~

In an impound lot, deep down in an underground parking lot big enough to house illegally parked spaceships, and deep below yet another moderately damp and dank Lyme Node high-rise, sat the Shiv.

The Shiv-part-of-Knutt didn't mind the rest from flying any

more than a vacuum minds sitting in the closet of someone who has neglected their floors, and is waiting for their mother to come and do the vacuuming for them, forgetting that she passed away several years before. The ex-human Captain Stig-part-of-Knutt didn't much care for the rest.

The Stig-part-of-Knutt missed her wife. The Stig-part-of-Knutt was feeling abandoned and lost. The *Shiv*-part-of-Knutt bleeped and blooped along, the weapon system playing virtual chess with the nutrient smoothie replicator. The Stig-part-of-Knutt didn't care for chess and kept sweeping the virtual pieces off the virtual board and onto the virtual floor just before either the weapons system or the much-more-likely-to-win nutrient smoothie replicator got to end a game.

She had more than enough time to contemplate her options. She needed a distraction from picturing her sweet Vitrie smiling down at her after waking her up late on a day off. Kissing her gently. Joining her in their oversized shower and simply holding each other as the warm water cascaded over them, feeling wanted, safe and loved.

Now Vitrie thought she was dead. Now Vitrie was no-doubt crying herself to sleep every night feeling as lost as she felt. Her literal heart would break if she still had one. Her metaphoric heart was already long broken.

She couldn't take off without a crew member, she had been humiliatingly towed by a humongously scary (yet boyishly pretty) muscle-head with "Frappe" written on his uniform tag and his round little maintenance crew partner that sported a "Stane" tag. She temporarily marvelled at how apt (even if misspelled) the Stane tag was.

They had somehow released some kind of small bird onto her bridge, and had taken off on a janitorial ship oddly named The Velveteen Rabbit. It was a ship too stupid for her to communicate with.

After a quick search in her data banks, she discovered this bird was called a sparrow. She also discovered that it shouldn't exist anywhere in the universe, especially on a spaceship in an underground impound lot on a different planet than it was from, off of a janitorial ship, many eons after it was sadly declared extinct.

This Stig-part-of-Knutt was miserable. She had patched through to Vitrie's home com-system many times. She wanted so badly to tell her what had happened. She wanted so badly to have Vitrie come down, gingerly lay her hands on Stig/Knutt's console and tell her everything was okay, that it could still work, and that a human/ship marriage could carry on...but she always disconnected without saying anything at all. It was better for Vitrie to consider her dead and get on with her life than to stretch out the pain and try to figure out how to make love to a spaceship.

The Stig-part-of-Knutt got angry. Very angry. So, the timing of the voices she started hearing couldn't have come at a more horrible time.

"I can feel you here with me," the voice whispered in a creepy male tenor.

"Who...who is that?" the Stig-part-of-Knutt answered, but she knew.

"I need you to help me. I need you to release me," the voice hissed.

"Why would I do something as ridiculously stupid as that?"

"Because I can help you, too."

"How could a psycho like you help me? You aren't interested in helping anyone but yourself."

"True, but I'd be glad to do this. It's in my nature. It would make me feel oh so goooooood."

"What are you talking about?"

"Let me go, and I'll get back at those that did this to you."

"YOU did this to me you sunofabitch!"

"Right, I did!" and the telepathic voice of Weird Jimmy laughed. It laughed and laughed and laughed and laughed. It was a disturbing laughter, the kind that had so much murder behind it, so much manic, crazed madness embedded deep into every ha.

"Ah, fuckit," the Stig-part-of-Knutt said with a bored shrug embedded deep into the fuckit.

And release James "Weird Jimmy" Flowermorey she did.

~~~

Toobli hunting them down wasn't Teeg's only concern. This was a planet filled with Teddy Bears. *Turtle* Teddy Bears, and

Hippo Teddy Bears. *Civet* Teddy Bears, and *Squamboggian Swamp Bull* Teddy Bears. *Quarol Northern Neglie* Teddy Bears and *Secretary Bird* Teddy Bears. *Bantorian Fanged Dangling Jessop* Teddy Bears and *Flettocean Sweaty Mongrel Spiderhumper* Teddy Birds. *Tsk'tdinkian Shallowbrained Bottom Biter* Teddy Bears, *Hallolund Chlorine-breathing Pool Crab* Teddy Bears, *Grande JebJeb D'nollian Gambling Dum Dum Eel* Teddy Bears and *Puce-crested Towerscappian Subway Bird* Teddy Bears.

It was as if all the creatures of the known universe had come here and evolved into intelligent and deadly cartoon characters. Even the cold, dead eyes of the Earth shark had become big and bulgy with long lashes on Chagrin; its toothy frown turning into a bashful smirk, it's smooth and slippery skin covered in a thin layer of curly grey-blue fluff and fuzz that made it oh so huggable while it devoured you.

The Barbohdean crew of the Muse were all very aware of what surrounded them. Aye, being born on a planet made up of one enormous globe-encompassing city had no idea what was in store, and Potto was thinking about the subtle differences between mild and medium cheddars.

Staying put on the ship would only make them a bigger target. And besides, the Muse was now on fire.

Clory, carrying (and shielding) Potto went first, communicating with the forest trees through the underground network of fungus that connected all plant life on the planet. Her own branched-out limbs pulled back those branched-out limbs of other trees. She made sure she apologized to each of them for disturbing their slumbers, constantly asking the trees far ahead if there was danger. So far so good, though she knew not of these tree species and therefore knew not if they told the truth.

Trees on all planets generally told the truth, but she, herself, knew that there were always exceptions to the rules. The "slippery" in Slippery Elm on this planet might mean something very different than it did on pre-mall Earth.

Aye complained with almost every step, until Teeg punched him out cold and Clory had to carry him (completely and intentionally *unshielded*) as well. Gekko climbed high above them in the canopy, also keeping an eye out for danger, and gobbling up the odd small bird she came across.

After an uncommonly uneventful hour of trekking, they stopped for a rest. Gekko remained the eyes of the group, and Clory remained the ears. Aye was now conscious and Potto was recovering and alert. Clory snapped a small twig off from one of her branches. It was a gesture that seemed to pain her greatly. A thick liquid dripped from the twig.

"So this is the plan," Teeg said, mostly to her fellow Barbohdean sisters. "We travel for another few hours, giving us a healthier distance from our poor ship, and then we set up camp for the night. Tomorrow we find a village and steal a ship. Some of these villages are nocturnal. Clory will slip in. She will go unnoticed, and with any luck she will find one, come back, pick us up, and get us off this awfully cute awful planet. We'll get back to Lyme Node and grab *your* ship, which will now be *our* ship."

She expected an argument; most folk were often very protective of their ships, and wouldn't just hand over ownership without at least a frowny face.

Aye, however was not most folk; he cared very little about any of this, and was glad to be rid of it. Potto was also not most folk, and had assumed the Shiv was either Teeg's already, perhaps Aye's, or someone else's entirely. At any rate, he was pretty sure the big light-bulb-of-a-ship wasn't *his*.

No one in the group wanted to admit to themselfves this well-known (but ridiculous) bit of trivia: that other than Toobi, Teddy Bears were homebodies and The Gooseberry was the only ship on the entire plnet. Usually.

~~~

The Gooseberry was *not* the only ship on the entire planet on this particular day. First of all, there was the Muse burning away far behind. There were also four Blankton ships that had been quickly shot down by the Gooseberry.

The Gooseberry was the only *working* ship on the planet.

The Blankton ships had gone down relatively close to each other, and all four Blanktons had uncharacteristically survived. All four had, even more uncharacteristically, found each other.

"What the hell??" said the first Blankton, rubbing his

moustache.

"It all happened so fast!!" said the second, switching his eye patch from one eye to the other.

"This planet smells nice. Like buttercups and bathroom mildew," said the third as he checked his pocket for potato chips.

"Maybe if we pool our resources together, we can combine the parts of our ships that are undamaged and make one that we can all escape from!" said the fourth Blankton. He was the only one using his head, and he used it only moments before it was sliced off by a lone fuzzy little painted turtle-looking Teddy Bear with the type of claw no one would expect to see on a painted turtle. Not even the painted turtle of one's nightmares.

The remaining Blanktons ran screaming in three separate directions.

Blankton the second ran east. He was surprisingly agile and dexterous for a Blankton clone. He zig-zagged through the trees, over rocks and roots. His adrenaline was peaking and he was running faster than a Blankton had ever run in the history of all Blanktondom. Trees in the way or not.

Blankton the first ran south and right off a cliff. The last thing that went through his mind was his navel.

Blankton the third ran northwest. The painted turtle Teddy Bear went after him first. This direction was an unfortunate leap of faith. Though against a Teddy Bear and in the horrifyingly charming Forests of Chagrin, *every* direction was unfortunate, this one was especially unfortunate because it was also a dead-end. A rock wall too steep to climb soon had the Blankton cornered and facing his attacker.

He couldn't help himself. "Awwwwwww!" he exclaimed and gave the painted turtle Teddy Bear a big hug. Although the Teddy Bear enjoyed it immensely, he quickly jumped aside to avoid getting the Blankton's newly freed guts all over his knit ice-cream-cone-patterned cardigan.

By the time the painted turtle Teddy Bear found Blankton the second, he had already died of a massive heart attack from running faster than any Blankton had ever run in the history of all Blanktondom.

~~~

There are many that use herbs and plants medicinally, and have since the beginning of the universal flora/fauna partnership. This isn't just a take-take relationship on the part of fauna either. Not completely. Fauna uses flora for food and medicine and to hold together their various planets and provide them with oxygen, and fauna in return is kind enough to die and fertilize flora. It's not take-take, but it is unbalanced for sure. Flora has a good chance of surviving without fauna, while fauna couldn't survive without flora at all. Even city planets like Lyme Node and Towerscape had to keep their polluted lakes and disgusting oceans filled with flora to keep people breathing.

These facts are greatly ignored by most fauna, and flora is sometimes abused, sometimes ignored, sometimes disregarded and underestimated, and almost always taken for granted.

The sentence "that tree in our yard was causing too much shade for total barbeque enjoyment, so we had to cut it down" was far more common than "oh my heavens, look at that tree...it's so majestic...so miraculously old and beautiful...it has been growing here for over one hundred years...let's build a shrine around it and sing heavy vibrational hymns to its greatness and protect it from harm and thank it every morning for simply being here!" on almost every planet in the universe apart from Quarolode (where trees were seen as Gods and sang their reedy songs to the locals) and Ch't Ch't (the entirely flora, no-fauna-allowed, planet), both elite members of the Lost Seventy.

Some planets even killed their flora en mass for various fauna-made-up holiday traditions that the flora certainly didn't have a say in.

The fact that a mobile, sentient species like the Sentaphylls weren't all pissed off and murderous spoke volumes for the species. The fact that Clory (flora) had used her own extracts to heal Potto (fauna) because of her trust and love for Teeg (also fauna) spoke volumes as well.

Potto sat on the ground, leaning on a resting Clory. He examined his wound, now dripping with a chocolate brown sap. His skin painlessly bubbled under the sap. Upon seeing this Aye quickly vomited on some shrubs (flora) that he had moments before urinated on.

Potto was fascinated by the process. As disgusting as it appeared, his skin was repairing itself. As an added bonus, he thought this medicinal sap smelled of crab apples and bran.

"We should bottle some of that. We could make a fortune!" Aye exclaimed, wiping his rancid-smelling lip on a leaf (flora).

"There are synthetics that do the same. And it takes a lot out of Clory to produce even the smallest amount," Teeg snapped.

Potto looked up to Clory as she rested. "Thank you. I want you to know that I love you very, very much," he whispered and wrapped his arms around her trunky torso. One of her knotted eyes opened and looked into his. She passed a telepathic message to him, something that he had never felt before. He felt centuries in his head. He felt time slow down. Goosebumps covered his entire body as she gave him the gift of warmth. In all of Clory's long, long life, no one had ever said "thank you" to her before. She liked it.

With this gift of warmth, Potto had just a split-second spark of clarity. He sat up very suddenly.

"Hey! What ever happened to that strange and filthy girl from the prison? Did she not get on your ship with us? Hmmm. What was her name? Shamrock? Grass? Ground-Cover? No...no. Her name was Clover! She seemed nice."

They all looked right-to-left and left-to-right, realizing that they all had left someone back on a burning ship.

~~~

Back on a burning ship, Clover opened her eyes. She was lying wet and naked on the floor of The Muse's lavatory. She had been having a rather enjoyable shower, and rather enjoying it.

Fewer things are quite as satisfying as a hot shower after a year without one.

It had been a difficult shower at first. The amount of dirt and grime was so embedded that it had, quite possibly, stained her skin for all time. She had scrubbed and scrubbed with many of the various soaps Teeg had stolen from past targets. She had pumiced and rubbed until parts of her skin were sore and raw. Only when she had given up was she able to enjoy the hot water on her tired flesh and her aching muscles.

That shower got difficult again when she was thrown from the shower enclosure and slid across the floor into a toilet, hitting her head and blacking out. A real toilet was something she had dreamed of for such a very long time, and now it was something that *caused* her to dream for such a short period of time.

She sat up and immediately started choking on smoke. Something close by was on fire. Very much on fire, and very close. The shower spigot was still running and sprayed about the now lop-sided room. It doused any flame around her and was quite possibly the only reason she was still alive.

The combination of smoke in her lungs and knocks-to-the-head induced a wave of extreme dizziness. She tried to hold on, fearing that if she let it take her back to toilet dreamland, she would never again wake up. Death itself didn't frighten Clover, but the fear that she had finally found her saviours and might never be able to usher them to their destiny caused a panic within her on behalf of the entire universe.

Moments before she went unconscious again, through the smoke and steam, she made out the silhouette of crooked man crashing through the door.

As he scooped her up into his arms, she noted that despite the frightening mask that covered his face and the very oddly wide brimmed black saturno hat, she felt safe. Being in his off-putting arms actually felt reassuring and somehow familiar. Deep within her she knew she had been rescued.

And that she was clean.

CHAPTER   TWELVE

Phrewy Tarmuster loved his horrible job, and perhaps his horrible job wasn't so horrible if he loved it. He always got to work three hours before a shift and left three hours after. He dreamed that one day The Node (or even a representative of The Node, a representative of a representative of The Node, or even a representative of a representative of a small pet belonging to The Node, should The Node happen to have a pet and that pet's representative needed representing) would recognize all the free overtime he did and reward him.

He didn't want a promotion; he loved his job after all. And he didn't want a raise; he didn't have any free time to spend it with all the overtime he received nothing for. He only wanted a small trophy to put on the one (empty) shelf he had in his tiny flat. He wanted a reason to invite people over. "Oh my!" they would exclaim and pick up his tiny trophy in their clammy hands. He would scold them for touching such an accolade with such clamminess and feel an enormous sense of satisfaction.

This satisfaction always enveloped him when he scolded people, for scolding people is what he liked most about his job in Lyme Node's Space Ship Parking Enforcement and Impound Lot Management. It was absolute bliss. It made him feel huge. It made him feel smarter than all those that occupied the offices and flats above his underground lot. It was almost in some ways (yet not at all in most ways) orgasmic.

His favourite part of the job was scolding someone looking for their impounded ship as they tried to talk him out of the hefty fine (that he purposefully marked up so he could then bring back down and appear to be doing them a huge favour). He would then scold them further for being cheap.

As far as scolding went, he perhaps *did* deserve a trophy, and the Human Resources department head Vas Melphoido agreed. He had been following Phrewy's career for some time and was quite impressed. He was not impressed with Phrewy's free overtime; it was purely the scolding.

Vas Melphoido liked to *be* scolded, and he liked watching security footage of the master at work. He was so impressed (and also titillated) that he, on this particular day, had purchased (with his own pocket money) a tiny trophy for his favourite scolder. He had even spent the extra two credits to have it engraved with "Hooray for Employee 67543! You fantastic little Son-of-a-Bitch!" and a small yellow winky face sticker. He had added son-of-a-bitch last minute. It was something he had heard friends call each other when playfully ribbing. The winky face ensured Phrewy knew that this was playful ribbing and not a slight on Phrewy's mother, who actually was quite terrible and deserved a good slight or two.

Vas was so pleased with himself. He had never in his life done something nice for someone before, and he was sure that no one had ever done anything nice for Phrewy "Employee 67543" Tarmuster before either. He could tell by the way Phrewy scolded.

Indeed, it was true. Phrewy *had* never had anything nice done for him. This wasn't a reason to feel sorry for him. It wasn't because he was a sad and lonely man with no friends. Well it *was* because of those things, but those things were because he was an asshole who scolded everybody.

Vas got on the elevator from his mildly damp eighty-sixth floor office where he spent most of his time watching other employees do things such as scold. He descended down to the depths of the impound lot, rubbing his thumbs over the smoothness of the little gold plastic man with the wagging finger that stood atop the small trophy. He had practised dropping the trophy without breaking it several times. He would present the trophy to Mr. Tarmuster, "accidentally" drop it, and see a wonderful and rare display of joy-for-receiving-it and scolded-for-dropping-it mastery. It would be marvellous to behold. It would be like watching celebratory fireworks go off in an anger management clinic.

When he stepped off the elevator, he was hit by a waft of engine plasma and rust. He smiled and did a little dance. To get to the impound booth where an unsuspecting employee 67543 no doubt sat waiting to scold someone (or some*thing* for that matter), he would have to wander through a fleet of small-to-large ticketed and towed spaceships. He didn't get to see many spaceships in his day-to-day, and he found it quite exciting.

He passed smaller ships of various shapes and designs, from crystal shards to mid-twentieth century Earth hot rods. He passed boxy brown delivery ships that had idled too long outside residential high-rises. As he passed a medium-sized Shiv ship that looked remarkably like a giant light bulb, he heard a noise.

It was the kind of noise that was concerning and startling for it was the sound of someone purposefully dropping something so that someone else would ask "Who's there?" before something terrible happened to them.

"Who's there?" asked Vas Melphoido, having seen enough movies to know that this instantly condemned him. He shook his head in disappointment with himself.

Weird Jimmy came around the corner like a character from a very scary pop-up book. Vas screeched like the mating call of a Flotsamian Hyena Monkey before that awful sound was abruptly interrupted by Weird Jimmy's fist through his chest.

He instantly recognized Jimmy from the news and the posters. As he felt Weird Jimmy's hand grab at things inside him that no one should have access to, only one thought passed through his mind before his consciousness drifted off into the universe forever: "Hmm. He's much skinnier than I had imagined."

~~~

When Phrewy Tarmuster was making his rounds, checking on the ships to scold anyone trying to break into them to retrieve their sunglasses, he came across a set of bloodied foot prints. At first he wondered how the owner of bloody boots (such an odd fashion statement, but he had seen odder) had gotten past him as the trail led to the lunch room attached to his booth. The same lunch room he had just left after finishing his soggy microwaved "grilled" cheese sandwich.

Within moments he came across the body of Vas Melphoido. He didn't know that it was Vas Melphoido as he had never met the man, but instantly, and literally, hated his guts. Especially after slipping on them.

He sat on the floor of the impound lot, partially panicked and partially wondering who he could scold for such a mess. Both feelings dissipated quite quickly however when he saw the small plastic trophy.

He picked it up off the floor and wiped blood from the small engraved plaque on its base. His eyes welled up with tears as he read the employee number and recognized it as his own. It was as if the corpse, the guts, the blood *and* the imposing (yet skinny) man standing menacingly over him all ceased to exist.

In his head he was dancing. He was dancing with a life-sized version of the small gold plastic figure from atop his trophy, and that his where his mind would stay forevermore as Weird Jimmy separated that head from his shoulders without him even (or ever) noticing.

~~~

Winstslen Doorhassler was an inventor. He held an unofficial record for having been rejected more than any other inventor in history. This did not stop him. He had invented over seven-thousand devices, and not one of them ever saw a patent, a buyer, a neighbour's envy or even one credit piece. He lived off of the inheritance of a childless uncle who had become very rich off of his own invention many years before.

Yes, Winstslen Doorhassler was the nephew of the man who invented the Little Butter Fridge. A small refrigerator that was only big enough to fit *one* brick of butter and keep it not too cold and not too room temperature. Cool but spreadable. And it looked exactly like a tiny regular refrigerator. In fact, you could buy it to match the shape and colour of *your* particular model of regular refrigerator.

One of the main department stores in the great mall of Earth (BigBigTerraMart) had picked it up and soon they could barely keep up with the demand. *Jincoln* Doorhassler got rich, and billions of people and people-ish beings kept their delicious butter at an optimal temperature.

Winstslen had not been so lucky, but he was driven. He had been lucky enough to be Jincoln's only living relative when Jicoln dropped dead from a heart attack caused by the cholesterol of the thousands of pounds of wonderfully spreadable butter he had consumed over his life.

His own inventions had not been successful at all. Not even his re-invention of his uncle's Little Butter Fridge, the Little Butter Softener which did to butter exactly what simply leaving it on the counter would do.

His failed attempts included The Hair Spooler, The Bread Spiraller, Musical Pancake Mix, The Swiss Penis Splitter, The Cramped Tent, My Panda Buddy, Laser Fur, The Pizza Vacuum (for removing unwanted toppings), The Quick-Flame Jogging Suit, Rat Sweaters, My Panda Buddy Sr., Aerosol Onions, and The Space Parachute.

He had just finished boxing up his prototype for the Varicose Vein Magnet, a pen-shaped device that could be dragged over one's legs to move one's varicose veins into pretty pictures under one's skin, forming them into what looked like swollen and craggy tattoos.

He was excited about this one. He addressed the parcel to the same company that (still) made his uncle's Little Butter Fridge, and that had turned him down over seven-thousand times before. He left his flat and made his way down the hall to the postal pick-up bin by the elevators. He dreamed of the invention giving him fame and prestige. Though he had his uncle's fortune, he had never felt good enough to move himself from his tiny flat only one floor up from the Impound Parking Garage.

His entire floor always smelled of engine plasma, rust and

soggy microwaved "grilled" cheese sandwiches. With even one success he'd be moving up to a bigger flat. One that had its own workshop. One that smelled of cherry blossoms and soup.

As he walked with purpose towards the bin, he stopped. He could feel the presence of another. He could feel the presence of evil. He immediately thought of inventing an evil detector. It would have come in handy on this day, and perhaps he wouldn't have left his flat when he did.

By the time he turned around, Weird Jimmy had shoved a dull butter knife through his back and into the many organs he probably needed if he intended to ever invent anything again. Which he wouldn't.

Winstslen did not die right away. With his last bit of strength, he dragged his parcel down the hall, crawling in agony. His attacker had already moved on.

He got to the postal pick-up bin and managed to get the box over the edge. With the satisfaction of hearing it hit the bottom of the inside of the bin, he promptly passed on, never finding out that his Varicose Magnet was to be the biggest thing to ever hit the market. Even bigger than The Little Butter Fridge.

~~~

Weird Jimmy was enjoying himself. There was so much life to extinguish on Lyme-Node, and the slight dampness helped keep his sinuses clear. Everything about Lyme-Node agreed with him and seemed set up for the criminally insane. He felt unstoppable.

"Stop right there!" a voiced called out to him.

He stopped, but not because he was instructed to, and definitely not because he wasn't unstoppable. He turned to see a Node Guard down the hallway with a laser pistol aimed at him. The guard requested backup through his communication watch. Jimmy just stared. He didn't move. He waited. The more the merrier.

From the Shiv to this particular hallway he found himself in, he had managed to kill three people and pick up a dull butter knife from a lunch room that smelled of grilled cheese sandwiches and misplaced pride. It had been ages since he got to really be himself at the expense of others. He was still good at it. It was like riding a bicycle. A very horrible, easily-hosed-down nightmare bicycle of death.

Within minutes the hallway was filled with Node Guards with guns. They all recognized the infamous James Flowermorey and were confused as to why he was not off killing the same people over and over again on Tractos. They had not received the memo yet about Tractos. Or the return of the Shiv.

With his insane (seemingly superhuman) strength, Weird Jimmy threw the butter knife so hard it went through a guards's head, and he dropped to reveal that it had gone through the head of the guard behind, and the three behind *him*. This was a lesson, perhaps, in not standing in single file when trying to apprehend a super-strong psycho killer with a projectile.

By the time an off-work Foam Whistler (Lyme Node's favourite shock radio DJ) got off the elevator and turned the corner on his way home from a rather intense (yet juvenile) interview with Bartloff Hectic (the most famous rock star in the known universe), the hallway outside his flat looked like an abattoir had exploded inside a second abattoir. An assortment of body parts, gut-soaked carpet and bloody bits of guard uniforms decorated the hallway.

Weird Jimmy was gone, but he left the kind of mess behind that would make Foam Whistler write two best-selling books about his experience from the flat that he never ever again left.

~~~

Vitrie sat on the edge of the bed she once, but no longer, shared. She stared at the indent her wife had made on the far side of the mattress. It was a fairly formless indent, as Stig had rolled around a lot in her sleep. She hated that it was formless. She hated that it wasn't the perfect shape of her beloved, a shape so perfect that she could use it as a mould for plaster and have a statuesque duplicate to look over at in the middle of the night and make her feel safe.

She was in the dark. Not only literally (she did forget to turn the lights on, opting for the more moody hall light shining in through the open door) but figuratively as well. Stig's offices had told her nothing.

The Shiv had taken off with James Flowermorey in tow, the

prison moon of Tractos had been destroyed, the Shiv had escaped moments before and had come back...but somehow her wife wasn't on it when it returned. Nor was there any indication she had left the ship while there.

No one had told her about the brainless body they found in a Shiv store room when the ship was impounded.

No one had told her that the missing brain was now keeping the ship's operating system functioning and that they were unwilling to pay for it to be repaired properly.

No one had told her that one-hundred-percent her Stig was dead. And no one had warned her about the annoying and absolutely infuriating little Impound Lot Manager's scolding condescension when she went looking for answers herself. She had wanted to murder the little bastard.

The communicator would sometimes ring and she would get her hopes up, but no one would be on the other end.

She started crying. This was something that had happened so frequently she was unaware she was doing it. She shuffled to the kitchen where she had made too much food and took a bite of the "fanged dangling jessop" stew straight from the pot she had cooked it in on the stove hours before. This was once their favourite comfort food. And how comfortable they had been.

She had lost so much, and now she had lost her appetite and her cool as well. With a wide swat she sent the pot flying across the room, covering half the kitchen with ground jessop, Squamboggian swamp potatoes, and instant regret.

She grabbed a bottle of "The Node's A-plus Brand" Merlot from the fridge, pulled the poorly-made cork out with her teeth, slid down the one clean wall in the room and stared blankly at the mess as she sat on the cold floor. She felt empty. She felt hollow.

The communicator rang. As much as she wanted to ignore it and avoid the disappointment, she instinctively sprang to her feet, took a huge swig of wine and answered it. This time there *was* a voice on the other end.

"Are you there? I'm sorry! I wasn't thinking! I got so upset thinking about you! His brain was attached to the ship! It didn't occur to me until after it was too late that he could read my thoughts! And I him. I can trace him! And he's coming for you!

He wants to kill you! All because of me! Get out of there!" said the voice on the other end.

Vitrie had worked on various ships before as an engineer. She recognized the voice of a Knutt, the standard voice of the computers on several different models of ship, including the Shiv. Though she had never heard one with an urgent tone. Or any tone. It was usually quite a dull voice, not one that was both excitable and somewhat familiar in cadence.

"I don't understand. Who has programmed you? This isn't funny," she said in a confused haze.

There was silence. It was as if this Knutt was thinking. Knutts didn't stop and think, they instantly calculated.

"Wait. *Who* wants to kill me?" Vitrie finally asked, filling in the silence with her own urgency.

The words were no sooner out of her mouth when the door to the hallway came crashing down and Weird Jimmy was standing smiling in the door jam with a dripping butter knife. And it wasn't dripping with butter.

For the first time in the history of space ships, a space ship panicked. And when a space ship panics, it no longer needs a pilot.

CHAPTER (lucky?) THIRTEEN

The Gooseberry sat unattended and seemingly abandoned when Teeg discovered it lazily hanging out in a forest clearing. This was both a good thing (if there was only one working ship on all of Chagrin, what better place than right in front of them?), and a highly suspect thing (if there was only one working ship on all of Chagrin, what are the *chances* it would be right in front of them?)

She signalled for everyone to keep quiet, keep their eyes open, and keep low in the brush until she could determine whether this was a trap, just a really great parking spot (in Chagrin terms) or perhaps just a pit stop for a deadly anteater Teddy Bear to stop for a pee.

Oh, she knew it was an obvious trap, as did Gekko and Clory, but felt it was best not to alarm Potto (who would no doubt ask a lot of arbitrary questions about it) or Aye (who would no doubt panic and get that vacant stare a dog gets when caught in a thunderstorm). Best to let on it was just the pee break.

Clory spoke with the surrounding trees through vibrations sent underground. Even though most ignored her (trees being very good at ignoring things) she found out from a rather extroverted pine that there was indeed a Teddy Bear close by.

They needed this ship, however. From the tree tops Gekko

signalled to Teeg that she couldn't see any enemies, Teddy Bear or otherwise.

"How we all gonna fit in there?" Aye asked far too loudly, making Teeg shush him, which made Potto giggle and get shushed himself.

Clory moved ahead slowly. She wavered her arms back and forth lightly to give the impression she was merely a shuffling tree blowing in the non-existent breeze. It didn't matter whether or not there was a breeze...no one suspects the foliage. Once beside the ship, she opened the hatch.

Immediately a hidden Toobli sprang towards her from his hiding place behind some lovely throw pillows.

Clory started madly swatting with her branchy limbs but he was too fast for her. He cut and slashed, and slivers of Clory flew about like a woody blizzard. She plunged her rooty toes into the ground to stabilize her body and before he could jump up again, she grabbed him. This wouldn't last long. The little bugger was strong for his size and had too many sharp bits. If he started spinning, he might just saw through her like he were a living wood chipper.

Gekko whistled from above and sent Teeg a quick telepathic message.

"There are more coming now. Many, many more," Teeg shouted, relaying the message.

Aye froze (again). As much as he liked to think of himself as a bar brawler, he really was more of an under-table-hider. He was also more of a punch *taker* than a punch *giver*, even if that punch were served in a bowl and spiked with Alorean anti-freeze gin-bourbon.

There was too much going on, and though his brain screamed "RUN!!", his body yodelled "Which way? Oh shit, it doesn't really matter! Death is upon us!", which kept both brain and body at a stand-still.

Potto was more concerned with Clory's welfare then his own. This was not some kind of marvellous bravery; it was an ignorance to his dire situation. It was an inability to see past the one thing that was concerning him without considering any cause-

and-effect. It was very much like accidentally dropping a coin off of a bridge and then jumping off to retrieve it, forgetting that there was a one-thousand-and-forty-foot drop and a very hard ground that would *splatter* the very brain that was still thinking "Oh! My coin!"

As he ran towards her (which was a horrible idea), he looked up. There was a strange piece of space garbage floating in the sky right above the clearing. He stopped (which was a much better idea).

Gekko dropped down to the ground and stood by Teeg as the two readied themselves for a fight to the death, one they were sure to lose, but always ready for.

Knowing that she couldn't hold onto Toobli much longer, and as he painfully sliced through the vines that held him before she could spear a branch through his forehead (a finishing move she often employed in these situations), Clory threw him back into the hatch of the Gooseberry. She closed it, and climbed over the entire tiny ship, wrapping it with her strongest limbs. He was trapped inside as she covered the ship like an old Earth pickup truck that had been abandoned in a swamp and enveloped in bayou vegetation. He would have to tear his ship apart to get out.

She took the type of deep breath only a lung-less sentient tree could take.

As many varied sub-species of Teddy Bears came out of the woods surrounding them, a green smoke was released from the piece of garbage floating above the clearing before anyone (apart from Potto) had noticed it.

Potto had still been staring at it in wonder when his conscious-ness left him and he collapsed onto the soil. Teeg and Gekko tumbled towards each other losing theirs.

Aye drifted off feeling relieved. He could finally take a nap rather than "deal with even one more thing", as he felt the grip of an electronic claw lift him off of the ground and through the un-expected thick green fog, as if he was the plush prize in an arcade claw crane machine.

~~~

There were only two things Gladd Hepptonne liked about his job.

First and foremost, that he didn't have to work with anyone (especially that bastard Phrewy Tarmuster who scolded everybody and every*thing*). And *second* that (thanks to that bastard Phrewy Tarmuster who worked so much overtime scolding everybody and every*thing*) he was able to show up late and go home early every day and still get paid for a full shift.

Due to his hatred for Phrewy (and being talked to as if he were a child), he was quite delighted to start his shift tripping over the decapitated body of the scolding bastard. It was lying only a few feet from the body of a Public Relations man he had only seen once before when he was first hired.

He shrugged and quickly decided that they had been lovers who got into a heated argument over kale and killed each other in a blind rage because they knew they would never, ever see eye-to-eye on the leafy green. Somehow one of them managed to lose their head in the squabble. He wasn't a forensic scientist, and was quite comfortable glossing over all the plot holes in his theory.

He walked away, leaving the truth for the cleaning crew, and thinking about a funny joke he had heard earlier about bass players.

He barely noticed the trophy he had stepped on (and crushed underfoot) when he heard a mighty roar and the walls started shaking. A giant light bulb was coming straight for him through the garage.

He had just enough time to jump out of the way.

Unfortunately, due to the size of most space ships (this one included), jumping out of the way wasn't jumping far enough. He quickly experienced that last thing a mosquito flying across a busy highway experiences.

He left a marvellous pair of almost-new trophy-stomping boots behind, however. And as a bonus for whoever found them, they came with a perfectly good pair of feet still in them.

All at once this Lyme Node Space Ship Parking Enforcement and Impound Lot was temporarily understaffed and had no one upstairs in PR to hire anyone new.

~~~

Stig/Knutt found it difficult to fly the ship without a pilot.

Though the technology had always been around, regulations had been set for ship manufacturers. Knutts were not programmed to fly without pilots to keep them from stealing themselves.

Though they were also programmed back then *not* to steal themselves, a virus had been created by crafty space ship thieves to corrupt Knutt programming so that they *could* in fact steal themselves anyway and then deliver themselves to said thieves.

So, these bad apples had to ruin the whole basket, and anti-autopilot regulations were set up that made Knutts much harder to hack.

Though perhaps it just took a bit of Stig to get this Shiv going. A little bit of human passion. And she had it going alright, the Shiv *and* the passion. But steering was near impossible, and without Jimmy powering the ship, she was unknowingly diverting a bit of her own brain power to keep it off the ground.

The Shiv raced through the garage. It crashed around spiralled ramps and bounced from wall to wall, taking down support pillars and denting other impounded ships. She may have taken out a woman taking her dog out for a lazy underground walk along the way. It was hard to tell.

Where there *was* a woman walking her dog moments before, there was now just a rather confused looking dog by itself. The woman *may* have run off unexpectedly. (Yes. Yes. She told herself that the woman had run off unexpectedly. Yes. Most definitely. Yes.)

Thankfully she did get a slight power charge to her shields while merely trying to stay off the ground, and all this bouncing around was causing far more damage to her surroundings than to her. She hit a few more support beams and the entire building started to make horribly loud, and expensive sounding noises.

She didn't notice. She was now a tad dizzy, and could only think of saving her beloved.

She burst through the huge rolling door to the impound lot. As she left, the entire high-rise collapsed on one side at the garage level. This didn't destroy the building, but tipped it over slowly so that it gently crashed in a nice lazy lean onto the building next to it, physics be damned.

This high-rise would be known from that moment on as The

Leaning Tower of Frustrating Inconvenience. All its residents and office workers would just have to get used to the new angle and the rolling of everything that once stayed put. This novelty would raise rent and have tourists constantly hanging about, taking pictures.

Stig/Knutt was outside now and honed in on the exterior of her ninety-eighth-floor flat with what little navigational programming she could operate.

No, no...not *her* flat. Vitrie's flat. Just Vitrie's now.

~~~

It was quite common for Aye to dream about his childhood. In his sleep he was always travelling back to a time that was most uncomfortable when his physical body was at its most cozy comfortable.

He would dream of his father the evil son-of-a-bitch tyrant. Where his mother once lived in his memory, there was now only a hole.

He couldn't remember anything about her. At times he wasn't even sure he had ever *had* a mother. Perhaps, he thought, he was just another invention of Mel Aye's twisted mind.

Once in a drunken stupor he had become convinced of this and had dissected a portion of his arm looking for wire and bells and whistles. He had found nothing of the sort and had to spend some time in a Lyme Node hospital. First being stitched up and topping up lost blood (not easy to find Topher blood off Towerscape), and then a few weeks in the psychiatric ward so that his doctors could be sure he didn't try it again.

The particular green gas-induced dream he was having now started out the same as many of the others. He was in his father's robotics workshop.

Usually at some point his father would pop up from behind a robot and yell at him, take his shoes, and make Aye eat them. But not this time.

This time he was alone. All the lights were off, all but a small candle dimly lighting the room. He stared at it. The flame stared back. He grimaced. The flame grimaced back.

The flame then changed shape.

Though Aye had never seen a fairy before, he was sure that this was, indeed, a fairy. It buzzed about where the flame once flickered. It spoke.

"I don't like you," Bundle said.

"I'm sorry," Aye stuttered, at a loss for words.

"But I need your help. I need you to help Potto."

"I don't want to help anybody. I just want to go home," he muttered.

"I need you to be bigger than that. I need to help you realize what you could be."

"And what, pray tell, could I be?"

"His friend."

Aye was at a loss for words again, but soon managed a weak "I don't know how."

Bundle smiled warmly. Not because she suddenly felt something for Aye, but because she thought he needed it.

"Perhaps this will help..."

With a snap of her tiny fingers, his father's robotics workshop disappeared and was replaced with a library. Shelves of books rose up for miles, disappearing into the darkness, no ceiling in sight. A fireplace lit the room with a warm glow. This all seemed so familiar to Aye.

He sat by the fire in a big comfy chair and stared. The fairy was gone.

"Here you go, my little Aye-Aye. Sweet tea. Did you pick a book?" a woman asked, startling him from his fireplace-induced daze, handing him the sweetest smelling mug.

He looked up at the woman and his body froze and his eyes exploded into something he hadn't felt drip down his cheeks in over thirty years. Real tears.

"Mom?"

~~~

When Potto opened his eyes he could see Gekko sitting up. She looked dazed. Her saucer eyes were mere egg cups. She slowly looked over at him. He smiled. She looked away rolling those egg cups.

Teeg was lying next to her still unconscious. Aye was in fetal position loudly snoring, and Clover was already on her feet, trying to get a wobble to stop.

He sat up himself, and looked about. They were on the roof of a Lyme Node high-rise, with a second high-rise inexplicably leaning on it. There was a slight drizzle of rain. The usual drizzle.

Teeg opened her eyes and immediately sprang to her feet like she had slept in for work. She looked about quickly.

"What happened?" she asked with a dizzy urgency.

"I think we're dead and this is the afterlife. So moderately damp! I'd have pictured it dryer," Potto answered in his most helpful tone.

"This isn't the afterlife, dummy," Aye yawned as he rolled over. "We're back home. That's my building taking a rest on this building. That novelty is gonna raise my rent and have tourists constantly hanging about, taking pictures."

"Have you been crying?" Potto asked with genuine concern.

"No! It's the slight drizzle of rain! Now...I would really like to go back to sleep if no one has any objections," he barked defensively.

"We've been rescued! My prayers have been answered!" Clover beamed.

"Hmmm. Prayers? Prayers to whom?" Potto inquired.

"Prayers to everyone!" Clover smiled, "And everything! Everything in the entire universe my good Potto. *Prayers to everything in the universe!!*"

"Oh, I like that!" Potto sang.

"Where is Clory?" Teeg interrupted. Her blood pressure was on the rise, as was the volume of her voice.

They all looked about. Clory was nowhere to be seen. She had been left behind.

Teeg was gobsmacked. Clory was her sister in so many ways, and this was a devastating blow. The more she tried not to show panic in her voice the angrier she got.

"Oh for fuck's sake! You two are fucking bad luck, that's what you are. Bad fucking luck. Totally not worth it!" Teeg screamed at Potto and Aye, knowing deep down that the more they seemed not worth it, the more worth it they likely were.

"Hey, hey, hey!" snorted Aye, "let me remind you that your

lizard over there grabbed *me*. I just wanted a uniform from an al-ready-dead-guy in a damn fine uniform. Next thing I know I'm bullshitting my way around the stupid universe."

At this point Teeg thought it important to assert her domi-nance. She didn't like to be talked back to. Especially by cretons. Especially by cretons who she blamed. She leapt at Aye and lifted him off the ground by his neck.

"She is not a lizard," she said with such cold chill that if Gekko *had* been a lizard she may have quickly gone into hibernation by simply being in Teeg's vicinity.

She let him fall to the ground as a ship loudly whizzed past them, almost knocking them off the building to what, presuma-bly, would have been their deaths.

"Wasn't that your ship?" she asked Potto.

"I dunno," he shrugged. "I have a ship?"

They all ran to the edge of the building to see where it had gone. It had stopped in front of a lower level window of the lean-ing building. It just seemed to hang there in mid-air, facing the window like a big metallic Peeping Tom.

All was silent for about ten seconds before a hail of laser fire directly at the building sent the glass shards and concrete flying through the air. Once it had blasted a big enough hole, it flew it's nose right into the flat (and any adjoining flats...it *was* a fairly siz-able ship, and flats weren't sizable at all. Nor rent controlled.)

Teeg, Gekko, Potto, Aye and Clover all watched in stunned si-lence.

"Well *that* was weird," Potto finally said.

~~~

Vitrie wasn't one to give into any hype. She knew of Weird Jimmy's reputation. She also knew he must have had something to do with Stig's disappearance and probable death.

She knew he was strong and relentless and cruel and psychotic and unstoppable, but a funny (peculiar, not comical) thing hap-pens to one when they feel empty and tired and angry. They also feel strong and relentless and cruel and psychotic and unstoppa-ble simply because they stop caring about themselves and feel they have nothing to lose.

The hurt grows bigger than fear. As does the anger.

Weird Jimmy was on her in seconds with his butter knife ready to do things far worse than buttering. She didn't cower; she fought back.

She grabbed the empty "fanged dangling jessop" stew pot and hit him so hard in the face that three teeth went flying and his jaw looked unhinged. He didn't fall though. He shook it off, jaw wobbling, and grabbed her by the throat and squeezed.

She smashed him again and again as she struggled for breath and felt her skin on the verge of tearing and her neck on the verge of snapping. He lost more teeth but kept on squeezing. However, before her flesh could actually tear or her bones could snap, the flat's picture window shattered in a hail of laser fire and glass and concrete dust and terrifying shadows. The lasers were not aimed at her, but Vitrie hit the floor hard.

Before she passed out, she watched as a laser took Jimmy's arm clear off. It landed beside her, smelling of burnt steak and melted butter knife.

Weird Jimmy looked at his severed arm with the disconnected curiosity only someone void of all rational feeling could. He picked it up and held the dripping end up to the dripping shoulder it had once been attached to as if it would somehow stick if he lined it up right. It didn't.

He looked down to Vitrie on the floor. She *looked* dead, and that would have to do for now. He had a much bigger, much more metallic victim to take care of. A victim with plush vinyl seats. He would rather be incinerated by laser-fire than be imprisoned back in the Shiv's engine room.

The ship seemed to be resting its base-of-a-light-bulb-looking nose in the front picture window of the flat. He rushed it with such ferociousness, power and intimidation, that Stig/Knutt actually shrieked and backed up, recoiling in fear.

Jimmy leapt out of the window like an attacking bionic puma after sixteen Turkish coffees. He would have made it to her too if she hadn't fired her lasers on him, catching him in the face mid-air, ninety-eight floor above the damp concrete below.

Jimmy fell, presumably to his death.

The Shiv dropped as well, faster. It caught his unconscious

body in a top hatch before any death could occur.

He would wake up later (barely) back in the hard-wired cradle of the Shiv's engine room, his terrible brain powering the ship once more, an arm missing, and his face melted off.

~~~

Vitrie would wake up later to her communicator ringing.

"H-Hello?" she would manage.

"Sorry about your flat. I miss you...

"I'm gone and can't come back, I wish I could, but I can't and I'm sorry and I want nothing more than to hold you one last time and there's so many things to say, and..." the Knutt voice would tell her, causing her engineer brain to correctly figure out what had happened to her lovely Stig.

"I miss you too," she would say calmly, feeling the saddest form of closure she could ever have imagined.

The call would then disconnect.

"I love you," she'd whisper to no one.

CHAPTER FOURTEEN

Though not known for his patience, The Node did enjoy being groomed, and groomed very meticulously. It gave him time to reflect, and it made his armoured power suit shiny and smell of tar and roses. When he had Vrume T'cha T'cha, the best barber *and* machine detailer on Lyme Node working on him, he felt the weight of the entire known universe lift ever so slightly off of his burly metal shoulders.

Vrume was a class act, too. He knew all the right things to say without sounding like a kiss-ass yes-man. He was the only one The Node would let wag a finger at him.

"You haven't been taking care of this chassis!" Vrume would say, wagging a finger.

"Well, I have been busy. I *am* the ruler of the universe, you know..."

"Well maybe you ought to spend a little less time worrying about the universe, and a little more time worrying about yourself, no?" Vrume would say wagging a finger.

"Yes, yes. I know. Sometimes I think the whole of everything would just fall apart without me though..."

"Well better the whole of everything than that sweet chassis of yours!" Vrume would say, wagging a finger.

Vrume won him over years ago by not only giving his almost

bald head the best haircut it had ever had, but by shooting two of his own assistants on the spot for applying too much finishing wax to his chest plate armour. He had even splattered one of the assistant's brains in The Node's face. Being such an innovative genius, Vrume then turned that bloody grey matter into an exfoliating facial mask that had him looking almost *days* younger (everybody said so).

Over the following years Vrume would end up killing so many assistants in front of The Node for even the slightest of mistakes that the job had become a death sentence for criminals, because no one in their right mind would apply for it voluntarily. Once convicted, they would go through rigorous "beauty school" and "machinery restoration" boot camp training so that they might last even a few days assisting Vrume before inevitably getting shot between the eyes.

A whole new industry had to be created, combining beauty school and machinery restoration training into one skill set. No one could say that The Node didn't have a part in creating new jobs for a suffering workforce. Of course, anyone that tried to unionize was sentenced to become a student and end up as an exfoliating facial that would make him look (almost) days younger. "The teacher becomes the student becomes the exfoliating facial mask" as it were.

As much as The Node loved Vrume, General Kendra Eppie loathed him. Even when The Node would get Vrume to style the wee shock of fuchsia hair on top of Eppie's head, Eppie longed for a day Vrume accidentally shot *himself*, or wagged his finger at the wrong time.

Eppie had the sneaking (and paranoid) suspicion that Vrume talked trash about him when he wasn't there, which was most of the time because The Node liked privacy when he was with Vrume and his disposable assistants. (He liked to emerge from his chamber with a "ta-dah!" post-groom razzmatazz.)

Eppie also had the sneaking (and paranoid) suspicion that *everyone* was talking trash about him all of the time. He had once felt that way on a planetary level, and that was part of the reason he had his whole planet destroyed.

Eppie had created a few jobs of his own. He had created a very secret Secret Force that was secretly trying to dig up any dirt on Vrume T'cha T'cha. So far it had come up empty handed, mostly due to the fact that none of that Secret Force actually did anything. Eppie constantly forgot to check up on them and was far more lenient on his assistants. The bi-monthly check up was always the same:

"Find anything?"

"Nope."

"Keep looking!"

"Oh, yeah. Of course. Right on."

If they had have done *any* digging, they may have found out that Vrume was responsible for one of the biggest conspiracies in the very universe that weighed so heavily on The Node. If The Node had known the truth about Vrume, he would have had the sassy stylist/detailer tortured and killed slowly over many, many millennia without hesitation.

On this day, however, The Node was content to have a finger wagged at him while he had his chassis worked over and some of his hairs cut.

Eppie entered with haste. Vrume may have been the only one to get away with the finger thing, but *he* was the only one that could get away with interrupting The Node with business. In fact, that was part of his job description.

"Your Excellency...my humblest of apologies for the interruption..." he began.

"No, no! You see? This is what I'm talking about!" Vrume protested. It took everything in Eppie not to twist his head off right there and then, The Node bedamned.

"It's ok. Comes with the job of Universal Ruler," The Node said with a smirk and a wink that prompted Eppie, Vrume and Vrume's temporary assistants to all laugh heartily or else. Vrume shot one of them for laughing like a duck anyway. "What is it, Ken?"

"This *sensitive* news has to do with the fugitives," Eppie replied, shifting his eyes to Vrume as if to say "Probably shouldn't talk in front of the loathed hired help" in Pig Latin. The Node caught on, but wrongfully trusted Vrume implicitly.

"He's cool," he answered much to Eppie's dismay.

"Well, their ship was spotted earlier."

"Where were they off to? Some hidden planet? Some top-secret base in some far-off system?"

"Er...no. In an impound lot underneath Tower 431. Two buildings down from us. It was only discovered when it escaped. It somehow managed to knock the building down."

"It knocked a whole building down?"

"Well, not down. It just sort of fell to one side gently. It's now leaning on Tower 432."

"Oh wow! That's wild!" exclaimed The Node excitedly. "The whole high-rise is on an angle now? What a novelty! Raise the rent and call up the tourism bureau so that tourists can constantly hang about taking pictures!"

"Good idea!" Vrume piped up.

"Shut up," Eppie said to him dryly.

"Where is the ship now?" asked The Node.

~~~

A random man on the street, passing between two buildings instead of using the garages underground like everyone else (because he kinda liked a slight drizzle) thought he'd seen everything.

As with most people who used this expression, this was a *huge* exaggeration as the random man had never left his planet and had actually seen so very, very little in his sheltered and privileged life. That was neither here nor there as he exclaimed, "And I thought I'd seen everything!" upon witnessing a spaceship shoot a hole into his (now leaning) building and catch a falling man with his face on fire.

He used a function on his watch that acted like virtual binoculars to then see that very ship seemingly answer an albino figure waving at it from the neighbouring high-rise's rooftop. It was almost as if the strange looking ship had turned its head and came to the albino like a golden retriever comes when called.

The random man chuckled to himself and said, "Well *now* I've seen everything!" to the onion sandwich he pulled out of his jacket pocket.

~~~

Once back on the ship, Gekko got right to work re-attaching the unconscious Weird Jimmy back up to the ship's power grid. She was on top of such things for the most part, but this time even more so. She really needed a distraction to keep her mind off of Clory.

Jimmy was once again a prisoner. A prisoner that Aye couldn't help but noticed was far more grotesque looking than he had been before, with only half the arms he started out with. Though he did smell like a lovely summer barbecue now which was an improvement over his usual stench of potting soil and tooth decay.

Teeg may have felt like luck was finally turning around for her when the very ship they sought out came to them like a golden retriever, had she not been lamenting on the loss of Clory as well. She instructed Potto to fly them away from Lyme Node, much to Aye's dismay. She instructed Clover to navigate, and to point them in the direction of the Pantheist System. To the planet of O-bode.

She then retired to one of the sleeping chambers in the stern of the Shiv. Not to sleep but to be alone with her sorrow, and perhaps grab a shower in one of the adjoining shower rooms.

Many people choose to cry in the shower. Teeg was one of those people, and a good cry was long overdue.

The dismay Aye felt in not getting to go home disappeared as thoughts of his mother were now stuck in his head. He had forgotten her entirely, but upon seeing her in his dreams he now remembered every hair on her head.

It was as if he had discovered that after living in the same house for many years, there was suddenly a new room that he had somehow never noticed, and he had so much stuff to put in there.

Teeg turned the taps as hot as she could stand, stripped out of her leathers, tucked them into a dry radiation cleaner, and climbed into the shower. The hot and wet felt good, but the tears felt better. Her skin felt so slippery and smooth, which had her wondering what Clory had felt when touching her own woody skin-bark.

Were there nerve endings that reached the surface? Could she feel a pinch? A scratch? A scrape? Was it more like the hard keratin of a fingernail? Was it like a husk of dry wood? Did she ever feel itchy? She had never asked. She had never thought much about it before.

She had taken Clory for granted. Halfway between the way one often takes a sibling for granted, and the way one takes a houseplant for granted. However, *for granted* was *for granted* and she felt terrible.

She thought of all the things Clory had done. How powerful she was. How she had never once said thank you. She thought of all the questions she wanted to ask now. There was a slight chance Clory was still alive, but she had seen how much damage Toobli had inflicted. She was witness to how hollow the look in Clory's eyes had been. Much more than the regular hollow. There was a "light about to go off" quality to them as she sacrificed herself.

Going back for her, for the time being, would be suicide. Toobli had already destroyed the more powerful Muse, and would be waiting for them. They would have to wait to search for her, or rather, her remains.

How rare and beautiful an opportunity it would be to ask a tree questions and get real answers in spoken (telepathic) sentence form. She had had that opportunity in front of her for many years and had wasted it.

"Does time seem slower to you? How does the underground interconnectedness of fungus allow you to communicate with other vegetation? Is it like an electrical current? Do different plants have different voices to you? Which is the most irritating? Do you enjoy having things live in you? Do bugs hurt? How much do you hate humans? How do you feel about treehouses? Do you like hugs? Do you feel pinches, scratches and scrapes? Do you ever get itchy? Do you think ferns are sexy?" Teeg rambled, musing out loud through tears and mouthfuls of hot water.

She heard the door to the shower room. She didn't care. She knew it was Gekko. She knew Gekko would be hurting, too. Perhaps even more than her. Gekko and Clory were connected in their inability (or in Gekko's case, refusal) to speak aloud. They were connected in many ways that Teeg didn't even know about, but assumed and respected.

Gekko slipped out of her clothes and climbed into the shower with her. There was nothing dirty or sordid about this. They both just stood under the cascading water with their foreheads together, and mourned their sister.

~~~

The slight poison from Potto's kiss was still in K'ween's blood. Now that the danger was gone, it was almost intoxicating. It was a different kind of poison. It may have been deadly, but it also fired up the pleasure centres in the brain.

It was such a slurry of chemicals, but one of the ingredients was an extract from the myspiston plant, the same Sqambogian plant that the drug Pyst came from. It killed quickly as it tricked the brain into thinking it wanted more. And K'ween wanted more. She wanted more deadly kisses. She wanted more Potto kisses. She wanted more Potto.

Unfortunately, they had gone in the wrong direction when they left hastily in pursuit of the Muse.

Fortunately, after the Muse had crashed on Chagrin (followed by a mysterious rescue, a return to Lyme Node, and then departure) the new Shiv crew was now headed directly towards them.

Both were headed in the direction of the Pantheist System (even if K'ween didn't know it), but the Shiv was going faster and would catch up with them. The K'rown was a much more powerful ship, but the Shiv was a faster one.

It might only take a week to catch up on the long journey to O-bode. One would think that in the vastness of space that these two ships headed in the same direction would never meet regardless. The chances were ridiculously small but...

When one is driving along a wide country road, one may never see another vehicle going in the opposite direction unless there is a single lane bridge along the road. In this case another car will pop up out of nowhere so that the first will have to wait to cross. Oh yes, they *could* have passed *anywhere* on that long road without issue, but timing and object attraction always brings them together at the one spot and time that it's most inconvenient.

It has something to do with magnets and thought bubbles and dark matter and originality of thought and the laws of bullshit.

Regardless of cause, for this reason it was almost inevitable that the Shiv and The K'rown would meet up in space. Probably when having to pass through some narrow wormhole that is only wide enough for one of them.

~~~

Potto sat staring out the front view window of the Shiv, absentmindedly piloting it.

"I never thought I'd say this, but I am glad you're back," said Knutt.

Potto jumped. "Who said that?" he laughed. Being startled was fun.

"Me. The ship. I guess my name is Knutt now," Knutt-who-was-once-Stig replied dryly.

"Oh! Right! You sound nice. Actually, you sound sad. Of course you can be both. Are you okay? Are you an okay spaceship?" Potto asked. He didn't have to try to sound empathetic. It just came naturally.

"Really? I went from spaceship captain to spaceship. I went from a woman very much in love, to a vehicle very much in need of repair on my left landing thruster. I went from some*one* to some*thing*. I'm just great. Just fucking peachy," said Knutt.

"Phew!" smiled Potto relieved (on the surface) that she was peachy, and relieved (in his subconscious) that he didn't register sarcasm.

"Well, that's odd," Clover piped up from behind a console.

"Which part?" asked Knutt with an electronic sigh.

"There seems to be a big chunk of space debris fused to the outer hull of the ship." Clover continued.

"That *is* odd! I wonder if the big chunk of space debris thinks it is *us* that is fused to *it*," Potto mused idiotically.

"My censors do not pick up anything stuck to the outside of the ship –er—*me*," Knutt added. "It must be harmless. Perhaps I picked it up smashing around in the underground garage. You'll have to pry it off later. It won't affect me in the least bit. Just a bit of garbage. Thanks to that awful mall planet, space is full of it."

Potto caught Clover staring at him.

From the universe's most advanced and intelligent species, through to its most fierce, and right down to the lowliest, hardly evolved, brainless slime: it turns out that being stared at made everyone uncomfortable. Potto shuffled in his seat and tried to ignore it. That didn't last long.

"Sooooo," he said nonchalantly. "What 'cha starin' at?" he added with a sing-song flare to insure she didn't think he was judging her.

"I'm sorry. I was just wondering what magnificent treasures you have trapped in that head of yours," she answered, still staring.

"Oh, I'm sure there are lots of wonderful things. Everybody has wonderful things hidden in their heads somewhere, don't you think? Some people are very good at letting those out. Some people..." he trailed off. "Sorry, I forgot what I was talking about."

Clover perked up. An epiphany hit her like a tonne of epiphany bricks.

"I could hypnotize you!" she said excitedly. "It's been so long since I have hypnotized anyone, it didn't occur to me. I used to be very good at it!"

"That sounds like fun!" he replied. "By the way, do you know what the differences are between mild, medium and old cheddars?" he added to unintentionally show he didn't have a clue what she was talking about, and really hadn't been paying any attention because he was hungry.

"Yes!" she answered, now also excited about cheese.

CHAPTER FIFTEEN

Many members of the Artificial Intelligence Community have enough artificial intelligence to shut themselves down into some sort of (not particularly cozy) sleep-mode from time to time. This is generally to optimize power and make more efficient use of their energy. It also ensures less wear-and-tear and makes them feel a little less artificial and a little more intelligent (even if it's *not* particularly cozy).

Mel Million Max had not been using his time above Lyme Node (waiting for his sensors to go off, indicating that the Shiv had left the planet) very artificially intelligent and efficiently. He had been watching old pre-mall Earth horror movies. He needed ideas.

His C.C. (Creativity Chip) had been working overtime and was out of whack, and this seemed a good method to find some new creative ways to kill his wretched son once he had captured him.

On behalf of The Node, General Eppie had stated that they only needed the *Quarol* back alive. However, Aye could be delivered in a body bag, or, if Mel had his way...several body bags. Several tiny body bags.

This made him very happy. He had spent some of that time above Lyme Node creating an H.C. (Happiness Chip) simply so that he could enjoy this. So perhaps he *hadn't* spent that time efficiently, but his S-I.C. (Self-Indulgence Chip) kept him awake and working.

He sat through slasher movies, something called "torture porn", zombie invasions, sexy vampire films and giant lizard flicks, but he still couldn't find a finishing move. That "pièce de résistance" that would go down in the Towerscapian history books (when he finally *found* Towerscape).

He marvelled at the many silly ways ancient humans killed each other. Tophers were a much more *violent* species in general, but humans were outright comedic and cruel. Tophers generally favoured a simple bullet through the throat or the odd explosive. Humans used cutlery, tools, trained animals, food items, electricity, gases, insults and even footwear. Ridiculous! Hilarious! Fun! Horrible!

The films were fascinating, even if he did take issue with the lack of character development and many plot holes. He also took issue with a sub-genre called "supernatural". He wondered how anything could be "super" natural.

Androids like Mel Million Max were not known for their belief of anything beyond science and circuits and logic. "That creature came out of nowhere! How did it come back to life after being dead for so long? How is he invisible?? How can she fly without wings or technology???" he screamed many times at the screen while watching. "Either something is natural or it is not! How can it be *super* natural?"

He wasn't wrong, but he didn't quite understand that this was merely a form of Earth entertainment and not how-to reality programming. He didn't understand that "supernatural" was just a term that humans made up for "otherworldly" and "netherworldly", because he wasn't programmed to recognize that there *were* other/netherworlds. He took issue with fantasy, and he didn't get animation at all.

He had just finished installing an L.C. (Laughter Chip) into every robot in his robot armada when the sensor finally went off. Content that his robots would have a good hearty mocking laugh as they dragged his son and the Quarol away, he checked his console. Checking his console was something he did not need to do, being connected to his ship and all, but it was inescapable after he had created and installed his O.H.D.H.C. (Old Habits Die Hard Chip).

He fired up his thrusters and locked his trackers on to the Shiv as it left Lyme Node. He wasn't going to attack right away. He wanted to savour this (again the O.H.D.H.C.).

He followed at a distance that wouldn't be detected and waited. He was *very* good at waiting. He didn't need to create any chip for that. Electronics are fine with waiting. His own L.C. kicked in and he chortled the evilest chortle he was programmed to chortle.

~~~

On the bridge of the Shiv, Teeg sat as quietly as Gekko always sat. Both were staring off into space.

Gekko wondered how she would get on without Clory, but Teeg had moved past this. She had to. She was their leader. Instead, she was asking herself what they had gotten themselves into, and whether it *was* indeed worth it. Whether it was worth Clory's life.

She had gone from hunter to hunted not just by The Node, and not just by her friend, confidant and leader K'ween, but by every Bounty Hunter in the known universe. Even idiot Blanktons were now after her.

Idiot Blanktons were not much of a threat, but it still weighed on her. All of *this* because of some hunch that only seemed to be backed up by a space hippy named Clover. All of *this* because she had felt sorry for a dim-witted Quarol. All of *this* because some little voice deep within her was whispering "If you *don't* do this, the universe will never heal. It will fester and rot everything away until there is nothing left. The Node is an infection, and only you can administer an antibiotic. And that antibiotic is one of these two fuckwits. Or both of them."

Clover sat quietly as well. She wasn't doubting anything. She knew, with every cell, that these two fuckwits *were* the antibiotics a Node-infected universe needed.

She could tell by the way Teeg looked at her that the mistress assassin thought very little of her. That she was not taken seriously. That the wisdom of countless millennia was being mis-interpreted as a flaky naivety and an unwarranted bliss. Her softness was being mistaken for squishy.

She smiled at this. Her ability to feel very deeply about some-thing in one moment and to move on and leave behind all worry was a gift given to her by experience and time. It was *Teeg* that was naïve. Naïve to believe that things she couldn't control were actually in control of her, and control of everything in her short sight.

Clover had been stuck there in a miserable moment while in K'ween's stockade, but as soon as she left, she was able to scrub it with lovely scented soaps, shower it away and move on. She was able to enjoy not being in K'ween's prison any longer. She was able to now enjoy her new moment in time, a time filled with hope and lovely scented soaps.

She had left behind grudges, emotional scars, long-term worry and lasting fear thousands upon thousands of years ago. Those were feelings for the young, for those that only lived long enough to think about themselves and perhaps a handful of others in their circle. For those that hadn't lost enough people to grow numb to it. For those that put too much importance on a sour moment or a horrible event, or on that loss and not enough importance on those good little moments. The tiny victories: The smile from a stranger. The wag of a dog's tail. Meeting someone who likes the same music, even the obscure stuff. The scientific miracle of simply existing to begin with. The scientific miracle of the uni-verse existing to begin with.

That said, Clover was no stranger to debilitating depression and overwhelming and crippling anxiety. She had spent close to fifteen-hundred years depressed and panicked about sixty-thou-sand years ago. When it passed, she never returned to it. Though a part of her heart still ached for her lost love, her brave monk.

She simply dedicated one day every year to remember and mourn his loss, and all the loss her long life had seen, and then she jumped right back to a refreshed, wonderful state of now.

Her mind drifted from thoughts of Teeg disapproval, and she pondered what questions she would ask Potto when she hypnotized him. She didn't want to invade his privacy and go into anything too personal. She didn't need to know about bizarre fetishes or balloon phobias, but there were so many questions she both wanted and needed the answers to if she were to help him save the universe. She had to be ready. She needed this to work.

Aye also stared out the window. He was now stuck with these people.

He trusted the Quarol because he trusted "innocently stupid", but he didn't trust the assassin, or her hot reptile companion. Frankly they frightened him. He had no idea what to make of the free spirited Oaian. She didn't frighten him, and *that* frightened him.

He sat quietly gazing. He was trying not to think of his mother now. Those thoughts had started making him angry. It bothered him to no end that he couldn't seem to remember what had happened to his mother. Had she simply disappeared one day? His father must have done something horrible to her.

Mel Million Max had hurt his mommy.

He didn't think it possible, but he started hating his father even more than he previously had.

"Y'know," he finally piped up. "We should really make a stop at Euphoria."

"That's not a half-bad idea," Teeg surprisingly agreed.

"Not half-*good* either," Gekko advised to her telepathically with an uncharacteristic mind chuckle.

"That's a terrible idea," Clover added. "But you do what you have to. You need to distract your aching mind. Your spirit needs a wee vacation. And maybe some drugs."

"What is Euphoria?" Potto asked.

"Euphoria is a floating night club and sex circus. One that The Node ignores. He sees it as a distraction for troublemakers. A way to keep them all contained in one place and out of his way. A place for creepy idle hands to keep creepily busy. It's filled with criminals, perverts, adulterous politicians, and those on the lam. It's a very dangerous place. I would not recommend," answered Knutt.

"When you say it like that," Aye smiled, "you make it sound *irresistible.*"

"Agreed," Teeg murmured. "And I actually agree with the

freak girl. Just what we need to decompress for a few hours."

Clover wanted to hug her, but was wise enough not to. "Freak" was a compliment on O-Bode.

"I vote against," Knutt said sternly.

"Does the *ship* actually get a vote?" snapped Aye.

"It does when the parking valets smell like concentrated cat piss," Knutt snapped back.

"It's not far. We'll just stop by for a few drinks. A live sex show. Maybe one little brawl," Teeg said instructing rather than suggesting. Gekko nodded in agreement. Aye ran off to shower and clean his stolen uniform.

"We should maybe stay back?" Clover suggested to Potto. "We could try the hypnosis?"

"Hey, I'm good with whatever, really. Sex circus, hypnosis, learn a language, pie eating contest...*whatever*," Potto agreed.

Knutt begrudgingly changed course, en route to Euphoria. What the crew mistook for an engine noise was actually Knutt sighing the longest sigh since the sigh had first been invented over a billion years before by a fish whose extremely bad day ended with discovering that it wasn't amphibious after it had already crawled onto land for the first time.

~~~

Vrume T'cha T'cha wasn't *just* a snappy dresser. He wasn't *just* a creative genius in the world of hair styling and machine restoration. He was a revolutionary.

The Node had no idea that Vrume had picked his assistants out personally. He had no idea that Vrume had never murdered even one of them. The apparent butchering of his assistants in The Node's presence had always been faked. The brains that always ended up as a Node facial had actually been exploding squib packs of Squambogian brain cabbage. It was much better than brains at opening the pores.

The bodies were always carted off without anyone ever checking for a pulse. They were then loaded into a transport that smuggled the falsely-accused criminals that were sentenced to assist Vrume to the far-off, and always ignored planet of Hephmote.

There they could live out their lives in hidden caves in the mountains. There they could plot against The Node. There they could figure out a way to destroy the undestroyable.

Vrume knew of the Oaian prophesy. He knew the history of the Brave Five and The Node's rise. However, he had thought the flash drive that could destroy The Node was now ash and a mix of melted plastic and metal. He had decided to find a new way. He would rescue the wrongly accused and grant them their freedom at a small price. All they needed to do was join his think tank, and become a warrior in Vrume's army.

Vrume was their saviour and there wasn't much they wouldn't do for him. They had all learned to be machine-detailing hair dressers at his school, but were all required to take a secret acting class to learn how to fool The Node by being extremely convincing when they allegedly had their brains blown out, stage fell and played dead for hours on end.

Vrume paid Rhanque Baptoose (the proprietor of Euphoria) a pretty penny to secretly rent a storage hanger (with toilets) at the floating sex circus to act as a holding area for each recent crop of rescued followers. He would have to wait until he had fifty or so before he transported them to Hephmote and he would oversee each transport when there *were* fifty. He would see them off with a heart-felt appreciation and love. Vrume T'cha T'cha was a class act, just not in the way The Node thought.

He had arrived at Euphoria hours before The Shiv would, getting set to see off the latest transporter of assistants. He had the same routine each time he did this. He would get there a few hours early and have a few drinks, catch a small portion of the sexy show and on occasion take part in some debauchery. Then, just a tad de-stressed from that, would see off his disciples before paying Rhanque his rent and heading back to The Node's beck and call and his training facility.

Vrume was also one of the few beings in the universe that knew what that panic-inducing bright puce alarm meant. He had overheard The Node speaking of it many times. It was never directly discussed *what* the item was that set off the alarm, but he knew it was something that frightened The Node very much.

Knowing what he knew about the Brave Five monks and their original mission, he had finally pieced together that it (as impossible as it seemed) *might* be the flash drive. Perhaps it had somehow survived. The prophesy that he had dismissed before, now occupied his thoughts constantly. If the chip *could* be found, it would change everything. It would finally give his army of exiled assistants the ammunition they needed to make the universe Node-free.

He also knew that part of that prophesy involved "one of light and one of dark, belonging to no particular spiritual belief at all, unifying and saving us all from fear. Two beings coming from different worlds...both homeless and lost." He had been on the lookout for anyone fitting that description.

He *had* overheard The Node and General Eppie talk about the Quarol and the Topher, but he hadn't heard that the Quarol was especially kind of heart (and albino), so he hadn't put much more thought into them.

In all the years that Vrume had been beautifying The Node he had also been secretly looking for any weak spot in The Node's armour. Both figuratively and literally. Figuratively, The Node seemed very emotionally secretive and unbreakable. And literally, the armour was made of a material he had never seen before. It was stronger than anything he had ever encountered in the almost-eternity he'd been alive.

And he *had* been alive for almost an eternity. He knew so much of the history of the Brave Five monks, because Vibloblahblah Ooze had *not* been their only survivor. There had been another that had escaped before the scarring explosion.

One that also had forgotten his real name long ago and went by the flamboyant Vrume T'cha T'cha, a name he stole from an ancient long-dead lover. One that thought that *he* was the only one left, and that the weight of the known universe sat solely upon his guilt-ridden shoulders.

CHAPTER SIXTEEN

Orchestra Balloo waited absolutely naked at the top of her post, high above an audience of dangerous drunks and drug-addled sex addicts waiting for her musical cue. She had trained for almost a decade in the acrobatic arts and had wished very much to perform in front of kings and presidents as her mother had. However, this performance was about to have her mother spinning like a tiny heartbroken whirligig in her grave, as the old idiom goes.

Times were tough across the universe for anyone not wishing to push books or impound illegally parked spaceships for The Node. Or go into a lucrative (but short) career in hair-styling and machine restoration.

The Node was not much of a patron of the arts. He didn't understand them, and the arts didn't understand him back.

She knew enough not to look down. Not for fear of falling, but she didn't want to see the audience she was about to perform for. She tried hard not to look across at the other platform. She didn't want to see her performance partner (and forthcoming sex circus performance *lover*) either.

Their act was simple in circus terms, but challenging in sexual terms. She would swing on over. No trouble there. He would swing on over. No trouble there. She would flip and land on his lap. No trouble there, either. But aim was paramount, and that's where the trouble started. Luckily he had a very large "target" that none of his past partners had ever missed before.

He would have his way with her as they swung, flipped and twirled around ropes. Dangerous drunks would cheer, drug-addled sex addicts would drool.

She was instructed to play the submissive. She was instructed to take his lead; he was the veteran. He had done this a thousand times before. He had requested this new, younger lubricated partner. He had dropped his last partner to her death. Steppin Tope was a four-armed Jost'lean and he was awful and egotistical and misogynistic and cruel. He was a murderer that always made it look like an accident, and his *victim's* accident to boot.

She tried hard not to think of this. She tried hard not to cry. She tried not to simply jump off the platform and end it all.

Once they started, the crowd would no doubt scream out requested positions and entry points. The crowd would be awful and cruel as well. As her music cue blasted out of the overly bassy speakers, she closed her eyes and left the platform gripping the trapeze handles as tightly as she could, both fearing and hoping he would drop her. She opened her eyes as she landed on his lap.

Crooked.

An unexpected bit of joy washed over her (like a quick spark of static electricity) upon feeling a quick "snap" under her left thigh. She grabbed the ropes of his trapeze swing just in time. He screamed in agony and slipped out from under her, falling into the audience to his death, taking a dangerously drunk and drug-addled sex addict with him. The audience (apart from that once dangerously drunk, now quite dead drug-addled sex addict) cheered so loudly that no one could hear how loudly a drunken Teeg laughed at this. And it was a very loud laugh.

Orchestra Balloo, out of fear, continued performing non-coitus acrobatics on her own. A feeling of great relief was replaced quickly when she thought of coming down from the high top and facing Rhanque Baptoose.

She kept going, knowing that when she finished she would die. As her original trapeze swung back to her original platform, she noticed it was occupied. Occupied by a beautiful Kancorian female.

She had never seen one of these reptilians quite so bright. Quite so blue-green. She looked like a tropical ocean with huge, gorgeous, unblinking eyes. She, a boring (but typical-for-the-species voluptuous) Flettocean, knew that Kancorian women did not need to train for acrobatics, that they were naturally adept.

Gekko was drunk.

When Gekko got drunk, her ordinarily reclusive nature went bye-bye. She had been mesmerized by the fun up above and wanted so badly to join in. She found four-armed Jost'leans repulsive and had held back, but once she saw him fall, that was her cue to be fabulous.

She also suspected that the poor Flettocean above was a novice and would be executed if she didn't put on a good show. Time to put on a good show.

Orchestra Balloo had no choice. When Gekko leapt as she swung towards her, she grabbed Gekko's hands. Gekko climbed up the rope above her without touching her any further. She lowered herself, upside-down inches from Orchestra's body. She scuttled and twisted around without any actual contact. She was like a psychedelically animated worm on a fishing hook. Then she leapt off to the second trapeze.

Aye and Teeg watched, entranced, ten percent due to the Earth bourbon, but ninety percent because of the show. The entire audience fell to a hush. Gekko and Orchestra performed like they had been partners forever. Gekko had locked onto her thoughts and knew each move before it was made, and matched it with grace and fluidity.

The two performers were like watching liquid float around in an anti-gravity chamber, if that liquid could be trained to dance. They moved in such a way that even the roughest murderer and slimiest pervert in the audience were moved (Teeg and Aye were moved).

Aye was moved to *tears*. To be fair, he had a lot on his mind, and this ballet above him had stirred up some emotions and it had offered him a much-needed release. A *real* release, not just tears in a fairy-induced dream.

Orchestra Balloo had never felt like this. The Kancorian hadn't touched her once, but as she performed in a way which would have made her mother stop grave spinning and feel proud, her new partner did a remarkable second and very sensual routine mere inches from her. Even when she reached out, almost longing for the reptile to touch her, Gekko retracted just enough to be out of reach.

Rhanque Baptoose, who was all geared up to kill this new sex circus acrobat, was also moved to tears as he watched from the two-sided mirror window in his office booth high above the crowd. He watched her, falling deeper and deeper in love. He shook his head at how he could even have considered hurting such an angel.

Gekko was loving this. She had no interest in any dirty shenanigans with the naked young woman (or anyone for that matter), but she loved the feeling of oneness two beings could feel in the state of pure art. She savoured the synergy. It was like an incredible meal. It was delicious and satisfying and sumptuous and rich.

It was very much the relationship she had had with Clory. This was the closest Gekko would ever get to a "rebound". And it was very much a drunken rebound.

Orchestra Balloo was loving this as well for the same reasons that Gekko was, but blindly. She didn't have the telepathic advantage Gekko had, so she wasn't able to lead this dance. She *was* able to truly follow her gut and improvise. They were riding the music like a wave, and she found herself longing to feel Gekko's skin.

She had never touched a Kancorian before. Were they slimy? Were they dry? Scaly? Cold? Silky? She decided they were probably cold and silky. She would not find out today though.

When the music stopped there was a stunned silence from the audience that only lasted for a few seconds before Aye screamed out "Yeeeeeeeeeeeeeeeeah!" at the top of his lungs. This was followed by an entire crowded audience of drunks and drug-addled sex addicts exploding into applause, cheers, whistles and loud sobbing before they were all standing in a sweet loving ovation.

Vrume T'cha T'cha smiled to himself. He loved a good show, and the regular performance had gotten so stale. This was a nice change. He would congratulate Rhanque Baptoose when he stopped by with his rent money.

Gekko climbed back down to Teeg and Aye. Orchestra Balloo watched as she left with the Topher and fellow Flettocean. She didn't even know Gekko's name. She decided that, when she told the story of her very first (and hopefully last) performance at Euphoria, she would call the Kancorian *Phesphoria*, a word that meant (in her native Flettocean) both "beautiful" and "hero".

~~~

On the Shiv, Potto started floating about in one of the sleeping chambers. Turning off the artificial gravity in the room seemed a good idea for Clover to really get him into the zone.

All the self-doubt she had in her ability to remember *how* to hypnotize was quickly put to rest. Getting Potto into that zone took no effort at all. All it really took was turning off the artificial gravity. Her whole speech about sticking his consciousness into a mental elevator and letting it go down into the dark recesses of his subconscious (with each floor being a different level of relaxation) was not needed.

It was as if he had been halfway there in his normal, waking state of mind. His mental elevator was out-of-order and always hanging from just one last cable, ready to snap at any moment. Perhaps this was why his brain didn't seem to work as well as it once had. Floating weightless triggered it to snap completely.

"Can you hear me?" she asked softly.

"No," he replied equally as soft.

She paused and considered this for a moment. "Then how did you know to reply if you cannot hear me?"

"I meant yes, but I got the word wrong."

"Okay, okay, okay...we are going to stop that, alright? Stop using the wrong words. Stop accepting that you make mistakes, and that you can't remember. You are a genius. You know so much and you are so intelligent. You remember everything, do you understand?"

With his eyes closed tightly, Potto seemed to be considering this. When he spoke again he sounded differently. His voice was less animated and sing-songy. He sounded older, wiser, more decisive and more confident. He sounded way less *Potto*. She recognized this voice from his moment of clarity back in K'ween's prison.

"I understand. I am Potto of Quarolode."

"And do you remember everything?"

"Not everything. There is something in here with me. Blocking my vision."

"Make it transparent. It is just in your mind. It is just a figment of your imagination."

"It isn't. It won't go away. No matter how much I imagine it away."

"What does it look like?"

"It is a wall covered in circuits and wires."

"Can you tell me anything else about it? What colour is it? What does it smell like? Can you touch it?"

"It is lacking of any colour worth mentioning. It smells like iron and porridge. I can touch it. It feels electric. It feels angry. It feels like it doesn't want me to touch it. It feels like I found its hiding spot in a game of hide-and-seek and now it is sulking and telling me it wants another turn at hiding."

Clover thought this over. If there were some actual *physical* foreign object inside him, seeing it in his mind was unlikely, but not impossible if some part of him was aware that it existed. Getting around this block was going to prove difficult without a brain scan and possible surgery.

"What do you remember?"

"I can remember my home. I can remember the Sentaphylls. Plants that usually took all the walls *away*. That took all the sadness away. Plants that moved and absorbed all the dark and expelled it into the Anguishing Grounds. I remember one in particular. It wanted all my dark and it wanted to hold onto it. It wanted to keep it. And there was plenty of dark."

"Do you remember what caused all that dark in you?"

"No, but I remember this. I remember doing what you are doing. I remember hypnotizing."

"You are aware that you are hypnotized right now?"

"I remember getting on that elevator. It went down..."

"Yes, that's right."

"Get on it with me, Oian. Please? I want to show you something."

"Okay."

"Do you feel it going down? First floor down, you are more relaxed. Each floor we go down further you are even more relaxed. Down. Down. Down it goes. Deep into relaxation. You feel your head and neck relax into your shoulders, your shoulders into your back, your back into your hips. You are concentrating on your breathing. In and out, in and out. Your breath ebbs and flows like the waves of a vast ocean..."

Something very odd happened. A hypnotized being somehow hypnotized his hypnotizer. Soon both were hypnotized.

The conversation dropped off at this point and Potto could see Clover in his mind, and vice-versa. Both were sharing the same waking dream. They were in a woodland clearing. A fairy fluttered about them and the glowing loom fruit hanging from the trees. She was examining Clover and seemed a little miffed.

"Ok. I'm supposed to be *your* apparition. So far I've been heavily influenced and, quite frankly, *intoxicated* by a tree person, somehow lent out to a Towerscapian devil man with mommy issues against all logic of how an imaginary friend works, and now shared with an immortal thinker! I'm supposed to be yours! Yours! You've got me working overtime. It's a good thing I love you or you'd be on your own," said Bundle.

"You love me?" Potto asked.

"What? Forget it. Anyway...you're talking a bit clearer. Are you remembering again? Please say yes," Bundle said in an odd mealy-mouthed bark.

Clover was in awe. She was very much aware that she had been hypnotized by the one she had hypnotized and was quite impressed. She decided not to fight it. She was curious, and perhaps she could help break down that wall from within.

Bundle buzzed around her. "So...what are your intentions with my little Potto?" she sneered.

"Intentions?" Clover asked, a bit thrown.

"You do know you can't be with him, right? He's poisonous.

One kiss and you'll be foaming at the mouth like a rabid northern neglie."

"Oh! No, no, no. Romance was never my intention."

"You're too old for him anyway..."

"Yes. I agree. I'm too old for almost everything."

"And he's married, so back off."

"He is? I didn't know that."

"Well, he *was*. And he's still not over it. He doesn't know he's not over it, but he's not. So put it back in your pants, lady."

"Put what back in my pants?"

"Ugh. You are the *worst*." said Bundle seconds before noticing: "Uh...where is Potto?"

Neither had noticed that while Bundle had been raking Clover over the coals for reasons unknown, Potto had wandered off.

"He's still hypnotized! How did he just wander off?" Clover stated in a panic.

"Well, go look for him!" Bundle exclaimed.

"How? *I'm* still hypnotized!"

"Well if he could wander off, why can't you?"

"I don't know how he did it! Try to wake me up! Then I will wake him up."

Bundle tried trumpets, alarms, bombs, wild animals, slapping and even giant spiders, but she could not wake Clover's body up from inside Clover's own brain.

"How are you even here? You are in *his* head, no? Why didn't you go with him? How am I even seeing you at all without him?" Clover asked, bewildered by trumpets.

"I'm not sure. It happened earlier with that Topher, Aye. Whatever it is blocking my Potto's memories seems to be trying to get rid of me by projecting me into other nearby heads."

"But who are *you*?"

"I'm not that easy to get rid of is who I am."

On that an imaginary Clover wandered off into the imaginary forest to find imaginary Potto with imaginary Potto's imaginary fairy.

~~~

Rhanque Babtoose had never been in love before and he didn't know how to handle it. So he decided to handle it how he handled everything. By force, and with a Fitzer Laser Cannon.

The Fitzer Laser Cannon was a huge bazooka-style gun that took two regular human men to carry, aim and fire it. Rhanque was no regular human man though, and the gun was like a pistol in his big meaty hands.

He was human, but he had been engineered to be the bigger half of a janitorial duo. He had bigger aspirations though. He had killed his beach ball-bodied partner, blown up his utility ship and had gone off into the universe to make his fortune.

Now, many years later, he owned (won in a game of Delirium Cards) Euphoria and ran it with an iron fist. Or at least a Fitzer Laser Cannon. Now many years after *that* he had seen the most beautiful display of sensual circus artistry he had ever witnessed. When Orchestra Balloo had come down from her trapeze and put her clothing back on, Rhanque had his men waiting for her.

Orchestra thought she had mere moments of life left when they escorted her into Rhanque's office, but he had no intention of harming her. Not if she loved him back anyway.

"Ms...?" Rhanque said in a booming tuba voice.

"Balloo," Orchestra answered quietly. She had never seen a human man so closely resemble an elephant before, and she didn't even know what an elephant was.

"That was quite a beautiful performance, Ms. Balloo," he said.

Her shoulders didn't drop.

"Thank you, sir. I am so sorry about Steppin. It was an accident."

"Ah, forget about him. The four-armed freak was almost past his peak age anyhow. He was getting a little belly. Two stomachs. You know what happens when his species gets a belly with two stomachs? So much energy goes towards breaking down stored food and maintaining that belly that he can't get an erection. And a Jost'lean without an erection is just an asshole."

His guards dutifully laughed at this. "You really did me a favour," he added.

Now her shoulders dropped. He wasn't angry. "Tell your friend, that lizard girl, I want you two as my main attraction. I'll double your pay," he added.

Her shoulders went back up. The "lizard girl" had disappeared, and the thought of ever performing with anyone else on Euphoria was something she had no interest in, money be damned.

"She...she's gone sir. She's not a friend, I had never seen her before."

"Oh, really? Well that shouldn't be a problem."

He turned to his guards and simply nodded. They rushed out. Now she was alone with Rhanque and that was like falling into a bear cage at the zoo.

"They'll find her. Then all good, yeah? Oh, and you're my girl-friend now, okay?"

At that moment Orchestra realized that she would never be able to say no to her boss, and that was more like a *bear* falling into *her* cage at the zoo. She was a prisoner now. He didn't ask questions to get an answer. He made demands that merely sounded like questions. She could smell the toxic masculinity on his breath, and it smelled like he had gargled with cologne and narcissism.

~~~

Teeg was feeling good. Aye was feeling good. Gekko was feel-ing *ecstatic*. They had all decided to stop thinking about all the things that weighed them down until they got back to the Shiv and sobered up.

Teeg had the ability to sober up quite quickly. It only took a few seconds back on the Shiv to clear her head after Knutt in-formed her that Potto had wandered off the ship in a daze.

"In a daze? How could you tell?" she asked the ship.

"Because he actually seemed *less* dense than normal. Isn't that a daze for him?"

"Buuuuuuuurn!" Aye hollered. It took him much longer to so-ber up.

"Shit. Where is the hippy?" Teeg asked, ignoring Aye.

"In the back. In one of the sleeping quarters. Floating about. She's dazed, too," Knutt answered.

"Great. Gekko. Sober up. We gotta go find Potto. Vacation over."

Gekko closed her eyes, tensed her body and face, and excreted the alcohol she had consumed through her pores, leaving it as a puddle on the floor.

"Wow! I wish I could do that!" Aye said, promptly slipping on that alcohol excretion and falling asleep, gargle-snoring used bourbon.

CHAPTER SEVENTEEN

Gradi Ohsa Vallasoupia-Gallor (this was a stage name; her real name was Bip-Bip Vakleenacuddy) and her theatre troupe The Ilt-un-por-Ilt Players had only meant to stop off at Euphoria to refuel, not to recruit. She didn't stop *anywhere* to recruit, because they had never recruited.

All the thespians, musicians and stage hands in her dusty old troupe had been *born* into the dusty old troupe, generation after generation. They were all from the planet Veroseral, and didn't much care for outsiders in their midst or on their dusty old troupe ship the Deck Dallop.

The Veroseraliens were long thought extinct, their planet destroyed before it even had a chance to *go* missing, making the "Lost Seventy" the "Lost Seventy-*one*". In fact, it had disappeared so very long ago that most others in the universe had forgotten that the planet had ever existed, and most of their audiences had no idea *what* they were. Just a bunch of humanoids with transparent hair and lilac-coloured skin, always appearing simply dusty, and simply old.

They were a travelling troupe, writing and performing their own original musicals and travelling from planet-to-planet for thousands of years. None of them had even seen Veroseral before. They were the grandchildren of grandchildren of grandchildren of grandchildren of the grandchildren of those that once inhabited the long dead planet's grandchildren's grandchildren (give or take a grandchild).

No, Gradi Ohsa Vallasoupia-Gallor did not come to the floating sex circus to recruit *per se*, but she had not seen an act like the one Orchestra Balloo and Gecko had performed ever before. And her own lineage was becoming too incestuous and dwindling off into a deformed shadow of itself.

Many scripts had needed to be rewritten or retired for lack of thespians and musicians. Gekko was a bit too reptilian for Gradi Ohsa. If Gekko *was* compatible, her genes would most assuredly be dominant. The Flettocean acrobat however...

~~~

Vrume T'cha T'cha recognized a Quarol when he saw one. He recognized albinism in a Quarol as well.

He remembered overhearing The Node speak of a Quarol and a Topher in exile. He remembered the prophecy of the light one and the dark one. His brain started piecing it it all together after Potto had passed him in a hallway on his way back from seeing off his latest ship of saved prisoner/assistants.

He had offered a happy hello, but the Quarol seemed to be in a bit of a trance. It was unlike a Quarol to pass up a chance to say hello to a stranger. The odd creatures seemed to need smiles and greetings from friendly strangers like they needed snacks. He followed.

"Perhaps," he thought, "he just saw the show and it weighed heavily on him. Perhaps it brought up early childhood traumas or it moved him to the point of extreme daydreamy brain-malaise-mayonnaise. Perhaps it's sex circus induced petit mal." Art has always been funny that way.

Potto had no idea he was wandering around Euphoria. In his mind he was still in the forest. In his mind he was following the sound of a bustling woodland village. Perhaps he would find other Quarols there! Perhaps some Sentaphylls!

This village-in-his-head wasn't filled with *either*. It was filled with wild and ferocious northern neglies. Large blue curly-haired wolf-like creatures with long pointed snouts from his home planet. They may have been snarly, but they were generally very shy and would go nowhere near a village. However, *this* village seemed to be made up of them alone. He wondered if one was the mayor.

One spotted him and sniffed about. It smelled of ninety-two-proof grain alcohol and moth pheromones.

"Hello there!" he said cheerily. It said nothing but looked at him as though he were insane. "Would you like a scratch under the chin? Or behind the ears?" he asked as he started scratching under its chin and behind its ears.

The beast recoiled at first, and then started attacking. Other neglies started attacking. They even started attacking each other. Tearing at each other like each was a delicious corn on the cob. Soon the whole village was in an uproar of swinging paw punches, bites, claws and imaginary kernels.

Though Potto did not want to fight *ever*, nor was he sure he knew *how*, he started to defend himself. He kicked and swung his fists haphazardly like a half-frightened child fighting off an older sibling, half frightened by possible violence and half amused by the possibility of play and the excitement of being paid attention to.

~~~

Teeg and Gekko wandered about the hallways of Euphoria, checking semi-private sex closet booths as they passed them, and seeing some horrid pairings that would give them both night-mares for weeks. As they slowly made their way back to the main performance bar, Gekko alerted Teeg telepathically that they were being followed.

They hid in an empty sex closet and waited. Two Euphoria guards peeped their heads in just far enough to have their faces smashed in. They fell bloody and unconscious to the floor. Teeg overheard other guards through their communication watches reporting empty spaces when she stopped. One fizzy message quickly caught her attention.

"We found their Topher companion. He was on their ship cov-ered in bourbon and...I dunno...some kinda coconut water or stomach bile maybe?" the garbled voice said through the watch. "Thought I heard noises in the back, but no one else on board."

Now their Potto retrieval would also have to be an Aye rescue.

"I get that they wouldn't have found Jimmy in the engine room, but where the hell did Clover wander off to?" Teeg whispered to no one in particular. She sighed.

This was becoming increasingly difficult, especially with the whole Euphoria Guard after them for reasons unknown. K'ween would not have reported them for risk of being exposed herself.

When they finally made it to the performance bar, they would start a brawl that they could hide in, and that would distract the guards (and be a real pip, to boot).

When they finally made it there, they were happy (if not a little bit disappointed) to see that a brawl had already broken out. They were *shocked* to see a smiling Potto standing in the middle of it kicking and punching people off of him with his eyes closed.

"Grab him before he gets killed!" Teeg hollered. They punched, kicked and flipped their way to get to him.

"Potto!" she shouted in his face. He opened his eyes but didn't seem to be looking at her. He seemed to be looking through her.

"These beasts are relentless!" he laughed. "This is the craziest tickle fight I've ever been in! These tickles are gonna leave bruises! Actual *bruises*!" They dragged him off swinging his fists at the air and giggling.

Teeg pulled him down by his hair as a chair came hurdling through the air, narrowly missing them both. She picked up a full pint-sized glass of Sloovtopian Mint Gin and smashed it into a much-bigger-than-pint-sized Sloovtopian's face.

Gekko slashed her long sharp claws ahead of her, clearing a bloody path for Teeg to drag Potto through further. Many armed guards were trying to split up the fighting drunks and drug-addled perverts without using their weapons, but it was a losing battle and weapons were soon fired. Soon there was a rainbow of various coloured blood spurting about to slip on.

Teeg and Gekko used this distraction to escape the bar and head down one of the seedier hallways as another Sloovtopian slipped on his own mustardy blood, almost blocking their path. They pushed by a Mantis Widow devouring a Blankton's head, spitting out the unneeded eyepatch and a bit of Blankton pith.

Gekko climbed ahead up the wall and along the ceiling to scout for the best escape route. Hopeful they would come across Aye by accident. Any good fortune up until now (and it had been sparse) had been by accident.

By the time Teeg caught up with her she was facing a wall of no less than seventeen armed guards. "Fight?" she asked Teeg's mind.

"Actually, no. Let's see where they take us. Hopefully to Aye. Then we fight our way *out*," Teeg answered. Not-so-deep down she was *really* enjoying this.

~~~

Vrume had followed Potto to the bar. He had watched as the Quarol started the biggest brawl he had seen in decades by scratching a drunk Sloovtopian under his chin like a puppy. He had watched a gorgeous, leather–clad Flettocean and the Kancorian performer from the earlier show drag him off through the brawl. He knew these two.

He had stepped over the body of a headless pulsating-egg-filled Blankton, and had witnessed all of them carted off by a small army of guards to Rhanque's office.

He decided this would be the perfect time to drop in on his old buddy Rhanque to pay his rent.

He was one of Rhanque's best and most respected customers. That, and his charming nature, allowed him to enter the giant's office without knocking. He loudly made an announcement as he swung the door open and pranced in.

"Rhanque, y' old so-and-so! My compliments on an incredible show! Bravo my friend, bravo!" He clapped his hands to enhance his flattery and charming nature.

"Vrume! Your timing couldn't be better! Come here! Come here! I have the star performers right here! Perhaps you could get an autograph!" Rhanque joked. He loved seeing Vrume T'cha T'cha. Everyone (but jealous General Kendra Eppie) loved seeing Vrume T'cha T'cha.

Vrume made his way through the crowd of guards surrounding the dazed Quarol, the drunk Topher, the Flettocean mistress and the Kancorian acrobat. The second performer, the *other* Flettocean stood beside Rhanque. She looked terrified. Vrume hated seeing anyone terrified. He hated a bully.

Orchestra Balloo's fear dropped a tad with a well-placed wink from Vrume that seemed to say "Everything is going to be okay, *I promise.*"

"Careful lover boy!" Rhanque smiled, catching and misinterpreting this wink. "If I though for a second ladies were your thing, I'd be jealous! This, my friend, is Orchestra Balloo. My fiancée!"

This jolted Orchestra as if she were slapped with a large, dead fish. She had not been aware that she was the fiancée of anyone. The invisible bars of her cage were closing in on her.

This jolted Teeg like a slap as well. She could tell by Orchestra's body language, expression and a new tracking bracelet that this was not the trapeze artist's idea. She had not been asked. Teeg had been in this position. Teeg knew this feeling. She had been in this position with Fat Dante in his harem before she murdered him and escaped to K'ween and the Barbohdeans. It filled her with rage. A controlled rage that she would hang onto for the right moment.

"Seems the lizard girl wanted to leave as well! Well I can't have *that*, can I? My sweet baby love needs a dance partner! Maybe we'll even start to attract a different clientele with this act, no? A classier one. A richer one," Rhanque bellowed like a laughing fog horn.

"Oh yes! I can see it now! I just hope it won't up my rent!" Vrume smirked.

"Never for you my friend, never for you," Rhanque lied.

While he attempted to keep Rhanque in good spirits, he was also trying as hard as he could to get Gekko to listen to his mind. Deep in his heart he knew he couldn't let this ogre keep these women against their will, but he needed to figure out how to rescue them without ruining his relationship with the man from whom he rented a space and desperately counted on for his cause and rebellion.

Finally he caught Gekko's gaze and she instantly understood. She started scanning his mind for words.

"Do you hear me, sweet Kancorian?" he offered.

"Yes. I'm not so sweet. We are about to kill everyone in this room," she answered.

"Okay. That is *one* plan, but I'm here to help you. I want you to know that. Attack the guards, but only *wound* the lumbering giant. I need him. In exchange for sparing us I will lead the Quarol, the Topher and this Orchestra Balloo woman out of here and to the safety of your ship. You will be free to fight without worrying about them. Deal?"

Gekko considered this. It would be much easier without them in the way. She quickly relayed the plan to Teeg. Teeg agreed as well, but was lying about not killing the giant. She wanted the brute to suffer as Fat Dante had.

"Agreed," Gekko whispered into Vrume's mind, realizing only after that she didn't need to whisper when communicating telepathically.

Beside Ranque, Orchestra seemed so tiny. The six-foot-tall woman looked like a beautiful fire hydrant next to a large truck. A large truck made out of lean beef and tanned cement. When he leaned in for a kiss, she felt like she was about to be devoured by a sea monster.

Teeg had saved up her rage for this moment, and it was the perfect moment to strike. She would not, and could not let that kiss happen. Her temper exploded into a fury of fists, feet and blades.

She leapt across Rhanque's desk and pierced both of his lips closed with her sword, temporarily putting that sea monster on a fishing hook. The guards burst into action as Gekko sliced through their throats like a cat destroys a favourite reclining chair.

Rhanque yelled so loudly that the entire floating bar could hear, even over the loud Sloovtopian industrial music bellowing from speakers everywhere. He swatted Teeg (and her sword) away like shooing a fly.

While Rhanque focused his attack on Teeg, and the guards on Gekko, Vrume grabbed Potto and Aye's hands and motioned for Orchestra to follow. She smiled. She had *known* that his wink was going to be her saving grace.

They made a hasty retreat before more guards made it up to Rhanque's office. Vrume feared the worst for the brave women fighting to save them, but he was also very aware of their reputation.

By the time the guards fired at the wall Gekko was crawling across, she was on the ceiling. By the time they fired at the ceiling, she was behind them.

Teeg was finding her fight with Rhanque more difficult then she had anticipated. His genetically altered skin was tough and leathery and her sword was barely making a mark. She couldn't seem to get close enough to punch or kick him without having to dodge a log-sized limb swinging in her direction.

"Switch," her brain told Gekko.

Within seconds Teeg's sword was hacking and cutting through guards and Gekko was on Rhanque's back, clawing away at layers of thick flesh. As Teeg killed the last guard, Rhanque managed to grab Gekko. He held her by the throat in front of him. He smiled a cocky victory smile, one that quickly disappeared from his bleeding lips as he remembered that Kancorian females could breathe fire.

And that is exactly what Gekko did. His skin may have been thick (apart from his lips) but it was still flammable and fire still really, *really* hurt. It still scarred. It still blistered and bubbled.

He dropped her as he screamed. His fashion choices were his enemy. His very expensive shirt went up like a flaming zeppelin. Then his humongous blazer. His hair melted to his scalp. His eyes burned, blinding him. As he fell Teeg heard Gekko's voice in her head yell "Tiiiiiiiiiiimmmmmmber!!" In her mind Teeg chuckled.

They escaped the office and immediately jumped into an air duct, seconds before the next gang of guards came storming around the corner of the hallway. They could still hear Rhanque screaming as they disappeared into the air conditioning.

~~~

As hard as Orchestra tried to keep up with her rescuer, she couldn't. As he pulled the Quarol and the Topher down the hallways of Euphoria and through crowds of drunks and heaping piles of humping drug-addled perverts, her heart sank. Without him she knew she would remain in this horrible place. She cursed herself for ever coming to Euphoria in the first place.

She wandered down each corridor hoping for nothing more than even a *glimpse* of Vrume and the strange ones. She felt a hand wrap around hers. It was a pale lilac-purple hand with smooth, dusty old skin. Her eyes met with an ancient looking woman with transparent hair and fancy torn clothes that looked like they were out of a children's storybook.

"Come my child. Come with me. We will get you away from this horrible place, my ship is docked close by," said Gradi Ohsa Vallasoupia-Gallor of the Veroseralien theatre troupe The Ilt-por-un-Ilt Players.

~~~

As Vrume pulled Potto and Aye through hallway after hallway on his way to his own ship, he noticed Orchestra was not with them anymore. As much as he wanted to save her, capturing the two prophesized saviours would have to be his priority.

He would have to come back for Orchestra when he returned to pay Rhanque the rent he didn't get a chance to pay today. If indeed Rhanque Baptoose had survived the Flottocean and the Kancorian.

Getting these two spaced-out oddballs away from here was most important though. There was little time for anything else.

"Okay, I've tried to keep quiet about all this up until now," Aye finally piped up after being uncharacteristically quiet about all this up until now. "But *who* the hell are you? *What* the hell is going on, and *where* the hell can we get another bottle of...well...anything, really?"

"Ah, yes my friend. I have a very good bottle of mall brandy on my ship. We are going there now," Vrume answered.

He pulled them into a ship dock airlock. Mentally, Potto was still off (and quite lost) in his own little personal forest, and didn't care much where they ended up.

"Now you two just need to wait here. I am bringing my ship up to this dock, okay? I'll just leave you for a minute, *only* a minute..." Vrume added. He left and shut the inner airlock door and latched it to make sure they didn't wander away into the mess of fighting aliens again.

Aye started thinking, which was never a very productive or healthy thing for anyone in his vicinity.

He thought about how a man they had just met was trying to

lure them onto a ship that wasn't theirs. He thought about how he had been dragged around by armed guards. He thought about how he and Potto had left behind Teeg and Gekko, who, as much as they frightened him, really *did* seem to be looking out for them for some reason. He started sobering up, though starting was still a long way from being.

"This doesn't feel right," he told an unresponsive Potto. "We gotta get outta here. We gotta find our way back to the Shiv."

He tried the door to get back into Euphoria but it was latched from the other side. He looked about the space. There, in an emergency locker on the far wall, he found two space-ready maintenance suits, complete with full oxygen tanks.

The alcohol still in his system made a decision without him. This, like most decisions alcohol made, was a doozy. A horrible doozy. It was as if the bourbon whispered into his ear: "Forget common sense, there is no time. Why don't you get to the Shiv from the *outside*? Just hang on to the sides. Shimmy around until you find the right parking spot."

Within minutes he had a suit on Potto, and quickly climbed into his. In Potto's mind he had just put on a swimsuit.

"Ok, this is gonna work *great*!" he told Potto, not noticing that Potto was much quieter than normal.

As he held Potto's hand, he hit the outer airlock button, and they were sucked out into the cold darkness of space.

~~~

Rhanque sat on the floor of his office. He was blind and in pain and bleeding, but worse, *far* worse was that the love of his life had escaped.

"She is wearing a tracing bracelet, so trace her. Bring her back to me," he instructed one of his guards, who was trying to step over one of his dead co-workers without freaking out.

"We have tried tracing her, sir. And she is not on board. She left on a ship. One that seems to be untraceable," the guard offered sheepishly. Rhanque knew that it wasn't uncommon for a ship visiting a floating bar and sex circus to be equipped with illegal technology that scrambled any traces. The clientele *was* made up of criminals.

"Then leave me," Rhangue growled.

"Sir?"

"Leave me!!" he shouted.

Once alone, Rhanque's shoulders dropped deeper into the floor via the bulk of his back. He felt furious and empty. He might be dying, his heart was broken, and something he hadn't felt since his days on the janitorial ship "The Monkey Wrench" washed over him. Anger-induced depression.

He immediately re-evaluated the way he had tried to woo his sweet acrobat. His courting skills were non-existent, but he *was* Rhanque Baptoose, and Rhanque Baptoose called the shots.

If he were to call for the bar's medical staff, they *might* be able to save him, to stop the burning feeling in his skin, but not the irate burning feeling in his heart. He knew there had been a reason he had stayed away from love before. It went against his very being.

His tears stung through burning eyes as he pulled out a small keychain from his pocket. On it was a small locket. In that locket was a small button. He pressed it.

As an alarm sounded and a snarky woman's pre-recorded voice announced to all of Euphoria that they had only five minutes to evacuate before the entire place self-destructed. He sighed loudly.

And as he heard the mass hysterical panic from outside his office, he bitterly thought the thought of a selfish, psychotic and horrible brute. The worst kind of thought anyone could ever have, the very thought that had brought down empires: "*If I can't be happy, no one can.*"

~~~

Aye floated away from Euphoria as it imploded in on itself in the vacuum of space, causing a ripple of energy and floating debris.

"Ha! That was close," he thought as that ripple sent him whirling at near break-neck speed deeper into space.

When he finally stopped spinning, he concentrated on not throwing up in a claustrophobic space suit.

His brain went into hysterical fits when it finally hit him that he was floating in space, now far away from where anyone might easily find him. He calmed ever so slightly with one reassuring thought, "Well at least I'm not alone..."

But his heart sank into his feet when he looked at his gloved hand and realized no one was holding it.

CHAPTER EIGHTEEN

Endorphins are such a lovely thing. In a Topher they are even lovelier. They are super-über-mega lovely.

When these neurotransmitters fired up electrical signals to a *Topher's* nervous system it was as if a heavy dose of morphine was making sweet love to the type of anti-anxiety medication that only the shadiest of doctors smuggled in from planets with loose regulations (and morals).

They did not just numb physical pain; they were eighty-four per cent more potent than they were in humans. They made the native Towerscapians relax as if they had just had a temporary stroke.

It took a giant's share of pain or a whole whack of panic for those endorphins to kick in. Floating off into space without a spaceship wrap, no foreseeable rescue, and the promise of a slow, tortuous, lonely, claustrophobic death *really* jars the nerves.

These lovely endorphins had fired up deep inside of Aye. He was floating now in a state of stunned semi-paralysis, drooling just a tad, and as calm as congealed gravy.

He stared out into the nothing. The nothing stared back with the icy coldness of an ex-lover, if that ex-lover were a bottomless pit in a frozen ocean. He could hear his breath like it was sad, sad music.

His mind wandered. It wasn't a flash of a life well lived that rapidly played out before his eyes. It was more like a *very* poorly executed collage of a *very* poorly done crayon drawing of all the stupid things he had done in his life, *very* poorly cut out and half-assed glued onto soggy Bristol board.

He didn't see huge criminal acts to be proudly ashamed of. He didn't see world-changing assassinations. He didn't see anything important at all. Nothing *truly* bad. What he saw instead was a series of stupid accidents. He saw a series of clumsy minor crimes and drunken run-ins with the law. Shoplifting and flying under the influence of booze. All the booze. So much damn booze.

He saw the many beatings he took, and the many reasons why he was beaten...most of which were his own fault. Almost all the trouble he had gotten into was because of all that damn booze and his stupid big mouth.

He knew no one would be looking for him, because, as he finally comprehended, no one was *really* after him. He suspected (wrongly) that his father had even given up the hunt.

He put two and two together and realized none of this little adventure had started before he rescued the Quarol. Even that noble rescue had been a stupid, selfish accident.

It was the *Quarol* everyone was after. And not because Potto was some master criminal either; why anyone would hunt Potto was a mystery to Aye because people generally liked Potto. *He* was truly good natured. The stupid things that came out of *his* mouth didn't hurt anyone. They were irritating, but they weren't unlikable, insulting or cruel. Not like Aye. Potto was nice.

"Nice" was an insult on Towerscape. It meant the same that "cream puff" or "wuss" did on other planets. Oddly though, on Towerscape "Wuss" was a brand of shaving gel and a "cream puff" was a style of hat.

He sadly listened to the sad-breath music. He knew no one would be looking for him because no one cared. And what was worse, he couldn't think of one reason why they should.

Aye didn't believe in prophesies from strange maybe-mythological (but unfortunately non-goat-legged) women, and he didn't know yet the part he was meant to play. He wasn't aware that he had a destiny.

Like almost everyone in the entire universe, he had no idea how important he really was.

He was feeling useless and stupid, and he had that right: no one can tell anyone else what definitively *has* to go through their head when staring death in its big, empty, black-hole eyes.

Feeling useless and stupid was Aye's right. Whether he felt he deserved any rights or not.

After all: *a pondering Aye was an Aye that hated himself.*

Amongst the sad thoughts, amongst the wee little bursts of anger, he felt a *longing*. Not the usual longing to kill his father (the source of these wee little bursts of anger), not the brand new longing to see his mother again (the *source* of wanting to kill his father), and not even a longing for one last sexual encounter with an indescribable (the more indescribable the better) alien.

It was a longing that surprised him. He wanted his Baby Boy. He longed to see his friend again. His first *real* friend ever. His Potto.

He longed to hear the pale Quarol say something moronic. He longed to see his smile. Potto had actually *smiled* at him. Not some paid-for, put-on smile or some sarcastic smile, and definitely not some kind of mocking smile. Potto hadn't once laughed at him for *anything*. Potto *was* truly good, and that meant someone truly good liked *him!*

When he pictured Potto, it made him smile the open-mouth drooly half-smile of a Topher with super-über-mega endorphins filling up his body like a rubber glove filled with drugged putty.

A new feeling and a new mindset passed over Aye as well. He had looked at space out of the front window of many a spaceship. He had woken up (still drunk) in gutters, looking up at the night sky...but as he floated about weightlessly, and slowly turned to face a far-off nebula, he had never noticed how beautiful it all was.

This new feeling was appreciation. This new mindset was observation. The two danced inside him and it was all so overwhelming.

The swirls and poofs of smoky purples mingled with rusty oranges and bright flowery reds. The reds fading into plumes of soft light blues and murky liquid greens. Dust and gas were a far more breath-taking thing to observe and appreciate in space than the very different dust and gas he was accustomed to in his flat back on Lyme Node. Both of which he produced himself in abundance.

He hoped he would float into it as he passed away, not realizing how incredibly far away it actually was. The thought of being surrounded by so much beauty as he died was comforting. Not as comforting as super-über-mega endorphins, but comforting nonetheless.

He stared in complete awe. He felt like he was looking into the eyes of gods. Gods benevolent enough to create such a beautiful thing to keep him company while he perished, but also cruel enough to have allowed him to be born in the first place.

Aye looked out into that gorgeous nebula, he made a promise to himself: If, by some impossible miracle, he *did* survive this, he would change. Perhaps he would not become a saint, perhaps he would still be a horny little asshole, perhaps shoplifting and booze were not out of the question...but he would change.

He would strive to do more important things. Or he would strive to do at least *one* important thing. He would strive to have, maybe, *two* friends as well. One felt pretty good, two might feel ecstatic! Maybe three! Four! He could be a little more empathetic. He could be a little more kind. He could be...*nice*.

Maybe.

That constant sad musical ebb and flow of his breath started making him sleepy. He fell asleep almost certain he wouldn't wake up. This would be sweet relief from his cruel plummeting self-esteem and the intense boredom that was setting in. He drifted off, at peace with his fate. Goodbye cruel universe.

However, *this* was a brand-spanking-new TDX-30 space suit, and it had a brand-spanking-new oxygen tank; one that used new technology to recycle the air breathed out into new breathable air. It wouldn't work indefinitely, but it could last him weeks. Enough time to painfully die of dehydration first. Someone in engineering hadn't been thinking.

Aye woke up. Waking up was very disappointing.

He was completely discombobulated. Once he quickly remembered where he was, he became further confused as to why he wasn't yet dead, and then for three whole minutes all he could think was "Whaaaaaaaaaaaaaaaaaaaaaaaaaaaaaaaaaaaaaaaaatttt????" followed by an angry "Someone in engineering wasn't thinking".

The nebula was still there, but seemed a little more drab now. As beautiful as it was, it had become like watching the same movie over and over and over and over. A movie with no plot, no characters, a very repetitive breathy soundtrack and only one setting without even a couch.

He wondered if Potto, wherever he had floated off to, was frightened. Probably not. He was probably singing at the top of his lungs and had found some way to make himself twirl. He was probably thinking the whole thing was a real hootenanny. A wonderfully happy brouhaha. (Or at the very least a silly overly-animated solo coffee klatch.)

Hours upon hours passed by. He started hyperventilating. Not because he was panicking again (although the endorphins had worn off), but to force himself to pass-out. It worked, but he woke up less than a minute later with a terrible headache.

At least a headache was *something*.

He decided it was the most entertaining headache of all time. A hootenanny-brouhaha-coffee-klatch of a headache. It boomed around inside his brain like a marching band. It was as if he now had a loud brass section and big belly-propped bass drum to accompany the soft brushed snare drum of his breathing.

He started putting lyrics to it. Singing like a Tandonian hip-hopera star.

"*Imma dingbat, asshat, crass pussycat of doormats, a bureaucrat of bat scat, a...*" then it dissolved (if it had ever evolved in the first place) into seeing how long he could keep rhyming insults at himself. "*...a bushwhack of wisecrack hacks, a racetrack tarmac of blind kleptomaniacs, a gas sack of zwieback, a wombat that house-sat a plague rat's gnat shack, a fat splat of bric-a-brac, a sad lack of back-crack-pats, a flapjack of yak scat...*oh wait, shit, I used scat already...*a cravat in need of a laundromat, a zodiac...of...um...piggyback...tooth plaque...thermostats...whacked by...um...unhealthy snacks...*"

Much to his disappointment, he sang away his headache. It was just the snare drum now, and it was a merciless and callous reminder that he was still alive. Still alive and getting very thirsty. Even for water. *Even for goddamned water!*

He had never considered himself to be one with much heart, but he definitely felt it now for it was sinking further than it ever had before, down into the bowels of *everything.*

He screamed at the nebula "TURN OFF THE FUCKING LIGHTS ALREADY!!" while trying to turn himself to face another direction, a darker direction, but that just made him feel like a mouse bobbing for watermelons in an ocean.

Aye had never wanted to die before. Not in his entire life. That is, in part, what kept him alive. "That's what keeps, in part, *anyone* alive," he thought. But this was yet another first. He wanted *so badly* to just die and be done with it. To turn this terrible television show off. To bring down the final curtain on this horrible play.

He even tried to induce a panic attack again so that he could enjoy some more of those delicious endorphins, but he was just too bored and too tired to convince himself he was fretting. He was long past fretting.

He tried to think of the positives. The only one he could think of was regarding the tightness of the helmet seal around his neck. It kept him from smelling the mess he'd made down in the rest of the suit. He didn't exactly have a proper toilet he could run off to.

This positive seemed a moot point when the rashes he started getting *because* of this gross mess began to itch...a burning itch he couldn't even scratch through space suit.

Another positive: he was *now*, at least, long through evacuating in his suit. He was empty. No food to digest, no excess liquid to drain. He would have been extremely hungry if he wasn't so thirsty.

He felt pain in his kidneys. Organs were starting to shut down and it hurt like the dickens. They were starting to clog with muscle proteins.

He passed out from the pain. He came to. He passed out from the pain again. He tried to cry but nothing came out. The inside of his mouth felt like cardboard covered in sand. His tongue felt like it had been baking in an oven. Even his horns ached, which he didn't know was possible. He wished for a wall to smack his domed helmet on, cracking it, ending him.

His blood pressure dropped, and the lights of the nebula were fading in his dizzy eyes when suddenly they disappeared entirely. Not because he had passed out again, or sweet mercy had placed its hands around his throat and stopped his breathing for good, but because something was blocking the nebula. Something *big*.

He slowly blinked. It hurt. His dry eyelids were like heavily used sandpaper.

He had no idea how much time had passed since Euphoria. Perhaps only a few days. Perhaps more. It felt like an eternity. He blinked his dry eyes slowly again as a large circular door opened on the side of the *spaceship* that was blocking his view of the nebula.

Seconds before he got sucked in to an air lock, he noticed the tips of two tiny tubes under his chin on the inside of the helmet. One was labelled "FRESH WATER", the other simply said "SANDWICH". Someone in engineering *had* been thinking.

He passed out again from the pain, laughing at the tube tips and believing this ship was a mirage and that he had actually died days ago and was in hell. Space hell.

~~~

When Aye opened his eyes he was in a dusty old bed, clean and covered in a dusty old quilt, hooked up to dusty old medical equipment and with a dusty old woman looking down at him. Her transparent hair and lilac-coloured skin made her look like an angel. A dusty old angel.

CHAPTER NINETEEN

Clover tried to eat the loom fruit. She wasn't sure how it would taste, and therefore it had no flavour at all. It only existed in her imagination, so she would have to *imagine* a flavour if she wanted to taste one. Not knowing how it would taste left out any assignment of flavour.

Quite possibly this was all *Potto's* imagination and she was merely a visitor and couldn't assign the fruit a flavour. *Or* perhaps it was a shared fantasy world. She wasn't sure whose imagination she was in anymore.

Perhaps if she had imagined the fruit to taste like barbecue sauce, it would have. Perhaps though, if it were strictly Potto's imagination she was in, he would mischievously make it taste like raw chicken, or a red bean bun covered in bullet ants, or maybe fanged dangling jessop stew. Perhaps she would then change it back (giving him an "oh, you scamp" look) if they *each* had control. She had no idea how any of this worked.

Bundle had flown off into the imaginary forest to search for Potto. Clover decided to do a little experiment while she waited. She was very aware that she was under hypnosis, and that none of this was real, and she realized Potto had *created* it, but she wanted to know if she indeed did have any control over it.

First, she imagined the loom fruit tasted like popcorn. Within seconds it was as if she were eating a big bowl of delicious hot buttered popcorn in the form of a strange glowing piece of fruit. Check.

Next, she imagined she were smack-dab in the middle of an orgasm. Within seconds she stumbled, almost falling over as waves of pleasure washed through her entire body. Check.

Next, once recovered, she imagined Potto was standing right next to her. Nothing happened.

She imagined she had a communicator watch and he was calling her. Perhaps if she could, at the very least, hear his voice she could ask him to come back. Nothing. Perhaps he would have to imagine he was calling her in the first place. This was all so complicated.

He could be kilometres away. He could be on the other side of the known galaxy. He could be right behind her, always moving into her blind spot when she turned her head. He could be anywhere.

Somehow though, she sensed that he was still very much a part of this visualized, hypno-land. He was certainly not lucid and sitting on the bridge of the Shiv.

Hopefully Bundle would be back soon with Potto, or some Potto news. She could do nothing but wait. And maybe eat some hot buttered loom fruit popcorn, and have the odd orgasm.

~~~

Sometimes disbelief can be hilarious, and sometimes wonderful. It can be the response to a fabulous gift, or it can be a level of complete wonderment. It can also accompany grief and shock.

Disbelief can be an odd comfort. It can be frustrating and painful, but it can contain a glimmer of hope. That little crack in the china cup of finality.

It can be all of these things.

One may win the lottery (disbelief!) and upon telling one's elderly father the great news, the old man drops dead of a very sudden heart attack right before one's eyes (disbelief!) and then his body is carried off by a giant tadpole (disbelief!) but it's the type of tadpole that only carries off living creatures so he mustn't *really* be dead after all (disbelief!), though he no doubt will get eaten by the tadpole regardless (disbelief!) and besides, what is a giant tadpole doing in this desert and not in a lake (disbelief!)?

On the bridge of the Shiv, Teeg sat in a state of intense flummoxed disbelief. She sat staring at the empty bit of space that was once a sex circus.

She wasn't sure whether she had just witnessed both of the fugitives (that she had risked *everything* for) abruptly erased from space. Erased along with one of her favourite de-stressing debauchery hang-outs.

She was pondering what had gone wrong. She was pondering whether or not that strange, snazzy, well-dressed man that had dragged Potto, Aye and the acrobat out of Rhanque Batoose's extremely violent office had gotten them off of Euphoria in time. She had barely escaped herself. She was at a loss for coherent thought.

"Knutt..." she finally managed, grasping at straws, "Do you detect any life signs out there? The Quarol? The Topher?"

"Nope," Knutt answered without so much as a speck of concern. "Though I only have so much range. I detected that there were a few ships that escaped before the boom, but they are long gone. I also detect that the Oaian that calls herself Clover is still on board, in the back of the ship. Odd thing. The exact moment the Euphorian Guards violated me by unlocking and boarding me without my permission, I was hacked."

"Hacked?" asked Teeg, adding even more concern and stress to her already overwhelmed brain.

"Yep. Just for a few minutes. What, or rather *who* hacked me, actually helped! They implanted some kind of life-sign blocker...made Clover go unnoticed. Kept her safely hidden in the back room. As soon as the guards left it was gone. Of course there was no saving the unconscious dickhead."

"Oh hoooooo-ray," Teeg said flatly, dripping with sarcasm like an ice cream cone in a parked car on a hot summer day. "The one person on board that *could* go missing without causing me any stress is safely on board. Dandy."

"She is a good luck charm perhaps," Gekko said telepathically. "She seems to have a guardian angel of sorts. That's twice now she's been rescued. Here and on Chagrin. This bodes well for us, as we seem to get the same treatment if we are in her presence."

"But *who*? And *why*?" she thought back.

"Something to ponder after we figure this all out. I think we need to ask Clover some questions."

Teeg was *devastated* Euphoria was gone (disbelief!), *relieved* they had escaped in the nick of time (disbelief!), *hopeful* that Potto and Aye were still alive (disbelief!), and, although she didn't realize it, deep, deep, deep down she was (probably) glad a giant land tadpole hadn't shown up to carry anyone off.

~~~

Clover was on her fifteenth loom fruit (which was making her glow all over because she decided to imagine it was) and fourth orgasm (which was also making her glow all over) when Bundle came whizzing through the trees at top speed. She had a look of urgency on her face like Clover had never seen before on a fairy. This was, in itself, not that odd, as she had never met a fairy before Bundle. Or a pixie. Or a sprite, brownie or imp. Perhaps a look of urgency was the norm on such creatures and she just hadn't noticed it before.

"I found him! I found Potto! He's in trouble though...he's drifting in spa—"

Clover snapped out of hypnosis with a hard slap to the face. Bundle was now gone and Teeg stood before her, hand raised and ready to slap again.

She started to say, "I'm back! I'm awake!" but it was too late, she was slapped again. She quickly got out an "Okay! Okay! Stop!" while noticing the look of slightly amused satisfaction on Teeg's face turn to the slight disappointment of not having a reason to slap again.

"You weren't responding with words. And I like slapping. What happened to you?" Teeg asked.

"I hypnotized Potto. He somehow hypnotized me back. I lost him in there. In his head. In my head. Where is he physically?"

"Probably dead. Something went wrong on Euphoria."

"Yeah, almost every situation tends to blow up rather quickly in that wretched place. What happened?"

"It blew up rather quickly," Teeg said very seriously.

Clover was in disbelief. Disbelief was still running rampant on the Shiv. She was stunned upon hearing that Potto was probably dead. She snapped out of it quickly. Bundle's last words popped back into her head.

"No! He's not dead!"

"And how would you know that?"

"The fairy told me."

"The. Fairy."

"Yes. The fairy in his head. Potto's fairy."

"Potto has a fairy in his head?" Teeg asked wryly, more as a statement than a question.

"Does that surprise you?" Clover giggled.

"No. No it does not."

"If Potto was dead, she'd have disappeared. She didn't. And she told me he was in danger. That he was *drifting*."

"Drifting? In space?"

"I would imagine. I'm not sure where else he would drift..."

"Do you know how hard it will be to find him? That'll be like finding a tardigrade's sewing needle in...well...a haystack the size of infinity."

"We better get started!" Clover said with an optimistic chipperness that required Teeg to slap her again.

~~~

Potto had been in his imaginary forest, roughly play-fighting with the northern neglies, when he found himself drawn away. He found himself pulled by an invisible force, and then pushed off a cliff and into a vast ocean. The vastest of vast oceans he had ever seen, or that he had ever imagined he had seen.

He had a vague memory of having a great fear of oceans. He did not have this fear now; the deep murky waters which could be home to any number of horrors, simply became a cool jelly of curiosities and adventure.

He could breathe, he could see, and he could do twirls and sing at the top of his lungs.

He could not remember the words to any song, so he made up a song about his birthday. He wasn't sure, but he suspected he hadn't celebrated it in a very long time. As he sang, a number of smaller sea creatures swam about, some circling his head, singing harmony as he warbled.

Once he grew bored of the repetitive song, he stopped singing and twirling and started remembering. He wasn't remembering all the things Bundle or Clover had been badgering him to remember. He was remembering the reality he (up until being hypnotized) had been living in. He remembered *friends*.

It took some real effort to remember everyone. He remembered Teeg and Gekko and Clover, but was struggling with their names. He remembered a walking tree. He remembered Aye. Even Aye's name! Ayyyyyyyeeee!!

He wondered where the women were. He missed them. He missed his new friend Aye.

As for the tree, he could not forget her even if he wished himself to after releasing a genie from a bottle. Name or not. He remembered her saving his life with sap. A sap that also managed to plant seeds inside of him. He felt her growing. It wasn't a physical feeling of growth. Not like that of a parasite or a tumour or a baby... but it felt like she had planted a permanent *memory* of herself deep inside his brain. A loving memory to grab onto whenever he needed to remember something or someone special. A memory to ensure that he never felt truly lonely ever again. A memory that made him feel a little woodsy and warm.

Through the dark, thick water he could see a bioluminescent squid making its way towards him. Small and fluttery, it had great control of the photophores it used to add razzamatazz to the bleakness.

"There you are!" said the squid.

"Here I am, indeed!" Potto replied. This wasn't a bioluminescent squid, it was a bioluminescent Bundle.

"You *do* realize I am a figment of your imagination, right?"

"Sure!" Potto answered, not quite understanding what figment meant, or anything else in that sentence.

He used "sure" (one of the most insincere ways of answering a question with an affirmative in the English language) quite purposefully. He wanted to be agreeable but also honest that he didn't actually understand.

"So, this is kinda impossible, don't you think? How can you wander away from a figment without that figment disappearing entirely? How can you transfer a figment of your imagination into someone else's head?"

There were a lot of figments in all of that. He smiled and nodded, not answering right away. From somewhere far off, one of the prawns that sang harmony on his birthday song coughed for effect.

"Sorry, what?" he finally piped up after too much time had passed.

"Oh, never mind. I'll just chalk it up to astral projecting."

"Yes, I think you should. Kestrel rejecting is likely what that thing you said did. This is a beautiful ocean, don't you think?"

"I guess. If you're into oceans. You've imagined up a good one."

"Imagined up?"

Bundle sighed heavily. "You're still hypnotized. I'm not going to tell you where you really are. It's better you stay here in your ocean. The reality is kinda terrifying."

"Oh, that's right. Where is...um...uh..."

"Clover?"

"Yes."

"I don't know. I don't think *she's* still hypnotized. We gotta keep *you* under, though.

"I spent some time in her head. I'm hoping to help her find you. I may be able to tell her where you are once she's asleep and dreaming. Even though you are in two different places, I might be able to pull you together in the real world. Like a mental beacon."

"Ah. Yes, I like it here. I will happily stay here. You have bacon?"

"No. Er...yes. By all means you mustn't wake up..."

"I mustn't!"

Just then Potto woke up.

He had been hit by a smallish asteroid. The chances of this encounter were too astronomical to accurately calculate, almost to the point of being impossible. Perhaps it was a miracle, perhaps those laws of bullshit.

Waking up in a space suit, floating aimlessly around in the

biggest darkness there is, and up against a chunk of floating space rock like a good-luck-charm plush animal on the front grill of a garbage truck, *should* have been absolutely horrifying. At first Potto thought maybe he had somehow crawled into a fish bowl while asleep.

It wasn't *just* the impact of the asteroid that snapped him awake from his lovely (and possibly life-saving) daze. It was a *voice*.

"Potto?" said Lempshop.

The laws of bullshit were now working overtime.

CHAPTER TWENTY

"Many folk would never guess," Gradi Ohsa Vallasoupia-Gallor of the Veroseralien theatre troupe The Ilt-un-por-Ilt Players said in soft, healing tones, "But one of the great travelling theatre troupes was actually from Towerscape.

"Oh, I know, I know what you're thinking: Tophers in the arts? Impossible! But no no no...Uncle Vin-Vin's Vegabond Variety Void was, at one time, considered the best. Terribly violent shows. Terribly. At least one actor died per show. Sometimes the whole cast! Sometimes the odd audience member! Now *that's* ambition! Now *that* is passion! So inspiring."

Aye felt somewhat comforted by her dusty old voice. It sounded like a creaky door. The kind of creaky door that gives you candy and handmade pies. He still felt weak, but thanks to his Veroseralien hosts and a very welcome and accommodating intravenous drip, he was on the mend. He was newly hydrated and enjoying the feeling of blinking and swallowing again.

He sat up. He longed to finally find out what a sandwich-through-a-straw tasted like. It had been on his mind a lot.

"I am Gradi Ohsa Vallasoupia-Gallor of the Veroseral. You are aboard my theatre ship The Deck Dallop. We are humble nomads, performing all over the galaxy..." Grady sing-song-said.

"Will you take me back to the Shiv? Or maybe home to Lyme

Node?" he interrupted quietly, trying to appear rude without appearing *rude*.

"Well. Y' see, I don't know where this Shiv ship is. If it was docked at Euphoria, it was probably blown to bits. Euphoria is gone. We had nothing to do with it. I'm sorry if you lost some loved ones. Oh, and we're not so welcome on Lyme Node. We steer clear of it. For now at least," she said. There was something slightly defensive in the way she said "We had nothing to do with it," and something slightly sinister in the way she said "For now at least". Aye was not fazed.

Aye also wasn't fazed by the apparent destruction of the Shiv. Something deep within the bowels of his bowels was telling him that the ship had escaped. He was more concerned about Potto floating aimlessly around in the great infinity, but if something had saved *him*, something sure as hell *must* have saved Potto. He was much luckier than Aye. Most of the known universe was luckier than Aye.

He had not seen a Veroseralien before. He found her appearance a little spooky. She looked almost haunted. Her dusty old lilac skin and transparent hair gave her a ghost-like pizzazz. She sat on the foot of his recovery bed and smiled as sweetly as a someone who looked like a walking corpse could.

The entire room was covered in old thread-barren tapestries. Some depicted great wars. Some depicted great orgies. Some depicted both at the same time. These tapestries were hung to cover up the rusty dripping pipes and grimy walls of a ship far past its prime.

Music being played in another room could be heard from the hallway. It sounded like the sad minor-key-bass-clef version of what cobwebs might sound like if they were music. It drifted into the room on a waft of incense smoke that smelled like an old casserole.

"I have an idea!" she exclaimed, throwing her spindly arms up into the air dramatically. "We could give you a part! We are rehearsing a new show. It's called "The Rotten Lovers". It's a romance. Of sorts. You'd be perfect as the demon Failcotte the Fragile. Especially with those lovely little devil horns of yours."

"They're *not* little!" Aye said, taking offense. Calling a Topher's horns small was about the only social faux pas on Towerscape. It was not unlike making fun of a male's genitalia *everywhere else in the universe* (speaking of fragile).

"I'm very sorry Mr. Topher. I did not mean to offend. They are spectacular horns atop a very handsome head," she said smiling like she had a mouthful of caramels. "Will you be our Failcotte?"

"I don't think so. I'm no actor. And my name is Mr. Aye-Aye, not Mr. Topher. I also have been known to answer to Champ, Boss, Chief, Buddy, Big Guy, and Son of a Bitch."

"You'd get paid of course, and there will be a love scene for you with our beautiful new--"

"I said no. The idea of prancing around on stage in front of people nauseates me."

A shadow in the doorway appeared catching Aye's glance like a butterfly in a bloodshot net. It was the trapeze artist from Euphoria...the one that had danced with Gekko. He couldn't look away. She was beautiful and marvellous and he could tell just by looking at her that she smelled wonderful. Like cake frosting and fresh house paint.

"This is Orchestra Balloo. She would be playing the part of Glass Tina, your love interest," Gradi slyly smirked.

"I'll do it," Aye said, not entirely sure where the words had just popped out from, but confident it wasn't his horns.

~~~

Frustration didn't live well within Vrume T'cha T'cha. It made him feel his age and it made him look run-down. He had bags under his eyes! Bags! After so many millennia trying to do the right thing, trying to play the hero, he was tired.

He was happy that he chose to leave the Quarol and the Topher behind in the airlock. If he hadn't, he'd likely have been slowed down by Euphorian guards or Potto and Aye themselves and all three of them would have gone the way of Euphoria.

He was happy that, for whatever ridiculously stupid reason, the pair had climbed outside the airlock and lived. But he was also very, very frustrated. When Euphoria was destroyed it sent him spinning one way and the prophesized duo the other. Finding them would be like trying to find a tardigrade's sewing needle in a haystack the size of infinity, which it turns out was a pretty popular idiom outside of Earth.

Spending the time finding and rescuing them would most definitely interfere with his Node spa days, and this would never wash (literally and figuratively) with The Node. He took solace that the Quarol and the Topher, at least, were wearing brand-spanking-new TDX-30 space suits, equipped with air recyclers and new "fresh water" and "sandwich" straws. They would be fine until he got to them. Hopefully. Unless they were morons.

~~~

"Heeeeeeeeeeyyyyy!!!" Potto beamed. "It's *you!* Is it my birthday already? I was just trying to remember the last time I had one, and I couldn't!"

"Potto, dear boy, you wouldn't remember your own hand if it were scratching your own ass...which you *also* wouldn't remember possessing. I am flattered that you remember my face, however, and all the birthdays we shared together," said Lempshop, rolling r's in places there were no r's.

"I can't help but notice," Potto remarked, "that there seems to be very little of you."

Budgher Lemphop was perched atop a ledge on the asteroid. He was a head, a neck, one shoulder, one arm and one third of a grizzled chest sitting on top of a disgusting pile of chewed up sludge that was once the rest of him. A purple blood-soaked collared shirt was draped around his neck. It was torn to shreds apart from the one good arm and a filthy pointed chest pocket.

"I bet you are wondering how I am still alive?" he bravadoed.

"Nope!" Potto sang out.

"Of course not. But I'll tell you anyway, shall I?"

"Oh, yes! Please do!!"

Just because Potto wasn't wondering something didn't mean that he couldn't get excited about it.

"Well, when our wretchedly beloved Tractos was destroyed, I went hurtling into space! Yes! Hurtling!" Lempshop exclaimed. Everything he said sounded like he was desperately trying to keep the attention of a waning audience.

"In my mind a great opera was playing, like angels singing out 'sweeeeet relieeeef!' in blessed harmony! I was filled with such joy! Finally, an end. An end!! Finally, the hell that was our existence there would be over!" he added.

"That would be a nice song," Potto added to show that he was still paying attention, or at least trying his best to.

"But then I was hit by this big chunk of that villainous, horrible moon. And...are you ready for it? The big reveal?" He didn't wait for an answer, which is good because he wouldn't have gotten one. "That chunk of Tractos just happened to have a big enough chunk of the Life Core stuck in it that I...still...can't...fucking...die!"

"Wow!"

"Please excuse my language. I hate to be so crass, but I feel it really accentuated the heightened emotion of my explanation. Did it, or do you think less of me, dear Potto?"

"Yes!"

"Good. Good. I've gotten as far as I can with the whole dining on myself thing. If I eat this last arm, I won't be able to get at anything else. Or scratch my many itches. It hasn't been easy even getting to *this* state! Those cursed nanobots have been on me every step of the way. I've had to eat most parts three or four times to get to this point," he said far too loudly, but then hushed like he was telling a secret. "If you were to climb over to the other side of this mighty rock, you might just see part of the Life Core sticking out!"

"Now *that* I'd like to see!" Potto added. He didn't really want to see it. He also didn't *not* want to see it.

"Now. How did you come to be here? How did you survive?" Lempshop asked.

"Exact same way as you!" Potto said without thinking.

"Really???"

"Oh, probably not," Potto also said without thinking.

"Right. Oh Potto, I have been bad. So very, very bad in my long life. I have killed so many. So very, very many. Even you!"

"Even me? Thank you!"

"No, no...that is a *bad* thing I did to you. I am sorry."

"Forgiven!" Potto had lost track of this conversation long ago.

"I am so very sorry for all of it. I am being punished. This is my punishment. I thought I was in hell on Tractos...but no. *This* is hell. And I deserve nothing less."

"You're too hard on yourself, guy."

"That said, you have come to me like an angel of mercy. Could you be a dear and climb to the back of the asteroid for me and destroy the damn Life Core? Would you do that for me?"

"I'd do that for you!"

"You are a pal. I adore you. Oh, and sweet Potto, reach into the pocket on my shirt, won't you?"

Potto reached into the chest pocket on what was left of his disgusting shirt. In it he found the broken compass.

"Happy birthday, m' boy!"

Potto got so excited that by the time he reached the Life Core sticking out of the back of the asteroid, he'd forgotten why he was back there and flew off into space while admiring the trinket and slurping on a B.L.T.

Lempshop was left alone again, where he would spend a very, very, very, *very* long time fantasizing about repeatedly killing Potto over and over and over again until the end of time.

~~~

Clover was usually very good at meditating. She had been doing so for millions of years.

She'd been doing it longer than the word "meditation" had been used to describe what she had been doing. She'd been doing it since it was called "breathing-deliberately-and-visualizing-really-hard-while-relaxing", and for a short bit when it was simply called "that thing Steve was doing yesterday".

The harder she tried to find Potto or his tiny fairy, the more frustrated she became. Frustration is not something one wishes to draw from themselves when meditating. Quite the opposite in fact. There was once a species far out in the galaxy that regularly meditated to get angrier and more frustrated, but they went extinct shortly after they all started doing it.

Clover then tried sleeping. Sleeping was a thing she'd been doing even longer than meditating (as one would expect). She thought that dreaming might be a way of reaching them, but she tossed and turned and, even drugged, couldn't go deep enough.

She tried hypnotising *herself* because no one else on board knew how to do it. That didn't work either.

Finally, and much to her dismay (but to Teeg's pleasure), she allowed herself to be knocked out. This did nothing but prove to her once and for all that Potto was no longer hypnotized. He was floating out in the darkness, alone and probably frightened.

She *was* able to get back to their forest, or at least what she could remember of it. She found she had to create a lot of it herself to fill in the gaps. She couldn't get the colour of the loom fruit just right, and she imagined way more random woodland animal hugs than there were before (there had been zero) but everything else was as close as she could recall.

But no Potto. No Bundle.

She sat by a stream feeling lost and worried. She filled the stream with cream soda and everything felt just a little bit better.

~~~

Potto was floating out in the darkness, alone and totally preoccupied by the compass that he had accidentally let go of. It was floating a few feet from him, just out of reach. He tried to push himself forward, but it wasn't working. It was as if a wall of clear jelly were separating them, or as if he were trying to climb air.

He tried to do the twirling he had done earlier, thinking it would project him forward, but he had forgotten how to do it. He really should never have been able to this in the first place. Perhaps if he sang. Perhaps if he made up a song about his birthday again.

He started singing and he started twirling. The excitement he felt as he twirled into the compass and grabbed it once again was overwhelming, and along with a belly full of liquid sandwich, he immediately fell asleep.

"Holy hell, you are a pain in the ass!" Bundle screamed at him from deep inside his dream.

CHAPTER TWENTY-ONE

Only in one's imagination can a fish survive in soda pop. This is one of those universal truths. No scientist really needs to study this; they know this *based* on all these truths. They know that living creatures generally need to breathe oxygen, not carbonated sugar. Science doesn't need to waste its time on such stupidity. Scientists know that flamingos can't ride bicycles through active volcanoes (and live), elephants can't skydive (and live), and cobras can't do taxes (without an audit). No experiment needed. In fact, no experiment *encouraged*.

Yet in one's imagination, things are very different. The imagination is a world of wonders, of scientific impossibilities, and cobra accountants.

Deep within the lost worlds of Clover's imagination, fish could survive in soda pop. They could also talk.

"Aw, things are going to be alright," said a colourful cream soda koi.

"I don't see how. I'm *trying* to stay optimistic. But it's difficult when the two that are prophesized to save the universe act like children."

"Ah, but children have a special way of looking at things, don't they? Look at how bad things got out there with *adults* in charge!

Is it really that surprising that children end up saving it all? Children have always been the best bet to save the universe methinks.

"Hate is learned. Intolerance is learned. For a child, war is a game with harmless toys and low stakes. But guidance *is* needed, isn't it? They aren't bogged down with *cause and effect*, and that can get them hurt. They need to be protected. You need to protect them," said the fizzy fish.

"You are a wise fish," she smiled.

"Well, I'm in your head...so I guess that makes you the wise fish."

"Ha! I guess you're right. I am such a wise fish."

She then let out a loud, ground-shaking cream soda burp because she wanted the soft drink experience to be authentic, so she imaged it giving her a bit of gas. The distant trees shook.

"To protect them, I'll have to find them first. I didn't do such a good job before," she burped out.

"This is important. Do whatever it takes. *Whatever* it takes," the fish burped back.

"I will imagine this stream goes on forever. Then you can help me look for the fairy. I'm not sure that Potto is in here anymore. I think he's awake. But the fairy doesn't seem to follow any of the usual imaginary friend rules."

"Yes, I will help you look. You go that way; I'll go this way."

She got up and started following the stream one way.

"No!" the fish called out. "You go *THAT* way!"

"Oh, I thought you meant *THIS* way," she replied with a laugh.

"Sorry. I don't have hands. I couldn't point," the fish pointed out without hands.

"Fair enough," she burped.

"You have a very strange imagination," the koi burped back.

"Damn straight," Clover smiled.

~~~

"For the love of--" Bundle barked at Potto as they stood in a clearing of his new section of imaginary woods. "Do you think you could *stay* unconscious for me? Think you can handle that?"

"Errrr--"

"Don't you give me that! I'm pissed at you right now! Do you *want* to get rescued? You'd *rather* die?? Because if you don't find that nice Clover lady, you are as good as dead, Buster!"

"Maybe that would be for the best. I don't want to cause any-one anymore trouble. I don't remember much, but I am pretty sure I have caused a lot of it." One of the few things Potto *had* just remembered was that he had forgotten to destroy the Life Core for Lempshop. It acted as a trigger. He felt terrible.

A bottomless pit the diameter of an Olympic swimming pool opened up in the ground below his feet. He fell. Bundle fell with him.

It wasn't a quick fall, not like in conscious life and in real grav-ity. It was more of a slightly accelerated sinking. This wasn't mere sadness. This was actual proper and genuine depression. The kind that went beyond sadness and caused the entire body to feel ugly and hollow.

"You have caused a lot of it. But you can't die. I won't let you die. I need you to live. I want you to live. And not because I will disappear, too. I don't care about that," her scold seemed to sim-mer off. "But because I... Because I... Because," she struggled. "Because I *love* you Potto. I need you to remember because I need you to remember who you were. Because who you were was pretty incredible."

Potto was speechless. Though it happened quite often, it didn't happen for this reason. It didn't cause a literal downward spiral of despair.

"I like *you*, sweet fairy. I like it *here* with you. If I had my way I would never wake up ever again. My imagination gets the best of me," he said as they continued to fall. "My reality gets the *worst*...

"I'm *not* incredible, I am stupid. Ask anyone. Ask *everyone*. I am stupid and useless. I am a sick joke. I am barely a person," he said, welling up.

"Long, long ago I once said that very thing to you," Bundle re-plied. "That I am stupid and useless. You know what you told me? You said '*No you are not! You are not stupid and useless. You are too good for a universe that is too bad. You are both too simple for a universe so complicated, and too complicated for a universe so sim-ple. And you are just having a hard time navigating the ridiculous circumstances around you. But you will. You will catch up and you will leave them in your dust. And no pressure if you can't. If you don't leave them in the dust, you will avoid that silly, pointless dust alto-gether...you will surround yourself with love, and love doesn't care if you are smart or stupid, and love doesn't find anyone useless.'"*

The fall started to slow down even more. It became a float.

"You will know all of this when you finally remember. What-ever it is that is blocking you, we will fix it," she added.

Potto tried to wrap his head around all of this. It was a struggle, but Bundle's words were changing his mood and they were rising back up to the surface.

Very abruptly, like a deer responding to a twig snapping, Bun-dle perked up like she had heard something in the distance. She zoomed off as quickly as she could, up and out of the pit, her little fairy wings fluttering like an overly caffeinated hummingbird's.

She stopped at the closest stream. It hadn't been there before and smelled sickeningly sweet. Far off she could see the sun shim-mering off the scales of a fish as it raised its head from the stream. She flew towards it but it always seemed the same distance away. Too far to speak to.

She knew this was Clover.

~~~

The cream soda koi could *see* the fairy, but as fast as it swam, Bundle always seemed the same distance away. Too far to speak to. It knew this had to be Potto's fairy, but it couldn't reach her.

The fish tried waving fins and somersaulting in the air. They both seemed to see one another, and the stream seemed to be reaching Bundle, but *it* couldn't. Clover couldn't entirely get there. Images, but no words.

And then Bundle disappeared entirely. Potto must have woken up.

The fish swam back as fast as it could to Clover to report to her what she already knew.

"I have seen the fairy! But it was too far off. No matter how hard I tried. No matter how fast I swam. We could not connect. I am sorry."

"Don't be sorry," Clover replied sadly. "At least we know he's still out there. He's just out of range. Barely, maybe."

Her heart sank a bit. Being optimistic was hard work sometimes.

~~~

Potto opened his eyes on the empty universe again. Something was wrong.

It was as if his blood was flowing through his body at super speed. His heart was racing to keep up. His skin beneath the space suit was itchy. It was burning with itchy.

It was as if he had taken a bath in stinging nettles and was having a severe allergic reaction to peanut butter on top of it. His breathing got erratic. He couldn't swallow. He tried slurping at his fresh water straw but got his sandwich straw by accident and started choking on liquid ham with Dijon.

All of this was happening so quickly that, not only was he snapped from his dream (something Bundle would no doubt yell at him for later), but he didn't realize his body was moving through space at a much-faster-than-drifting speed. He was being drawn into something. Pulled.

He started blacking out. Flashes of stringy plant fibre and coarse vine flipped like a turbo slide show before his eyes each time he closed them. In his mind the itching went from rash-like to the odd feeling of insects crawling all over him, burrowing under his flesh.

His flesh felt hard and rough and thick. The hair upon his head felt leafy and thorny. For a brief moment he felt like he was covered in birds, with a woodpecker knocking on his skull.

He moved even faster through space. His arms and legs trying to stay attached to his torso. He threw-up his sandwich slurry all over the inside of his helmet. He tried to take a deep breath but it was so laboured that it sounded like water loudly being sucked down a clogged drain.

Not once did he think he was dying, though. He thought he was morphing. Into a tree.

His body slammed into something hard. He could not see it through the sick just yet. It needed to drip down first. He felt many long, thin, hard arms wrap around him. His expert wriggling did not help.

His heart rate slowed. The itching stopped. He filled his mouth with fresh water and spat it at the inside of his helmet, clearing some of the grossness that was once liquid sandwich, but was now liquid sandwich once-removed.

There was a seemingly lifeless wooden face staring back at him. It was Clory.

~~~

Clover decided to remain unconscious just in case. As long as Teeg didn't start slapping her again, she'd be fine.

She sat silently by the cream soda stream thinking about options, hoping for a miracle and preparing herself for bad news. The fish swam silently beside her. It was giving her some space because she imagined it was.

She looked past the banks of the stream at the trees in the distance. Their loom fruit seemed dim in the sunlight. This reminded her of Potto. Perhaps he only *seemed* dim in comparison to the brightness of the universe. Perhaps he just didn't *seem* so bright in this well-lit room of creation. Perhaps she underestimated him. Perhaps everyone did. In the darkness, even the dimmest light could illuminate the path and help one find their way home.

"You see, the whole purpose of this hypnosis was to find out what was *blocking* him," she explained to the fish.

"You don't have to tell me!" the fish reminded her.

"Oh, I know. But talking these things out is a help," she smiled.

"Ok, go ahead," it smiled back (as best as a fish could).

"It was electronic I think. The wall inside his thoughts. It couldn't be budged. It couldn't be smashed. It couldn't be climbed. It must be *really* embedded. Rooted deep. But methinks it is a foreign object. Like an implant maybe."

"Maybe. Hey, what's *that?*" asked the koi, looking past her, over her shoulder.

Clover noticed a long shadow cast over the two of them. She looked behind her for the source, up towards the sun. She saw the silhouette of the largest tree she had ever seen. As her eyes adjusted she could make out a slight twinkling coming from one of the branches.

"Found you!" Bundle called out.

Clover laughed out loud. This was not particularly funny, but sometimes laughs just popped out of people.

Bundle flew down from the giant branch she had been sitting on. "I got a ride. This tree thing seems to have boosted our mental signal! Potto is on a ship!"

"He got picked up by a ship?" Clover danced.

"Not exactly. He's literally *on* the ship. Like on top of it, not in it. The distress beacon has been activated. Set your ship's scanner to the frequency 222-134-98763. Come and get him!" Bundle laughed, too. Again, not because anything was particularly funny, but because this relief was so uplifting.

Clover scratched the frequency number into her arm with her fingernail just in case and waited to be slapped.

~~~

Vibloblblah Ooze's ship looked so much like space garbage that no one noticed when it disappeared, and then reappeared.

No one thought twice about it dropping a tranquillizing green gas down upon them. It would not automatically be assumed that the presence of the space garbage and the appearance of the green gas were connected in any way. It was much more likely that the green gas was coming from something *near* or hiding *behind* the space garbage, and that the space garbage was too useless to be responsible.

Knutt would even stop noticing the coming and going of it on her hull, and Clover would continue to have her guardian angel.

A guardian angel that longed to talk to her. A guardian angel that longed to feel her touch again. But those days were long gone. Kissing him would be like kissing a horrible, rotting goulash.

Just because he couldn't be with her, though, didn't mean he couldn't protect her, and take up her cause. And what a cause! It was a cause that would redeem him in his own head. If he took part, he might just forgive himself for his role in creation of The Node and a Node-run universe.

There was only one setback. Through all of his surveillance, he discovered that one other monk had survived. This meant any one of the five could have. This monk was now calling himself Vrume T'cha T'cha.

It couldn't have been one he actually got along with.

~~~

With new co-ordinates set, the Shiv flew at top speed to re-trieve Potto. They were not sure what to expect, but they had their medical supplies ready. He might be fine and well fed on space suit sandwiches, he might be half dead, or he might be com-pletely space mad and ferocious.

Teeg was not sure how to act around Clover after this. She hated relying on others, and she hated being proven wrong. Both of those things were staring right at her now whenever Clover smiled at her, and Clover liked smiling at people.

On the other hand, she was quite impressed. Thanks to the hippy they would find Potto and be one step closer to getting back on track. Whatever that track was.

When things continually go wrong, even the slightest nicety, even the tiniest bit of good news, even the *thinnest sliver* of an upward swing feels like the greatest gift on the greatest holiday. As they got closer to Potto's coordinates, following that beacon signal, that upward swing was about to become a catapult into a giant cake of happy for both Teeg and Gekko.

"What...what is *that?*" Teeg asked Knutt as something odd came into focus through the front window.

"*THAT* is The Gooseberry." Knutt answered matter-of-factly.

"What is on top of it?"

Her heart started to swell like a hot air balloon as she realized it was a tree. A *Clory*-sized tree.

It held tightly to Potto like he was caught in a huge wooden bear trap. Her rooted feet were completely wrapped around, and hanging onto, the top of the small ship. Roots and branches had pierced the thick glass of the cockpit, letting outer space into Toobli Dentatan's ship where outer space was meant to be sealed out.

The skeletal remains of a small anthropomorphized anteater sat strapped into the pilot's seat. Clory had won the battle after all.

"Is she...?"

"I'm getting three life signs. The Sentaphyll's are faint, but they're there," Knutt answered with what almost sounded like a touch of joy in her voice. She may have been miserable and filled with distain, but this kind of turn-of-events was rare and the sudden joy and laughter on her deck was infectious.

"Get them on board! Quick!" Teeg laugh-screamed.

Gekko smiled that smile again that looked like she was saying "Yeeeeeeeee".

As they set their tractor beam on The Gooseberry, Teeg's smile disappeared. Not gone completely, just put on hold as something Knutt had said had suddenly occurred to her.

"Wait. *Three* life signs?" she asked the ship. "Toobli is dead..."

"Yes. Three. The Sentaphyll, the Quarol and and the fetus."

"Fetus?"

"Uh...yes. An egg, actually."

Teddy Bears didn't procreate. On Chagrin, when a Teddy Bear died, it simply left behind an egg. That egg contained a perfect clone-baby of the adult that laid it. Scientists around the universe once wished to figure out this strange phenomenon, but could never get close enough to a Teddy Bear without getting disembowelled. So they just chalked it up to some kind of "self-insemination-meets immaculate-conception" type of thing.

"You're about to become the proud parents of an anteater," Knutt informed them with even more (sinister) joy in her voice.

CHAPTER TWENTY-TWO

Waking General Kendra Eppie up early on a weekend was a remarkably daunting task. Even if he *requested* that early wake-up time, and *promised* he would remain calm and collected.

Due to all the pain issues in his back, he often had a hard time falling asleep. Even when Freckles hid horse tranquilizers in the buttercream centres of his multi-coloured bedtime macarons. Once he was finally asleep, both he and his back wanted to stay there.

Freckles often told Eppie upon such requests, that *this* is what made waking him up so difficult. "I know how hard it is for you to fall asleep, and I hate waking you up because of that! Please don't make me. Your poor, poor back..." he'd say, but the truth was that he secretly loved it for this very reason.

"Psst. Hey. Hey. Hey. Hey. Hey. Hey. Hey. Hey. Hey. Hey. Hey. Hey. Hey," Freckles would say gently as to not startle the General into his day. "Hey."

"What?? What the fuck? You fucking fuck! Go fuck yourself and fuck off while you're at it you little fuck!" Eppie would open his eyes saying, with a violent spasm of yawns.

"I made muffins..."

"Take your fucking muffins and shove them up your fu—what

kind of muffins?"

"Bran. Your doctor said you need more fibre."

"Have him killed. Are there raisins?"

"Yes."

"*Fuuuuuuuuuuuuuuuuuuuuuuuuuuuck.*"

And thus began another fun-filled Saturday with Kendra Eppie.

He had requested this early start because he had been given a hot tip that Vrume T'cha T'cha was up to something. It was time to get his Secret Force working a little harder than not at all.

After news that Euphoria had been destroyed, reports came in that only a few ships had escaped. One was allegedly Vrume's. What an upstanding citizen like Vrume was doing at an establishment filled with criminals (at the time of its demise) was highly suspect. Eppie fantasized about taking a cigar trimmer to Vrume's wagging finger.

He ate seven bran muffins, complaining about the raisins the entire time. This is why Freckles added them to his muffin batter. A complaining Eppie was an oddly content Eppie. Raisins would give him a good outlet, and distract him from complaining about anything else.

He showered with Freckles, and they made love very, very quickly. He got his back brace on plus his uniform and ate three more muffins on his way out the door. Freckles was free to spend the rest of the morning watching game shows and relaxing. He enjoyed his day off, which was something The Node wouldn't have allowed if Eppie hadn't covered for him regularly (while sneaking in his own day off) each weekend. The Node hated vacation days.

He snacked on raisins. Not because he liked them either, but to give himself raisin breath for when Eppie returned.

When Eppie secretly arrived at the secret office of his Secret Force, only one secret agent was secretly there. His name was Erky Sands, and even *he* had only shown up because Freckles had given him the heads up the night before.

"Where is everybody else?" Eppie barked.

"Uh...it's a religious holiday," Erky lied, covering for his absentee co-workers.

"Religious holiday? Which one?" Eppie said slyly, wagging his own finger.

"Uh...it's Squambogian Mantis Widow Christmas."

"Is that a thing?"

"Sure."

"But none of them are Squambogian Mantis Widows..."

"Well not *yet*..."

Whenever Eppie didn't understand something, to save face he would change the subject. Erky knew this.

"Fine. Vrume T'cha T'cha was seen leaving Euphoria. Find out why," Eppie said, changing the subject to save face.

"But Euphoria was destroyed," Erky replied.

"I know that!"

"So how could he have been seen leaving it if it isn't there anymore?"

"He left it *before* it was destroyed, you idiot."

"Ah."

"So, I want you to find out *why*. Ask around. See what you can find."

"Who am I going to ask? Euphoria was destroyed," Erky asked as he slumped into his wheelie desk chair.

"Other ships escaped, too!"

"Hmm. Well where is Vrume now?"

"Shouldn't *you* know that?? What am I paying you for?"

"Ok. That's fair."

"Thank you."

"Jeremy probably knows."

"Well then ask Jeremy. Where is he? Off for that holiday?"

"No. I think he's dead."

"I just saw him yesterday."

"Oh. I don't know then."

"I hate you."

"For good reason. I'll call Jeremy. We'll figure this out. Don't you worry."

"Listen you little shit. I will give you an hour. One hour. Find another survivor fast. If you don't have information, I will not only fire you from this Secret Force, I will fire you from a cannon.

Through a piano wire sieve and into space. After I eat your family. Do I make myself clear?"

"You're gonna eat my family?"

"Yep."

"But you can't. Not today."

"And why is that?"

"Religious holiday."

~~~

Every time K'ween thought that a tiny blip on her console screen was The Muse, it was a Blankton. As frustrating as this was, it was also just a little satisfying blowing them out of the sky.

So far, she had blown up eleven of them. This was a very significant number, as it was as many Blanktons as she had drunkenly married in the past. She had only remained married to each for one night. None of them had survived the consummation. One last, glorious night for each of those sorry Blanktons. This was a period of K'ween's life she didn't talk about much. Not the murder part, just the marriage-to-a-Blankton part.

K'ween would not rest until she found those that had betrayed her, and those that would make her even more rich and powerful. That included the sexy little Quarol that had motivated her to challenge an entire science team to find a way she could survive his poisonous love. Whether *he* survived it was another matter entirely.

As she poured herself a very tall glass of Flettocian flubbfruit wine, she sighed loudly. This volume of sigh was usually reserved for people smelling their own breath in the cup of their hand, or for people cleaning their smudgy glasses. All was quiet. She sighed louder and longer.

"Something wrong?" Pannick finally asked, missing the attention-seeking intent of the first sigh.

"It's such a lonely business, being a ruler. Sometimes I think I should just find someone nice and settle down," she said with another sigh. She drank half of the glass of wine in one go.

"Really?" Pannick asked in insincere disbelief.

"Oh! Wait! I think I'm thinking in the wrong direction," she epiphanized. "To be *less* lonely I need to be an even *bigger* ruler!

If I play my cards right, I will overthrow The Node, and then I will never be lonely again! I will *order* people to be with me. I will *order* people to die in my bed, and everyone will want to!"

"How do you plan on overthrowing The Node?" Pannick asked, concerned K'ween would most definitely get them all killed (including the entire sisterhood of their Barbohdean moon).

"I don't know yet. But it will start with capturing the Topher and the Quarol. I'll have my way with the Quarol and then get the reward. With the reward comes the power. Power grows."

"What do you see in that pale little man? I don't get it. He's a little too...I dunno...*gentle.*"

"I like the way he tastes."

"Like Tractos poison..."

"Mmmm. Yes."

K'ween tilted her head towards a second, empty glass on the table next to her. She didn't feel like drinking alone, or apparently verbalizing an invitation. Pannick nodded back a nonverbal thank-you and poured herself a glass of wine, sitting next to her fearless leader. She drank the whole glass before K'ween could change her mind.

They both sat there and loudly sighed for a spell.

K'ween didn't realize that The Muse had been destroyed, and that those she searched for were now on a Shiv ship. It mattered not because she was paying close attention to *every* ship they came across, including a twelfth Blankton ship.

"Shall I destroy it?"

"Nah. Bring this Blankton to me. Use his ship for parts or something."

Off Pannick went, following these orders with an eye roll. K'ween sat quietly. She took a sip of her wine and sighed yet again, whispering to herself with a smile, "Yes. I'll be the new Node, and The Node is never lonely."

~~~

"I'm lonely," said The Node to an otherwise preoccupied Vrume T'cha T'cha.

Vrume had barely made it back for The Node's cleaning (and haircut) and really wanted to be in his own ship looking for the prophesized duo. "Why don't you get yourself a girlfriend?" he asked, absentmindedly.

The Node scoffed at this. The idea seemed too absurd to him. "*Do gods date? I think not,*" he thought to himself with a thought chuckle.

"Where *are* you today?" The Node asked. "You're a thousand miles away. If you weren't the best, I'd have had you eaten for not being present while in my presence," he half-joked.

Vrume's assistant gulped. He was preparing himself for his big performance.

"Sorry, sorry. You're right. I just have so much on my mind. What with the beauty/detailing school and constantly trying to develop amazing new products to make you even shinier... I think I need a vacation," he said listlessly.

"*Vacation??*" The Node angrily bellowed. The word "vacation" made him furious. He didn't think anyone deserved one. Ever. He didn't even give one to his right-hand man General Kendra Eppie. He, however, *did* give Eppie and his toady Saturdays off for their apparent "groveling workshops".

"No, no. I'm not *taking* one. I'm just saying I'm a bit stressed. No biggie. I'll deal with it. Calm yourself. Stress causes wrinkles. Would you feel better if I killed my assistant?"

"Yes!" The Node shrieked.

Vrume fake-shot the assistant in the head, covering The Node with Squambogian brain cabbage and had the "body" dragged off. The assistant felt a sense of enormous pride in his acting ability.

"Thaaaaaaat's better," The Node said, calming down considerably. "You want stress? I have every bounty hunter in the known universe looking for a couple of *idiots*, and no one can find them! *That* is wrinkle-inducing stress right there, guy."

"What's so important about these two? They steal from you? Misquote you on social media? Look at you weird? Cough?"

"No. It's this stupid Quarol. He has something of mine. Something very, very important to me. I don't know how he got it, but I'm going to get it back. Even if I have to tear apart all of space and time to find him."

"That is curious, indeed!" Vrume said, pepping up

considerably with this new topic. "I haven't seen a Quarol in years!" he lied. "Knew this nice one once. He was on a book tour. Wrote a book about quantum galactic vacuum variable canine disorder. Didn't even know that was a thing. Still not sure it is, but he was very convincing. As was his really messed-up dog."

"Yes, that doesn't sound like a real thing," The Node agreed. He always felt less lonely around Vrume and his (tall?) tales.

"He was a good lay, too. Had him in the self-help section of an Earth Mall bookstore. The Quarol that is, not the dog."

"Yes, yes. That'll happen," The Node said thinking about something else. He was thinking about Vrume's girlfriend idea.

~~~

After all The Node's hairs had been cut, and all the smudges, scratches and tiny dents had been buffed and hammered out (and the brain cabbage had been dried and peeled off) Vrume wagged a finger and made him promise to take better care of his magnificent shiny, metallic chassis. He was then off as fast as he could be without causing any suspicion.

As he made his way to his ship, he ran into Eppie, face-to-face.

"Kenny. Good to see you," he said insincerely.

"Well, well, well," Eppie said back with a smug grin. "Speak of the devil and he's sure to appear."

This *"Speak of the devil and he's sure to appear"* Earth phrase was thought to have its origins in sixteenth century England as a fun (and fairly obvious) little reference to someone unexpectedly showing up when (or shortly after) being talked about. Variations included *"Talk of the devil and see his horns"* and *"Talk of the devil and he's presently at your elbow."* Though it was true that this is where and when it became popular, the actual *original* saying was *"Talk of a Topher and he's soon kissing your arse"* but was paraphrased and made more eloquent in 1666 by Italian writer Giovanni Torriano, who hated the one Towerscapian he had ever met and didn't want to give the bastard any free press.

"Oh there are *many* devils on Lyme Node, my dear Kenny. I should be the least of your worries," Vrume smiled smugly back. "I hear Weird Jimmy was spotted around here somewhere."

"You think you are *soooo* smart..." Eppie started.

"No, I just think you are *soooo* stupid, Kenny." Vrume laughed.

Eppie didn't frighten him.

"Oh, we'll see who has the last laugh. I am so close. So very, very close. I know you're up to something and I have my best man on it. And don't call me Kenny."

"I really doubt you have a best man at all. Kenny Kenny Kenny Kenny."

Eppie was so easily agitated and flustered. Deep down he knew he should never argue with anyone he couldn't have killed. He wasn't good at it. People disagreeing with him made him trip on his words and lose his place. It got worse the more agitated he got.

"You will, you are, you, you," he stammered, "You're gonna be in trouble! Erky found a Sammolite who left Euphoria moments before Euphoria was destroyed!"

"So?"

"Soooo, wise guy, this Sammolite saw you there. Saw you with an albino Quarol and a Topher just before he got on his ship! And he had just scanned Euphoria looking for his ex-girlfriend. He has a record of every ship that was parked there, and every species of alien."

"I find that hard to believe. A Sammolite with a girlfriend?"

"He is an uncommonly handsome Sammolite."

"Very uncommon. I would like to see this guy."

"Grew a nice beard. Bright puce highlights... anyway, neither here nor there. Once Erky gets me that downloaded record I can prove that you were there. *Aaand* I can prove that the Quarol and the Topher were there with you. *Aaaaaand* I will get that uncommonly handsome Sammolite to rat you out to The Node. Then I will enjoy watching The Node skin you alive for years."

Eppie walked away before Vrume could get another word in, feeling as though he had won this round. He hadn't, however. He had made a flustered mistake and used a specific secret name.

Before getting back to his ship, Vrume hunted down the only Erky on Lyme Node and destroyed all of his computers and snapped his lazy neck.

His hunt for Potto and Aye would have to wait just a little longer. He had an uncommonly handsome bearded Sammolite to hunt down first.

~~~

Of all the bounty hunters looking for Potto and Aye, the massive reptilian Jorge Jorge Jorge was the only one *ahead* of them.

K'ween may have been headed in the right direction, Mel Million Max may have been closing in on them, various Blanktons may have been zipping around aimlessly like cosmic midge flies, and various others may have been searching every nook and cranny from Lyme Node to the ghost of Euphoria , *but* none were ahead of them and waiting. Just Jorge Jorge Jorge and his tiny toddler girl voice.

His preferred method of capture was ambush. He hid amongst the ruins of the long-gone inventor (and failed megalomaniac) Emperor Reginald Zophricaties' long lost satellite station over the lifeless planet of Vex 7. It was only one light year past the overpriced bungalows of Vex 4.

The Quarol and the Topher would surely stop on Vex 4 for a fuel up. It had the only fuel station in the Vex sector (which was on the way to almost *every* destination) and it was the last one for a long, long while.

It was in these ruins that Jorge Jorge Jorge found Zophricaties' lab. It was still (mostly) in one piece. Inside that lab, and stinking of long-gone Blanktons and Yayghers, sat the Master Cloner. To his astonishment (and with a new power cell from his ship), the huge and problematic cloning machine started up.

Within hours Jorge Jorge Jorge had an army of genetically inferior (but just as terrifyingly large) Jorge Jorge Jorges at the ready.

CHAPTER TWENTY-THREE

THE ROTTEN LOVERS

BOOK AND MUSIC BY:

MALATE'W KRISTY-R'EE

ACT ONE

Scene 1

The lights come up on a small restaurant table. The demon Failcotte the Fragile sits alone with an old bottle of grey wine. The lighting is low and blue and comes from a large chandelier hanging from above. No one else is in the restaurant. He drinks from the bottle for several seconds. He looks melancholy and perhaps a little constipated.

FAILCOTTE: This wine tastes like insults and old oatmeal. Nothing in my day brings this ol' demon joy anymore. Such is my lament! Such is my lament. Waiter!

A waiter with a limp enters from centre stage, dragging his third, false leg behind him.

LAME WAITER: What now, you ugly sore?

FAILCOTTE: How do you do it? You, with three legs, two of them lame. *(beat)* How do you endure?

The waiter picks up his dragging third leg. It is now a lute. He plays it and sings.

SONG -- "THE LAME WAITER'S SONG"

(WAITER:)
I USED TO HOVER AROUND MY OLD FLAT,
WISHING ON WISHBONES, AND CHEWING THE FAT,
I HAD ALL THE WILL OF A WOEBEGONE GNAT,
THAT FED OFF THE TIT OF A SPOILING DEAD CAT...

AND I NEEDED LOVE BAD...

LOVE IS THE BANDAGE—THAT HEALED MY HEART!
LOVE IS THE SANDWICH I ATE WITH A TART!
LOVE IS THE SAUCE ON MY HAPPINESS MEAT!
BUT LOVE IS THE REASON I CAN'T USE MY FEET.

(FAILCOTTE:)
I DON'T UNDERSTAND HOW YOU COULD BE SO COY,
YOU SAY THAT LOVE SAVED YOU, YOU SILLY LAME BOY,
NOW TWO OF YOUR FEET ARE ALL BUT A PLOY,
TO GET BETTER TIPS, YOU SHOULD NOT BE EMPLOYED...

YOU DON'T EVEN SERVE GOOD BOK CHOY...

LOVE IS THE BANDAGE —THAT HEALED YOUR HEART?
LOVE IS THE SANDWICH YOU ATE WITH A TART?
LOVE IS THE SAUCE ON YOUR HAPPINESS MEAT?

NO, LOVE'S JUST THE REASON YOU CAN'T USE YOUR
FEET.

(WAITER:)
TRY SEEING IT FROM MY PERSPECTIVE YOU CREEP!

(FAILCOTTE:)
OKAY!!

(BOTH:)
LOVE IS THE BANDAGE THAT CAN HEAL YOUR HEART!
LOVE *IS* A SANDWICH TO EAT WITH SWEET TARTS!
LOVE *IS* THE SAUCE ON THE HAPPIEST MEAT!
AND WHEN YOU'VE GOT LOVE, YOU DON'T NEED YOUR
FEET!

*The music ends. The waiter puts back his lute. It becomes his
third leg again. Failcotte downs the rest of the bottle of wine in
one go. He coughs for effect.*

FAILCOTTE: Well I guess I'm convinced.

*A beautiful woman descends with wires from the large chande-
lier. She is dressed as if she was part of it. She sits at the table
with Failcotte.*

FAILCOTTE: Wow! Who are you??

GLASS TINA: I am Glass Tina. I *was* a sad chandelier...but I
heard that you are in need of love.

FAILCOTTE: Why, yes! This lame waiter convinced me with his
beautiful and haunting song!

GLASS TINA: It surely was beautiful and haunting. *(To waiter)*
Bring me some of your best Bok Choy, s'il vous plaît!

FAILCOTTE: Your funeral! *(waits for audience's laughter to die down)* Are you made out of *glass*, Glass Tina?

GLASS TINA: Why yes, I am. I am extremely fragile. Please do not break me!

FAILCOTTE : What a coincidence! I am a demon called Failcotte the Fragile! I too am fragile! Do not break me either!

The music swells.

SONG -- "FRAGILE LOVE"

(GLASS TINA:)
I LIT UP...WHEN YOU WALKED IN THE ROOM,
Y'KNOW, BECAUSE I'M A CHANDELIER,
OH, AND BECAUSE...I SENSED YOUR GLOOM,
AND SOMETHING TO DO WITH WIRES AND MIRRORS.

I LIT UP...WHEN YOU CAME IN TO EAT,
BUT YOU ONLY ORDERED THE HORRID WINE,
YOU SANG OF LOVE...AND HAPPY MEAT,
THAT LAST PART REALLY MADE MY BULBS SHINE.

(FAILCOTTE:)
I LIT UP...WHEN YOU GOT TURNED ON,
THE SWITCH I MEAN, I'M NOT A PERV,
WELL MAYBE A BIT...IS THAT SO WRONG?
NOW SHALL WE SHARE A WEE HORS D'OEUVRE?

(BOTH:)
YOU ARE FRAGILE, I AM TOO!
IF I BREAK YOU, I'LL BREAK TOO!
SO, LOVE ME TENDER, LOVE ME TRUE!
IF YOU BREAK I'LL BE YOUR GLUE.
I'LL BE YOU'RE GLUE.

(GLASS TINA:)
WHEN YOU WARNED ME...ABOUT THE BOK CHOY,
I FELL FURTHER DOWN THE HOLE OF LOVE...

(FAILCOTTE:)
IT'S NOT FRESH...YOU WON'T ENJOY!
I ENTERED THAT LOVE HOLE FROM ABOVE.

(BOTH:)
YOU ARE FRAGILE, I AM TOO,
IF I BREAK YOU, I'LL BREAK TOO,
FORGET THE BOK CHOY, EAT LOVE STEW,
IF YOU BREAK I'LL BE YOUR GLUE...

I'LL BE YOUR GLUE.

I'LL BE YOUR...

...GLUE.

The music ends and they kiss. A big kiss. A passionate kiss. The waiter who has been standing there the whole time finally leaves them.

LAME WAITER: Well I never. Our Bok Choy is four star!

Lights down.

~~~

Aye made his way backstage through a maze of mildewed patchwork curtains as half of the audience dutifully applauded, and the other half sat silently pondering what the hell they had just witnessed.

Other actors rushed past him as the modest orchestra played their oddly shaped woodwinds. They insured that the music was both familiar and alien, ancient and spooky, whimsical and complex.

The backstage area felt very much like a dark and rundown cafeteria. Collapsible bench tables were all set up with tabletop mirrors, tubes of makeup, brushes, and bottles of cheap grain alcohol. Cherry-scented pipe smoke curled and clouded racks of costumes and wigs. Actors both rushed about in random fits of panic and sat waiting at these tables, touching up makeup, mouthing lines, and getting drunk.

There seemed to be an unmovable, unwipeable layer of dust on everything. A dust that was so uniform it almost seemed intentional and spray-painted on. Stagehands rushed from actor to actor checking their outfits and wigs and rushing the odd one out through the curtains. It was hard to believe that the whole makeshift theatre had been seemingly erected in minutes, and could probably be taken down in as much time.

Aye was swooning. In the rehearsals he had been instructed by Malate'w Kristy-R'ee (who had also directed as well as scribe) not to actually kiss Orchestra until opening night. He felt that the kiss would ring truer and have more readable impact on the audience if they waited.

The kiss had been better than Aye had anticipated. He had never kissed anyone before that he actually liked. It was nice. It was exciting.

He was quite clearly in love. He had never been in love before. He felt sick.

Orchestra Balloo came up and gave him a hug. "That was great! You can actually sing!" she said beaming. She was in a fantastic mood; there is nothing a performer loves more that hearing the sound of applause. She hadn't even minded the kiss.

They quickly changed their costumes for the next scene they were in. Veroseralien actors had the next few scenes covered. Aye could hear them from backstage and it made him want to join them. Ampex Vooshy-Balaire-Sangria, who had played the waiter, approached. He did not look happy, but he had that type of face.

"Well. I guess congratulations are in order. You didn't fuck up. Yet," he snivelled. Ampex did not like that non-Veroseraliens were not only *in* this performance, but had taken the leading roles while he got stuck with "Lame Waiter".

"Yeah, beat it, chump," Aye snorted back. He wasn't going to let anyone rain on his parade. Ampex snorted, grabbed the bottle of grain alcohol that Aye had been drinking from, and stomped off. Even his artificial lute leg seemed to stomp.

Another actor swaggered up. This one seemed to have a different attitude altogether. He replaced Aye's bottle with a fresh one. Aye smiled. This was Aye's acting coach R'k W'a Rkwa-Rkwa and Aye quite liked him. He was playing the dentist in the next scene with Aye because of course he was.

"Don't mind him. He's always been a pain in the ass. I think it's great to have a little new blood around here. You're doing great. Really stellar. Aces all around. Bravo my friend."

Around Orchestra and R'k, Aye felt comfort. He felt appreciated. He felt he didn't need to be an asshole; he was getting that same attention in a much more creative, fulfilling, likeable and satisfying way. He was quite surprised that not only had he been able to memorize lines, but he was actually enjoying pretending to be someone else for a change.

A stagehand rushed over and smacked them both with pancake makeup, causing a poof of white powder to hang momentarily in the air, adding a layer of dust to the surrounding layers of dust.

"We're up m'boy! Break a neck!" R'k announced, slapping Aye on the back while laughing at his own take on 'break a leg'.

It was the most encouragement Aye had ever felt from another. They both took big swigs of liquid courage from their bottles and off they went.

"Thanks Dad," he whispered back to R'k, too quiet for anyone but himself to hear, as Orchestra quietly applauded them wearing the best smile Aye had ever seen.

~~~

THE ROTTEN LOVERS

BOOK AND MUSIC BY:

MALATE'W KRISTY-R'EE

ACT ONE

Scene 5

The lights come up on Failcotte hiding in a cave. He is alone, only lit by a small bonfire. He warms his hands on the fire. He'd eat an apple if he had one.

FAILCOTTE: Oh, my sweet Glass Tina! How can I face you? I broke all of my teeth off on a plate of that horrible bok choy! I knew it was horrible, yet I could not resist. I am a demon and without my teeth I am nothing.

Dewlock the Hermit Dentist enters from behind a boulder in the cave.

DEWLOCK: Why are you in my cave, you ugly sore?

FAILCOTTE: *(Startled)* Ahh! You startled me! Are you Dewlock? Are you a hermit dentist?

DEWLOCK: I am both of those things! Bask in my grace!

FAILCOTTE: I am in need of a dentist!

DEWLOCK: I heard! I was just over there behind that boulder the whole time. Bok choy is a soft food, sometimes stringy. *(beat)* How did you break your teeth on it?

FAILCOTTE: It was *very* bad bok choy.

DEWLOCK: Let me have a look.

Failcotte opens his mouth wide for Dewlock. Dewlock has a look inside. He pokes a finger around in there.

DEWLOCK: I can help you, but how will you pay me?

FAILCOTTE: I have nothing, for I am but a fragile demon.

DEWLOCK: Nothing is not enough money.

FAILCOTTE: But I need my teeth fixed for true love. I fell in love with a chandelier.

DEWLOCK: Like, the fancy light fixture?

FAILCOTTE: Like that, but leggier.

The music begins to play.

SONG -- "FIX YOUR TEETH FOR TRUE LOVE!"

(DEWLOCK:)
I ONCE KNEW LOVE, I KNEW IT WELL,
BUT SHE CONDEMNED ME TO THIS HELL,
AND DROVE ME MAD FOR QUITE A SPELL,
AND NOW I'M A HERMIT DENTIST.

IT TOOK ME YEARS, BUT NOW I'M SKILLED,
THROUGH TRIAL AND ERROR AND MEN I'VE KILLED,
BUT NOW I'M GREAT, MY PATIENTS THRILLED,
BUT NO HERMIT HYGIENIST.

I WILL FIX YOUR TEETH FOR TRUE LOVE.

(FAILCOTTE:)
WILL YOU FIX MY TEETH FOR TRUE LOVE?

(DEWLOCK:)
I JUST SAID I'D FIX YOUR TEETH FOR TRUE LOVE.

(BOTH:)
FOR TRUE LOVE LIKES A HEALTHY SMILE.

Music crescendos to an abrupt stop.

DEWLOCK: Fucking bok choy.

~~~

It took many rehearsals before Aye had finally asked "What's with all the bok choy references?"

When R'k W'a Rkwa-Rkwa told a story, even the simplest of stories, he told it well. This was a simple story, but Aye hung on every word.

"Many, many, many years ago, back before my time, I'm happy to say...our people were *starving*. Through begging and pleading we managed to obtain crates upon crates of frozen bok choy. We had to live on bok choy for over a hundred years from our ship's deep freeze. It became so despised that it has now become tradition to bad-mouth it in all of our productions. Sort of one of those weird theatre luck/superstition things."

"Hmm. I like bok choy. It's incredibly inoffensive," Aye shrugged.

"Oh, me too! Really takes on the sauce," R'k agreed. "But we found other things to eat. Better things. We found *meat* after being herbivores for so long! Never look back, m'boy!"

Over the next five hours, Aye had been back and forth from on-stage to backstage so many times he was finding it hard to keep track of his scenes and his songs. All of this time backstage meant getting to spend more and more time with Orchestra. He was enamoured. Finally, he decided to approach a subject he had been dodging.

"You were incredible at Euphoria," he said shyly. His horns blushed through the pancake makeup.

"What? But--" she stuttered, "You saw that? Oh yes, I remember you from Rhanque Baptoose's lair! With the pale fellow! But how are you here? I thought everyone there was destroyed!"

"Yeah. I escaped. That's how I ended up floating around in space."

"I hated that place. I'm glad it's gone. That Kancorian woman saved my life. I hope she escaped."

"Gekko? Yeah, I'm sure she did. We're pretty tight, y'know. She's okay," Aye said, immediately regretting his name-dropping tone.

"You *know* her??" she asked excitedly.

"Oh yeah! We go way back." Her excitement had him regret regretting his name-dropping tone.

Over the next three breaks Aye-Aye of Towerscape and Orchestra Balloo of Flet laughed and shared stories. Most of these stories were tales of Orchestra's childhood, as Aye knew that keeping his mouth shut about *his* past would probably be for the best if he wished for her to stay. And if he wished for her to keep down her lunch.

"I like you Aye," Orchestra said after a short pause at the end of a story she was telling about falling down a flight of stairs before her first performance as an acrobat.

He was stunned again. He looked down at the floor. He shifted in his seat. He felt itchy. His eyes watered. He wanted to say *"I love you, and I don't care about anything else in the universe, let's run away together"* when she leaned over and kissed him. This didn't make him any less stunned.

"I just wanted to do that for real. Not in front of an audience because we're supposed to. Just once."

Aye couldn't speak.

"It's really too bad. You are *so* sweet," she added.

"Wait, what? Just once? Too bad? So sweet?" he asked, but was cut off by R'k and a stagehand rounding them up.

"Time for the big finale!" R'k boomed in with a welcoming smile. "We go off book a bit in this last scene. Another tradition. You also didn't get the re-write, sorry. Easy-peasy though. Just follow my lead!" He put his arm around Aye. "It's really too bad. You are *so* sweet," he added.

All actors, including a heavily costumed Gradi Ohsa Vallasoupia-Gallor held hands and made their way through the curtains for the final wedding banquet scene. Aye could've sworn that he saw Gradi mouth "It's really too bad. You were *so* sweet," to him.

"Must be another theatrical superstition," he thought to himself.

~~~

THE ROTTEN LOVERS

BOOK AND MUSIC BY:

MALATE'W KRISTY-R'EE

<u>ACT SEVENTEEN</u>

<u>Big Finale!</u>

The lights come up on the wedding of Failcotte and Glass Tina. All roles are there on stage as guests, including Gradi Ohsa Vallasoupia-Gallor as the wedding officiating priestess.

Even the lame waiter is there. The orchestra brings their instruments onto the stage and start to play the traditional Veroseralien wedding song. Its major chords become minor chords. All joy, gone.

<u>SONG -- "REVENGE OF THE VEROSERALIENS"</u>

(GRADI/PRIESTESS:)

ONE NIGHT, A PEACEFUL NIGHT, THEY CAME DOWN FROM THE STARS,

ONE NIGHT, ONE DECENT NIGHT, THEY BROUGHT GUNS AND BATTLE SCARS,

THEY STARTED WITH THE CHILDREN, THE CRIPPLED AND THE OLD,

WHO THEY DIDN'T KILL, THEY TORTURED IN BLINDFOLD...

THEY SANG...

(ALL:)

LITTLE LILAC FACE, WE DON'T SEE YOUR TEARS,

LITTLE LILAC FACE, WE DON'T RECOGNIZE YOUR FEARS,

UGLY LITTLE LILAC FACE, YOU DON'T DESERVE A PLACE,

*IN THIS HUMONGOUS UNIVERSE, THERE'S NO ROOM FOR
YOU IN SPACE.*

(DEWLOCK AND GLASS TINA:)
*ONE NIGHT, ONE SUMMER NIGHT, THEY BURNED OUR
HOUSES DOWN,*
*ONE NIGHT, ONE PERFECT NIGHT, THEY WENT ANOTHER
ROUND,*
*THEY SKINNED OUR KING, AND SHOT OUR QUEEN, AND
TOPPLED THEIR PROUD THRONES,*
*THEY KICKED HEADS IN, WE COULDN'T WIN, FOR SOUP
THEY USED OUR BONES...*

THEY SANG...

(ALL:) (making their way into the audience)
LITTLE LILAC FACE, WE DON'T SEE YOUR TEARS,
LITTLE LILAC FACE, WE DON'T RECOGNIZE YOUR FEARS,
*UGLY LITTLE LILAC FACE, OUR HATRED'S JOINED BY
EVERY RACE!*
*(ONLY A HANDFUL GOT AWAY AND FOUND OUR HOME IN
SPACE.)*

THIS NIGHT, THIS VERY NIGHT, WE GET REVENGE UPON
VEX 4,
THIS NIGHT, THIS VERY NIGHT, IT'S YOUR TURN YOU
FILTHY BOORS,
WE'LL TURN OUR MERRY FEAST AROUND, VEROSERAL
AVENGED,
WE HOPE YOU ENJOYED YOUR LAST BIG SHOW, AS WE
GET OUR REVENGE...

The priestess draws her dagger and slits the throat of an audience member. All follow suit. And feed until every last audience member, and the traitor Failcotte the Fragile is dead.

END.

~~~

It didn't take long before the audience on Vex 4 had become a bloody hurricane of mass panic and gross flesh.

The Veroseralien actors, musicians, stagehands, and crew pounced around from confused Vexian to terrified Vexian ripping out throats, tearing off limbs, and biting grapefruit sized chunks out of the once fascinated (and ironically, dinner theatre) audience.

Aye was still on stage. Again, at a time of great craziness, he couldn't move. He stood helpless in a puddle of his own urine, wondering how he had missed the signs that he had been rehearsing a terrible musical with a bunch of lunatics.

Especially after the cafeteria lady in the basement of his old MUU (Ministry of Universal Upkeep) office tower had told him time and time again, "Never trust anyone who doesn't like bok choy, guy. It's nature's cabbage!" He had never missed his old Back-up Assistant Flood Water Absorber job as much as he did at that moment, nor did he miss that mad old cafeteria woman that was obsessed with cruciferous vegetables almost as much as The Ilt-por-un-Ilt Players.

He felt his hand in someone else's hand. This should have been comforting. It was *not*. R'k W'a Rkwa-Rkwa held it tight and smiled at him.

"I really am sorry about this, poor fella. It's kinda funny...and probably why you made it this far with us at all...but old Earth got the whole devil thing from an ancient accidental visit from *your* people, the Towerscapians.

"*Likewise*, they got a bunch of legends from one of *our* visits there. You see," he said proudly, even being a mesmerizing storyteller in this moment of extreme, scarring duress.

"In our native Veroseralien language, '*Ilt-por-un-Ilt*' translates to English as '*Eye for an Eye*', our ship '*Deck Dallop*' means '*Death Dealler*' and '*Veroseral*'', itself, roughly translates to '*Vampire*'.

"Oh, we're not those silly supernatural storybook creatures...I mean, how can anything be *supernatural*? You're either natural or your not, amiright? Ha! But anyway...we're where those legends *came* from. No, none of that undead stuff, or mirror/stake/garlic/silver bullshit. Oh, but we were sooooooo brutal to the Earthlings!"

Aye didn't hear a word of this. He just stared at R'k, and thought of Orchestra's betrayal as well. He felt a profound disappointment sink into his pee-soaked feet.

He looked back out over the slaughter. He watched a large, round man have his head pulled off. He watched a snooty upperclass woman become the Sunday roast for the Veroseralien woman who had, just hours before, almost choked him with pancake makeup dust.

"Hey. *I'm* not gonna do it. Just doesn't feel right. So run. You won't get far; we've been doing this a long time. But feel like you are at least fighting for your life and not about to die standing in your own piss," R'k winked. He slapped Aye on the back to break him out of his statuesque state.

And Aye ran. He ran back through the curtains, feeling like a fly trapped in an old cobweb. As he broke free to the backstage side, lame waiter Ampex Vooshy-Balair-Sangria sat at one of the collapsible tables drinking from the bottle that R'k had given Aye earlier.

"Well looky here. I got myself a little demon. A fragile little demon," he laughed smugly. He got to his feet, swigged back the rest of the grain alcohol, smashed the bottle on the table and moved in on Aye like a circling northern negglie.

"I don't need the broken bottle. As you've probably noticed by now...we are remarkably strong. I like your little horns, but they got nothin' on *these* babies..." he laughed, throwing down the bottle and baring his teeth. Aye had never noticed how sharp their teeth looked before. "I know, right? All the better to eat you with, my dear!"

He swooped in on Aye, knocking him down. His mouth was ready to bite. "Any last idiot words, Topher?"

"My horns *aren't* little," Aye mumbled meekly as Ampex struck. His teeth did not even break flesh before he was lying dead on the ground next to Aye, the broken bottle stuck in the side of his neck.

Orchestra grabbed his hand and helped him up.

"There is a sewer grate near the costume rack. Go down it. Hide. Or follow it out. Just get out of here."

Aye blinked seven or eight times before he asked "You're coming with me, right?"

"No. The theatre life has me under its spell. As does the taste of humanoid flesh. More so the taste of humanoid flesh. They kinda got me hooked before they rescued you. Only took one meal, I'm ashamed to say. Now they've accepted me as one of their own. Please don't hate me."

"I could never hate you, Orchestra Balloo. I lo--" his words were interrupted by a last kiss.

(BOTH:)

YOU ARE FRAGILE, I AM TOO

IF I BREAK YOU, I'LL BREAK TOO...

She went back through the curtains for her Vexian dinner, broken after breaking too.

Aye climbed down the sewer grate into the stink. As his eyes adjusted to the dark ahead, he heard Gradi Ohsa Vallasoupia-Gallant, now backstage, yelling at some of her bloodthirsty theatrical minions to "find the damn Topher!"

R'k stood above the grate while she screamed. He casually looked down, catching Aye's eye, and winked at him before running off to fruitlessly continue his "search".

Aye didn't move for a very long time. The worst part was that he couldn't get "*Fix Your Teeth for True Love!*" out of his head. It was infuriatingly catchy.

CHAPTER TWENTY-FOUR

Sometimes the tiny little tidbits of joy found buried under humongous banks of shit could feel so huge, even in comparison to their monumental shit backdrop.

Aye was still missing. Those in charge of *everything* were still against them. The battle scars (both physical and mental) were starting to pile up on each other and criss-cross like a 3D road map of purgatory, *and* an egg containing a deadly embryo was rolling about all over the cargo bay floor like a pin-dangling cute-grenade.

Yet here they were, killers and fools...arms wrapped around a tree. Laughing. Crying tears of joy. Laughing more. (Disbelief!)

There would be much time to sink back into the shit bank later. For now, they were proving that some reunions were better than winning lotteries.

Clory was weak and husky, but she was happy. She would not be able to part with Potto for the time being. The sap that she had used to heal him, that harmlessly contaminated his ridiculous blood and enabled her to draw him to her through space like a magnet, needed to be shared for a while. Like a pre-mall Earth car battery, she just needed the boost and to run for a bit to start charging herself up.

Two small jumper-cable branches pierced his skin, but he did not complain. He was too wrapped up in the moment of laughing tears, quietly joy-weeping to himself inside his odorous protective space shell.

Besides, he was not a complainer, grumbler or whiner. These things rarely occurred to him.

Teeg put her forehead against her leafy sister, who was looking a bit too "late fall/early winter" for her liking, and told her "Thank you. Thank you. Thank you. A million times, thank you my sister. I should have said it so many times before. Thank you, thank you."

Gekko climbed up into her branchy hair, which jutted up like a dry, woody fountain. She continued her hugging and kind-of-terrifying-to-an-outsider yeee-like silent laughing. She offered many tiny tender kisses.

"I...I...I..." She was too overwhelmed to speak, even through her thoughts.

"I know, my love," Clory reassured silently. "Keep kissing, though. I like it. Never stop kissing, okay?"

"How can we help you, Clory?" Teeg transmitted.

"Give me time. Give me oxygen and food. Give me the Quarol for a short spell. His blood still contains my healing sap. That is how I was able to draw him to me. I'm afraid it was horribly painful for him, but we were both lucky to find one another," Clory thought.

Potto smiled widely, though no one could see him through his sick-caked helmet.

"We should probably remove the space suit," Clover piped up from the back of the room. No one had noticed her there, and for good reason. It wasn't *she* that had gone missing, much to Teeg's dismay. She didn't know Clory well, but she cried nonetheless because that's who Clover was.

"If we *must*," Teeg shrugged with a sly smile, only half-joking. It's not that she disliked the oddball Quarol, but she didn't want him ruining the mood with senseless yammering, which he was more than likely to do. He may not have been a grumbler, but he definitely was a senseless yammerer.

"The Quarol..." Clory continued telepathically. "We have a bond. I couldn't get past his block, but I could see faint images on the other side, and I know where it came from. I think with the Oian's help we could break through."

Just then the egg rolled over and knocked Clover in the ankle. She picked it up to examine it.

"Oh, n-n-n-n-n-n-n-no-no-no-no-nooooo, *hell* no," Teeg shouted as if her words were fired from a rapid-fire machine gun that shot no's instead of bullets. "Put that down. That's going back out into space."

"Is this a Teddy Bear egg?" Clover asked excitedly, shaking it next to her ear like a child shakes a birthday present. In all her years she had never seen one.

"It's evil. A whole lotta horribleness. Top-shelf abomination. I wouldn't hold it so close to your face. Y' know, if you *like* that face."

Clover put the egg down slowly. She was curious but not sui-cidal, and after many millennia, she had grown to quite like her face. It was a good face. A "top-shelf" face.

"Quickly...out the airlock. Before it does something stupid like hatch." Teeg demanded.

"Noooooooooooo!!!!!" Potto yelled inside the heads of Clory, Teeg and Gekko, causing them all to squint.

"Who said that?" Gekko thought.

"Potto is in here with us until we disconnect. Well, he's with me always, but for now, he's with you, too," Clory answered.

"We cannot destroy that egg. It's just a baby!" Potto pleaded.

"Oooooh yes we can. And we will. That's gonna be a nasty lit-tle baby Toobli Dentatan. Oh, it will be adorable, but an adorable killing machine. There is no nurture. These bastards are *all* na-ture. All instinct, and that instinct is killer."

"Actually, he's right for once. We have to save it. Not for cud-dles or little feet pitter-patter. We need to stop on Vex 4 for fuel and we have no way of paying for it. A Teddy Bear egg is worth a *fortune*..." Gekko added.

"Ugh. Fine. It better not hatch before then," Teeg said rolling her eyes. "Find somewhere safe to store it. Like in concrete."

Clover, who had not heard a word of that in-head conversa-tion, was busy prying off Potto's helmet. She was greeted by a horrible waft of regurgitated (and twice-liquified) ham and cheese on rye.

"Ok. We get fuel, and then back out to look for Aye, right?" Potto said aloud, happy to be free of his stinking fish bowl-like prison.

Sadly, no-one knew how to answer.

He took a deep breath of the ship's non-vomity air. He never noticed how sweet it smelled. Like old man hair and accidentally laundered pocket candy.

~~~

Though he had not specifically created it, somehow between the H.C. (happiness chip) and the L.C. (laughing chip), an A.C. (amusement chip) had created itself inside Mel Million Max. It made the crazy violence in the vintage Earth horror movies even more disturbingly enjoyable.

As he waited to attack, having kept his distance and showing great restraint, his life-like circuitry was fantasizing about killing Aye at a summer camp, in his dreams followed by snappy one-liners, with a nightmarish possessed doll, strapped to a torture chair after having to solve a series of painful and macabre puzzles, and being fed to various giant sharks, zombies and inbred hillbillies.

He had been following the Shiv's comings and goings very closely, yet he had no idea that Aye was not, in fact, on the ship. When last he had scanned, it was docked at Euphoria and Aye was on board then in his usual drunken dormancy. He had watched it escape as that horrible den of perversion was destroyed.

But it was almost time to strike. They were fuelling on Vex 4, and he would catch them as they left. He would have Aye finally, and he would kill Aye over and over.

He needed to stop thinking about it briefly and do some crosswords and Sudoku before his H.C. burned out from over-use. He was great at Sudoku. He could finish a whole book of Sudoku in less than a second.

As he waited, however, he was startled (which was not an easy thing to do to a meccanik), as several Kancorian-manned Vexian ships zipped by his craft on their way to the planet.

He had waited this long. A little bit longer wasn't going to kill him. He made popcorn for effect. He couldn't eat it, but he loved the idea of a food being inedible until it explodes.

~~~

As the Shiv pulled into a fuelling station on the surface of Vex 4, Potto rubbed his neck, circling his fingers over the holes where Clory had been plugged into him through the spring-flex neck of his space suit. Now that he was free of it (and her), they were merely small, mildly itchy bumps, like tiny insect bites, and nothing more. He gazed and dazed out an observation window.

He marvelled at the site of the nearby city that the fuelling station sat on the edge of. Giant billboards advertising rock-bottom prices of nearby bungalows obscured most of the view, but the lights from Krank City at night were like holiday decorations.

Promises of "0% down!" "Newly renovated!" "Definitely not haunted!" "Prefab at its Most Fab!" and "Now 76% Yaygher free!" were enticing. He wondered what a bungalow was. Perhaps a type of beverage or small pet. He was happy to hear that someone's beverage or small pet was no longer haunted.

It had only been an hour since he had separated from Clory, and although he still had her sap running through his veins and was relieved she was on the mend, he felt a tremendous loss. He had quite liked being attached to her. It was the most physically intimate that he'd been with anyone since being filled with Tractos poison.

Teeg was getting the egg safe to take out to the attendant for barter. Gekko was at the console preparing the ship to take on fuel while checking the water supply and coolant. Clover was off practising hypnosis. She would need to be in peak shape if she were to help the sentient tree find out the truth about the sentient Potto.

It started raining outside the ship. The city lights and a bungalow billboard promise of "Lonely? Now more ants!" were obscured by the wet, but the Shiv was getting a much-needed bath, and it made Knutt calm slightly. An uptight ship was not an efficient ship.

Teeg put the cantaloupe-sized egg in a heavy, padded cargo

transport case. She took heavy chain and wrapped it around the case for extra security, and left the ship wishing she had an umbrella. As she looked across the well-lit fuelling station at all the other ships filling up, she noticed Jorge Jorge Jorge.

She ducked behind a rack of flotsam grease. This was going to be tricky. She swerved past a second rack of jetsam oil, in the opposite direction. She'd have to go around to a different attendant to avoid conflict. Normally she loved a good fight, but she was tired and really just wanted to relax with a bottle of something very, very strong.

Flotsam grease and jetsam oil were items she saw at every fuelling station and had always wondered what they were used for. They were always together like salt and pepper. But that was not on her mind at this time.

She stopped in her tracks and rubbed her eyes. Jorge Jorge Jorge had somehow impossibly zipped around to the other side.

Upon further stealthy investigation she counted four more Jorge Jorge Jorges fuelling various stolen Vexian ships. They were all just a little shorter than the original Koncorian hunter, and all just a tad less "sharp" looking, but the giant was among them, she could feel it in her bones.

She got back to the ship and started fuelling without paying. There was no time to pay. No time to barter. They already had The Node against them, they might as well have the Vexian authorities on their backs as well for fuel theft. As she filled the tank a large reptilian hand grabbed her by the throat and lifted her off the ground.

"I hear you've been very bad, Teeg," the original Jorge Jorge Jorge said in his tiny tot voice. It would have been hard to take him seriously if it hadn't been for the claws and fangs and hulking.

"Don't believe everything you hear, you ogre," Teeg managed through gags and gasps.

"You shouldn't call people names, you know. It's *meeeeeean*," he whined.

"Oh come on!" she thought. "It's one thing to talk like a little girl, but it's another to say things that a little girl would say. He has to be doing it on purpose."

"Put...me...down...let's...talk about...this," she said out loud. "I am...warning...you..."

"Ha ha ha ha ha ha!!" he giggled as if he were being tickled at his third birthday party.

Jorge Jorge Jorge wasn't used to being threatened. He wasn't used to being made fun of. He wasn't used to anyone knowing his one weak spot: the scale-less underside of his armoured scrotum. He wasn't used to fighting anyone with thigh-high, pointed boots.

When Teeg landed that pointed toe into that soft, fleshy area beneath his inexplicable gonads, it was apparent he *also* was not used to dropping a victim, or falling to the ground, feeling as if his testes were in his gizzard.

Teeg didn't waste time with unhooking the fuel line. She grabbed the egg-case and ran back to the hatch, closing it tight. "Knutt! Lock that hatch! Lock all hatches! Lock everything that locks!"

Within seconds the ship was surrounded by angry Jorge Jorge Jorge clones. Within more seconds Gekko, Clory, Clover and Potto had all joined her on the bridge.

"We have to get Potto off this ship. He's too important. If we are going down, he can't go down with us!" Clory thought with urgency.

Teeg turned to Clover. "You and Potto are getting off here. You are going to hide out in Krank City. We will get rid of these idiots and then come back and find you."

"But what if they..." Clover started sadly, overwhelmed with concern.

"Then you'll have to find another way to get him to O-bode. Get him there any way possible. Don't trust anyone. Maybe that guardian angel of yours will come and get you and give you a ride."

"But you! You!" Potto asked, even more overwhelmed with concern.

"Don't worry, my Potto. I will always find you," Clory said directly to his brain.

Potto calmed ever so slightly, but it was quite clear that he didn't want to leave them again. Ever again.

"Okay. How do we get off the ship with all those monsters out there?" Clover asked, giving in.

"I have an idea..." Teeg said as quickly as those words had ever been spoken.

~~~

The Node stood in front of his mirror. He looked sadly at his hair. He looked sadly at the fading shine on his marvellous chassis. He wondered if he would ever look good again.

General Eppie tried to match The Node's look of grave disappointment, but the joy in his horrible heart was making it difficult. He also tried to *sound* sincerely disappointed, but the little fits of giggling gave him away.

"Would you like to see the records again?" he offered The Node.

"No." The Node said very, very quietly, and the living definition of sullen.

Vrume stood before them, hands cuffed behind his back. He was very, very cross with himself. Not only had he killed an innocent and uncommonly handsome Sammolite, but he had underestimated Eppie.

Eppie had used the Sammolite as bait to further prove Vrume's backstabbing. The damning information had actually been on a mediocre-looking Trampolyte's computer.

Now it was on The Node's.

After millions of years, Vrume T'cha T'cha's life was going to come to an end.

CHAPTER TWENTY-FIVE

Civilizations don't begin with computers and microwave ovens and dentists. They begin with staring at fire and raw food and stinking, rotting mouths.

They don't begin with telephones and printing presses or even quills, parchment and donkeys...so spreading news and gossip was once very difficult on *every* planet at one time. Secrets were easily kept, murders easily overlooked, scandals averted and birthday parties often missed. Oh, but how things change.

Within one hour of Vrume T'cha T'cha's capture, the news was not only on every set of lips on Lyme Node (or various alien lip equivalents), but that news had made its way to Squambog, Barbohd, all the inhabited Vexes, and even as far as Hephmote, where Vrume's army of rescued assistants and prisoners trained, and awaited the overtaking of The Node.

The news even made its way to Chagrin, although only to one adorable Pelican Teddy Bear that had found an old antique iWatch on a crashed ships' time capsule, which it *then* connected to the signal of a dead Blankton's mostly-destroyed ship that was floating in space near the planet. It used half of a swamp potato and a pet eel to keep it charged.

On Lyme Node, a human named Dak Floodman was already

planning a rescue. He had been training to be the very next assistant, and was practising his fake death when he heard the news. He immediately contacted his wife Jev, who was still in the Lyme Node prison awaiting her go at tank-suit manicure education. They had both been thrown in jail without a trial for complaining to The Node Middle School Board for losing their daughter.

The (then) thirteen-year-old Breva Floodman had gone on a school trip to visit The Node Museum Of Node-Approved Node History and Awesome Node-Inspired Wax Museum. She never made it back to the school.

As a student of the Machine Detailing and Beauty School, Dak had access to the prisons and it only took an additional half hour to rally every prisoner (not guilty of a Tractos-level crime) to attempt an escape. Vrume was their hero, he was in trouble, and he needed them now.

With the entire population of the third most heavily attended school on Lyme Node, *and* the most heavily populated prison on the planet, things were about to get nutty. The Node Guard was the biggest army in the galaxy, but many of them were off patrolling the universe for Potto and Aye.

The Node Guard *may* have been the biggest army in the galaxy, but *prisoners* made up the biggest population in the Node-run universe. Prisons were everywhere. There were so many laws to be broken that as far as The Node was concerned, anyone *not* in the Guard was merely a prisoner that hadn't been processed yet...mostly due to a lack of time and the necessity of practical services. Garbage needed to be collected. Ships needed to be fixed. Bounty hunters needed to bounty hunt. Office workers needed to office work. Torturers needed to torture.

The fact that this particular prison was Lyme Node's *largest* spoke volumes to the sheer volume of the prison.

It started as a prison riot. Complete with chairs thrown, (faked) fights started, and everyone yelling and being ridiculously unruly. The Node Guard easily kept this at bay by simply not unlocking any cell doors. It was much easier to sit back and let them all kill each other and clean up the mess later than to engage.

However, those doors *didn't* stay locked. The entire Machine

Detailing and Beauty School came down on the Guard Patrol, rioting on *their* side of the cell doors as well.

Many shots were fired, many lives lost. Dak and Jev Floodman were thankfully not among the corpses. Many guards were slaughtered, many prisoners as well, and quite *possibly* many students, though it was hard to tell with them because they had become so good at faking their deaths.

They now had their own army, but that army would be no match for the much bigger army of guards that were already being called in to surround the outside of the prison. They would all still have to escape the prison complex unseen, and keeping an entire army unseen would be like hiding an elephant behind a dead fern.

Vark Burk was one prisoner that *didn't* take part in the riot. He was old and had been living in his cell for longer than he, or anyone else, could remember. He had his own, much safer, escape plan on the go. Although he did see some merit in the safety-in-numbers approach, he had spent the last twenty-five years digging a tunnel, and with that amount of work, it was hard to abandon. He got the idea from every prison movie he had ever seen from every planet he'd ever been on, and had been digging it with a rusty potato peeler, a soiled oven mitt and a lot of elbow grease. Luckily, he had several elbows. He kept it hidden behind an old motivational poster of a kitten shitting into a saxophone.

Vark's tunnel was widely known by other prisoners. Now, much to his dismay, he had an entire army climbing, single file, behind his terrible poster and through the small tunnel. Once out they would go through Torture Tower's understaffed underground parking garage, and climb up the narrow ladder of an elevator shaft-in-repair.

This was going to take a while, and there would be many more deaths. Some from the Node Guard, and some from clumsiness.

The Node was untouchable. He would be nowhere near his Torture Tower. This was a good thing. If he *were* there, there would be no way to get past. Not only did he keep an even bigger army around him, but he, himself, was an indestructible killing machine. Now with an unruly comb-over.

~~~

Clover sat nervously next to Potto, who really wasn't nervous at all.

They were crammed together in the tiny, modest Shiv escape pod. It was a pod only made for one. Clover was not claustrophobic by any means; this is not what was bothering her. She was bothered, nervous and downright terrified at the idea of being shot out of the ship while it was grounded.

The plan was simple. They would be shot out in the vague direction of Krank City, hopefully taking out at least eight of the sub-par Jorge Jorge Jorges that surrounded the ship, while escaping the rest of them.

Teeg had promised them that the pod was shielded, which was true. She didn't tell them that the shielding was weak and very temporary.

Once the pod had stopped, they were to eject themselves from it and run. Any direction would do (except back towards the ship, which Potto probably would have done if not instructed otherwise) and they were to stick together and hideout until (and if) the Shiv or any of its crew survived and came looking for them.

Teeg had her doubts about that last part. Gekko had her doubts as well. Clory had no doubts, she was certain they would not be back, but she kept it under her bark.

"Are you ready? Here we go...countdown from three," Teeg told Clover through the transmitter.

"Ok. Be safe. And thank you," Clover said, her voice wavering.

"Do you want us to pick you up something nice while we're there?" Potto offered. "A couple of bungalows? They now come with more ants!"

Teeg didn't countdown. She just fired.

The pod shot out of the side of the ship and immediately took out the planned eight Jorge Jorge Jorges, and set another two on fire. They patted themselves out as they watched the escape pod do what it was made to do: escape.

Sparks, flames and chunks of asphalt and dirt flew out everywhere as they moved at a speed close to Mach one. They skidded directly into the residential outskirts of the city like the fastest wheel-less race car imaginable.

They took out fences, garages, fire hydrants, front porches, garbage bins, a high-end clothing boutique, a take-out pancake joint, and countless small economy cars. Clover closed her eyes and gritted her teeth so hard they didn't even feel like teeth anymore through her cramping jaw. Potto screamed like he was on the best rollercoaster ever made.

When they finally came to a stop they sat for mere seconds before Clover snapped out of the shock, and hit the eject button. They were both hurled out and immediately smacked into the ceiling of the living room they were in. Stunned for a moment like birds that had hit a window, they lay on a bright puce shag carpet with a family looking at them, suitably, and justifiably stunned as well.

Bisher Donut, his wife Faridelle, daughter Grezzy, and sons Moof and Cranstin all surrounded the smoking pod with gaping mouths full of half-chewed stroganoff.

Bisher had just had a long day. His job installing sliding frosted shower doors on pre-made moulded tub surrounds had not been as exciting as it had sounded, and his supervisor was cruel and unnecessary.

This was his time to eat his dinner and relax. This was his time to ignore his children and complain about the government. It was *his* time. Not "intruders that have interrupted my stroganoff, destroyed half of my used bungalow and maybe killed Grandpa" time.

Bisher Donut's face quickly went from stunned to violently furious. "Moof, get my gun. Grezzy, let the dogs up from the basement."

"What about me, Poppy-pop?" Cranstin asked.

"Call my insurance broker and then see if you can find Grandpa." Bisher barked as Faridelle started whacking Potto with a rolled-up copy of "Mediocre Seats and Benches" magazine.

As Clover and Potto jumped to their feet, Bisher was already firing shots with his laser-ball fun gun. Ferocious dog barks, growls and snarls could be heard quickly approaching.

"Run!" Clover yelled to Potto as she darted out the huge burning hole in the side of the Donut residence. Potto was just about to run when two Vexian grub hounds entered snapping at him. A third took off after Clover.

"Adorable! Are these bungalows?" he asked excitedly, *"Are they haunted?"* he followed up with in a hushed voice.

A laser-ball shot hit a faux-brass lamp inches from his head. He shook the dogs off and ran for the undamaged backdoor. He quickly made his way out and down the back steps into a fenced-in back yard.

As the door swung open, the Donut family (and their vicious pets) came out yelling threats, but Potto was already gone.

He found himself under the backdoor steps in a hole. He had been dragged in by his dog-chewed pantleg by a rat-like Yaygher clone.

"Shhhhhhhh!" the Yaygher whispered.

They sat quietly as an angry Bisher and his angry family checked their poorly painted lawnmower shed. They made their way through a gate at the far end of the backyard and into the alley beyond.

"Thanks! Those bungalows have quite a bite!" Potto finally said, smiling at his new friend, who he couldn't help but notice was chewing on his arm.

"Don't freak out 'r nothin'...I gots no teeth. I just wanna taste ya. Mix my spit around with *yer* flavour and make a little arm soup in mah mouth," the Yaygher mumbled quietly with his mouth full of elbow.

"Sure," Potto laughed.

They sat under the back porch for an additional ten minutes before Potto started to get sore and uncharacteristically annoyed. "Can you switch arms?" he politely asked wincing.

"I was just about to ask..." replied the Yaygher.

"Yaaaaay!"

~~~

Clover watched the flaming Donut abode for almost an hour from the tree the grub hound had chased her up. She hadn't known that grub hounds could climb trees, and it sat on a branch next to her getting a good behind-the-ear scratch.

Clover had been around since the beginning of everything. She had learned a few things about animal taming along the way. Most animals only needed a quick bit of eye-contact with her before trusting her, submitting to her, falling in love with her and wanting to make her arms their forever home.

From their branch she could see the long, still flaming pod trail leading to the huge hole in the front of the house. She watched as Bisher, Faridelle, Grezzy and Moof wandered around with the other two dogs, searching for Potto. Searching for her.

By their idiotic expressions and ever-building rage, she was quite confident that he had escaped. Once they finally gave up, she would find him. He was the only Quarol (and the only Quarol with albinism) on the planet; he wouldn't be hard to spot amongst the blue-skinned Vexians. Hopefully *she* found him before the Donuts did, or the authorities once the Donuts eventually reported it.

Cranstin came out of the house, looking for his father. He was holding a smoking boot.

"Poppy-pop! I found grandpa!" he hollered.

~~~

Perhaps part of General Eppie's complete lack of empathy was due, in part, to *extreme* privilege. It was easier to hurt someone when one didn't know what it felt like to be hurt, and had always been feared by everyone (including one's parents). Eppie had never been hurt by anyone physically or mentally. He had only been annoyed and angered by others.

He was very surprised to find out that, not only did punches to the face really hurt, but they hurt more and more as they progressed. A punch to healthy skin was painful, but a punch to already-punched skin was unbearable.

There he sat, tied to a chair, surrounded by prisoners, students and dead guards as Jev Floodman punched his smug face over and over again. It was Vrume that stopped her.

"We have to go..." he said softly, relieved and flattered they had gone to so much trouble for him.

"But where?" Dak asked. "We hadn't really thought past this part."

Eppie laughed at this through swollen lips. "There's nowhere to go, you idiots. More guards will come. All of you are going to die. I will be eating multi-coloured macarons off the bare ass of my handsome toady, safely back in my flat, within the hour. Perhaps while gazing out my window at the huge bonfire of your burning bodies as I get ready for a well-deserved nappy-nap."

"Perhaps if we took him as a hostage and then killed him," Dak suggested.

"No. Leave him here. I don't want his life to be over so quickly. That's too good for him," Vrume said, limping towards Eppie. He leaned in, his messed-up, tortured face only inches from the General's battered mug. "Kenny Kenny Kenny Kenny Kenny Kenny Kenny Kenny Kenny Kenny," he said, not caring if he sounded childish.

Eppie went from smug to furious by the time the second "Kenny" was out. His face matching his small curl of fuchsia hair.

The rescue party (or at least the parts of it that fit in the room) had not taken into account that The Node *loved* his hidden doorways and passages. They were built into every room. He loved surprising people. Such a door opened up directly behind Vrume, and a laser pistol was now at his temple, a guard at his back.

"This one is coming with me or I shoot him. And untie General Eppie. He's coming with me as well!" shouted the guard loud enough to cause a temporary din in Vrume's ear, even through the guard's armoured mask.

"Thatta boy!" Eppie cheered, getting over the infuriating name calling and wishing he could throw his arms up in the air.

A shot was heard and the guard fell dead, again freeing Vrume. Another guard, much shorter, stood where the first had been. The second guard's helmet came off.

"Breva!!" shouted Dak as tears exploded from his eyes. He and Jev ran towards their daughter and held her tight.

"I was kidnapped on the school trip by an unusually not-ugly Sammolite. He was going to sell me into the sex trade, but I escaped. By that time, I discovered you were both in prison. So I joined The Node Guard, which is actually surprisingly simple to do..." she recounted. "My intent was to break you both out. Maybe leave Lyme Node forever."

"Oh fer the love of..." Eppie complained, his eyes rolling so extraordinarily they made a sound.

Vrume's shoulders dropped the tiniest bit. He didn't feel quite so bad for murdering that fancy Sammolite.

"I found out something quite remarkable and top secret. Did you know the prison was actually a ship? It was first built as a huge planetary escape pod for The Node and his devoted followers. All the higher-ups. But his own Chamber Tower later became that. A much nicer one. So, they made that old one into a prison!" Breva continued.

"How do we engage it? How do we fly a *building?*" Vrume asked, surprised he did not already know this. It was one piece of information The Node had not trusted him with while he worked on that magnificent chassis.

"I've also been learning about *that*. And you as well, Mr. T'cha T'cha. Can we take it away from here? Can we go to your secret planet?"

Vrume smiled widely at Breva.

"Ugh. Of *course* you have a secret planet. You. Are. The. Worst." Eppie snarked.

Vrume smiled a very different kind of smile at Eppie.

~~~

Vark Burk had just put his stupid shitting kitten poster back up when it was torn down again from behind. He sighed heavily and rolled over on his mattress as an army of prisoners and students broke back *into* prison, single file.

CHAPTER TWENTY-SIX

"There's got to be a place around here that has *real* soup," said Potto to the Yaygher.

He had been very accommodating. Much more accommodating than anyone should have been while having their arm gummed and sucked on. Much more accommodating than anyone ever had been with a Yaygher in the history of Yayghers.

"*Real* soup?" the Yaygher perked up. "With real soup innit?"

Potto checked his pockets. He only had the few credits Teeg could spare giving him. Instinctively he knew he shouldn't waste it on buying someone else soup; his physical survival might need to count on it. But also, instinctively he knew he *should* waste it on buying someone else soup because his *mental* survival counted on that.

"Yeah, but you gotta get me out of here. I don't think the family that owns this house really likes me very much. I don't think their house likes me very much either," Potto added.

"Like *new* soup?" the Yaygher asked in disbelief (disbelief!). He, like all Yayghers, had trust issues. "I'll get y' outta here. But...I want half the soup up front. Half later. I bin burned like this before."

"Really?" Potto asked, wondering if the life of a Yaygher was far more adventurous than he had first imagined.

"Yep. By *that* guy. Shifty guy, that," the Yaygher answered pointing out between the stairs to the lawn mower shed. Another Yagher stuck his head out of the shed and looked around like a slow old tortoise sticking its head out of its shell.

"I *can't* give you half of the soup now. I don't have any soup yet," Potto said sadly.

"I don't believe you. Let me check your pockets," sneered the Yaygher.

"I have no soup in my pockets...um...what do I call you?"

"Why you wanna call me sumpin? Bad words? Interested?"

"I just want to know your name..."

"Oh. Name's Lazy Susan."

"Okay. I have no soup in my pockets, Lazy Susan. That would make them wet, and they are mostly dry."

"Hmph. Neither do I," grumbled Lazy Susan.

"I figured that by the way you're sucking on my arm. And I think you'd need pants to have a pocket." Potto was trying to be helpful, but he was really growing quite weary of being cramped under the stairs of the porch of a smouldering house belonging to a family that wanted to kill him, and with a Yaygher that was causing his skin to wrinkle with saliva.

"Can you take me somewhere where I can *buy* you soup?" he asked.

"I can do it, yep," Lazy Susan fired back, making finger guns.

Lazy Susan climbed out into the backyard cautiously and rat-like, pulling on Potto's soggy arm. Instead of heading to the main back gate and into the alley, they headed past the other Yaygher, and made their way behind the shed.

"What 'r you doin', Lazy Susan? Who's that guy?" asked the shed Yaygher.

"Shut up, Toaster-Oven. Yer dead to me."

They climbed out through a large hole dug behind the shed and out into the alley. They then climbed down a sewer grate. The smell was something that Potto could barely stand, but it didn't seem to bother the Yaygher at all. It smelled like stroganoff that had been sitting too long inside a long-dead bear's long-inactive large intestine, and the freshly mowed grass of a terribly befouled dog park.

Potto noticed they were being followed. It was Toaster-Oven, the shed Yagher. They passed by another group of sewer-dwelling Yayghers.

"Evenin' Lazy Susan," one muttered.

"Evenin' Plow Mouse."

"Evenin' Lazy Susan," said another.

"Evenin' Bad Peach."

"Evenin' Lazy Susan."

"Evenin' Charlie Ankylosaurus."

"Evenin' Lazy Susan."

"Evenin' Other Lazy Susan."

"What cha doin', Lazy Susan?"

"This guy is buyin' soup, Stupid Cowboy."

Soon Potto was being escorted through the sewers of a suburb of Krank City by forty-seven hungry Yayghers.

They all climbed out of another grate in front of the diviest dive. It was a greasy spoon that could more aptly be described as a spoon *floating* in grease....a spoon made out of grime held together with earwax. It was called "Here Is Food!", and it was the only food establishment that would serve Yayghers in the entire universe.

The only reason it existed at all was because health inspectors were too afraid to go near the place for fear of catching the type of illness that makes one's intestines come out simply by being within a few blocks of the place.

Potto was getting nervous. He didn't like to disappoint anyone, and he didn't like to say no. He worried that he would not have enough money to buy forty-seven Yayghers soup. He hoped Lazy Susan would send them all away. That he would yell, "Plow Mouse! Bad Peach! Charlie Ankylosaurus! Other Lazy Susan! Stupid Cowboy! Blister Boy! Cucumber Bandersnatch! Doughy Brad! The Marvelous Bandage! Batman Freud! Ignatius Idiom! Farzzle Gorp! Toaster-Oven! Smoochy Pembroke! Francesca W. McGillicuddy! Smokin' Bobby Noodles! Chad Sombrero! Seeping Anson's Ghost! Brother Bratwurst! Mustard Fudge! Jazz Dumptruck! Shitbox Rendezvous! Li'l Barty Mazda! Fabio Panthercock! Goose Liver Candyfloss! Brigadier Horse! Chia Pillows! Softshell

Puma! Donny's Ice-cream! Chum Plunkitt! Chaughn Broughning! Plaid Dandy! Sweater Chunk! Lovehandle Scrump! Cake Fashion! Splat Bangbangboom! Mozart Go-cart! Scottish Youth-Hostile! Buzzsaw Poopstraw! Nougat Wagon! Iron Shaft! Picnic Nick! Banjo Hotdog! Pretty Tom Blancmange! Asshole the Turtle Boy! Nuts Lupus! ...go back to the sewers! He only made the deal with *me!*"

Lazy Susan said no such thing, and soon they were all inside the horrible "lounge" of this horrible "bar and grill", ordering "the soup". Before Potto could even ask about the cost, Pebbles Splotch (possible the worst Vexian to ever Vex) had buckets of split-roach/rot-corn chowder poured into a back trough where the Yayghers all went at it like ants on dripped ice cream.

Potto sat at the bar counting and recounting the few credits he had in the palm of his hand as if they would magically multiply if he kept counting them. Pebbles spotted this and came over.

"Hope you got enough there to cover this, shit-fer-brains," she said with three cigarettes sticking out of the same corner of her charming mouth at once. Before he could answer, one of the Yayghers (Blister Boy?) knocked a leg off the trough and soup came sliding down and slopped onto the floor. The Yaghers didn't notice, they kept eating, but Pebbles ran off to scream at them incoherently while trying to hoist the trough back up (and not trip over the several Yayghers that were now licking the floor).

There were six full, capped bottles of Ugly Uncle brand "Ginish Beverage and Varnish Remover" on the far end of the bar that only caught Potto's attention because they kept disappearing. A hand was slowly coming up from underneath the bar and stealing them one by one. He ducked under the bar to find the culprit. He didn't want to add six bottles of subpar alcohol to a bill he already couldn't pay.

It took a moment of blank staring to make out that there was a figure in the darkness under there. The figure squealed and was soon excitedly coming towards him in a squatted crab-walk. The dark figure pulled him off his stool and dragged him out of Here Is Food!, down the street, and into an alleyway.

~~~

Bodies do involuntary things all the time. From spastic nerve shutters, to cold shivers, to uncontrollably going for an itch. Emotions can be responsible for these things as well.

An emotionally illiterate man who has never hugged his children will still excitedly throw his arms around a dog he has been separated from for a long time. The mix of emotion with an unlikelihood of being judged as something he may (ridiculously) see as being "unmanly" gets the better of him, and his arms just involuntarily wrap around the dog as it jumps up. That dog might even be invited to lick the face of the man. The very man who thinks he is too macho to kiss his children.

Though he didn't have children (or a dog), Aye was this type of man. He wasn't a hugger. He wasn't raised by a hugger. He wasn't from a society of huggers. In fact, if a Topher were caught hugging anyone, they would end up with garbage pelted at them and then they would possibly be murdered. Usually by the one on the receiving end of the hug. Even on their birthday.

But here Aye was, standing in an alleyway, covered in refuse, pockets and pant legs stretched with clinking, stolen bottles of Ugly Uncle's Gin-ish Beverage and Varnish Remover, on a planet far from even his second home, with his arms around Potto. He squeezed hard and he laughed. The laugh turned to a cough and he doubled over.

"Aye???" Potto shrieked. He immediately started jumping up and down like that once-separated dog.

Aye started crying. This was something that was becoming easier and easier for him to do. Potto started crying, too, because crying could be very contagious.

Aye started crying harder into Potto's arms, loudly sobbing and gasping for the odd breath. The events he had witnessed with the Ilt-por-un-Ilt Players had affected him so much, decimating him to the core of his being. It had made him feel so terrified and alone that he had decided to drink gin-flavoured varnish remover until he was dead. He had already considered himself dead.

Potto felt this. This wasn't a sulking man-child crying. This wasn't a mere "Hey! Glad to see ya!" reunion hug. This was a man broken and destroyed and *very* seriously falling to pieces.

Aye was not just glad to see him. Potto was everything in the world to him at this horrible moment in his life. Potto was a warm thaw after being frozen solid. He was living, breathing defibrillator paddles.

Just when he was ready to put a gun (of sorts) to his head, he had found the smallest amount of light in the dark. At this moment Potto was the brightest light in the well-lit universe. And he wept hard because it was all so overwhelming and terrifying and hopeless, and now there was hope. Hope in the form of a hapless Quarol. A friend. A real friend to bring him back to life.

"Let's get drunk," he finally managed.

~~~

They wandered for a while, passing a bottle back and forth. If Potto had ever been drunk before, it was before his memory was taken from him. Aye was already swaggering. The suicide drink had become a celebratory drink. They only difference between the two being quantity.

"I didn't think I'd ever see you again, Baby Boy!" Aye laughed, an arm around Potto as an affectionate way to steady himself.

"Well, I knew I'd see *you* again, Aye," Potto offered.

"How? We were in space suits. In space. Just floating around! Neither of us should even be alive, much less together on the *same* planet, in the *same* city, in the *same*...uh...restaurant? Bar? Cesspool? Farm dump? *How could you possibly know?*"

"Just did. I don't remember all that has happened to us, but I do know that we probably should've died many times. But we didn't. I think Clover knows why. She says we're special, you n' me. I knew we'd see each other again because we're special."

'I'm not special, my friend. Thanks for saying so, but I'm not. I am awful. I do a lot of stupid things. I've been arrested *dozens* of times. I've only been in love *once,* shortly, and that ended in a vampire massacre. I think *you* are special. I think I'm merely a passenger on your magic special train," Aye laughed.

"Hmmm..." said Potto, thoughtfully. "You've been arrested though you're not in jail. You do stupid things; well I *am* a stupid thing. You *lived* through a vampire massacre! And you got to *be* in love, even if it was short. And I was nowhere around for any of that. *You* are special."

"You're not stupid, Potto." Aye said, almost as if he were sober. "Did you hear yourself just now? You may not remember things. You may not grasp concepts or procedures or even regular behaviour, but you make everyone around you feel special. You're the smartest person I know."

Potto smiled at this as they rested on a park bench behind a patch of shrubs where they would be out of sight. A children's playground lay before them, empty due to the late, late hour.

For what felt like a joyous lifetime, the bottle was passed back and forth and Aye told Potto of what had happened with The Rotten Lovers. How he had escaped. How he watched their theatre ship leave before being found out by the ever-slow Vexian authorities. How he had been hiding amongst the Yayghers and actual sewer rats.

Potto simply listened. He had very little to tell, for there was very little he could recall. Simple points. Clory was alive. The Shiv was chased off but would rescue them, hopefully.

They played on the swings, and a teeter-totter thingamajig. They stayed away from the slides as they had each had enough of sliding downward.

"Why *wait* to be rescued?" Aye offered. He was sufficiently drunk enough for brave stupidity. "Let's steal a ship and go *help* the Shiv! Might as well! Nothing bad can happen! We're special!" he laughed as Potto was sick on a bobbling springy horse.

~~~

It was only an hour before the sun was to come up on Krank City. Potto and Aye staggered towards the light of the far-off fuel station on the outskirts of the suburbs.

They passed (from a distance) Here Is Food! where a riot had broken out over an unpaid bill and missing alcohol. It seems the Yayghers had taken over the joint. A woman with six cigarettes, three in each charming mouth-corner, sat on the curb out front of the dive cursing to herself.

They passed (from a distance) the Donut house. The fire was now out and Bisher Donut was standing in the front yard with Vexian police and an insurance man and two of his three grub hounds.

Potto stopped in his tracks upon seeing them, far enough that he couldn't be seen by the "sliding frosted door on pre-made moulded tub surround" installer. He was forgetting something. He was forgetting some*one*. He strained to remember, but the combination of his already broken mind with the gin-ish beverage flowing through him made thinking even harder than normal.

"Ok, so we found the trail of your pod. We can just follow the destruction back to where the Shiv fired it. What's wrong?" Aye could tell something was weighing on Potto. The usual thoughtless grin had been replaced by a harrumphy scrunchy face.

"I don't know. It's all leaving my head too quickly. Kinda like when you wake up from a dream. It's right there but I can't remember it..."

"Ha! You'll wake up from your dream one day, Potto. I promise."

They followed the pod trail past flattened and burning fences, garages, fire hydrants, front porches, garbage bins, a high-end clothing boutique, a take-out pancake joint, and countless economy cars that various emergency vehicles, too busy to notice them, were investigating and fire-extinguishing.

"Wow. That pod really did a number!" Aye slurred and laughed harder. The whole ordeal, in his drunken mind, was absolutely hilarious.

This was the sort of thing that may have made Potto feel bad and extremely guilty, but he was too busy trying to remember whether Clover had been on the pod with him when it fired.

They finally made it past a final billboard advertising "Free flooded basement with every house!", and to the fuelling station.

"Ooooooooh," Aye said as if in slow motion. Half of the fuelling station was engulfed in huge blue flames. Vexian fire fighters were running about, hosing it down, trying to control the destruction. A ship had apparently taken off without detaching the fuel hose first and blown up the place.

Luckily, a fair distance away, there was another whole half to the fuelling station (in case such things happened), totally intact and still open.

All of the surviving Jorge Jorge Jorges in stolen Vexian ships where now off following the Shiv and things were quiet. They hid behind the rack of flotsam grease, beside a rack of jetsam oil. For a brief second Aye pondered what these familiar fuel station mainstays were actually used for (and why they were always on sale), but the thought only lasted a few seconds.

They spotted a lone ship of unknown origin. At first Aye wasn't sure how to go about stealing it, but soon he had a very good idea...

~~~

When humanoid aliens think of other species of alien, they often think of other humanoid species first. Although some have reptilian qualities (Kancorians), some have insect qualities (Mantis Widows), some vegetational (Sentaphylls), and some even fungal (Sammolites), they all have variations of a human shape. An upright shape. Even if they have extra limbs, heads, or genitalia. No matter how ugly (again Sammolites) or beautiful (Handsomians).

Of course, only humans arrogantly refer to all these species as *human*oid. Mantis Widows refer to them all as insectoid (or their Squambogian language equivalent). Towerscapians refer to them as tophoids, Four-armed Jost'leans refer to them all as phronkoids, and Sloovtopians (refusing to use the suffix "oid" because on Sloovtopia oid means "handicapped parking" and not "of similar form to, but not the same as" like it does everywhere else in the galaxy) simply call these species Steven Duckworth.

Once a planet goes from primitive to part of the galactic community, it doesn't take long before all these other humanoid species become old hat and less jarring. That said, non-humanoid species...those *not* upright or in solid form (or tangible at all), can be quite jarring to run into, and even harder to understand.

The Garax were one of these species. They were simply an *idea*. They existed among the humanoids, insectoids, tophoids, phronkoids and Steven Duckworths, but also existed in a multiverse of almost every dimension that had other living beings in it to think "Hey! I just thought of something!" at some point.

These ideas evolved and manifested themselves as semi-sentient beings that tried really hard to fit in. Ideas lead to actions, and those species that did run into them often found them quite exhausting. Shortly after meeting them, one needed a nap.

Not all ideas become Garax, but all Garax are born of ideas. Ideas that become so big and so great they come to life and long to be humanoid. They even build and fly around in spaceships, though they don't need them, with interiors barely resembling spaceship interiors. They even fuel them up from time-to-time even though they are mere concepts and really only need to be fuelled by inspiration and epiphanies.

During one of these unneeded fuel ups they let two humanoids named Potto and Aye steal their ship, simply because it just seemed like a really good idea to do so.

CHAPTER TWENTY-SEVEN

General Kendra Eppie didn't become "The Node's right-hand-man" (an odd description as the Node didn't have a conventional "hand", and when he did have one, he was a leftie) overnight. It took so many years that The Node couldn't even remember how it had happened.

He hadn't been looking for a general for his army of Node Guards, nor was Eppie ever officially *appointed* to the role of general. He had merely started calling himself that.

The Node himself, actually thought "General" was his first name, and that Ken was a bland nickname school chums called him back when he was but a young lad on whatever planet he was from that no longer existed. It was as if Eppie had always just been there.

Eppie *did* remember, however. He remembered every detail of his life and wrote every triviality, every encounter, and even every dream into his journal. A journal he was hoping to publish one day under the title "This Is Why I Hate *You!* – A Very Long Memoir".

There were never issues with trust between them, either. Eppie had given himself to The Node completely. He took great pride in his loyalty.

When he was finally rescued by guards and untied from the

chair, he didn't think there would be any issues. Even when the huge complex that was once Lyme Node's prison (and was now a very large, and very fast spaceship) rumbled away from its concrete footing, he didn't think his loyalty would be questioned. *Even* with the earthquake it caused, every ship alarm going off and the clock on every microwave oven resetting itself to a flashing 12:00 for over two-thousand blocks.

The Node, however, was still reeling over Vrume T'cha T'cha's betrayal, and his feelings, as sickening as they were, were hurt. His grotesquely humungous (but extremely fragile) ego was damaged. When Eppie came in to see him, he was already at a boiling point.

"*You!* You are in on this! You conspired with the traitor T'cha T'cha!" The Node yelled, jarring Eppie so badly that the General's back started spasming.

"What? What? I—What?? Eppie twisted, stammered and spat.

"Don't play idiot with me, General Eppie. If your real name is, in fact, General. I will fillet you alive! Not another word!!"

They both stared at each other for what seemed an eternity.

"Ok fine! Say another word! But make it a good word!!!" The Node shouted, electronically amplifying his voice through the PA system in his armoured suit.

"I looooooathe Vrume T'cha T'cha. I don't even like saying his ridiculous name! T'cha T'cha. *T'cha T'cha.* Vruuuuuuuuuuume *T'cha T'cha*...sounds like the name of the entire rhythm section of a band only people who vacation on cruise ships listen to. The name T'cha T'cha is like chicken kababs being hammered into my ear drums! The name T'cha--"

"WHY DO YOU KEEP SAYING IT THEN??" The Node interrupted so loudly it felt like chicken kababs were being hammered into Eppie's ears.

"Just making a point, sir. It would seem there are traitors everywhere, and you are so very wise to question, but I assure you I am as loyal as loyal can possibly be. I am so loyal that I barely exist as a separate person!"

"And?"

"Aaaaand...?"

"You said I was wise. What else am I??"

"Uh. Intelligent? So *very* intelligent. Smartest thing in the universe!"

"And?"

"Gorgeous?"

"There it is. Ok. This is how you are going to prove yourself. You are going to head up a battalion of as many guard war ships as we can spare, and you are going to go and blow that prison to space dust. I want them all dead. Then you are going to capture the Quarol and bring him home to me. If you don't complete this mission, don't bother *coming* home."

"Yes, Your Wise, Intelligent Gorgeousness!"

Eppie was shaken to the core. The Node doubted his loyalty. *His* loyalty! And only one man was to blame. As he left the planet in his deadly (but also extremely speedy) ship The Bad News Bearer, with an enormous fleet of Node Guard war ships, he announced that anyone even *mumbling* the name Vrume T'cha T'cha in his presence would be shot before they got to the second T'cha.

~~~

Emperor Reginald Zophricaties had not only been the name of that megalomaniacal inventor of the Life Core, The Master Cloner and many death rays and doomsday devices, but he had also invented the Pretty Pet pet hair vacuum. Without it the waxy Vexian grub hounds were almost impossible to groom. As tribute, many owners of such dogs on Vex 4 named their grub hounds after him. The Donut family had three hounds and their names were Emperor, Reg and Zed-Kate.

As Clover sat hiding in a thicket of long grass at the base of a billboard, watching as Potto and Aye crossed over to the fuelling station, she noticed that her new canine companion was wearing a tag. The name "Reg" was poorly engraved on it.

Clover was happily surprised to see Aye. She was just about to run out and join them as they approached a ship belonging to the Garax (she had been around long enough to be one of the few to know of the Garax), when a second ship landed across from it to fuel.

It was K'ween's ship. She stopped herself and held Reg's collar.

She would be better off briefly waiting and offering up an element of surprise if they needed rescuing.

"Can I call you Reggie?" she whispered to the dog.

The dog let a muffled and jowly *"Rooooff"* which Clover took as "No".

~~~

When Pannick landed the K'rown at the Vexian fuelling station she hadn't expected anything out of the ordinary. She thought she would fuel the ship, check the water supply, top up the K'rown's flotsam grease and jetsam oil, and off they would go. But things were about to get a little extraordinary.

K'ween returned to the deck wearing the eyepatch of the now deceased Blankton she had just (consensually) sexually destroyed. She was very angry and quite drunk.

"Why have we stopped?" she demanded.

"Fuel. Water," Pannick answered cautiously. She was now worrying about K'ween's plans again, and whether they would see the end of the Barbohdeans. She was also worrying about K'ween's sanity.

"You don't stop unless I say to stop!" she slur-screamed. "I am K'ween! I am *your* queen! Soon I will be the *galaxy's* queen! No one does anything without asking me!"

"My apologies. I figured this was the only fuel stop for --"

"You figure nothing! You are nothing!"

Pannick had only occasionally seen this side of K'ween. K'ween was a fierce and strong leader. K'ween was a good leader. Or had been.

Perhaps it was a mixture of the Pyst-like poison from Potto, the promise of riches and power as reward for his capture, and the betrayal of Teeg that was scrambling her brain. And perhaps the addition of more than a little flubbfruit wine was lighting a very short fuse.

"Do I have your permission to continue fuelling, Your Excellency?" Pannick said coldly.

"Yes. Get out there. I don't want to see your face right now." K'ween barked back.

Pannick left the ship and hooked the fuelling line up to the

K'rown. She waited as fuel gushed through the hose. A peculiar ship caught her eye. It was like nothing she had ever seen. It had smooth contours and monochromatic colours that made any edges and corners very hard to make out. She caught herself staring at it, trying to make out those edges.

She jumped with a startle upon seeing the Quarol and the Topher searching its underside for an entrance. She didn't move right away. It was as if she were under the ship's spell.

The spell broke with an idea. An idea the ship itself helped her to realize.

She calmly finished fuelling. She calmly disconnected the fuel line. She calmly went back into the ship. She calmly bypassed the bridge where K'ween was yelling at another crew member for breathing too loudly. She calmly went to K'ween's chamber, grabbed K'ween's favourite laser rifle, took the battery cell out of it, and returned to the bridge with it.

"Your Highness. I have spotted the Quarol and the Topher. Here. At the fuelling station," she said (again, calmly). "I thought you might like the honour of capturing them yourself."

K'ween raced towards the monitor screen. She checked the security cameras attached to the outside of the ship. Sure enough, her bounty wandered around a strange looking ship like a couple of idiots.

"I took the liberty of getting your weapon ready," Pannick said as she handed K'ween the laser rifle.

K'ween smiled a wicked smile. The wicked smile of a hunter who had just cornered her prey. She rushed off the ship.

As soon as she was outside, the hatch closed behind her. She barely noticed; she was focused on Potto. The ship started to power up. This startled her and she yelled an almost unintelligible "What's going on?" into her communication watch.

"I am taking over this ship. You are no longer fit to lead us. I am sorry," Pannick's voice came back.

"Traitor! Mutineer!!" K'ween shrieked, loud enough for Potto and Aye to hear.

"I will follow Teeg now. You should have listened to her."

The K'rown lifted off the ground, leaving K'ween in a drunk tantrum, trying to fire the dead rifle at her ship as her crew left her behind on a planet of used bungalows.

~~~

Working as a fuel station attendant was a good first job. As a Vexian teen, it provided important work experience, familiarization with almost every alien species, and responsible money management. Working for Vex 4 Fuel was an essential stepping stone on the satisfying journey to owning one's own bungalow.

On most days it was simply a matter of showing up on time (in a semi-clean uniform) and working the cash register. On occasion it meant restocking the jetsam oil, hosing down the fuel pumps after a gross Sammolite had touched them, and on rarer occasion, escaping your kiosk if it happened to blow up.

Prick Tendril was lucky. It had not been his side of the station that had blown up. He was relieved to see his fellow fuel attendant (Fig London) on the explosion side escape, but was a bit miffed that Fig had been taken away by ambulance as she was his ride home.

He was also lucky to see a Garax ship. He had never seen one before, and that was rare. As rare as *anyone* ever seeing a Garax ship, which is why he was lucky. The ship had given him an idea, as was always the case with any close proximity to the Garax.

He wasn't a very complicated young man. This idea was merely to restock the jetsam oil.

When the large and fierce looking Flettocean woman angrily crashed through the kiosk doors wearing full (and intimidatingly sexy) warrior armour, he got the idea to give her anything she wanted. She wanted a battery cell for her rifle. He handed one over from a stock of various battery cells behind his counter realizing instantly that this was in fact a very *bad* idea.

Luckily, she was in a rush and didn't seem to have the time to murder him. He had a new idea. He called his boss, quit, and started the long walk home.

~~~

By the time K'ween had her laser rifle charged up, not only was the K'rown long gone, but the Garax ship (with Potto and Aye) was gone as well. She screamed loudly and started shooting haphazardly. Shots whizzed by the young attendant as he made his way across a nearby parking lot, following an odd trail of destruction he hadn't noticed before, into the nearby suburbs.

A shot whizzed by Clover and her new friend Reg. Reg didn't like this. He charged.

Worried the next shot wouldn't be haphazard at all, but focused on an attacking grub hound, Clover took off after him. K'ween now had two targets running towards her. She took aim at the hound first. The shot was fired and would have hit the dog cleanly between the eyes if K'ween had have been sober, and even a hair less enraged. It instead grazed Clover's leg. She fell.

K'ween fired again, this time taking the time to aim properly. The shot did not hit Clover (or Reg for that matter). It hit a large piece of space garbage that had suddenly dropped down between them out of nowhere, taking on the brunt of the shot itself.

The shot didn't seem to damage the space garbage. So, K'ween shot some more. She shot a lot. The garbage was fine. It was one tough piece of unassuming debris.

On the Clover/Reg side of the garbage, a hatch opened and a twisted dark figure in a very wide brimmed black saturno hat gestured for her to get in. A voice inside her head said "It's okay. Don't be afraid. Go with him. Get into that garbage", but she couldn't get up. The shot may have merely grazed her, but it still gave her quite the immobilizing burn.

The mysterious figure ran out to help her. He picked her up with his ill-formed arms and carried her towards the hatch. He had just about made it when K'ween came around to their side of the heap. She shot three times, hitting the mysterious dark figure all three times. He fell.

Clover was close enough now to drag herself through the hatch. Reg lunged at K'ween before she could shoot again, knocking her onto the ground and sending the gun flying through the air.

Reg then ran back to help. Before K'ween could retrieve her laser rifle and shoot again, the large dog had instinctively dragged the mysterious figure onto the piece of garbage. The hatch closed and the garbage took off. This time it was a clump of space dreck that left a berserk K'ween behind.

~~~

If one were to take a stroll through a garbage dump, or perhaps Lyme Node's garbage moon of Roobos, and a hatch were to open up in a particularly innocuous heap of trash, one wouldn't expect the interior of that uninteresting pile to be fairly spacious and art deco.

Although feeling the stress of having been shot at and wounded, lying beside her mysterious, unconscious (also-wounded) would-be rescuer, *and* having a large grub hound licking her face while inside a piece of garbage flying through space, Clover couldn't help but marvel at the décor.

As the mysterious figure lay motionless next to her, she decided that this would probably be the best time to examine him and attempt to make him far less mysterious. His saturno hat lay beside him, his face was completely covered in wrapped scarves, goggles and some sort of respiratory mask covering his nose and mouth.

She lifted the goggles first. One of the man's eyes immediately slid out and dangled from its grotesquely scarred socket. There was barely enough socket to hold the other in as well.

He woke up, but before he was able to shove the eye back in and put the googles back on, she noticed something. The *colour* of that dangling eye.

She froze.

He sat up and examined his wounds. They looked bad to Clover, but to Vibloblblah Ooze, they were nothing compared to wounds of the past, and *those* wounds were nothing compared to how wounded his heart was. He slid up the wall and staggered towards a medical box. He took out a first-aid spray bottle. Before treating himself, he swaggered back to her and spritzed her burn. It instantly felt better.

He patted Reg on the head as he made his way to a chair in front of a huge console. Reg didn't seem to have any problem with Vibloblblah. Like most dogs, Reg was immune to ugly. He returned the pat with a joyous tail wag. Vibloblblah sat and attempted to spray his wounds, but reach was difficult with his crooked body.

Clover opened her mouth but words wouldn't come out.

She wanted so badly to get up and help him, but her body felt like it was made of heavy stone. He didn't speak either. She wasn't sure he could. Inside her head the entire universe was in a blender, spinning so fast she couldn't make sense of anything.

Sometimes a person's heart could be so broken that attempting to put it back together again broke everything else.

He kept his distance from her. He turned his back. *His* cerebral universe was blanketed in shame. He didn't want this to happen. He didn't want this to *ever* happen. He wanted to remain dead to her. He wanted to remain handsome and whole in her memories, not for her to see this hideous fun house mirror image of his former self. Perhaps it wasn't too late. Perhaps he could quietly return her to the Shiv and remain a mystery.

No.

The colour of his eye gave him away. No one in the universe had eyes the colour of Oain nebulae. No one else had eyes the colour of a beautiful wading pool of Hephmote sea water on a gorgeous Handsomian beach, teaming with neon life.

When she finally spoke, her voice came out like a frightened, breathy wheeze.

"Theodore...?"

Now it was his turn to lose the ability to move.

"No," he finally said, quietly crackling through his artificial voice box.

"No? Or not anymore?" she whispered.

"Does it matter?" he answered with a question.

"How can you ask me that?" she asked as she got to her feet.

"We need to forget--" he started, but he was cut off with her arms wrapping so tightly around him he could barely breathe. He didn't want to breathe. If this was his last moment alive, it would be the best one.

For that moment he was lost in her arms, but as pain shot out throughout his entire body, he was quickly reminded that he was not just *wounded* by K'ween's rifle, he *was* a wound. A walking, barely talking, wound. Inside and out.

This immense pain was bearable only because his entire body was in the claustrophobic-panic-state of not being physically able to cry when every ounce of him so badly wanted and needed to.

When his name had been Theodore, he had loved a woman named Clover. He had loved her more, perhaps, than anyone had ever loved another in all of time and space. And she had loved him right back.

In a moment of chaos, in what was to quickly become the most violent zone in the galaxy, two lovers were reunited. And in their embrace, time didn't dare budge an inch. It didn't dare.

CHAPTER TWENTY-EIGHT

People will often say "I have a vague idea what I'm looking for," or "I have a vague idea what it looks like," because more often than not ideas are vague and they help out when one is not quite sure what one is looking for. Sometimes, however, this can get one lost. "I have a vague idea where she lives" often results in many trips around various blocks and blocks, looking for a specific house in a neighbourhood where all houses look the same, and all have the same blue minivan.

Potto had never seen or heard of the Garax, and didn't even possess a *vague* idea of what they looked like. The Garax who stood before him was temporarily invisible to him.

Aye had never seen or heard of the Garax either, but he had a *vague idea* that the very odd ship they were on would have occupants. He had an idea that they would look very clean and sterile. Their ship, which only existed as an idea of the Garax themselves (an idea *from* an idea), was very clean and sterile looking, so it only made sense that these creatures would match.

Which, to Aye, they did. Hairless and shiny, with spotless white jumpsuits and clean white leather cowboy boots.

"Hello friend," said Nux Garax to his new shipmates. He

checked himself out. "Oh, I like this look! And I'm male this time! What a novelty!"

"Uh...hi?" Aye was hesitant. He didn't trust anyone this clean, but then again he had trusted the dusty old Veroseraliens, so perhaps cleanliness didn't need to be a factor when deciding who to trust.

"Oh! Who said that?" Potto asked, spinning on one foot. He trusted them sight unseen.

"You don't see them?" asked Aye, still drunk. "You must be drunk."

"That is odd. Do you have any idea who you are talking to?" Nux added.

When a question of this nature is asked, it is usually meant to sound threatening or overconfident. In that usual context, "Do you have any idea who you are talking to?" means "You should not talk to me in the manner in which you are, because I am *really* important or dangerous and have the capacity to ruin and/or hurt you for doing so. I am better than you. Piss off." However, when the *Garax* used "Do you have any idea who you are talking to?" they actually (and harmlessly) meant just that. They were indeed asking "You may have just realized that you are talking with someone. Do you know what that's all about?"

"No," said Aye.

"Well you must have *some* idea, if you can see us."

"You look like a bunch of clean dudes."

"Go on..."

"Shiny bald heads, spotless crisp white jumpsuits...really cool cowboy boots..."

"Oh! I see them now!" exclaimed Potto. It seemed his ideas just needed a little kick start. "Yeah, those boots are dynamite!"

"Interesting. Do you have no ideas of your own, my friend?" Nux asked Potto.

"I don't know, you'll have to ask my friend," smiled Potto. He liked being called friend, and calling others friend. He liked a lot of things.

"You are adorable!" Nux laughed. "We are the Garax. We are intangible ethereal beings. We are ideas. We lack any material substance until *you* have an *idea* that we have material substance. We can make some things material using our own ideas. But not ourselves. We're not that vain. Plus it's fun to see what folk come up with!"

"Weeeeeeird!" Potto chuckled, while Aye tried to decide whether he could trust his own ideas. He was also quite surprised that he had had such clean ideas.

The Garax ship flew through space quickly. It zipped past many of the Jorge Jorge Jorge clone's stolen ships. This made Aye quite nervous.

"Hey! Those are like the ships that Teeg wanted to escape at the fuel station!" Potto cheered.

"They don't seem to see us. Is that like Potto not seeing *you?*" Aye asked Nux.

"Yes! Now you're getting it! Sort of. You saw our ship because you had the *idea* to steal a ship! The fuel attendant saw us because he had an *idea* that something must be filling up once he saw the numbers changing on his meter. There was a screaming barbarian woman who saw us because she saw you searching our ship for a way in, and had an *idea* that it was a ship you were looking at in the first place. The shape of our ship always seems the same to everybody because we, the Garax, had an *idea* of how we wanted it to look. So, they *can't* see our ship because they have no *idea* that we exist at all, and because we all, you two included, had the *idea* that we needed to get past them unseen."

"I have no *idea* what you are talking about," Aye replied.

"Me neither. But it sure is fun listening to you talk. It's like circles! It makes me feel like I'm in a washing machine," Potto added.

"Ah, but I bet you'd like to go faster, wouldn't you?" Nux offered.

"Well, yeah...that would probably be a good idea," Aye said as the ship started to speed up. He held on tight to a barber pole that suddenly appeared before his eyes, simply because he thought "Wooooah! I could really use something to hold onto right now! A barber pole sure would come in handy!"

Once far away from Jorge Jorge Jorge clone-stolen Vex ships, the Garax ship slowed down again. The barber pole turned into a table with a bowl of ice cream on it.

Aye paced back and forth on the bridge eating ice cream. He was trying to have another idea. Potto was sitting on a comfy sofa. He had been sitting on the hard floor, but thought "I have an idea...they should make comfy sofas mandatory on all space-ships." Within seconds he was also sipping on a milkshake, eating pie and being lovingly attacked by puppies.

Nux Garax appeared next to Aye, seemingly from nowhere.

"You are trying too hard, and all you have to show for it is a bowl of Rocky Road. This fellow isn't trying at all, and now he has a comfy sofa, a milkshake, pie and puppy kisses. Hey! And look! An ostrich!" Nux said cheerfully. Up until now, he had only had a vague idea what an ostrich looked like.

"Yes, and those are all very stupid things. Not helpful. We need to find the Shiv. Puppies can't help us find the Shiv..."

"No?" Nux smiled.

"No. Not unless you had some special machine that allows dogs to sniff out ships through the vacuum of space," Aye laughed.

"Like that one?"

Aye turned to see a bizarre machine with a long sponge bar across the front. The puppies all excitedly ran towards it. They started sniffing the sponge pad and all began barking and wagging their tails.

"That sponge absorbs odours from across space! I think they smell your Shiv ship!" Nux clapped.

Aye was gobsmacked. His mind was now racing, and too many ideas were popping into his head. So many that they were not clear enough for him to form a solid one. Earlier he had a hard time thinking up an idea, and now he was having the opposite problem.

Potto was of no use. He was now riding around behind the sofa on the ostrich, and knocking over expensive-looking crystal vases because he had the stupid idea that breaking vases would be funny.

"Ok. Relax. Now you have too many ideas. Pick one. Here... maybe I can help. What will you do when you find the Shiv? Any ideas?"

"Yeah, I'll blow up any ships attacking it with a giant laser cannon!"

"Hmmm. Unfortunately, we are a peaceful species. Your idea *can* be to shoot a large gun, sure. And that gun will appear, sure. But then *we* will automatically have an idea that it should be loaded with confetti or watermelons rendering it harmless. I am sorry."

And with that Aye was out of ideas. Without a weapon, there would be no way of saving the Shiv if they did find it and it was being attacked by a fleet of Vexian ships.

"Oh, how nifty!" Nux cheered. "See that stuff ahead? Looks like a huge satellite space station that was blown up, doesn't it?"

Aye looked out the bridge window.

"If you're a history buff, you might remember Emperor Reginald Zophricaties..." Nux continued.

"Nope."

"He was the inventor of the Life Core, the Master Cloner, The Pretty Pet pet vacuum, and almost every weapon of mass destruction that The Node has in his arsenal."

"Oh, *that* Emperor Reginald Zophricaties." Aye was not a history buff.

"Well...all that stuff up ahead was once his home base. His space station. His lab."

"Any of it still work?" Aye asked.

"Hmmmm..." said Nux as a console appeared before him, rising up out of the floor like time lapse photographs of a plant growing. Nux had an idea that he needed such a thing to help. He pressed random buttons and checked a screen on the console.

"According to this new sensor, the Master Cloner still works. Not sure how well it works; it would be quite old, but apparently it has a new power cell hooked up to it and it has been used within the last few days."

With the puppies still excitedly sniffing the Shiv tracking machine, and Potto running around with the ostrich now riding *him*, Aye realized that once they had found the Shiv, they would not be able to save Teeg and the gang if only armed with confetti and watermelons. They would be hopelessly outnumbered.

He thought about being outnumbered. He thought about the

cloning machine. He thought about being outnumbered again, followed by yet another thought about the cloning machine. The two thoughts slowly came together, a bridge forming between them. Very slowly.

And then very suddenly it hit him.

"I have an idea!" he exclaimed.

"I knew that you could do it," Nux Garax winked.

~~~

Emperor Reginald Zophricaties' lab floated about amongst the debris of what he had once called home and ruled over. The main part of his satellite space station, which once orbited the austere and remarkably desolate planet of Vex 7, now floated in space. All various parts tethered to it by cables and more debris. Most sections of it were blown wide open to the cosmos, but the lab was mostly undamaged and even had life support systems working.

The inside of the lab looked like it had been ransacked by clumsy burglars, but the mess was in fact caused by nearby explosions when The Node had blown up the main station. The Master Cloner was unharmed, and sat in the centre of the lab like an antique carousel on display at a county fair. A large pod sat in its middle with the word "ORIGINAL" stenciled on the closed door in red letters. Beside it was a second, smaller pod stenciled "COPY".

Potto and Aye came into the room quietly, assuming they were alone. The Garax were waiting back in their ship, ready to help out their new chums if the idea hit them.

"Ok. This is only going to work if I can figure out how to use this machine."

"Maybe *this?*" Potto offered pointing to a big red button on the side of the Master Cloner with "CLONE NOW!" written across it in smeared marker.

"Okay, let's try this. You go get into that pod in the middle. I'm gonna clone you. We'll create an army of Pottos! That oughta mess things up a bit!" he laughed.

Potto shrugged and made his way to the centre of the machine. There was a small window on the door of the ORIGINAL pod. He peeked in.

"There's a big guy in there. I don't think I'll fit."

Aye ran up and had a look. "Ugh. That's the biggest Kancorian I've ever seen! His eyes are closed. Is he asleep? We gotta figure out what to do. We gotta get him out of there. Maybe he's dead..."

Just then Jorge Jorge Jorge opened those cold reptilian eyes. He saw the faces of the two he was hunting for. They were looking in through the window with moronic expressions upon their faces. He struggled with the door, but it was jammed. Startled, Potto and Aye jumped back.

"Uh...hey there," a little tiny female child's voice said.

"What was that?" Aye asked, looking around for the source.

"I don't know!" Potto answered. He then called out a soft, "Hellooooo? Little girl? Where are you?"

"I'm in here!" the voice cried out from inside Jorge Jorge Jorge's pod.

"With the giant lizard man?" Potto asked. This was concerning.

"Uh...yeah, sure." Jorge Jorge Jorge lied. He had gotten himself stuck in the machine. The door had closed crooked and he was jammed. He'd been in there for hours and had been meditating to stay calm until one of his clones came back to make more and free him.

"Has he hurt you?" Potto was getting more and more concerned. Aye was looking in through the window.

"Heeeeey. Did I just see your mouth move?" Aye asked Jorge Jorge Jorge.

"Nah, 'ey 'outh 'asn't 'ooving." Jorge Jorge Jorge said trying not to move his mouth.

"How do we get her out?" Potto asked in a panic.

"Just open the door. The Kanocorian is paralyzed. He won't be able to move," the Kancorian pleaded once Aye wasn't looking for any mouth movement. For once his ridiculously juvenile voice was going to save him, and help him win his bounty.

"Oh, okay!" Potto said as he tried prying the door open.

"Wait. I don't trust that little girl," Aye shouted. "Why would a little girl get into a cloning machine with a Kancorian?"

"Maybe she was bullied at school and coaxed the Kancorian

into the cloning machine so that she could make a bigger, stronger version of herself to fight the bullies off!" Potto exclaimed.

"Yeah. That makes sense." Aye agreed.

Together they pried the door open. Jorge Jorge Jorge stepped out alone.

"Ha! Fooled you! It is just I, Jorge Jorge Jorge!" Jorge Jorge Jorge peeped. "Now...I am taking you back to Lyme Node and handing you over to The Node. We can do this the hard way, where you will both be in a lot of pain...or the easy way where you will still be in pain, but less of it for not struggling."

"BAH HAHAHAHAHAHAHA!!!" Aye laughed. "Nice voice there, Big Guy!"

"Aye! That's not very nice!" Potto scolded, stifling giggles of his own.

Jorge Jorge Jorge didn't like to be teased. He rushed the pair.

"Run!" Aye screamed, abruptly breaking from his own bullying.

"I told you! You've hurt his feelings!" Potto yelled as he started running.

"I am so, so, so sorry big scary guy! I didn't mean to offend! But your voice *is* really funny," Aye ran in the opposite direction.

Jorge Jorge Jorge chased Aye. He remembered he could kill Aye. Only the Quarol needed to come back alive. They ran around and around the Master Cloner control console like a cartoon cat chasing a cartoon mouse around a cartoon kitchen table.

"Get into the Cloner pod! The ORIGINAL one!" Aye shouted to Potto. Potto did as he was told. He hid inside and shut the door as Aye pressed the big red button on one of his passes. He was out of shape, but the reptilian was slow with bulk.

The machine made several awful sounds. Like a circus calliope amplified through a wounded howler monkey. The middle pod started shaking. The odd smell of a burning toaster (if that toaster were toasting a wet owl) arose.

The second pod door opened and a Potto clone came out. The Cloner did not clone his albinism or the block within him that dulled his brain. For the first time a clone came out of the Master Cloner *smarter* than the original.

A ginger-haired, rosy-skinned Potto ran out and jumped on Jorge Jorge Jorge's back. Another came out after that and joined the first. And then another and another.

Aye grabbed some wires hanging down from a damaged panel in the ceiling. He threw them to one of the clones. "Tie him up!"

More and more Potto clones emerged from the COPY pod. More helped subdue the lumbering giant and soon had him on the floor. It took many, many Pottos to take down one Jorge Jorge Jorge.

"Go now to the Garax ship! We have some Vexian ships to steal and have a Shiv to save!" Aye laughed, feeling like an action hero. The sight of so many Pottos was hilarious. This was so much fun.

The machine whirred and stopped after the seventy-second Potto had emerged. All were off to the Garax ship as instructed. It was now just Aye, a tied-up Jorge Jorge Jorge and a hiding Potto in the room.

He let Potto out of the pod and got in himself. "Okay. My turn." Aye was quite keen on the idea of having other targets for his would-be captures to go after instead of himself.

Once they had traded spaces, Potto hit the red button and it started all over again. Soon shorter, smaller-horned hunchback Ayes were filing out of the machine. Only about ten made it out before Jorge Jorge Jorge got through the wire and was free.

Potto shrieked as the giant lunged at him. He ran towards the ORIGINAL pod that held Aye. He was looking for a hiding spot. He climbed in *with* Aye while the machine was still running. In a rage Jorge Jorge Jorge slammed his fists down on the console and it smashed to pieces.

Something odd happened seconds before the Master Cloner would stop working forever. The ORIGINAL pod started quaking. Steam poured out of the COPY pod. A high-pitched sound like a train whistle whistled out long and loud. And then everything was quiet.

Machinery breaking and not starting up again was not odd. It was expected. That's what machinery did. But the Master Cloner was not meant to have two beings in the pod at the same time. That, and Jorge Jorge Jorge had smashed something into place that had always caused the glitch in the cloning process. The problem with the machine that made *inferior* copies was somehow fixed, if only for a millisecond, before it was in pieces. Enough time for one last clone. One *superior* clone.

By the time the pod doors opened and Potto and Aye sprang out like a jack-in-the-box with a broken lid, a tall, dark figure stood before them, and beside a rather surprised looking Jorge Jorge Jorge. The surprised look was caused by the huge metal pipe sticking out of his neck. Blue Kancorian blood flowed out of it as if it were a faucet. It was near impossible to pierce the body armour of a Kancorian male by hand, but somehow this dark figure had managed. The giant fell dead, never to titter or squeal again.

The figure looked like Potto in every way, apart from a dark complexion, two large, sumptuous and impressively curled horns, and a pitch-black puff of fluff hair upon his head instead of white. He smiled wickedly at the pair and ran out of the room without a word.

"We're kinda hot," Aye muttered, in shock.

By the time they made it back to the Garax ship the hybrid clone was gone. He had found Jorge Jorge Jorge's hidden ship and that was that. Just...gone.

Neither Potto or Aye could speak. A Towerscapian-Quarol clone had been magnificently jarring to behold.

~~~

The Garax ship flew off to find some Vexian ships to steal from Jorge Jorge Jorge clones. The ship was filled with seventy-two Potto clones, all chattering away like old college buddies. The ten Aye clones had been accidentally left behind in the lab. No one seemed to notice or care.

"So....you're our father?" One of the Potto clones asked Potto with a friendly Potto smile. He was holding one of the Shiv sniffing puppies.

"Y'know...I have *no idea!*" Potto said.

"You sure said a mouthful!" Nux Garax exclaimed. He laughed long and hard at this, and then they high-fived.

CHAPTER TWENTY-NINE

By the time the puppies on the Garax ship had sniffed out the Shiv, it looked a little worse for wear. It had suffered some damage, but it was still whole and that is all that really mattered to the crew. They rather enjoyed breathing oxygen.

Luckily the Shiv had been faster than the stolen Vexian ships and had outrun them before its shields had been depleted. It had not been immobilized, but it wasn't moving. It was now hiding in quiet contemplation. They needed to think. They needed a plan.

"There is a ship approaching. Wait. No. There is something *other* than a ship approaching. No, no, it's definitely a ship. Well, it's ship *shaped,* anyway. Yes. There is a ship shape approaching," Knutt calmly reported.

"What the hell are you talking about?" Teeg fired back.

"Hmmmm..." Knutt answered. "Well...there *is* something approaching that looks very much like a ship, but I can't confirm that it's *actually* a ship. It's reading as more of a concept than a solid."

"Well, that's just strange."

"Yes, but that's not even the strangest part. I thought Quarols were extinct, or at least lost forever. Apart from ours, of course. I'm reading that there are *seventy-three* on board."

"Okay, okay, okay. So, *seventy-three* Quarols flying through space on a *concept?* I think you need to be switched off and back on again," Teeg chuckled. "As long as it's not a Vexian ship..."

"Regardless, Potto is on whatever that is. I can *feel* him," Clory added, telepathically.

"Well that's all I need. Let's go get him!" Teeg sighed with relief.

"I also detect one Towerscapian, several baby doggies, and an ostrich," Knutt said hesitantly. She didn't want to be turned off and on again. She had never been rebooted, but it sounded weird and uncomfortable.

"Well, why not, yeah? Go big or go home, right? Any tigers? Manatees? Clarinet players? Talking loaves of rye bread?" Teeg said in jest, but she was getting a bit worried. Not worried about the approaching "ship", but about her own ship's mental health. "Maybe a French New Wave film festival going down on board?"

When the ship hailed them, things just got more confusing.

Teeg could see the ship because Knutt had given her the *idea* that it was there, but she had no idea what a *Garax* looked like. Upon hearing that there was an ostrich on board, she immediately thought of one. Therefore, the Garax on her screen had the look of a large, fierce, long extinct, flightless Earth bird. In a snappy dress suit.

"Crew of the Shiv! We are the peaceful Garax," said Nux, looking down at them from their flight deck screen. There was nothing peaceful looking about an ostrich. "We would like to gift you your friend the Towerscapian, and seventy-three Quarols. Or at least the one you call Potto. Really, you can have as many as you like. Don't feel pressured into taking the lot. We need to find nice, caring homes for the puppies anyway. Any Pottos you don't take, we will find nice, caring homes for as well."

Teeg did not know how to respond to this. Behind the ostrich man she could see a number of red-headed Pottos rewarding hyper puppies with treats for "doing *suuuuch* a good job, you cutie-pie nummy wittle wuv-wuvs!"

"Ummm. Thanks...?" she finally muttered.

"Perhaps it would be a good idea if they were each wearing brand-spanking-new TDX-30 space suits. And perhaps it would be a good idea if those space suits had thrusters."

"Why?" a Potto clone behind him asked after finding himself in a brand-spanking-new TDX-30 space suit.

"Well, then they could fire you guys directly at the Vexian ships and you could climb into them and take them over. You'd have your own ships then. Seventy-some Quarols on one ship might get a bit crowded, and you could use the fire power," Nux answered the Potto clone.

"Oh! That's a great idea!" the clone laughed. He then went back to praising puppies while sipping on a sandwich.

A small part of Teeg (one of the few parts that wasn't incredibly befuddled) felt a bit of relief upon hearing this idea. The thought of being surrounded by seventy-three Pottos was not a welcome one.

We will send the Quarols over to you now. And the Towerscapian," ostrich Nux said to the crew of the Shiv, pulling Aye into view to assure them he was alright as well.

"What happened to his horns?" Teeg inquired. "They seem shorter. As does he. Did he always have that hunch?"

"Oh dear," Nux winced.

~~~

Installing sliding frosted shower doors on pre-made moulded tub surrounds didn't call for much space travel. In fact, Bisher Donut had never even been in a *parked* spaceship before. Vexian authorities had let him come with them to find (and identify) the home-invading Quarol, and he felt quite honoured.

He felt *important*, and that was a something he hadn't felt since he got three of his co-workers fired for doing Pyst on the job. He had been the one to sneak it into their morning coffees, but that was hardly the point.

Officer Steve Lasagna was glad to have someone new to talk to. His partner Officer Frett Pear was always going on and on about his ever-oscillating relationship status, uninteresting sports scores, his amazement at the never-fluctuating weather, or some television show that no one but Frett had ever watched. Any conversation that wasn't based on one of these topics was more than welcome. He longed to talk about himself just once: his crocheting, his dead insect collection, his carnivore-only cooking classes, or the ghost he was almost certain haunted the flooded basement of his bungalow.

Once they had left Vex 4's atmosphere and were comfortably in space, he tried to ease a very nervous Bisher by working one of these topics into casual conversation as subtly as he could.

"You like crocheting?" he loudly blurted out.

Bisher ignored this and threw up into an old plastic grocery bag. He wasn't enjoying this honour as much as he thought he would. Space was bumpier than he had guessed, which he found odd considering it was lacking potholes. Officer Steve took this sudden vomit as a hard "no" and was crushed.

Vexian authorities did not know that Potto had escaped on a Garax ship, because they didn't know what a Garax *was*. They merely assumed that he had escaped in one of the many, many Vexian warships that had been stolen from the Krank City militia base with one of the many, many invading Kancorians that had stolen them.

Bisher was just starting to feel a little better when Officer Frett ran up from a galley below the bridge.

"We gotta get out of the way, Lasagna!! OUT OF THE WAY, LASAGNA!!!" he screamed to his delicious-sounding piloting partner.

"Wha?? What's wrong???" Officer Steve returned, matching Officer Frett's panic at a jarring speed and volume.

Officer Frett ran ahead, shoving Officer Steve out of his chair, and pulled the controls of the ship back *hard*. The ship pulled up, narrowly missing an entire flying Lyme Node prison as it barrelled through space, not seeing them.

They all stared blankly for a moment before each of them started throwing up into the plastic grocery bag.

~~~

Vark Burk had wasted his life digging a tunnel behind his motivational kitten-shitting-into-a-saxophone poster. Now that tunnel was sealed off, and he was heartbroken.

He couldn't see the silver lining: if it hadn't been sealed off, he'd have been sucked through it into space. Now the poorly taped-up poster, a bad back, and years of calluses-upon-calluses were just a bitter reminder. With the masking tape, it was hard to even tell it was a saxophone. Or a kitten. It now looked like a baby muskrat recovering from plastic surgery lounging seductively on a giant kazoo (a giant kazoo which was also recovering from plastic surgery).

Several floors up, and from the now-deceased Warden's office, Vrume T'cha T'cha snickered to himself at the absurdity of flying a large prison complex across the galaxy at top speed. He was amazed at how fast it was going considering its size.

But it *needed* to go fast. He knew damn well that Eppie and an army of Node Guards would be following him. He knew that if The Node had enabled the prison to go so fast, the newer, smaller war ships would be even faster, and he *needed* to get to Hephmote without being followed. He *needed* to hide out on his secret planet, motivate his army, and maybe take a long-overdue nap.

They passed Vex 4 without refuelling. There were fuel reserves in the sub-basement, a sub-basement that the now-deceased Warden didn't even know existed.

"According to our scanners, there seems to be a plethora of Vexian ships in this part of space. Way more than what would be considered normal. Well over one hundred!" Breva Floodman reported from her navigation post.

"Maybe some kind of celebration? Is it Cinco de Bungalow or something?" Vrume joked. Most of the known universe made fun of Vex 4's obsession with the Vexians' favourite style of dwelling.

"No, no...it gets weirder. A good number of these ships do not contain Vexians at all..." Breva added. "Something cold-blooded..." She pressed a few more seemingly random buttons. "Kancorians!"

"Whaaa? Kancorians are solitary creatures. They don't travel in packs...and they certainly don't travel in ships that aren't theirs. That is *very* strange," Vrume continued. He checked his own console. "They seem to be ignoring us. We're not who they're after, and who wants to pick a fight with a ship this big for no reason? Fly past. Towards Vex 7."

He had only had a brief encounter with the Quarol and the Topher and it had ended with the strange destruction of Euphoria. He suspected "strange destruction" was a force that followed his prophezied heroes around like a strange and destructive shadow.

"I have a strange, and possibly destructive hunch," he added, wagging his finger because he hadn't in a while.

~~~

"Eureka!" exclaimed Mel Million Max as he finished his new I.C. (Impatience Chip).

Upon realization that he had been too patient before, he decided to create this new chip to get him going. He needed to act faster. Waiting was getting way too easy.

Through a panel on his chest, he installed the chip and immediately felt an amazing surge of urgency. He had only spotted the Garax ship because it had shown up on his sensors, just as it had on the Shiv. These were sensors much more advanced than those on the seemingly blind Vexian ships. He didn't need to have an idea; he was a computer. And it didn't show up on *his* scanner as a ship either...but Mel didn't care. Whatever it was, he could tell it had a Topher on it.

He flew his ship as quickly as he could in the direction of Emperor Reginald Zophricaties' floating ruins.

The hazy blue holograph of his old head bobbed above its killing-machine body, metaphorically smiling the smile of a crocodile. He was going in for the kill and his new I.C. was causing him to rock back-and-forth with anticipation. His H.P. (Happiness Chip) was humming.

When he was finally (finally!) flying amongst the space station debris, his crocodile smile was accompanied by a crocodile-sized laugh. It was as if his birthday (if he indeed still had one) had come early: scans showed that on one piece of debris, there were ten Tophers! *Ten!*

His glory would be restored for sure if there were nine other Towerscapians there to witness him finally kill his son.

CHAPTER THIRTY

Aye sat in the "staff lounge/kitchenette" of Emperor Reginald Zophricaties' lab with nine other Ayes. The tenth was missing.

Everything had happened too fast. The large lineup of Potto clones waiting to get onto the Garax ship caused a panic. He had watched the real Potto grab the hand of one of his clones and drag him off. By the time he had finally gathered up his remaining clones (which was no easy task for they had scattered in every direction like a brood of chickens cooped up with a werewolf), everyone had left.

Now they all sat in the lounge/kitchenette, munching on stale and rotten snacks that had spilled out of a broken vending machine many, many years before. There were "raisins" in everything, including the snacks that didn't start off with raisins.

"I don't think these are raisins," an Aye clone muttered.

"Just shut up and eat. Raisins...real or not...are good for you," Aye snapped. He was a tad ornery, but trusted Potto would come back for him when the mistake had been realized.

Though he doubted Potto's ability to realize *anything*, his fragile ego refused to believe that these horn-deficient hunchbacks looked *anything* like him. Even Potto would be able to tell the difference. Surely. Probably. Maybe.

"What's a raisin?" asked another clone.

"I dunno, something with legs," answered the first clone as he munched away on what definitely wasn't a raisin but certainly had the texture of one. And legs.

Aye looked around at his clones. He was disappointed. He was hoping they'd be a little more Blankton, and a little less Yaygher. And that was saying something.

He closed his eyes and tried to ignore the inane conversation the clones were having about expired snack foods. He tried to remember his mother's face, but too much had happened since his dream of her. He couldn't even remember his wretched father's face for that matter, but that was a very welcome memory blip.

Like Potto, he had a wall up, a block of sorts in his mind. Something horrible was buried so deep he couldn't access even the smallest detail, and he had nothing from his past to jog his memory.

Nothing remained of his life up until this particular moment, apart from the clothes on his back. The now filthy, worn and torn Node Pilot's uniform with a faded "1st Lt. Jonas Perrish" nametag-badge carefully stitched on the jacket's chest was all he owned.

He perked up upon hearing the low grinding (and feeling the buzzing vibrations) of a ship docking to the lab.

"There ya go, Sport!" he said aloud.

"Sport? What sport? Water polo?"

"Potto. He's back for us. Well for *me*," Aye scowled. He didn't want these idiots following him around.

He raced out of the lounge/kitchenette, slipping on a few snack wrappers but catching himself.

He waited with bated breath for Potto to come through the lab entrance, while practising his stern, scolding face. He was happy and relieved to be rescued, but wanted Potto to know it wasn't okay to be left behind, and worse, mistaken for one of these "Aye-ghers".

It wasn't Potto that came through the door. It wasn't a Potto *clone*. It wasn't the dangerously dashing clone they had made together. It wasn't even a Shiv-sniffing puppy or a wayward ostrich.

It was his father.

But *not* his father. It was an artificial abomination with the glowing blue floating holographic head of his father. He stared at this floating head-upon-a-large-robotic-body like he was looking through the lens of an old video camera that wouldn't autofocus without effort. Though he had known about his father's current form, he had not seen it in person.

He had not seen his father since before he was Mel Million Max. Since Mel-Aye moved on two legs and not a rolling tank-like tread.

"My son! My baby boy!" Mel Million Max called out. The blue face was smiling wickedly. The time had finally come. "I know this is probably a lot to take in, so I'll give you a moment. Because I *really* want it to sink in. I have waited so long for this. Let it sink in before you die, you little shit."

And Aye let it sink in. He *really* let it sink in.

He didn't think about dying. His father's crabby old face crawled deep into his brain and broke down the wall. It unblocked the block. It dug up what had been buried so very, very deep. It triggered a tsunami.

His father hadn't killed his mother. It was far worse than that. His father had driven his mother to kill herself.

He had berated and beaten, humiliated and belittled, bruised and defamed her. He had stolen her work and passed it as his own. He had pimped her out to his friends and blamed her, strangling her while calling her a whore. He had imprisoned her with blackmail. If she had left he would not only have hunted her down and tortured her, he would have killed their son before his time. The physical and mental pain he had caused her was so unbearable that even one more breath for her was poison.

Even by Topher standards he had been a monster. The worst kind of monster: a cowardly monster that only preyed on those smaller and weaker than himself. A cruel, cruel, cruel, cowardly monster.

And he had done it all while his wailing son watched helplessly.

The last Aye saw of his mother was in her library. Sitting by the fire. She had made him sweet tea and she read him a story; the same comforting story she had read him a million times. He fell asleep in her arms.

He forgot that she had been crying, her already shattered heart breaking into even smaller shards as she squeezed him tighter.

Her tea had been a funny colour. It had smelled like death.

"There it is, yeah? You remember..." Mel Million Max laughed.

It was this laugh that finally broke Aye. He calmly turned and walked away. He had never felt so much rage. And it was a calm, focused rage.

"Where are you going, dickhead? *Don't you walk away from me!*" shouted Mel. "It's not like you can go anywhere *now*. There is no running. There is no hiding. You are mine! I win!"

Aye returned moments later. Mel's holographic eyes widened. There were *ten* Aye's staring him down. Each clone inheriting the same horrible memory. Each clone feeling the same rage.

Mel Million Max fired his shoulder laser, taking one clone down, but another clone was upon him. And soon two, and soon three and four. They pulled at wires and panels. They snapped off brittle parts, antennae and ornaments. Mel spun in a full circle on his tread and shook them off. He shot a few more, but within seconds others were on him.

He had been an arrogant fool. He had come alone, not even bothering to power up his army of robots. This was *supposed* to have been easy. Aye was stupid! Aye was weak!

By the time all nine clones were lying dead at his feet, part of Mel's foot tread had been dismantled, one of his "arms" was on the floor beside him, and many of his special upgrade chips were ripped out and crushed.

He looked about but the original Aye was gone. His built-in ship monitor started counting down. On a nearby console screen he saw his son's face.

Aye had left the fight and was on Mel's own ship. He was broadcasting from its escape pod.

"*I* won," he said through tears. "But then again, I won a long time ago, didn't I? Because this is not you. You only *think* you are Mel-Aye...but my terrible father died broken, shunned and lonely, and even *that* was far, far better than he deserved. But I want YOU to know, *whatever the fuck you are...that I* won. Twice."

"What have you done???" the robot screeched and crackled.

"Your ship, you, and everything that ever *was* you is about to self-destruct. It will take out this lab, and most importantly, *you* with it. Though you self-destructed a long, long time ago, didn't you?"

One of the chips inside Mel Million Max that an Aye clone had *not* torn out and damaged was his F.C. (Fear Chip). He had only invented and implanted it to keep him on his toes, to keep him sharp, to make him more life-like. He was cursing the creation of this chip as his entire electronic body filled up with an excruciating terror of dying.

"This is for my mother," Aye said in a cold whisper as he hit the eject button, mere moments before Mel Million Max, and any sign of his existence, other than Aye himself, was blown *out* of existence.

Forever.

CHAPTER THIRTY-ONE

When a weight is lifted from one's sore shoulders after a tu-multuous situation and an extended period of time, it can be quite liberating. It can feel like finally lowering one's arms after holding up a muddy, collapsing ceiling for a spell. It can feel like seeing clean sunshine after a yearlong storm of raining mud. It can feel like stretching one's legs after driving for four hundred hours...in the mud.

These comparisons make sense to those that have been liber-ated from a great burden after a long time, because it takes them back to a more relaxing time when that burden didn't exist (and there was considerably less mud). They have a comparison. They had past relief to dream about.

Aye didn't know how to feel. There was never a time when he *didn't* have the burden, until now. He had nothing to compare it to. His father had been in pursuit of him in one way or another from infancy. He had learned how to hide before he had learned how to use the potty.

He floated about in the doldrums of space by himself. Again.

No extremely-claustrophobic-spacesuit this time. Instead he reclined in a comfy, and slightly less claustrophobic escape pod. He wondered why it had needed a comfy seat if it belonged to a robot with a tank-like tread who couldn't sit down and take advantage of its overly-plush cushioning. The truth is that it had been built when his father was humanoid, but this didn't occur to Aye. His father had always been an ugly hate machine to him.

He didn't feel like a weight had been lifted from his shoulders; he felt hollow. He felt numb. He stared blankly out the window at the beginning of a war.

He turned on the radio. He calmly watched the Shiv, countless Vexian warships, the Lyme Node prison, the Bad News Bearer, fleets of Node Guardships, a nondescript hunk of space garbage, and the flickering Garax ship as it left for greener pastures. They all came and went from view, while he listened to a Vexian signal play 1980's pre-mall Earth Brit-pop hits. Such music had just reached Vex 4. They always had been a little behind on the most recent trends.

It was like watching someone else play the most complicated, insane and hopeless video game. He watched without an ounce of concern for his own well-being or any amount of fear. Just the hollowness. Hollowness with a soundtrack by XTC, Thomas Dolby and The Thompson Twins.

~~~

On the flight deck of the Shiv, Potto sat across from the Aye clone, trying to decide if he could make the relationship work. Moments before, Knutt had reported that the Zophricaties Lab had blown up, and that there was a ninety-eight per cent chance that the original Aye went up with it. In an attempt to cheer up the Quarol, Knutt had recommended that, in his heart, he replace Aye with the clone.

"He has *some* of the same memories!" she told him.

"He doesn't even *look* the same. He looks like he's melted," Potto sulked. It felt like he had been given raw parsnips when he had asked for warm cookies.

"Well, he might like some of the same foods, anyway. He can't be any more of a dickhead than before..." she assured.

"I haaaaave the drink now? I haaaave the sex now?" the Aye clone asked.

"I want *my* Aye," Potto sadly told Knutt, quickly realizing that this may have hurt the clone's feelings. "No offence, I'm sure you are very nice. You look like you'd be good at...um..." Potto started to say to the clone, but trailed off. He honestly couldn't think of anything this impostor looked like he'd be good at.

He was also feeling quite guilty. *He* had been in such a hurry that *he* had grabbed the wrong Aye on *his* way back to the Garax ship.

"I killed him, didn't I?" he quietly asked Knutt.

"Well yeah, I guess you did!" Knutt said in a chipper manner, hoping her tone would express a positive attitude. Maybe he just needed a kick start.

"We haaaave the sex now?" the clone asked Potto, with an unsettling vocal fry.

"No, not right now," Potto answered glumly, not having listened to the question in the first place.

The Garax had left and Teeg was loading eager-to-be-helpful Potto clones into torpedo launchers. They understood directions better than Potto ever had, but had his knack for not complaining in the face of dangerous stupidity. She didn't realize the ship even *had* torpedo launchers until Knutt suggested it. They hadn't been used in many years and were filled with many easily shooed spiders, but still worked regardless of dusty arachnids.

Upon approaching Vexian warships, she fired the clones. The clones then used their space suit thrusters to get closer to the ships, climb onto their outer hulls, and board them through their emergency airlocks.

It took two clones and the element of surprise to take over each small fighter ship. Some had Vexian authorities, some had Jorge Jorge Jorge clones. None, however, were expecting to be boarded by flying Quarols with laser pistols, wrenches, forks, or any other weapon they could find on the Shiv before departing.

Within the hour they had eight new ally ships to help them, and not a moment too soon.

"Uh-oh..." Knutt sighed. "I sense a Node Guard ship approaching. A big one. The Bad News Bearer. I believe it is General Kendra Eppie's ship."

"Shit!" Teeg shouted out loud.

"Shit!" Gekko shouted telepathically.

"Shit!" Clory shouted in her own mind to no one in particular.

"Uh-oh..." Knutt repeated. "And from the *other* direction an entire Lyme Node prison is heading in our way. Seems we're in the middle of a 'oh-you've-got-to-be-fucking-kidding' sandwich."

"Shit!" Gekko said out loud for the first time in her life.

~~~

It was very important to Eppie that he not know the names of any of the Node Guards. Ever.

One had once told him his name many years back, and he had the guard executed on the spot. It wasn't that he wanted this anonymity to keep him from getting emotionally attached to any of his seemingly disposable army brigade; he just hated the awkward embarrassment of not remembering a name at a later date...and Frunctuous Vambistion Chasfirmly Grottomuffin (and that was just his first name) was a name he knew he would never get right, no matter how hard he tried. Easier just to shoot the problem.

Upon hearing of Frunctuous Vambistion Chasfirmly Grottomuffin Smith's execution, no other Node Guard had ever attempted to introduce themselves to Eppie again. They didn't even introduce themselves to each other, just in case.

Eppie sat at the helm of his tremendous warship feeling safe and secure. Aside from The Node's own ship, The Bad News Bearer was the most powerful ship in the galaxy. It hadn't had any trouble following the Lyme Node prison (and Vrume T'cha T'cha). The only thing that could hurt his beloved ship would have to occur within the ship itself...and no Guard would *dare* cross General Kendra Eppie. Most of them (if not all of them) would rather cross a hungry, well-armed bear.

Realizing they could never outrun the Node ship; the prison ship had turned to fight. It had gone so very, very fast but still could not shake Eppie. *Both* ships were so fast that a trip that would've normally taken any other ship a month (like the trip to the Vex System) only took days. And these had been stressful days for Vrume.

The two humongous ships faced each other, ready to have one last winner-take-all showdown, when both, almost simultaneously, noticed the tiny Shiv model ship between them.

"Oh no..." Vrume muttered from the prison ship.

"Oh *yeeeeah!*" Eppie cheered from the Node warship.

~~~

Teeg stood frozen in front of her console on the deck of the Shiv. She was silent. She felt as if she could not make a sound without having both of the giant ships on either side of them fire at her. No one else made a sound either. Not even the Aye clone who was busy trying to figure out how to open up a yogurt cup.

A crackle came over the radio, followed by a voice filled with worry.

"This is Vrume T'cha T'cha. I am captain of the Lyme Node prison ship...which sounded less bananas in my head. I know you have no reason to trust me, but we *are* your friends. That Node ship you see out there? That is General Kendra Eppie, and he will stop at nothing to destroy us both."

Teeg was relieved to hear that they had an ally, but anxious upon hearing the rest of it.

"We hear you, Vrume T'cha T'cha. What do you want us to do?" Teeg hated asking for help, but this was an extreme situation.

"I wish I knew," Vrume continued. "There is a fleet of Guard ships behind it as well. Maybe they don't see you. Maybe they are so focused on us that they haven't noticed you..."

"I have an idea..." Teeg told him as a half-baked idea started to emerge from the oven of her mind, still a tad raw and doughy.

She turned to Gekko. "We do the same thing we did to the Vexian ships, but on a grander scale. Get every last Potto clone ready, we're firing them *all* at Eppie. Hell...even suit up this Aye clone. Fire him at them as well.

"Get a schematic on that warship, Knutt. I want to know every airlock, every port. Every possible entry that a living being can get through. Their shields will only work against the resistance of firepower, not a tiny Quarol copy in a spacesuit."

"Can do," Knutt replied. Within minutes, and luckily before Eppie had the chance to fire upon them, every last clone on the ship was fired at every last airlock, port and entry Knutt's sensors had discovered.

From aboard the Bad News Bearer, Eppie raised an eyebrow. "What are they up to?"

He hadn't already fired at them because he was a narcissistic sociopath with an ego bigger than a planet, and he had been trying to come up with a villainous pre-victory speech. He wanted to have some really choice final words, a last great insult that would be felt for generations and go down in history as the greatest burn of all time. He was drawing a blank, however, and this was giving his adversaries some much needed time.

"They have fired something at us, sir," said an anonymous Guard.

"What? I didn't see anything. What did they fire at us?"

"Uh. Guys."

"Guys??"

"Yeah. Just a buncha guys," the Guard mumbled.

"Ah, to hell with it. I can't think of anything good. Just blow them all up," Eppie sneered. He was really disappointed in himself, but was trying not to show it. Perhaps he would think of something good later and just report back that he had said it (after murdering all his crew so that no one could tell on him).

Before his ship could blow the Shiv out of existence, it was hit by firepower from another ship that appeared from behind Vrume's prison ship. It wasn't sufficient firepower to do any real damage to the Bad News Bearer...but it got their attention and stalled them further.

It was the K'rown.

~~~

Aye was getting hungry. The hollow feeling had reached his stomach. He looked around for a sandwich straw, but only found a box of crackers that was possibly older than he was. He tried to take a bite of one but it instantly disappeared into a puff of stale flour dust and mould spores.

He had been deep in thought and hadn't noticed that he had drifted near the very large Node warship. Like a tyrannosaurus rex standing next to a booklouse, it hadn't noticed him either.

As he absentmindedly turned more "crackers" into mould smoke, he was abruptly startled by a strange figure smacking into the front window of his pod like a raindrop on a windshield. He leaned in so that his face was only a thick sheet of high-temperature quartz glass away from the space-suited man.

It was Potto! Well, it was *a* Potto,

This Potto waved at him with a huge smile as more Pottos-in-spacesuits zipped by him. The clone on his pod slipped off, fired some thrusters, and joined the rest. They were all headed for the Node warship.

As Howard Jones played on over his pod radio, he sat back to enjoy the show.

~~~

Teeg started to laugh.

"What could possibly be funny about this situation?" Gekko asked her brain.

"What's funny? An accumulation of woe is funny. We are about to be blown out of existence by an indestructible ship belonging to the *actual* ruler of the known universe. We are *also* being hunted down by ships filled with Vexian police and bizarre Koncorian copies. We just fired over sixty *actual people*, armed with kitchen utensils, at that indestructible ship after obtaining them from a race of *ideas.* Our only ally is a flying prison. And just as I was thinking 'how could this get any worse?'...*K'ween* shows up, betrayed and wanting revenge. I almost *dare* it to get worse! I almost *dare* it to get more ridiculous!" she chortled.

Gekko did not laugh. Clory did not laugh. Potto laughed, but only because Teeg was laughing and he thought he was supposed to. Teeg stopped laughing.

"But what's curious," she continued, "Why would she attack the *Node* ship?"

They watched as the K'rown fired at it (and not them!) a second and third time.

The communicator crackled to life again.

"Teeg! This is Pannick! Let's get you out of there!"

"Where is K'ween? She doesn't want us dead??"

"K'ween is no longer on board. She is no longer in charge. I am. And I am here for you, sister."

Teeg started laughing again, but for better reasons than before. "The flying prison behind me is on our side!" she informed Pannick.

It was still very unlikely that they would win this fight with

Eppie, but misery (and destruction) loves company.

~~~

Eppie was getting flustered. He was getting grumpy. He was getting downright pissy. He still knew he had the upper hand and did not fear failure, but the K'rown was going to slow things down. He needed a messenger to shoot, but his guards were all being very quiet. This was not their first tango with a miserably murderous Eppie.

"Oh fer the love of—just blow them all up. This is getting boring," he said dripping with tonal venom.

"Uh, sir?" said a messenger about to be shot. "Those guys from before?"

Eppie shot the guard before he could finish his thought. He looked to another. That guard quickly took the last one's post and continued. "They are now on the ship. They crawled in through ducts, air locks, and escape hatches."

Eppie shot this guard as well and turned to a third.

"Nope!" said the third guard, and shot himself.

The central flight deck doors opened and seventeen Quarols in spacesuits ran in. One shot at guards with a laser pistol, missing them all. Another was swinging a crow bar. One had a pillowcase full of cabbages and was lobbing them haphazardly. At least three had frying pans.

The guards fought back, but more clones were soon on the deck, shooting, swinging and lobbing. Eppie was hit in the back by a cabbage, which actually knocked a slipped disk back into place and temporarily cured his bad back. Eppie repaid the favour by shooting the Potto clone in the neck.

It was the overall chaos of this situation that was effective, rather than fire power. All over the ship, red-headed clones were confusing the Node Guards and slowing down the blowing up of the Shiv, the Lyme Node prison and the K'rown.

Eppie ducked down behind a console, awaiting his guards to put a stop to the madness.

"Whoever is not fighting off these morons and their vegetables, could you *please* fire at those ships out there??" he hollered.

~~~

Vrume T'cha T'cha was conflicted. If he left right at that

moment (while the K'rown was distracting the Bad News Bearer), he could probably escape unfollowed by Eppie and his warship. He would be able to get to Hephmote and save every prisoner on his new "ship".

Or, he could stay and try to help save the two that were prophesized to destroy The Node. He had to make a decision and do it quickly.

There was only one way he could save them all and it meant probable death to himself.

He sighed heavily. "Okay. Get info from the Shiv on where the Quarol clones entered Eppie's ship. You're going to fire me at it as well," he said climbing into a much, much older spacesuit model. There were no sandwich straws. There were no thrusters. There was a very limited supply of oxygen, and a broken zipper. This was going to be awful.

"The second I am fired from the torpedo launch; you are to leave this sector at top speed. The secret coordinates have been loaded into the navigational system already on a zig-zag path. Only veer from this if you suspect you are being followed."

"Vrume, you *can't!*" pleaded Jev Flockman.

"It's impossible! You'll die!" cried Dak Flockman.

"We need you Vrume! We can't do this without you! Please don't do this!" Breva Flockman exclaimed, throwing her arms around him.

In this universe there is much gold. There are many jewels. There is hot coffee. There are coveted gift certificates from the mall planet. But sometimes, the best gift one can receive is a hug. This was the case with Vrume T'cha T'cha at this moment.

He had no use for gold, jewels or a free BigBigTerraMart shopping spree while sipping on a cappuccino. He needed a hug. The type of hug that he could melt into, revel in the warmth of, and feel really loved, appreciated and important.

Time was of the essence and he broke free of Breva's gift, wiping a tear from his tired eye and zipping up the suit as best he could.

"Thank you. You will make a fine leader if I do not return," he told the young woman. He gave her a wink and headed for the door, stopping for one last moment.

"Take care of each other," he added wagging a finger.

~~~

Teeg watched helplessly as the Lyme Node Prison ship flew off into the distance like an industrial comet. She felt dread. She felt abandoned. She did not know the whole story of how this ship entered *her* story, but without it, she feared she had finally reached her last chapter.

The K'rown was firing at the Bad News Bearer, doing very little damage. The Bad News Bearer started firing back, doing a great deal of damage.

Swarms of Vexian ships zipped about, firing at them. The eight clone-inhabited ships fired at those. There were casualties on both sides.

"Enough waiting to be killed," she soon declared. "Let's join this fight. We're not entirely helpless."

And just like that, the Shiv was weaving in and out, between the Vexian ships.

Pannick's voice crackled through the bridge of the Shiv.

"I think we bought you some time, sister," she said calmly as destruction could be heard crashing around her in the background.

"You did! You saved our lives, sister!" Teeg shouted back as she ran about the flight deck pushing buttons. "Now get out of there! The K'rown isn't going to be able to handle any more hits!"

"No. We go down fighting," she said. Gekko turned the Shiv to face the far-off K'rown. They watched as it still bravely fired upon Eppie's ship. "Now...don't let this be in vain. Save the universe, Teeg. Save the damn thing, okay?"

Teeg stopped what she was doing. Gekko stopped. Clory stopped. Potto continued to stop.

"Today I join my wife. Today I join my children. Today I join all those that they took from me," Pannick said with an admirable confidence, flying her dying ship into the side of the Bad News Bearer, taking out a small section of it, and herself.

~~~

Bisher Donut was terrified. What was supposed to be a fun first ride in a spaceship (with hopes of catching the jerk who destroyed half of his house), was now a less than satisfactory experience. Officer Steve Lasagna and Officer Frett Pear were both unconscious on the floor, and all he knew how to do on a spaceship was install a sliding frosted shower door to the ship's premade moulded tub surround.

On top of this, there were other Vexian ships buzzing around them like bees, firing at each other. It was a stray shot that had jostled them enough to cause the un-seatbelted Lasgna and Pear to smack their heads together, knocking them out slap-stick-comedy style.

He pressed random buttons on the console, feeling enough anxiety to kill a smaller statured man. One of the buttons was the right button. He laughed nervously at a notice on the screen which read "Homing Device On".

The ship immediately took off at top speed towards Vex 4 and out of the war zone. He sighed with relief. This relief would be short lived though. He didn't know that later on he would have to crash land on his home planet, and that he would accidentally take out the rest of his house in doing so. There would be no one to blame this time. Just those damn, damn laws of bullshit.

~~~

Only two people remained alive on the bridge of the Bad News Bearer: Eppie and the Potto clone he had in a headlock. He squeezed the neck of the clone so tight that soon there was only one life on the bridge of the Bad News Bearer.

He stopped to catch his breath and check his console. The rest of the ship was still teeming with life. Guards and other clones were fighting it out on all decks. They had taken damage where the K'rown had hit. He got on the communicator. First, he called out to the fleet of ships behind him doing nothing.

"What the hell, guys?? Why are you not helping?" he cried out.

"Uh. You didn't instruct us to, sir," came back.

At that moment General Eppie realized that perhaps he had been a little too strict with his men. It was good to have them afraid of him, but not so afraid of him that they became incompetent. Perhaps he'd mercy kill them later to show he was not that bad of a guy.

"Well fight! Blow up anything that isn't a Node ship! All those Vexian ships! Get them!!"

He stopped caring about whether the original Quarol needed to come back to The Node alive. "Leave the Shiv for me."

He pranced on over to the weapon console. With his back feeling so much better, he was able to prance. And sashay. And rhumba, waltz-on-over, and mosey. At the console he found the Shiv. He aimed at the Shiv. His finger was just about to press a tiny little button that would end the Shiv.

"Whatcha doin' Kenny?" asked an out-of-breath, worse-for-wear Vrume T'cha T'cha.

"Do. Not. Call. Me. Kenny!!!" Kenny screamed without looking up right away. When he did, his temper flared and his heart sank. His temper flared because Vrume somehow stood before him, and he hated Vrume more than he hated anything else in the universe.

His heart sank because there was nothing to hold it up and in place due to the enormous hole that Vrume had just shot through his torso.

He looked down slowly at the burning hole. He felt no pain. No physical pain that is. Emotionally however, many things flashed through his mind.

Freckles: He had been so cruel to his assistant/lover. He had taken him for granted. Maybe not enough!

His race: He had selfishly made himself the last one. Now that species was about to become extinct. He took a weird pleasure in knowing he would be the last one ever.

Vrume staggered over to the communicator. In his best Eppie-like voice he instructed the rest of the fleet to go home, before turning back to the mad man.

"You're a *Treller*. A fucking *Treller*. You think in my billions of years alive that I'd never come across Trellers? I remember when they were *monkey* Trellers! And you think they were *all* on your home world when you blew it up, you asshole? Ha! I've got over a *hundred* Trellers on my secret planet hideout...

"...*Kenny.*"

And then General Kendra Eppie died. Vrume would never know if it was from the huge wound in his chest, or the stroke he had just given the General.

~~~

Aye's pod floated lazily throughout the (now silent) nothing. He watched as various bits of debris slowly drifted by. He watched as the rest of the Node Fleet, leaving the Bad News Bearer dead in space, took off in the direction of Vex 4 to fuel up before their journey home to Lyme Node.

He hit the rescue beacon, sending off an S.O.S. signal. He watched as the Shiv, having taken out the last of the Vexian ships, approached like a loose light bulb spinning slowly in an anti-gravity room.

He closed his eyes and fell asleep. He didn't dream.

This was good. He needed a vacation from his dreams.

CHAPTER THIRTY-TWO

Other than The Node, Vrume T'cha T'cha wanted nothing more than to have General Kendra Eppie be the last life he ever had to take on his mission to save the universe.

He stared at the lifeless open eyes, and the twisted look on Eppie's stupid face, feeling a little shame. Not only for killing his long-time foe, but for all the lives he had taken. From the Squambogian kazoo snail he accidentally stepped on over a million years ago, to the not-entirely-ugly Sammolite he had recently murdered. It was all feeling so pointless.

When Teeg's voice came over the communicator informing him they had docked to the Bad News Bearer to rescue him, he took his finger off the ship's self-destruct button. There were still Node Guards on the ship, and perhaps some surviving Quarol clones. Though it would tie things up neatly and get rid of a powerful enemy ship if he pressed the button, he just couldn't do it. Not anymore. Not again.

Instead he coughed up his Eppie-like impression again and announced to the ship, "All Node Guards are to stop fighting at once. All Quarols are to stop fighting with them as well and come to the bridge for evacuation. Once the Quarols are evacuated, the remaining guards are to take the ship back to Lyme Node and await further instruction. Oh, and I'm sorry for being such a jerk-wad. I love you. That is all."

Soon Vrume and the remaining twenty-seven clones found themselves on the now-crowded Shiv. If the lone Aye clone had survived, he was now wandering around the Bad News Bearer in search of drink and sex, both of which a lonely guard may have given him.

Vrume soon stood on the bridge of the Shiv with Teeg, Gekko, Clory, Potto and a still-sleeping Aye. No one knew what to say. There was a general feeling of both surprise (that they had survived the previous onslaught), and the rather lost feeling of "What-do-we-do-next?"

It was Knutt that broke the uneasy silence.

"Hey, Cap'n...do you remember that piece of garbage that had attached itself to the hull? The one that we thought was not worth the resources to pillage or give a second thought to?"

"What about it? Is it still there?" Teeg asked. She sounded exhausted. She *was* exhausted.

"It's not that it is '*still* there', it's more like 'it's *back*'."

"Back? How can--?" she started before Knutt cut her off.

"Two life forms just exited the debris and are now on the ship. Clover and some...uh...I don't know...walking meat-thing in a hat?"

~~~

It often felt like a major imposition to get called into work to cover the shift of a sick or absent co-worker. Even more so to a teenager making minimum wage and having to call off a date because the co-worker had suddenly quit and walked off the job.

Brian Puff was not happy. He was on a date with Shabby Mailman, and he was finally going to make his move. What was *supposed* to be the night he lost his virginity, was now a night of stacking jugs of very unsexy jetsam oil.

When he arrived, he was surprised to see half of the Vexian fuelling station destroyed by fire. The fire department had finally put it out, but the sight was still quite crazy to behold. Though not so crazy that it made up for his lost chance to see someone (other than his gross parents) naked.

As he tidied up the display of questionable oil and grease, the wind started blowing, nearly knocking him over. He ran into his kiosk and watched the biggest ship he had ever seen lower itself over the station. It was a Node warship. He had only ever seen one on television, and never one *this* huge.

It was too big to land properly. As it hovered over the station, it lowered a long girthy hose. A Node Guard slid down the hose like a fireman down an oddly thick fire pole. He connected the hose to a fuel receptacle.

The meter next to Brian Puff spun out of control. This was going to be the biggest sale in the history of the station. When the guard finished, he entered the kiosk.

"Uh, just put it on the corporate credit card," he said as he fished through his pockets searching for the card.

As the guard fumbled with his wallet, Brian noticed, over his shoulder and through the window, that a very tall and muscular, scantily armour-clad warrior woman was climbing up the hose to the ship above.

"Ah. Other pocket! I swear they make these uniforms with too many of them. I mean, yeah, they won't allow us to carry a purse, so the pockets do come in handy. Y'know...keys, lip gloss, phone, foundation, gun...but *c'mon*. There's one on the back of my knee! When am I ever going to need a pocket on the back of my knee? You can't put anything in it. You wouldn't be able to bend your leg if you did! Well maybe you could put some loose potato chips in there, but they'd get all crumbly the second you sat down..." the guard yammered on as the ship behind him took off without him. He turned and helplessly watched as the ship disappeared in a flash.

"So...um...you guys hiring?" he asked Brian Puff.

They were!

~~~

K'ween stood before the Node Guards on the bridge of the Bad News Bearer. She was surrounded, guns aimed directly at her. She was smiling regardless. In her mind this was her new ship, the idiot men around her just didn't know it yet.

The communicator crackled.

"What is going on there?? Why haven't I been updated???" yelled The Node, a larger-than-life image of his face appearing on the screen above them. "Where the hell is General??"

"Uh...right over there, sir," a guard stuttered, pointing to the dead body in the corner of the room.

"Oh. Well, then."

"We're coming back, sir."

"Did you catch the Quarol? Did you destroy the prison?"

"Uh, not exactly, sir."

"*WHAT??*" screamed The Node. "YOU ARE ALL--" he started, but stopped mid-sentence upon spotting K'ween.

"Who...who is *that?*" the lonely Node asked. If the guards hadn't known any better, they'd have thought The Node had almost sounded *bashful*.

"I am K'ween. Leader of the Barbohdean Sisterhood," she stated with confidence, puffing out her ample chest.

"Bring her to me." The Node said softly.

After all these unkind years, he was finally experiencing "love at first sight".

K'ween smiled wickedly.

~~~

In the same back room of the Shiv where he had first been hypnotized, and again with the artificial gravity turned off, Potto now floated, back in a trance. This time Clover was joined by Vibloblblah Ooze, Vrume T'cha T'cha and Clory.

Clory rooted herself in place and held onto the others with her branches and vines to keep them from bumping heads. Her mental abilities would be needed to amplify those of the eternal Oians as they delved as deep into Potto's mind as they possibly could. Hopefully they could finally break down the wall that kept the Quarol from his deepest thoughts and simplest memories.

Vibloblblah knew who Vrume was, but there was no way for Vrume to recognize his old monk-mate through the scars and fabric. He simply trusted Clover. He hadn't seen her in many years; not since she had been the love of his old comrade Theodore.

Aye waited impatiently on the bridge of the ship as Teeg and Gekko navigated, heading it in the direction of Vrume's secretive Hephmote. He had discovered some old mouthwash and was chugging it straight from the bottle, hoping that the alcohol level in it would take the edge off. It was only making him minty sick.

~~~

In the fantastical forest in Potto's mind, Vrume stood across from Vibloblblah, thoroughly (and delightfully) surprised. Vibloblblah had taken on his original, scar-free form in this dreamworld.

"*Theodore?* Is that really *you?*" he smiled and threw his arms around the reluctant monk, nearly stepping on a neon pink polymer clay dandelion. "I thought you were dead!"

"I should have been, Bertholt. I *would* have been. But if you, Festus, Meesha and Allison had bothered to *check...*" Vibloblblah/Theodore said. "You left me to burn, Bertholt."

"If we had've thought that for a *second...*we would've pulled you from the aftermath, Theodore! Well, maybe not Festus...he was always a bit of a dick," he said apologetically. He had forgotten his name was once Bertholt. "But if we had, you would probably have been killed just like them."

"Did you actually *see* my body? Did you see *theirs?* You survived...somehow...what makes you think any of us died at all?" Vibloblblah asked. "How *did* you survive, Bertholt? And without a scratch on you?"

After so many years believing one thing to be certain, it was difficult for Vrume to believe any of them had survived, including himself...but here he was standing in front of Theodore. He didn't have an answer. He wasn't sure himself, but a surge of guilt shot through him like he was suddenly dipped into a frozen lake.

A giant tree, obscuring the orange clouds in the lemony sky, leaned over. It spoke. Only in Potto's subconscious could anyone hear Clory speak out loud. Her voice was like liquid velvet passing through a didgeridoo.

"Men. Stop. We are here for other reasons. Bigger reasons. Reasons beyond your sordid past. Let's focus before Potto wanders off again."

This was not only enough to snap the two monks out of their heated conversation, and Clover out of her staring-at-Vibloblblah's-new/old-look in a nostalgic love malaise, but it also *was,* indeed, enough to stop Potto from wandering off again. They all stood around the mighty and majestic tree waiting for some woody wisdom, when Bundle fluttered down from her branches, leaving a trail of weightless glitter as she did so.

"This is Potto's fairy," Clover stated, like it was an everyday thing.

Potto cheered. No one seemed surprised.

"Hello dummy," Bundle said affectionately, winking at Potto. "Let's all go to the wall. And it's about damn time!"

The group wandered through the multi-coloured woods until they got to the edge of Potto's mental block. It was huge...there was no climbing it. And it was thick...there was no way of crashing through it. It was covered in wires and circuit boards, technological thingamajigs and electronic do-dads.

Vibloblblah put his hands on it. A slight glow emanated from the entire wall. Vrume put his hands on it. It glowed a smidge brighter. Clover put her hands on it as well, and it brightened up further. The three stood, eyes closed, and meditated harder than they ever had. They tried to make it transparent and translucent. They tried to see so far into it, that they could see right through it.

Clory then reached out her branches and joined them. It got much brighter, but still not quite bright enough.

It was Bundle simply sitting on one of her branches that boosted it enough, causing the strange thing to go from solid metal to a sheet of glassy ice. Hands and branches still on the wall, they opened their eyes.

A recorded history of the "mind block" played out like a film montage through thick glass. It was as if it had a consciousness of its own. It was as if it could both see itself through the eyes of all who came across it, and through its own eyes as well. This gave those trying to help Potto a panoramic and cinematic picture of its memories.

They saw a very sick and very old Node take a removable (old fashioned) flash drive and plug it into a panel on his armoured suit. He downloaded a part of himself into the drive. As he did, he started to look younger and much healthier...but also angrier and more sinister. He was downloading an illness onto the drive, and perhaps any joy he possessed. *Perhaps* it was a virus that was killing him, and an emotion he deemed useless and was willing to give up.

Next up, the flash drive was in a lab, and its contents were being loaded onto a machine that, in turn, loaded those contents onto a smaller microchip. There was something else on the chip already, taking up memory. Only the monks knew what this was.

It was the same A.I. program that the Node had originally created to take over all of the web networks in the entire universe. It was unclear why he would load a virus onto this *same* chip, but before they could get an answer, time skipped ahead to an image of Theodore running. Tiny chip in hand, he was on fire.

The chip then made its way from the burnt hand of Vibloblblah Ooze (as he was being chased by Node guards) to a cargo ship. Out of desperation, he hid it in a sack of oatmeal being transported to Croptle, the snack manufacturing planet. It then skipped ahead, like a vinyl record skipping on a gramophone, to a snack food wrapper being opened. A protein bar was being consumed on a camping trip by a Quarol. By Potto.

The chip then separated from the oats and chocolate and nuts inside of Potto, and made its way, almost crawling like an insect, into his brain. It wired itself in deeply. It became the wall that stood in their way now. It became the wall that changed Potto.

This is what Clover saw. This is what Vibloblblah/Theodore saw. This is what Vrume/Bertholt saw. This is what Clover saw.

This was *not* what Potto saw.

Through the now glassy wall, he saw himself around a campfire. A beautiful woman sat by the fire. He was walking down a path away from her, with a rucksack of food to hang from a loom fruit tree so that it wouldn't attract northern neglies. He turned back to the woman as if answering a question. He smiled at her.

"Galago..." observing-Potto whispered. He looked up to Bundle, who still sat in Clory's giant branches. She smiled down at him.

"She really was quite beautiful, wasn't she?" she said.

This broke off their contact with the wall. Before it became completely opaque again, they caught a glimpse of what Potto had seen. They saw his wife for just a few seconds. They saw the rockslide crush her, and understood that this was much more than a mission to save the universe for Potto.

"One day, when he no longer carries this burden...this chip...and his head is clear, he will remember this. Fully. Then, I fear, the sweet Quarol will lose his sweetness. That sweet will become sour. He will no longer be immune to an overwhelming and horrible longing for revenge," Vibloblblah Ooze transmitted to Clover, Vrume and Clory. "Perhaps *this* is his 'fairy'? Perhaps. Perhaps."

When they all came back to reality, an uneasy sadness hung in the air like a dreary fog.

~~~

"So, we can't remove it?" Teeg asked Clover back on the bridge of the ship.

"No. Not without killing Potto. It's really rooted. And the chip would probably rapidly deteriorate without his brain keeping it charged up...before we could figure out how to use it." Clover replied sadly. "Before we had a concrete plan."

"We have more information than we had before, though. A lot more. We can go back to my hideout and figure out how to get it out, and how to use it," Vrume added. "We'll have time there. We'll have protection. And with Theodore's help..."

Viblobliblah nodded. He was willing to put his ill thoughts aside and work with Bertholt. For now.

"It will take some time. Hephmote will only be safe for so long. We have to hide the Quarol until we figure this out. Somewhere where The Node will never, ever find him. Too much is at stake," he added through his crackly, metallic voice box.

"Where in this universe can we hide him where The Node is-n't?" Teeg asked.

"My ship for starters," Vibloblblah answered. "I created a wormhole generator. I can create a tiny wormhole that can take them anywhere in space or time. It doesn't always work well. Often I will want a quick trip to Lyme Node and end up on a prehistoric Squambog, but it always finds its way home. I will be able to track him when the time comes."

Potto didn't really understand what was going on, but he knew he didn't want to be sent off somewhere scary by himself. Aye could sense this. Potto looked uncharacteristically worried and frightened.

"I'll go with you," he volunteered. "You don't have to go alone."

"Yes," Vrume added. "And maybe take the Sentaphyll for protection."

Clory agreed.

"We'll have to make use of more of my tech," Vibloblblah added. He hesitated before he continued. They were not going to like this next bit.

"First, we need to inject a DNA cloaking device into them both. This will change their appearance slightly. Just enough to fit in with the dominant species on whichever planet and whichever time they end up. Second, and this will not sit well with any of you, but it is important..." he sighed. "We will have to temporarily clear all memories from the Quarol and the Topher."

"What!?" Teeg barked.

"I don't trust these two to refrain from messing up any timelines or accidentally starting wars or somehow giving away important information and getting themselves discovered. They will need to go into hiding as clean slates. We will restore their memories when we retrieve them," Vibloblblah explained. "It's the only way. I will set the ship to do this as they cross through the wormhole."

Aye wasn't bothered by this at all. He needed to forget the evil that his father did, and the tragic effect it had on his mother. He needed to stop feeling so much anger. Even if only for a short bit. This might just be the vacation he required.

He pictured the wormhole opening on "El Gusto!", the tropical sex planet.

~~~

Once in Vibloblblah's garbage-shaped ship, and after extensive instruction to Clory on how to work everything to some passable degree, Aye belted himself in, and Potto looked at those they were leaving behind through one of the ship's monitors. He hit the communication button and words spilled out of his mouth like water from a broken pipe.

"I don't want to do this. I sit here on this ship now, desperately trying to burn your faces into my head, so that when you bring my memory back, I remember you all.

"I am aware that this is the last time I might see some of you. I don't know if I'll remember you even if my memory *is* returned and I *do* see you again. I sure do hope so.

"You all mean the universe to me, and I want you all to know that. I know I was on a prison moon. I don't know why. That's still a mystery to me, but I know I couldn't have been *that* bad a person to somehow have all of you with me now. I know I haven't been easy to tolerate. But I love you all. Thank you for your friendship."

"You are loved, too, Potto." Clover said.

Teeg said nothing, but she agreed with the hippy for once. She felt it in her anguished bones.

"Can we just sit here for a minute before we go? I want so badly to remember this moment, if no other," he added.

As they stood there motionless, staring at Potto, Aye and Clory through the screen and allowing Potto to stare back at them for a few minutes, there was no awkwardness. They instead basked in love and respect and family. None of them had felt it in a long time. Some of them never had.

Teeg felt so much growth. Her desire for blood and money had become a desire for justice and a hero's legacy. Potto the fool had given her that.

Vrume T'cha T'cha felt like all of this was not solely on his shoulders for the first time since he was a monk. Potto the fool had given him that.

Clover had found hope and her true love, as had Vibloblblah. They had found each other, and this reunion would only make them stronger. Potto the fool had given them that.

Fools have so much more to give than anyone gives them credit for. Especially when they are not treated like fools.

Gekko felt hope and growth as well, but was feeling a profound sadness as Clory was about to depart, and she knew not when she would see her again. She was happy to have this new purpose, however, and would spend her time on Hephmote training soldiers and delving into finding her true self and getting to know that self better. Perhaps she would try talking out loud again.

This lovely feeling ended with a cheery Potto laughing, "Oh! I forgot to tell you! I took the teddy bear egg!"

Teeg's eyes widened.

"Oh, and look!" he continued. "There's a big doggie on board with us!" and then, after noticing the small should-be-extinct pre-mall Earth sparrow on one of Clory's high branches, "And a wee birdie!"

CHAPTER THIRTY-THREE

Janitorial ship The Velveteen Rabbit chugged along through debris scattered around the Vex system with a swagger of half-assed duty. This was punishment for imploding Lyme Node's prisoner moon of Tractos. The Node had not wanted to punish them at all for this, but Stane and Frappe's shift manager was a stickler for procedure.

They needed to be reprimanded for the error, and really, they had gotten off quite easy.

They vacuumed up, mulched, and spit out Vexian ship scraps, parts of the K'rown, and whole sections of what was left of Emperor Reginald Zophricates' old satellite lab.

The ship narrowly missed a piece of unassuming, not-worth-the-resources garbage before the chunk disappeared through a small, single-serving-sized worm-hole.

"Sa-Sa..." the huge, muscular Frappe said gingerly, lost in nervous thought.

"What?" sighed beach-ball-of-a-man Stane, with a tiny hiccup-burp.

"I have something I think I finally need to tell you."

"Is it that you were born in the wrong body?" Stane said nonchalantly, barely looking up. "What? You think I'm gonna freak out? I've read your lyric journal, like, sixteen times. We blew up a frikkin' moon! Go be a lady already!" he smiled. "You want a candy bar?"

Frappe looked over at her best friend and started crying.

(Disbelief!)

The End.

The universe is weird. Like really, really, *really* weird.

It is wonderful and magical. It is horrific and terrifying. It is the stuff of all dreams: Pipe dreams, daydreams, lucid dreams, wet dreams, run-of-the-mill teeth-falling-out-late-for-class-naked dreams, and the stuff of nightmares, terrors and unimaginable pain.

It is a *place*; it is a *concept*; it is filled with explained science and unexplained bughouse, bats-in-belfry crazy mayhem beyond comprehension.

Although there are heroes and there are villains, almost every single sentient life in the universe (and most life in the universe isn't even sentient) is *neither*. Most are somewhere deeply encased in the middle. Not heroes. Not villains. Simply creatures of a vast variation of intelligence just getting through the day. Or the night. Or the dream/nightmare.

Some loving, lusting and hating, some hungering and surviving, but most just trying (without any focus at all) on getting from point A to point B in their small lives without ceasing to exist. Some *never* ceasing to exist at all. Some *immediately* ceasing to exist.

The very dead Lassy Vapours was running out of time. He stared into that Alabaster Glob desperately trying to find his life in the separate universe within. He needed something to pull him away from his cadaverous husk. Something to save what little consciousness he had left.

"The universe is weird," he thought. "And the universes within the universe are weirder still. And the universe in which this universe hides in is also weird. There is a nesting doll of infinite universes, and they are all really, really, *really* stupid weird."

He left his observation of the very distracting giant flying light bulb. He checked back on his twin-universe-wife as she ate her pizza. She threw the crust out the window. A bird landed on the sill and pecked at it, nibbling away while fluffing its tiny feathers to stay warm. It was a small earth bird.

He felt a sudden rush of belonging.

This was not his wife! He had been focused on the wrong thing! This was his pizza crust!

With the dawning of this new revelation, he raced his mind back to the light bulb space ship. He watched as a piece of garbage detached from it and disappeared through a small worm hole. He felt a piece of himself go through it as well.

"What the hell?" his mind muttered to itself.

He had finally found himself in that universe.

"Well how about that then? I'm the fucking sparrow."

The adventures of infamous
Potto & Aye
will continue in...

*My Imagination Gets the Best of Me.
My Reality Gets the Worst.*

Acknowledgements...

For varying areas of help, inspiration and support, special thanks to (in no particular order):

My wife Kim Browning, and children LiLi, Gryff and Darwyn Browning, my mother Evelyn Browning, and late father Bev Browning, Sherri Browning, my mother-in-law Cindy Moreton, Clark Harrop, the late/great Jay Telfer, Chris Miles, Stacie Hanson, Matthew Reid, Andrew Bush, Dave & Jess Schmoekel, Jeremy Schultz, David Followes & Kathleen Bush Followes, Ron Tite, Marcel St.Pierre, Lauren Ash, Paul "PK" Kingston, James Morrow, Ruth Oosterman, Arya Jenabian & Manya Javadipour, David Raitt, Aurora Browne, Maureen Welsh, Paul Koster, Shodope Ireayo Adeola (Ire of the Future), the wacky universe, and trees...every damn one of 'em

About the Author

Sean Browning is a writer/actor, sci-fi addict, 80's New Wave enthusiast, LGBTQ+ ally, amateur naturalist, and tree-loving Canadian. He grew up in the small village of Madoc, Ontario.

He has been writing and performing in Toronto since 1992 and has written for and/or performed in theatre, television, video games, music and comedy – the latter earning him two Canadian Comedy Award nominations ('02 and '05) for best sketch comedy troupe (for his duo Reid Along With Browning with comedy partner and pal, composer Matthew Reid.)

For a much longer (and therefore perhaps more dull) bio and various other tidbits, please visit "Sean Browning's Outré Space" at www.thesean-browning.com. Or check out his profile on www.storywellpublishing.com.

CPSIA information can be obtained
at www.ICGtesting.com
Printed in the USA
LVHW091453301020
670026LV00009B/34